MAR 17 2021

BLOCK
SEVENTEEN

BLOCK SEVENTEEN

KIMIKO GUTHRIE

BLACK STONE

PUBLISHING

Published in 2020 by Blackstone Publishing
Cover and book design by Kathryn Galloway English

Printed in the United States of America

First edition: 2020
ISBN 978-1-982678-40-1
Fiction / Literary

1 3 5 7 9 10 8 6 4 2

CIP data for this book is available
from the Library of Congress

Blackstone Publishing
31 Mistletoe Rd.
Ashland, OR 97520

www.BlackstonePublishing.com

To my parents and the Endo family

This is how one pictures the angel of history. His face is turned toward the past. Where we perceive a chain of events, he sees one single catastrophe that keeps piling ruin upon ruin and hurls it in front of his feet. The angel would like to stay, awaken the dead, and make whole what has been smashed. But a storm is blowing from Paradise; it has got caught in his wings with such violence that the angel can no longer close them. The storm irresistibly propels him into the future to which his back is turned, while the pile of debris before him grows skyward. This storm is what we call progress.

—WALTER BENJAMIN

PART ONE:

CONSPIRACY THEORIES

ONE

I can't find your grandmother.

She seems to be gone. But not just gone in the regular sense of the word. I see on my phone that, fifteen minutes ago, she "checked in" from some place I've never heard of between here and Texas. So apparently, she's somewhere. But I have no real evidence, in the old-fashioned sense, that she actually still exists.

Not that she's ever been fully *here*, really. It's difficult to explain.

I lean back against the side of your grandpa's car, which I've borrowed today for a job interview, enjoy the cool metal on my skin through my blouse, and light up a cigarette. I cough a few times—after all, I'm not a smoker, I just bought the pack when your dad left, needing some extra relief from the heartbreak—and feel the nicotine kicking in, softening my thoughts. My neck and shoulders relax as smoke twirls from my lips, painting a question mark skyward.

Standing here like this, I can't help but recall my very first memory.

It was the summer of 1979, so I would have been almost two years old. Your grandmother's version of the story goes that she accidentally locked me, along with the car keys, in the old Volkswagen in front of the Co-op on Shattuck Avenue in Berkeley. It was an unusually hot day, and for some reason all the windows were rolled up. She called your grandpa at the lab from a corner pay phone. He told her to call the police, that it was fairly routine for them to rescue babies from locked cars, but she refused, resulting in a small crowd of strangers collecting around the car, all concerned about my safety. Eventually someone else called the police, who quickly came and were happy to rescue me. Everyone clapped.

Every so often throughout my childhood, Mom—your grandmother—would relive this story. She'd bring it up out of the blue, at the oddest moments, as though it were never far from her. It was one of the few memories she ever discussed. For the most part, she hated memories, and did her best to avoid them.

"I still feel just awful," she'd say. "I should have broken the window right away."

"Or called the cops sooner," I'd suggest.

"I know, I know, but you know how I get around men in *uniforms*," she'd say with a flustered shudder. "Especially with my own little baby, you know? I guess I must need therapy or something!"

"Now, now, Sue, you were just stressed," Dad would chime in, his Louisiana accent slipping back. He and I both knew therapy was the last thing Mom would ever willingly do—our family generally looked down on prolonged self-reflection as a sort of weakness. "You were worryin' about little Aki, and just weren't thinkin' straight."

"Well, I just hope I didn't scar you too much," Mom would say with a mix of guilt and irritation, as though it were my fault she'd brought up the incident again. "I mean, jeez, it must have left a big impression if it's your first memory. *I* don't have *any* memories from when I was so young—none at all."

"Not necessarily," I'd rush to relieve her. "Memories are random. And it's not like I remember it well. I just remember the hot car and looking out and seeing you. The details are blurry. Maybe it wasn't even the same day as your memory, or maybe I'm just imagining it."

But the truth was, my recollection of the whole incident was perfectly clear.

From inside the car, I can see her pacing around the sidewalk in a short lime-green dress, one hand on her hip, the other clutching a small white purse. Every so often she pauses to wipe a trickle of sweat from her forehead. Finally she stops pacing and leans back against the car window. I watch her neck and shoulders relax. She seems to be breathing deeply. She turns and I see her profile: she's smoking a cigarette. Her short-cropped black hair frames her round face neatly as she pulls smoke into her lungs, closes her eyes, and tilts her chin to the sky. She looks straight out of a '60s film, except for being Japanese, of course, maybe playing a truck stop waitress on an afternoon break, or a femme fatale unwinding after committing some crime . . . I watch the smoke twirl from her lips and, ghostlike, disappear.

Why do some memories persist, no matter how much we try pulling them by the roots, while others fade or disappear entirely? The most persistent of all seem to be those we still don't understand—those that keep nagging at us because we're still asking ourselves: What happened, exactly? Whose fault was it?

Actually, I'm surprised how easily I'm recalling the details of my first memory now; recently, my memory has been hazy.

Like your grandmother, I'm not a fan of memories. We can't trust ourselves to be objective when looking back at our own lives; we're likely only to see what we want to in the present. At best, memories are good guesses—at worst, pure inventions, being tainted by our biases and having happened so long ago.

So then, what's the point of looking back at all?

Look to the future! Mom's voice chirps in my head.

Or is that a bird?

It's no coincidence that I'm thinking of my first memory here and now; at this moment, I find myself in almost the exact same position as Mom on that hot day in Berkeley thirty-three years ago—leaning against a car, smoking a cigarette, wondering what to do next. The main difference, of course, is that there's no baby locked in my car.

And I'm not parked in front of a grocery store in the city. Instead I'm alone, miles from the nearest store, out in the middle of rural farmland, parked on the shoulder of a dirt road, beside a creek, gazing out at an impressive orchard—walnut trees, your dad said they were.

The heels of my new pumps sink into the soft dirt of the road as I squint to get a better look down the dusty aisles between the long, neat rows of trees. I'd like to kick off my shoes and make my way down the ravine, across the creek, and up the other side, to wander freely among the trees, like your dad did the day he brought me here five years ago. But, just like that day, I feel stuck here on this side of the creek. It's a mysterious, though quite familiar, feeling.

My focus softens and I see, in place of the walnut trees, a green sea dotted with red. Back when your dad's family lived here, this orchard was a strawberry field.

Future, future!

It *is* a bird, I realize. I hear it more clearly now, singing a short, hopeful song, but I still can't see it. It must be hiding somewhere in the thick green of the orchard.

I should get back into Dad's car and drive back to my sublet while it's still morning, work on my résumé, or find something else at least slightly productive to do. Or the opposite—play hooky from my job-hunting for the rest of the day and drive somewhere entirely new, somewhere I've never been to or even heard of before, have myself a fantastically spontaneous, original experience.

But instead, I turn off my phone, shove it into my purse, and toss the purse through the car window. The mix of fresh air and nicotine is striking an invigorating, heady balance in my brain. My mind wanders backward again, this time to the confusing events of last year.

As I mentioned, my memory seems unusually clear today. It must be something about being here at this old strawberry farm—and talking to you.

TWO

The girl rests her head on the pillow of her mother's damp back, softly bouncing as bodies move together, arms rising and falling, the dancers' sandals click-clacking on the gravel ground in rhythm with the big, pounding drum. Low-hanging lanterns decorate the late-afternoon sky—she tries to touch one, small fingers grasping at the empty space above her mother's hair. The smell of the bonfire the men are lighting mixes with the smells of incense, the sandalwood perfume on her mother's neck, the grilled meats and vegetables and steamed rice cooking in the temple kitchen.

The music stops and the girl's sister rushes to them, begging their mother for something in words the girl half understands. The girl's brother and his friends approach, tackling each other, imitating the last dance, adding silly movements of their own—a baseball batter's swing, a tap dance shuffle.

Her brother sticks his face up close to hers, their moist foreheads touching.

"Having fun, Sumi-chan? See any spirits yet?"

"Tak!" she cries, grabbing and pulling his hair.

Everyone laughs.

"There's shaved ice, come on!" her sister calls; they all run off.

Her father's face appears. "Look, Sumi-chan, I saved this for you," he says, holding up a small, shiny circle.

Her siblings always rush to claim this treat when their mother prepares whole fish, but she's always left out, too small to compete. The eye stares back at her, unafraid. She grabs it and pops it into her mouth, biting into its crisp center, delighting in the sudden burst of sea.

A loud voice calls out and people return to the dancing circle, the bright reds, pinks, yellows, and greens of the summer kimonos a wild, blossoming bouquet.

Her brother and sister reappear, holding cones of red ice.

"Shave ice!" the girl cries, arching back, struggling to get down from her mother. "I want some!" Her parents laugh.

"Chotto matte, chotto matte," her mother says. Wait, wait.

"I'll get you one after this song," her brother assures her with a wink as the music starts. *"Go dance with Mama, like you practiced."*

Her father unwraps the cloth tying her to her mother, lifts her up and places her onto her feet. Her legs wobble a moment before gaining their balance.

"Come, Sumi-chan," her mother says, handing her a fan. *"Dance time-desu."*

The girl hides in the smooth fabric at her mother's calves, suddenly shy.

"Now, now," her father urges, nudging her into the light of the circle. *"Mama can't dance with you hanging onto her legs, can she? You dance, too. Don't you want to dance with our ancestors, who've traveled so far to be with us for Obon?"*

Separated from her mother's body, the girl feels a refreshing breeze on her cheeks. The music swells and the singer's voice fills the air, inviting her body forward, then to the side, feet apart and together, her fan reaching up and down, the way they practiced . . .

"Yes, Sumi!" her sister calls from the side. *"Just like that—keep going, keep going, you've got it!"*

Her mother looks over her shoulder. "Sumi-chan, jozu, jozu!" she and the other women nearby call, laughing as they dance. You're doing great, little Sumi!

The dance carries her around the circle, the movements becoming easier, more natural and in sync with the music and everyone, her feet feeling at once heavier on the ground and lighter in the air. She closes her eyes and sees her ancestors all around her, dressed in their bright summer kimonos, too, hears them laughing and calling out to her as they dance—it's a lively family reunion, humans and spirits together once again.

This is the girl's first memory.

THREE

The bird in the orchard has quieted, at least for now. I take another drag on my cigarette, this time without coughing, and admire the lacy patches of sunlight on the pale-brown ground beneath the trees.

Pointless as looking back may be, I think I'll take advantage of the surprising clarity I'm experiencing at the moment and tell you, as best as I can, what happened last year, starting with last fall. I feel I owe you that much.

It was a Monday night, I believe, last September, when your dad returned late from work, upset because he'd had to undergo a surprise security check after his shift. He sulked into the apartment, kicked off his shoes, stripped to his underwear, and began watering his plants, his face flushed. We were having one of our Bay Area second summers, and the apartment was uncomfortably hot.

"They said it was just routine," he said as he watered a plant by the couch, wiping the sweat from his cheek with a forearm, looking quite hunky.

"Well, don't worry then, I'm sure that's all it was. Are you hungry?"

"Nah, I don't buy it—they have their eyes on me. And now that new manager they just transferred out from Chicago has it in for me. Chuck. Real bastard. Would love to have me fired." Your dad worked for the TSA, doing security at the Oakland Airport.

He went to an assortment of brightly colored orchids he kept by the kitchen window, gently prodding the soil with his fingertips and stroking the underside of a new bud, then headed to the bedroom. I trailed after him, mopping the sweat from my belly with my tank top. I plopped onto our bed while he watered the tall, potted palm that stood beside it.

"So today I'm, god forbid, talking to this guy—looks Middle Eastern, has a US passport—as I'm doing a quick check on his bag, just having a nice, harmless chat, making silly faces at this cute little baby his wife has on her hip," he said, stepping out the window onto the fire escape, where he kept a few plants and a lemon tree. "And as I'm handing him back his bag," he called from outside, "here comes Chuck, practically sprinting toward us with his bright-red face on. Shoots me a look like I don't know my job and has the whole family step aside for questioning. Takes the baby from the mom's arms, checks its *diaper*—mom and baby are in tears by the end. Fucking disgrace. And I have to stand there and watch that shit."

He stepped back inside and returned to the kitchen. I followed him, gathering my hair off my neck into a ponytail.

"Later he catches me on break and threatens me with probation," he continued over his shoulder. "I say, 'Sorry man, just trying to be human. Oh, and trying not to assume every brown person's a terrorist—cause that's like illegal, right?' And he says, 'We don't get paid to be human, just to do our jobs. Go work at Starbucks if you wanna be human.' Total dickhead."

"Well, I guess he does have a point," I reasoned, grabbing a bowlful of edamame I'd prepared earlier. "I mean, being all hunky-dory with folks you're trying to intimidate *is* kind of counterproductive, isn't it?"

"It's not just that. I'm not some mindless worker drone—I have my own thoughts, and that spooks them."

He returned the watering can under the sink, grabbed a beer, walked to the living room, and settled onto the couch.

"I'm sure if you just keep your thoughts to yourself, things'll be fine," I assured him, sitting beside him with the edamame.

"Um, it's the twenty-first century—there's no more privacy. They probably have some microscopic bot inserted up my ass at this point." He chugged a good third of his beer and made a bitter face.

"So, what, they follow you on Facebook?" I asked, grabbing a handful of soybeans. "Aren't there privacy settings?"

"They do whatever they want—tap our phones, read our emails, whatever."

"But what would they be looking for?"

"For starters, I'm sure my films freak them out. And I just posted my latest. They probably think I'm a terrorist. Even though *they're* the real hijackers."

Your dad's passion in life was making short, artsy-political videos, which he posted online for a surprisingly decent following.

"So, what did they ask you tonight?"

"Usual questions, drug test; same routine. Good thing I stopped smoking pot. Maybe I should just quit that fucked-up place. I feel all out of whack. Probably from constant proximity to those monster scanners."

"And *how* would we live?" I asked, squeezing soybeans into my mouth and stealing a sip of his beer.

He slid down the couch so he was folded at an awkward angle, the smooth skin over his ribs creased, an empty edamame shell sticking out from his lips like a joint. I admired his handsome profile. Your grandmother once commented that he had the classic features of a samurai. I wasn't sure what that meant, exactly, and thought it was probably nonsense, but liked the idea anyway. He spit the shell into his hand.

"What shall we watch?" I asked, grabbing the remote control.

"Nah—not in the mood tonight."

"Well, we're not in some spy movie," I said, setting down the remote and crawling onto his lap. "We can't second-guess everything. Let's just go about our life and not worry."

He leaned his face into my breasts as I kissed his forehead and played with his hair. I could smell the fruity shampoo I'd recently bought.

"Oh, Mom flaked on our lunch date today. She just didn't show. I sat there a whole hour at the café, waiting."

"A whole hour at the café—man, sounds rough. The life of the unemployed," he teased, nibbling at my shoulder, getting a bit excited beneath me.

"Hey now, that was you too, not so long ago."

He slid me off his lap, dropped to his knee on the floor and took my hands in his, ceremoniously, looking like a fairy-tale prince in his underwear. For a moment his face was serious, then broke into his irresistible, dimply grin.

He squeezed my hands expectantly. "So?" he asked.

My throat and chest tightened.

The week before, during our five-year anniversary dinner, your dad had proposed to me. I'd wanted to say yes—desperately so—but had gotten flustered, and when I'd opened my mouth to speak, no sound had come. That whole week, I'd been pissed at myself for blowing the moment, and was waiting for another right moment to bring it up again.

I cleared my throat now, wanting to tell him my answer—this had never been a question for me, I'd known from a few weeks after we met that he was the one I wanted to spend my life with—but, just then, of all things, hot air blew forcefully down on us from the heating vent in the ceiling above our heads.

Shiro let go of my hands and walked to the wall to check the thermostat.

"It's set to *off*," he said. "What the fuck." He walked back to the couch and squinted up into the darkness between the grates of the howling vent. He had that brooding look I used to find so sexy, yet also troubling. "There's something wrong here. I'll check it out on my next day off. The heating unit's up in the attic."

"Attic?"

"That little space above our bedroom—remember? I put your old childhood boxes up there when we first moved in."

"No, not really. Well, let's just close this stupid vent for now," I suggested.

I stood on the couch and reached up, but it was still too high. He tried too, but was also a bit too short. We made fun of short-Asian-people jokes—even though we're both about average height—and considered getting the ladder, but we were tired, growing more lethargic in the oppressive heat, and decided to deal with it later.

I still wanted to give him my answer, but the right moment had passed again.

He seemed annoyed as he walked over to the kitchen and prepared himself a bowl of his favorite cereal, Cap'n Crunch, a childhood addiction he'd never outgrown and could eat at any hour. He stood leaning over the kitchen counter, scarfing down the bright-yellow squares as though he hadn't eaten in days, the naval captain on the cereal box beaming at me with a maniacally jolly salute.

FOUR

The next day, I was sewing at the kitchen table when my childhood friend Topaz paid me a visit. I was surprised; she hadn't called, and ever since she'd had kids, we hadn't seen each other much.

"Oh, Top, long time no see," I said when I opened the door. A dusky shadow hung over her features and her usually frizzy blond hair clung to her cheeks in brown, greasy strands, like tentacles. "Everything okay?"

"No."

As I led her to the kitchen, I noticed that, though it was still morning, the apartment was already warm and smelled of something rotting. I ushered Topaz to a seat at the table, pushing aside my sewing things as best I could. She immediately burst into loud sobs.

I stood there watching helplessly a moment before grabbing a box of tissues.

"Frank left," she said through her tears. "He says he's been shriveling up inside for the past two years and needs to *reinvent* himself, or some bullshit—" She paused, her blue eyes flitting around the kitchen. "What's that awful smell?"

"Oh, the heat's spoiling everything fast. Sorry, I'll take the garbage down," I said, moving to do so, but she stopped me.

"No, please stay." She looked up at me as though seeing me for the first time. "Nice dress—is it vintage?"

I looked down at the light-cotton, floral-print dress I'd recently sewn.

"No. I made it myself, actually. If you like it, I could make you one . . ." I motioned to the sewing machine and pinned fabric spread everywhere. After many months of unemployment, I'd managed to get part-time work sewing a few dresses a month for a small clothing boutique owned by a friend of Dad's. It wasn't much in terms of income, but I've always liked working with my hands, and it brought in some extra cash.

She raised her eyebrows. "Impressive," she said almost bitterly, then started to cry again, her nose beginning to run. "I hope it's all right I stopped by—I just really needed to see a friendly face."

"Of course; I just wish the circumstances were better, or . . . more pleasant," I stumbled, moving my fabric pieces to the couch to protect them from her mucus and tears.

"Apparently he would've left sooner, but he just couldn't figure out all the practical details, like where to go, how we'd split time with the kids, what we'd do about our shared gym membership . . . Isn't that pathetic? He said one day two years ago he came downstairs into the living room and saw a gaping hole in the side of the house. And in that moment he knew that the hole was him—that his body was here, but *he* was missing." She studied the wall of the kitchen as though seeing a Frank-shaped hole.

"So, where is he now?"

"With his new boss. And I'm sure they're fucking," she said, punctuating this revelation with a nose blow.

It wasn't as though I was very surprised about Frank leaving. He'd always struck me as secretive and restless, acting as though he thought he was better than the rest of us and wished he were somewhere else; it was only a matter of time before he went there.

"Hey, are you hungry?" I chirped, moving to the kitchen counter. "I could make us some cold soba noodles and cucumber. It's really refreshing in this heat. Or a fruit salad? I have this massive papaya I need to use before it molds. But I know some people don't like it. Do you like it? Papaya?"

She stared up at me as though I were an alien. I smiled, uncomfortable, a drip of sweat meandering down my back.

"See, Jane, that's what's so amazing about you. You're so. Fucking. Positive," she pronounced with a mix of admiration and disgust. "Even when your own mother abandoned you in high school, you were basically fine. I never once saw you cry. But are you really fine, or are you repressing some big, epic thing?"

I forced a laugh, which ended up sounding like a short, rude bird squawk. I was taken aback by these offensive, obviously overblown suggestions. But then again, that's what made Topaz Topaz: her exasperating but entertaining, even endearing melodrama.

Her phone began to ring musically from inside her leopard-print purse on the table. She slammed the purse onto the floor. "Fucking clients!" she spat. "I'm so sick of them—they can never make up their minds! Guess I should get going." But she kept sitting there, staring at the wall again, perhaps seeing Frank's hole.

"Fourteen years, Jane. Fourteen years of complete bullshit."

"I thought you said he was just shriveling up for the last two?"

"But doesn't that make the first twelve also meaningless?"

"Not necessarily. People change, right?"

She scowled. "What time is it? I need some whiskey."

"Not even ten."

I putzed around the kitchen, trying to think of something more helpful to say. I almost mentioned your dad's paranoia about his work being out to get him, but figured it wasn't the right time. Then I almost mentioned our anniversary dinner and his proposal, but caught myself. How thoughtless that would have been, to brag about my and Shiro's happiness when her marriage had just failed!

After her visit, I found myself still jarred by those comments she'd made about me and Mom. I couldn't focus on my dress and sewed a zipper on crooked.

Frustrated, I pulled out the stitches, put away my sewing things, took down the garbage, and made myself a bowl of cold soba and cucumber. But when I sat down to eat, I felt a pit in my stomach the size of a small stone. I could almost see its smooth, round form inside me, as though I had a video camera in my digestive tract and a monitor in my head.

I pushed my bowl aside and wandered the apartment aimlessly, eventually finding myself in the bedroom. I studied myself in the mirror: tired brown eyes, straight brown hair swept into a ponytail, arms dangling at my sides, pale, freckled skin, eyebrows in need of plucking. I imagined myself in a traditional white wedding gown, roses in my curled hair and an elaborate bouquet in my hands. But this struck me as unconvincing, even a bit absurd.

I thought of the small photo of Mom and Dad that had hung in our living room when I was a kid, the two of them huddled together on a busy San Francisco street corner after their city hall wedding, Dad in a tux and Mom in a formfitting minidress, platform heels, and a bouffant hairdo, clutching a bunch of wilted daisies. The image of them had always struck me as so romantic and bohemian.

I switched to picturing myself in something more retro, like Mom's wedding outfit—a cream-colored, satin minidress I'd make myself, along with a matching, round-collared jacket, à la Jackie O, perhaps. But this image didn't seem right, either.

Discouraged, I turned to the large window that opened onto a fire escape. One of your dad's blue uniforms from his work was draped over a chair out on the escape, drying in the sun, looking like a broken, empty man. The window was ajar, though the air from outside was no less oppressive than the air inside. Sometimes—I had no idea why—I imagined myself crawling out onto the escape and rushing down the stairs to the street, flames licking at my ankles. I wasn't sure, in this daydream, if I was simply fleeing a fire, or also running to something.

FIVE

That night, around midnight, I woke to find your dad sitting up in bed.

"It was gone the next day. Clean gone."

"Huh? What was gone?"

"You know, the deer."

I wondered if we were in a dream and resolved to pay attention to anything not following the rules of reality, like if he started hovering above the mattress.

"How could you know that?"

"I went back to check."

"You went back to check?"

"Yup."

"Wait, you mean you drove all the way out there again?"

We'd had a minor car accident involving a bizarre, grotesque road kill, the night of our anniversary, right after he'd proposed to me. I'd been trying not to think about it ever since.

I could barely make out his nod in the dark. "But what about work?"

"I called in sick. But it was gone. No trace at all."

I sat up beside him, looking for the sheets, which we'd kicked off in the heat.

"Are you sure you had the right spot?"

"Absolutely."

How he could be so sure about this, I didn't know. It had been dark, and the road had looked the same for miles—a winding corridor through redwoods alongside a creek.

"Well, I guess the city, or the dead-animal-cleanup people . . . or whoever deals with that, cleaned it up . . ." I suggested groggily.

"Yeah. Right. I guess."

"What about the antlers?"

"Oh—the antlers. Yeah, those were gone, too."

"Well, it was just a deer, Shiro. It was horrible, I'm not saying it wasn't. But you worry too much. You're making me worry. About all your worrying. Let's go back to sleep."

"I'm not worrying—I'm just intrigued by what happened. Aren't you?"

"Not really. These things happen all the time."

"*All the time?*"

"Well, okay, maybe not *all the time*, exactly, but taking a sick day to go back there, especially when you think your work has their eyes on you—"

"But it's obvious something more happened that night," he insisted, staring into the darkness as though still seeing the dead, mutilated animal. "You saw its guts, right? They were literally turned inside out. That wasn't just a normal road kill; that was some seriously fucked-up shit."

He was right, I had to admit. The scene had looked more like a surreal, botched surgical procedure than a road kill. I could still see the animal's tangled innards splayed on the pavement in the flashing red of our taillights, the gelatinous blobs and foamy pink scum. I recalled other road kills I'd seen in the past. The poor animals had just looked peacefully asleep, not disemboweled as though by some malevolent, mechanical force.

That stone-sized pit in my stomach contracted.

"Who knows what all happened that night? We'll never know. There's no point in looking back. Come on, let's go back to sleep," I repeated. I tried kissing him, but he pulled away.

"You really have no desire to pursue this further?" he challenged. It felt like a loaded question.

Just then my phone buzzed on my bedside table. It was your grandmother; she often texted at the strangest hours.

> Sorry about yesterday, sweetie. It's
> been so busy here and there and at
> the club. How about tomorrow?

Though your grandmother was seventy-five, she still worked a couple of jobs—one as a distributor in a pyramid scheme for an antiaging makeup line, which she loved because she could work remotely and received product discounts, the other as a part-time receptionist at a country club. But both seemed more like amusements than actual jobs, and I doubted either produced any significant income. She and your grandpa split up when I was a freshman in high school, and her second marriage failed as well, leaving her financially comfortable—or so I'd thought—with a nice condo across the bay in the upscale hills of Marin.

I replied:

I waited a whole hour at the café

Didn't you just eat?

That's not the point, I wrote, then deleted it.

Tomorrow's good. Want to come for lunch? I'll cook. Soba and fruit salad? I have this big papaya. It'll be good to chat. And I have something to talk to you about.

I wanted to tell her about Shiro's proposal, and my inability, so far, to give him my answer. But she didn't respond. I lay back down and placed my hand on Shiro's shoulder, but he was either ignoring me or asleep.

I noticed a faint, high-pitched sound coming from somewhere in the building. I could hardly make it out, but once I noticed it, my mind couldn't shake it. A cat mewing, it seemed. Probably hungry, stuck outside someone's door. The insistent, shrill voice was grating, and kept me from falling back to sleep.

Wake up, moron, I said to the animal's owner in my head. *Let the little guy in so the rest of us can sleep!*

But it kept on, the pathetic cries so subtle and slight, they managed to slip inside the cracks of my consciousness, eventually crawling their way into my dreams.

SIX

The girl plays with paper-thin shavings as they fall from above, singing along with Billie Holiday on the radio. Her father sits nearby on his stool, a lit cigarette dangling from his lips, his gray fedora hat pushed back. He balances a jagged piece of driftwood on his knee, his sharp blade and imagination working together quickly and confidently.

She found the piece herself, on a recent family outing to Santa Monica Beach. Usually, her father prefers working with harder, denser wood, but for this piece, he's making an exception. As he carves, she faintly smells the sea.

"You're sure you want a boat, not a bird?" he asks, glancing down at her. "This is your last chance to change your mind."

"Yes, a boat—I want to play sailing in the bathtub!" She stands, reaching for the wood, but he brushes her hand away.

"Careful," he warns.

She settles back on the floor, continuing to sing along with the radio and admire his skill as he works.

Her mother would sometimes tell her and her siblings that she had been a lucky picture bride. She'd been shocked to find her husband, who had moved to the US from her same fishing village several years before, so kind, and even more handsome in person than in the wallet-size photo he'd sent to her father. Many of the girls she'd met on the boat, and afterward in Los Angeles, hadn't been so fortunate.

"Papa has the face of a samurai," she'd say proudly, though only when he wasn't in the room; in his presence, she joked about his grotesque ugliness and complained that he was a want-to-be Renaissance man, or "Lenaissancu man-o," as she pronounced it, always trying everything but never settling on anything. "So American," she'd say, clicking her tongue.

"So I'm a good American—is that a crime? At least I can speak English. No one can understand a word you say!" he'd tease back. He and the kids would laugh.

This was the closest her parents ever came to showing each other affection—they weren't like the couples in the Hollywood movies, always kissing and hugging in public.

The truth was, the girl's father was a Renaissance man. He carved, played the flute, wrote poems, cooked, repaired appliances, ran the hotel with her mother—there seemed to be nothing he didn't do well, with ease, especially when it came to working with his hands.

He stamps out his cigarette now, blows smoke at the ceiling, brushes dust from the carving, and holds it out to her. "So? What do you think?"

Resting perkily in his hand, the toy boat looks alive, as though it's inviting her to play. She runs a finger along its smooth, freshly born surface. Her and her father's skin match the honey-gold of the wood, and she has the funny thought that it's made from both their flesh.

She lifts it; it's lighter, in color and in weight, than his other carvings.

She eyes a small, dark statue standing beside the family altar—a little man in a monk's robe with a bright-red baby's bib tied snugly around its neck. Her father carved it before she can remember. He once told her it was a god that protects babies and children.

She holds up her new boat for the statue to see. Though its eyes are closed, it seems to smile with approval.

"I love it!" she shouts, skipping and twirling the boat around the room.

Her father laughs, standing, brushing bits of wood from his clothes.

"Happy birthday, Sumi-chan—but put it down for now; I still have to oil it. And we have important business—the crabs have arrived, remember?"

"Can't I bring it with me?"

"You don't want to lose it, do you?"

"But what if Tak or Michi think it's theirs? And play with it?"

He takes off his hat and runs his fingers through his thick hair, furrowing his brow in pretend seriousness. "You're right, that is a risk. You'd better bring it. On the other hand, maybe you should start getting used to sharing your toys. You might be a big sister yourself one of these days . . . you never know what surprises life will bring."

She scrunches her nose, wondering what in the world her father is talking about.

He laughs again, disheveling her bangs. "Don't worry, Sumi-chan. All I'm saying is, sometimes life changes overnight . . . you never know when—"

"Is Mama having a baby?" she asks, her eyes lighting up. She jumps up and down, pulling his sleeve. "Is she? Is she?"

"Perhaps she is, Sumi-chan, perhaps. But not for many months. Come now—let's see about those crabs!" He turns off the radio and heads for the door.

She kisses her new boat, giddy at the thought of holding a soft, fragile bundle in her arms, and runs to the statue at the altar.

"Please keep our baby safe," she whispers into its ear. "And make it the cutest baby in the world—make it love to play with me!"

"Come, Sumi-chan!" her father calls from the hall.

She follows him down five flights of stairs, carrying herself in an upright, ladylike way, already thinking of herself as a big sister. In the hotel lobby, he leaves her for a few moments while he attends to business matters in the restaurant and behind the front desk.

As she plays with her new toy on and around the lobby chairs, she notices a white man dressed in a suit and hat, reading a newspaper by the front door. The way he peers over his paper at her father as he goes about his tasks makes her nervous.

When her father emerges from the kitchen, carrying three empty buckets, she asks him about the strange man.

"No one to worry about," he tells her with a wink, handing her the smallest bucket. "No one at all. Just a harmless man!"

The girl nods.

Together they walk, swinging their buckets, down the sunny but brisk streets of downtown Los Angeles. At the fish store they watch the freshly arrived lobsters and crabs climb on top of one another in their crowded tanks. The girl points at her favorites to be spared.

"Papa, this one's smiling at me; don't choose him! And this one—look, she's still just a little kid, probably. Leave her with her parents!"

He obeys, laughing along with the man behind the counter as he points only to the ones she allows him to sacrifice.

They carry their now heavy buckets back down the busy street, her new toy floating atop the single, anxiously squirming crab in hers. In front of the drugstore, the girl sets her bucket down, eyes the Ice Cream sign in the window, and raises her eyebrows at her father.

"What—ice cream, in December?" he asks. "Whoever heard of that?"

She makes a mopey face and kicks her bucket, startling the crab.

But when she looks up, her father is pulling a quarter from his pocket and tossing it to her, his eyes twinkling. He leans against a streetlight, adjusts his hat back on his head, a black curl resting on his forehead, and lights a cigarette, telling her to get them each a double scoop; he'll wait outside with the crabs.

They find a park bench and sit together to eat their ice cream, the winter air flushing their cheeks. The girl, still thrilled by the idea of being a big sister, swings her legs back and forth, licking her chocolate.

Such wonderful news, and on her birthday, of all days!

The buckets wait by their feet, the wooden boat jostling in the small waves as the doomed crabs poke their claws skyward.

SEVEN

The next day, as I was hand stitching the hem of a dress, my phone rang.

"Hi, sweetie," your grandmother said over a rattling hum. "There's this clothes shop I think you'll like—everything's one of a kind, all hand-made, just your type of thing. Maybe you could even sell some of your dresses there, who knows? My hairdresser told me about it. He always knows the latest. And it's not too far from you. Want to go?"

"Sounds expensive. And I have no money. And I should really finish this batch of dresses—"

"Oh, don't worry, we can just browse. Or, in an emergency, there's always plastic," she joked. "Anyway, don't I owe you a birthday present?"

"But I thought you were coming here for lunch?"

"Oh, okay, but you know what, Chris is moving—did I mention that? So I have to drive down to San Jose today and help out. He has to be out by the end of the month. It's gonna be such a pain for the kids. Plus, he's had some kind of identity theft."

Chris is your grandmother's stepson—your step-uncle, I suppose—who's married with children. He and I have never had much to do with each other. I wasn't sure why his needing her in San Jose made her available to go clothes shopping but not for lunch, but decided not to press the point.

"Chris and them are moving?" I asked. "Where to?"

"Probably Texas," she said more loudly, the hum in the background building to a roar.

"Texas?" I heard myself shouting.

"Yeah," she shouted back. "They give big companies like his all kinds of incentives to move out there, like no taxes!"

"Isn't that illegal?"

"Seems like, but I guess not!"

"Where are you? I can barely hear—"

"Besides, no one can afford to live *here* anymore!" she yelled, emphasizing the word *here* strangely—or maybe that's just hindsight. "I'm driving—call you back, okay?"

I pictured her Bluetooth clamped to her ear as she clutched her steering wheel, her petite frame dwarfed by the giant cabin of her SUV.

A little later, she texted me an address. I replied.

Can't you pick me up?

Oops, I'm already here getting my hair done.
That's why I'm on this side of the bay today.
Head's all wrapped in plastic. Meet in an hour?

Your grandmother had lived in Marin for over a decade, but remained loyal to her hairdresser in downtown Oakland, a Vietnamese man who kept her would-be-all-white hair a sleek reddish-black, cut in the latest styles. "He really understands me," she'd say when I asked why she didn't find a new hairdresser. "Plus, only Asian people know how to do Asian hair. You wouldn't understand because you inherited your dad's."

Shiro and I had just one car, an old Toyota Corolla he'd inherited from his grandfather, which he used to commute to work, so I was stuck with public transportation. I showered, threw on a tank top and shorts, downed a glass of water, and headed for the bus stop, leaving the unfinished dress spread out on the kitchen table.

After a bus ride too long for its short distance, I found myself walking several blocks, passing some depressed shops, a Korean restaurant, some seedy liquor stores, and a bunch of old warehouses looking long abandoned. I finally arrived at an especially tall beige warehouse where the address should have been. Google hadn't found it either.

The mammoth structure stood behind a barbed wire fence with a locked gate. Across the street, sitting by a pole, apparently untethered, a small but fierce-looking dog was staring at me. That pit in my stomach flinching, I called your grandmother.

"Oh, good, you're finally here?"

"Well, no. I'm standing outside a barbed wire fence in front of a huge warehouse where the address should be, and a mean-looking dog's staring at me, but there's no sign of any cute shops, no sign of the address you gave me. I wonder what this thing was built to store?"

"Calm down, Jane—do you see a green door?"

"Nope, no green door. I'm perfectly calm, just no green door."

"Really *look*. It's hard to spot at first. Right behind the old claw-foot bathtub."

"No bathtub either." Was she joking?

"Come on, Jane. You really have to *look*," she pressed.

"Maybe I'm not in the right state of mind to see this particular bathtub of yours," I quipped, sweat itching my underarms. "I just hope I don't get eaten by the dog before I find it."

"Oh, sorry, that reminds me—you actually have to go *through* the fence and around the corner to see it," she said. "There's a hole at the far right side. See it?"

I walked to the edge of the barbed wire fence. Sure enough, there was what looked to be a freshly cut hole, just barely large enough for a small person to wriggle through.

"I'm supposed to climb through a *hole*?"

"Yeah, I'm not sure why the gate's locked. But there's all sorts of ways to get in and out of places, Jane. Think creatively—the hole works beautifully."

Before I could ask her anything more, like if she had slid through this same hole herself, or if she had been the one to cut it with wire cutters she'd just so happened to have in her purse, she either hung up or we got disconnected. I squatted down and peered through, but all I could see was more of the giant, drab box of the building. It looked as though it was planning on swallowing me.

I made my way through, careful not to scrape my skin on the sharp wire tips, gave the dog across the street one last cautious glance, and walked around the corner. There rested an old-fashioned claw-foot bathtub, looking surprisingly natural in this setting, as though it had been there for years. And, just behind it, a bright-green metal door. The tub seemed set there to catch whatever spilled out from the door when it opened.

Cool porcelain brushing my thighs, I squeezed past the tub, noticing a small white security camera mounted above the door. I turned the doorknob, surprised to find it unlocked, pushed open the heavy door, and tentatively stepped into a long hallway.

My phone showed the dismal message: *network unavailable.*

"Mom?" I called out weakly, the door swinging shut behind me.

Opening the first interior door I came to, I entered a large warehouse space where techno music softly hummed. Circular racks displaying high-end looking, silky garments in a stark color scheme from white to silver to black were scattered about, and a few tables featured bags, hats, and other accessories. Long windows let sunlight into the space at a steep slant, reminding me of a church. In one corner, a cordoned off spiral staircase wound its way to an exposed second level that, after a few feet of flooring, simply stopped, as though construction had been indefinitely postponed.

I was struck by how large and relatively empty this place was compared to the cozy, packed little boutique where I sold my dresses. Located in a walkable shopping district, owned for decades by a sweet older couple, the shop always had a friendly, bustling feel. Jackie, the wife of the couple, always stood by the door to greet her customers, some even by name.

In contrast, this cavernous skeleton of a space had no obvious cash register area, or even salespeople; just a few solitary shoppers, who looked to be in their early twenties, roamed the floor with a quiet focus. I roamed among them, thankful for the relief from the sun, distractedly looking at some of the dresses for sewing ideas, until I saw the back of your grandmother, who was easy to spot, being the only senior in the place.

She was holding a black scarf up to herself in front of a free-standing mirror.

"Oh, Jane, you made it," she said to me in the mirror, her eyes wide. I was struck by how youthful her face still looked, evident even under the thick layer of makeup she always wore. Her antiaging products seemed to be working.

"Cute haircut," I said.

"You like it? It's not too hip for me?" she joked, fingering the tips of her new hairstyle, a wedge cut, nearly shaved in the back, with an asymmetrical bob in front.

"It suits you. So, how the hell does anyone find this place?" I asked, unable to hide my annoyance.

She turned to face me, her eyes flickering with excitement. "Isn't it *great*? It's an internet thing—you know, one of these new, temporary types of spaces. It roves around from here to there and fans just follow. It doesn't need an actual *place* in the old-fashioned sense—isn't that so liberating?"

"*Liberating?*"

"You know, not to be tied down anywhere. It just feels so . . . I don't know, *current*, doesn't it?" she asked, looking all around, blinking, as though she couldn't quite believe what she was seeing and all its potential ramifications. "Can't you just smell the *possibility*, Jane?"

I inhaled and detected a trace of something in the air—maybe tuna fish. I wondered if sometime in this place's past it had been a cannery. "I guess . . ."

"Hey, you should talk to them about carrying some of *your* dresses. You should have brought a few samples!"

I shrugged. The thought of doing business with "them," whoever they might be, struck me as a bad idea.

She seemed offended. "Well, suit yourself. Honestly, I can never guess what you'll like or hate, Jane. Oh, *Chris*," she said loudly, touching a finger to her Bluetooth and turning back to the mirror. "Yeah, yeah, I'll be there soon, don't worry. I'm with Jane now—*Jane*. Yes. I just had my hair done. My *hair done*."

Another shopper walked by, smiling aloofly at us.

"Don't worry, a couple hours, at most. I better get going, sweetie. Too bad it took you forever to get here. I can drop you at BART if that helps?" she asked, still talking to the mirror. It took me a moment to realize she was addressing me again. "Do you see anything here you like? Anything at all—my treat."

"I don't know, I haven't been here long enough. Can't Chris find someone else to help him? Like maybe his own mom?" I immediately regretted my words; I hated when I sounded jealous of my stepbrother.

"How about this?" she asked, offering the dark, silky scarf she was holding. "I like how versatile this is—you can wear it however." She brushed it against my arm. "Try it."

"No thanks. I'm not much into scarves."

She held the fabric horizontally and pulled it taut between her hands, as though she might be planning on strangling someone with it.

"Here, try it," she insisted, attempting to loop it over my head. I laughed awkwardly as I struggled to pull away, but she kept trying to restrain me.

"Stop it, Mom. What are you doing?"

She looked at me oddly, as though disoriented. "Sorry," she muttered, then bunched the fabric into a ball and tossed it onto a nearby table of accessories.

"Let's go," she blurted, swinging her purse over her shoulder and moving in her usual swift, no-nonsense manner through the warehouse. I followed, glancing over my shoulder at the abandoned scarf.

At the end of the space she leaned into a red button set into the wall and tapped her foot impatiently. Though she'd said this place was temporary, I had the feeling she'd been here before and had a nuanced understanding of its workings.

"You're sure you can't come by the apartment now, just for a bit?" I asked. "I still have a little sewing to get done, but I can cook us up something quick and we can chat. There's something I want to talk to you about."

"Not today, sweetie. Sorry, I really have to get going," she said as a giant garage door groaned open and a gust of warm air rushed at our faces. "I wish you'd finally get on Facebook—that would make things so much simpler."

We stepped out onto a busy street, complete with a local café, Wells Fargo, and Starbucks. Relieved to be free from that foreboding structure, I shielded my eyes from the bright sun.

"Why couldn't we just have entered from here?" I asked, irritated. "Instead of lurking around abandoned streets, crawling through barbed wire fences, and squeezing past bathtubs?"

"Exit only," she announced, donning her large, Audrey Hepburn–style sunglasses, looking like a glamorous insect as she marched down the street toward her shiny black SUV.

That day at the warehouse was the last I ever saw her—at least, in the flesh.

EIGHT

I suppose I should tell you, Little One, my given name isn't Jane. On my first day of middle school, I said it to my homeroom teacher as a kind of joke as she stumbled over my old name on her roll sheet. She seemed relieved. And that was it. It was great; everyone pronounced it perfectly.

"*Jane?*" your grandmother repeated when I told her a few weeks later. "Are you joking? What is this, the *1950s?*"

"Mom's right, Aki," your grandpa told me, looking worried as he set the table for dinner, still dressed in his navy-blue work suit. "You don't need to be ashamed of your heritage."

"*Ashamed?* My *heritage?* No, not at all. I just don't like the name."

Mom stormed into the kitchen and started banging around loudly.

"On the other hand, dear," Dad called to her, "Jane's a perfectly nice name. If she wants to change her name, I don't see what's so wrong with that."

"Of course you don't," she yelled back from the kitchen. "That's because you're a white male, Doug."

The next day I came home from school to find Mom on the couch, bent forward, her head cradled in her hands. When I walked in she sat up, startled. Her mascara was smeared all around her cheeks and her eyes were wide and scared—I remember thinking they were like a frightened child's.

As she set a snack in front of me later that afternoon, she touched my elbow.

"You're not serious about changing your name, are you sweetie?" she asked. "I mean, I'm all for a little experimentation, having a fresh start, even. And I know having a Japanese name can be a little . . . embarrassing sometimes. People not being able to say it right and all. But in this case . . . well, *Akiko* is your name. That's who you are: Aki. It suits you."

"It's kind of too late. Everyone at school already knows me as Jane now," I said, biting into a cracker. "So, oh well. Plus, I've never been a fan of my given name."

"Well, it's a bad idea, changing your name out of the blue like this," she said, her tone tensing as she began pacing the living room. "I'm telling you, it really is. When we chose your name, it was for a reason—did you ever think of that?"

"But you're not even into Japanese things. We barely even eat Japanese food or anything. And what about you? You go by Sue."

"That's different," she snapped. "That's short for Sumiko. I mean, come on, Aki, *Jane*? When we chose your name, it was for a *reason*," she repeated.

"Sorry, Mom, I just like Jane better, what can I say? And like I said, it's what everyone calls me now. Changing it back now would just be weird."

"But it's not good," she insisted. She stopped her pacing and looked at me, her face twisting strangely. "Not for you or anyone—did Michi tell you something that night? She always talks too much about things she shouldn't."

"Aunt Michi? No. I mean, she's told me some stuff, but never anything to do with this. Not at all," I said, laughing.

At the time I think I sincerely thought my new name was a random change—and a nice chance to start afresh. Now that I think about it, though, I suppose Mom was right; a late-night talk I'd had that summer with Aunt Michi, Mom's older sister, had affected me. After all, being named after a dead baby wouldn't be fun for anyone. Surely you agree?

"Babies died more often back then," Aunt Michi had reassured me that night, speaking softly so Mom wouldn't hear. "It happened all the time. Mama wasn't thinking straight. *Infanticide* is much too strong a word."

I still get chills when I think of those words now, all these years later. And of course I shudder to think what you must think of me. I don't blame you.

NINE

The Saturday after I met Mom at the warehouse, while your dad was at work, I woke from a nap to find our living room looking as though a hurricane had swept through—couch pillows, my sewing things, newspapers, jackets, and books were strewn everywhere. A plant had tipped over and the pot was now cracked, soil spilling onto the floor.

I ran out of our apartment into the hall and thought about finding someone in the building to call the police. What if the intruder was still in the apartment? Our building, built sometime around the 1920s, had just seven units, and most residents, like us, kept to themselves.

But after standing outside the door a few minutes and not hearing anything from inside, I stuck my head through the doorway, called out a few times, and, still hearing nothing, went back in.

My purse sat open and rifled through on the kitchen table, but as far as I could see, nothing was missing. Even my laptop was sitting there on the coffee table, right where I'd left it before lying down for my nap on the couch. I went to the bedroom and found a similar scene: our bedding, clothes, and books were scattered about willy-nilly, all drawers pulled open, even those on my jewelry chest and the file cabinet where we kept important papers, their contents scattered about. It looked as though someone had gone through our things, one item at a time, looking for something specific.

I went to put everything back in its place, but just as I began, I stopped myself. The apartment was now a crime scene, I realized, and the police would want to investigate the evidence exactly as it was. My heartbeat quickened.

I carefully backed out of the bedroom and returned to the living room to call the police, when I noticed something I'd missed at first.

In contrast to the chaos, some of our things—pillows, a few books, a framed picture, a DVD—had been neatly arranged into a small tower in the center of the floor. I was unable to look away; this stack of ordinary things looked disconcertingly meaningful.

Had Shiro been home? Could he have gotten off of work early and for some bizarre reason made this mess and built this tower? But why on earth would he do such things?

Telling myself not to panic, that there was surely some logical explanation for all this, I went back to the bedroom and sat on the edge of the bed, my hands trembling.

I decided the idea of Shiro having done this made no sense; he was still at work. It must have been some unknown intruder, with some specific agenda. After all, what kind of burglar takes the time to arrange random objects in such a way? The tower felt like a particularly perverted gesture—even personal, as though it had been built only to upset me.

To make matters worse, that cat in the building was crying again, this time louder. I wondered if it wasn't stuck outside someone's door, but trapped inside some small, stifling space, crying to be let out. The voice was so pathetic, so nagging and grating, it felt as though the little creature were perched on my shoulder, crying directly into my ear.

When Shiro got home, I was in the kitchen making dinner. I'd spent the afternoon cleaning. In the end, I'd decided against calling the police, since after all, nothing had been stolen. And the last thing I wanted was to think more about the disconcerting incident.

"What happened to the calathea?" he asked right away.

"The what?"

"You know, the plant with the striped, purplish leaves that was over there by the couch."

"Oh, that. I'll tell you in a bit. Ready to eat?"

"Lemme shower and shave first—have work cooties all over."

After he showered I stood in the doorway watching him shave, which he didn't really need to do; his skin was smooth as a baby's.

"So, today I'm patting-down some guy when I notice this other, older white guy standing toward the back of the line, getting worked up the closer he gets to the scanners," he said, pulling his razor along his cheek, plowing tracks of light-brown skin through freshly fallen snow. "He keeps looking all around, double-checking his bags, putting his hands in his pockets, pulling them out again—so, of course I have my eye on him. Not that I'm an actual BDO or anything, but—"

"BDO?"

"You know, behavior detection officer."

Now he was working on the sensitive area beneath his chin, making lots of fast, tiny motions with his razor. I had the urge to kiss him there.

"So, when it's time for him to take his shoes off, his hands are shaking so bad he can barely do it. Course by this time, other folks in line are noticing him, too—the guy's got suspicious written all over him. So, I ask him to step aside. After a few minutes, Chuck marches up, asks the guy a question or two, lets him back in line, then taps this *other* guy on the shoulder—some dude in his thirties or so, maybe Mexican, totally chill, just standing there waiting his turn—and escorts *him* off to the back. When the guy asks why, Chuck says his standard bullshit line about it being just a random search. Lets mister *psycho-killer white guy* back in line and hauls off the Hispanic dude for the private screening—classic, right?" He splashed his face clean and examined it. I wasn't sure what any missed spots would look like to him, since there was no hair to begin with.

"What's Chuck again? White? Black?"

"More like blue, with horns, twenty eyes, and a big ole iron club!" he joked, making a monster face and big bashing motions with his razor. "You know, like one of those oni." I must have looked at him blankly. "With the big iron clubs. Japanese demons. Don't you know your own culture?"

"Nope." Sadly, I've never been much exposed to that side of my background. Growing up, Mom had mostly preferred American things.

"Whatever. Chuck looks kind of like your dad, but younger." To your dad, every white guy over fifty looked kind of like your grandpa.

"So, what'd they do to the Mexican guy? Do you think he was guilty of something?"

"Nah, definitely no terrorist. They probably put him through the standard background shit, sweat gland monitoring, DNA sample, anal probe," he joked darkly. "In the end I bet they nailed him on some immigration issue. Maybe deported him. Maybe he's got kids here who are now fatherless—who knows? I swear, I'm gonna expose these criminals," he said with disgust as he rinsed his razor. "That'll be the one silver lining of this fucked-up job." He squeezed past me and disappeared into the bedroom.

"*Expose* them? What do you mean, exactly?" I called, but he didn't answer.

I waited until after our meal to tell him about the break-in. I mentioned it as nonchalantly as possible.

"Who the hell would do this?" he whispered, looking around the kitchen as though the intruder might still be hiding somewhere.

"I have no idea. It's really weird," I said, carrying the cast-iron pan from the stove to the sink.

"I bet it's my work. Dammit!"

"Your *work*?" I let out a surprised laugh. "Shiro, you don't—"

"That's what I've been saying. Man, I can't believe this!" he cried, pounding the table with his fist. The whole room seemed unsteadied. "I just recently posted that new video—and I bet I didn't answer those questions the way they liked. So now they're scavenging around my home trying to find something to pin on me—*those assholes*!" he shouted.

I was taken aback by his reaction. Your dad's a passionate person—that's something I always loved about him—but normally he didn't jump to such rash, paranoid conclusions.

He jumped up and ran to the bedroom, returned with his laptop, turned it on and waited for the screen to light up. My hands stiffened as I clutched the pan's handle.

"They probably went through all my files, too," he muttered.

"Come on, Shiro, what about the First Amendment? And what's that other one . . . about search and seizure? This isn't Nazi Germany; they can't just come barging into our house—"

"Oh, right, these guys are real sticklers for the Constitution," he snarked, sitting down, opening files. "So, what'd the police say?"

"I mean . . . this is really creepy," I stammered, "if you think your work—the *government*—is breaking into our house. Especially while I'm here at home, napping. I really think you're blowing this way out of proportion."

"Wait—you were *here*?"

"Yeah. On the couch. Sleeping."

"You were right *there*?" he asked, pointing at the couch.

I nodded.

He looked at me suspiciously a moment, then jumped up and ran his hands all over my body, as though checking for wounds. "*Jesus Christ!* Did they—did they do anything to you?"

"No, no," I assured, brushing his hands away, laughing nervously. I turned on the faucet and started scrubbing the pan. "I'm fine. We do live in Oakland, after all. It was probably just some kids looking for drugs. Anyway, I'm sure the United States government couldn't care less about your videos! Don't people post random stuff all the time? They have to respect people's privacy at least a little, don't they?"

He paused, taking a deep breath.

"Jane—no offense, babe—but you're being a tad naive, don't you think? Let me remind you, these are the same fucks working on technology to see your naked body—your *internal organs*—through your clothes. Through the roof of your house. From a *goddamn satellite*. Seriously, they can spy on your private parts from *outer space*."

He sat back down and looked at his screen again.

"Okay, let's just calm down a bit here," I said brightly, hearing Mom's voice as I lugged the iron pan back to the stove. I was so unsettled, my hands momentarily felt separate from me and the pan slipped, crashing loudly on the burner.

"I'm sure it wasn't your work," I said, lighting the stove, "or anything so significant like that. And even if it was, then why even call the police? Are the police so different from the TSA? I mean, if this is some huge government conspiracy, what good would calling the police even do?" I leaned against the counter, waiting for the pan to dry.

He glanced up at me. "You called the cops, right?"

"Yeah, of course," I quickly lied. "Of course I did, right away. But they said there was nothing much they could do, since, you know, nothing was taken."

"But they filed a report?"

"Sure. That's what they do, right? I just hope I didn't leave the door open before my nap. Sorry, if I did. From now on I'll double-check, I promise. Sorry."

"Oh, doors won't stop them," he said ominously.

"Come on, Shiro, we live in Oakland. It was probably just kids looking for drugs," I repeated, as though convincing myself. "Anyway, the police know, so all we can do is hope they find whoever it was and that it doesn't happen again."

Looking back now, the deception seems significant, but at the time, covering up the fact that I hadn't called the police felt effortless, like a natural instinct, though I had no idea why I was doing it.

His sweaty temples pulsed as he scanned his screen and fingered his trackpad. I could see all kinds of suspicions shifting around under his skin like busy bugs. I wondered what stolen information would look like to him; wouldn't it just look like nothing?

I turned off the fire on the stove, waved away the smoke, and went back to the table—suddenly he was sideways, and I was slumped on the floor, my head resting on the seat of my chair.

Shiro was bending over me, holding my shoulders. "Jane?" he was asking, his voice tender. "You okay, babe?"

"Not sure. Just really light-headed lately."

He helped me back into my chair. "Shhh," he soothed into my ear. "I'm sorry. I'm such an ass." He stroked my hair, which had fallen from its ponytail. "I've just been thinking about the crime; but it must have been terrifying, waking up to that. Being here sleeping while who knows what fucks were in here. Thank god they didn't do anything—you're sure they didn't touch you?" he asked, rubbing and squeezing my shoulders.

He placed a finger under my chin and searched my face.

"I love you," he mouthed.

"I love you, too," I mouthed back.

He planted a kiss on my lips—and I say the word planted deliberately; sometimes when he kissed me, I felt my body was made of soil. He sunk into me.

I wanted this random, disturbing incident to go away, and for neither of us ever to think of it again. But that tower in the center of the living room floor wouldn't leave my mind.

"I'm just glad nothing was taken," I mumbled into his shoulder.

"Look," he said, his breath warm on my neck, "maybe I should install a surveillance system in here, just to see what's going on."

"Surveillance system? In here? No way. You're kidding, right?"

"I just want to know who did this—don't you?"

"Yeah sure, but cameras in here? That'd be creepy. I don't want to live in a fishbowl. Promise you won't, okay?" I pleaded, pulling back to look at him, not knowing why I was so intensely opposed to the idea.

"Maybe you're right. Maybe that's just becoming one of them." He coaxed my head back onto his shoulder and continued stroking my hair in a steady, hypnotic rhythm. "Shhh. It's okay . . . we're gonna be okay. They're just trying to scare us, is all. That's their MO. See, what they want is to intimidate us. To keep me from rocking the boat. But we won't let them win."

"Win?" I yawned, suddenly exhausted, my eyelids heavy.

"They can go through our stuff, even get at our bodies—but not our intentions, our *beliefs*, if we're strong . . ." He kept talking, his voice sounding farther and farther away, and more surreal, transporting me to a trancelike state. I tried speaking, but it was no use; my voice leaked from my lips into a shallow, impotent pool on the floor.

My eyes closed and I saw an image of him still standing there, but now silhouetted by the sun, surrounded by a vast green field spotted with red. To his right stood a house with a green door and large front porch where a couple of kids played. I had the impression they were our kids. (Maybe one was you?) It was summer, I could tell by the colors, angles of light, and sweet scents of everything—and I was returning home from somewhere, dressed in an old-fashioned light-cotton dress, walking with an unfamiliar clarity of purpose toward him across the field, the heels of my shoes sinking into the soft earth. He stood waiting for me, arms outstretched, his hands covered in soil. I could see now the red dots were strawberries. We were both smiling.

"My shirt may be theirs when it's hanging in their locker," his voice out there in the kitchen continued, "but on my body it's a different animal, their power fades . . ." He went on like this, in a meandering manifesto of poetic, disturbing, conditional statements I couldn't follow.

Meanwhile I was getting closer to him on the field—as he reached for my hands I could smell the soil on his fingers. I had the blissful feeling of being home at last.

TEN

The girl tucks her toy boat between her clothes in her suitcase, hoping her mother won't notice. She's been told not to bring anything except clothes to wherever they're going. But she can't leave this toy behind—she has the feeling it might bring her to her father.

She shuts the suitcase and places it at the center of her bed. It looks funny there, all alone. It's early morning, and they're to report to the assembly center in a few hours. She doesn't know when, or if, she'll come home again.

She walks down the hall of the hotel and into the bathroom, where she finds her mother crouched awkwardly over the claw-foot bathtub.

Straining to peer over her shoulders, the girl sees what her mother is doing: laying out her kimonos carefully, one by one, along the bottom of the tub. The girl has only seen these a handful of times, as her mother only brings them out on special occasions.

"My mother made with her hands—no machine," her mother would tell her. "In Japan. Priceless. You can wear when you grow up."

Now her mother takes something she's had cradled in her lap and holds it up: the little wooden statue from the family altar. Standing about six inches tall, a bright-red bib around its neck, its face is round and childlike, expression serene, eyes closed.

Once she asked her father about it.

"He's a god," he'd explained. "O-Jizo-san. He protects babies and children, and all those who need help. And not just the living—he helps the dead as well."

"How?" she'd asked, touching its smooth brown cheek.

"Well, for instance, if for some reason a baby dies, he helps its little spirit cross the river, from the land of the living to the land beyond. He hides it in the sleeves of his robe, like this," he'd said, wrapping an arm around her, "so the demons there don't see it—great big blue monsters, with so many eyes, always watching!" he'd bellowed, playfully bugging out his eyes. She'd laughed but also shuddered.

"Otherwise the poor little spirit will be trapped in the riverbed for all eternity.

"He takes care of you, too, Sumi-chan—and all of us. So we must take good care of him."

"What about these?" She'd reached for a stack of small stones by the statue's feet, touching the topmost one.

"The trapped spirits spend their days stacking stones to give good karma to their families and to help themselves out of the river. But the nasty demons keep knocking them down again. But if we, the living, stack stones for the spirits here, like this," he'd said, motioning to the small tower, "we can help them change their fate. We can help bring Jizo to them, so he can guide them safely across the river."

Unsure what any of this meant, the girl had nevertheless always found the small wooden god's presence in their home comforting.

Now her mother says words in Japanese the girl doesn't understand and places the statue on the bed of kimonos, hesitating a moment before letting go. She lifts a large gray canister from the floor, shakes it generously over the tub, releasing a toxic odor, takes a matchbook from a silk pouch she wears around her neck, strikes a match, and tosses it into the tub.

The girl has to hold herself back from shouting out and lunging forward as the dragon-breath flames unleash, lashing dangerously close to her mother's slightly protruding belly.

Her mother moves back a few inches to watch the fire play out its elaborate show. At least Baby won't get burned, *the girl thinks.*

The kimonos are first to burst into flames, the brilliant sea-greens, wildflower purples, sunset reds, and autumn golds fast melting to brown and black, disintegrating to ash.

A mix of horror and sadness blooms within the girl.

The statue, though, resists at first, as if it does in fact possess some divine powers. Flames lick harmlessly, even playfully, at the cheeks, sleeves, and ankles, the serene face looking almost smug. The girl admires the strength of her father's carving.

But soon smoke rises from behind the sloping shoulders, like wings, and suddenly the small figure is alight. The once peaceful face grimaces for a flicker of a moment before disappearing into the flames, the dense wood giving off a sweet scent.

The girl imagines herself disappearing as well, like her father did the month before.

ELEVEN

Topaz and Frank's house had always been what you'd call "lived-in," but when I stopped by the next week, the place resembled our apartment after having been ransacked: brightly colored clothes, toys, art supplies, and half-eaten snacks were strewn everywhere. It seemed a rainbow had crash-landed through the window. A child's red potty sat in front of a TV playing an Elmo episode, like a beacon of clarity amid the chaos. Syndra and Millie, ages eight and three, lay on the floor camouflaged amid everything, ignoring the TV, staring at a phone and a tablet.

I tried saying hi to them, but Topaz whisked me through the mess to her bedroom and pulled me into the closet with her, sliding the mirror-door mostly shut, making it difficult to breathe. The musky air smelled of perfume and, oddly, peanuts.

"I think I'm gonna do something stupid to me or the kids unless I get some relief," she said through clenched teeth as we crouched on the closet floor.

"Why are we in the closet?"

"Only place I can think straight. I'm telling you, Jane, don't have kids!"

"Oh, Top, I'm sure things will—"

"Please cut all the nicey-nice crap, for once!" she snapped. Then she burst into tears. "Oh, god . . . I can't sleep, eat, work—my stupid clients are probably gonna leave me, too." The cool materials of her hanging clothes slid across my arm and cheek.

"Can you take some time off work, just for a few days?"

"And pay the mortgage? Sorry, Jane, but . . . you . . ." she said, choking on her tears, "really don't understand a thing about real estate. God, I miss the '90s!"

"What about your yoga and meditation?" I asked, feeling uncomfortable pressed up against her in the dark. "Do you still do that?"

"Yeah, yeah, but honestly, I'm sick of all that Buddhist *letting go* crap. It's easy for a bunch of bald monks up on mountaintops to find inner peace—they don't have kids pulling out their hair and pissing on the floor 'cause their *fucking father's gone!*" she shouted in my ear. "Tell me the truth, Jane: were you surprised he left?"

"Surprised?" I asked, my eardrum reverberating painfully. "I mean, of course—he was your husband." I let out a high-pitched laugh.

"That's not what I'm asking. I mean . . . did you ever like him? Tell me what you're really thinking."

"*Like* him?" I asked, buying time to think of an appropriate response. My thighs were cramping from crouching for so long.

"Mommy?" we heard Millie calling from across the house, rescuing me.

Topaz flung the closet door shut. "*Shh!*" she implored, her eyes flashing in the dark.

"Mommy?" Millie's voice called again, getting closer. We heard the pitter-patter of small feet. "Are you in the closet?" The pitter-patter continued into the bedroom. "*Mommy?*"

"Yes, honey, we're in the closet getting some clothes. We'll be out in a sec."

"Getting clothes?" Millie asked, perplexed.

"Hey, Millie!" I said in a big, dramatic voice. "Where's your sissy? I bet she wants to play hide-and-seek. Go tell your sissy you want to play hide-and-seek!"

For a moment I thought my plan had worked, but when I cracked open the door and peered out, Millie's big blue eye was inches from mine.

"Go tell your sissy," I repeated.

"No," she said, her voice tinged with anger.

"Come on, Top, we'd better go on out there," I reasoned. "Why don't I take the girls somewhere while you have some time to yourself?"

"*Time to myself?*" she whisper-shouted back. "Can't be alone right now. Doctor's orders."

Millie was trying to slide open the door now as Topaz struggled to keep it shut, Millie's *Mommy*s morphing into desperate moans, sounding too deep for her little body.

"Go watch some more Elmo," Topaz demanded.

"No!" bellowed Millie. "I hate Elmo!"

"*No one fucking hates Elmo!*" Topaz shouted back fiercely.

"Okay, everyone, let's all calm down a bit here," I chirped, sliding the door open, stepping out into the bedroom, thankful for the oxygen. "I know—I'll make snacks! By the way, why isn't Syndra at school today?"

Topaz opened her mouth in a silent scream.

"Yeah, snacks!" Millie was shouting, sounding like a three-year-old again, sashaying ahead of me. "I want Cheetos!"

I tried making mac and cheese from scratch, but the cheese in the fridge was moldy, so I settled for out of the box. When it was done, I carried bowls to the gals who were now on the couch, watching an anime show on the TV that seemed pretty inappropriate—girls with large breasts dressed in skimpily cut school uniforms, chopping off the heads of multiheaded red-and-blue beasts. They convinced me their mother allowed them to watch it, so I found my way back to Topaz in the dark of the closet.

I handed her some tissue and a bowl of macaroni.

"So, I think I'm gonna start medication," she said, sniffing over her bowl. "You know, some kind of antistress or antidepressant stuff. Just to get me through this."

"I'd think about that if I were you; that stuff's addictive. My mom's been taking antidepressants for ages and shows no signs of ever stopping."

"Oh, really?" she asked, pushing a skirt aside to get a better look at me. "Since when?"

"Since I was a kid."

"Before or after she left you?"

"I don't know. I guess before."

It bothered me how often Topaz referred to your grandmother's leaving—as though it had been such a defining moment in my life. Which it really wasn't. It wasn't even as though she had *left*, exactly; she just moved to a different place.

"Sorry, I don't mean to pry, it's just, back then meds were super strong and way less scientific than they are now, much more hit-or-miss.

And barbaric, like shock therapy or those Victorian treatments for hysteria. And super sexist."

"Yeah, I guess she was one of the pioneers in that department," I said, chuckling awkwardly.

"Well, it's gotten very refined now," she said, straightening her spine and lifting up a spoonful of macaroni. "There's zillions of options, depending on your specific, personal needs. It's a very complex, scientific process—so many minute factors to consider."

"Well, just try not to get addicted, there, dear," I joked in an ironic, mothering tone.

"Okay, Mommy," she answered in a cutesy baby voice, batting her eyelashes and pouting her lips. "I'll submit monthly pwogwess weports to you, I *pwomiss*."

We laughed.

We emerged from the closet, brushing ourselves off, breathing in the relatively fresh air as our eyes adjusted to the daylight, and found the girls in the living room. They were on the floor again, eating from a package of Red Vines, still watching their show. Now one of the schoolgirls, separated from her friends, was cowering in a corner, her torn skirt revealing too much of her ghost-white thigh, as several of the multiheaded, club-wielding beasts menacingly approached.

"Oh, yuck, I hate this violent anime stuff," Topaz said, grabbing the remote control and searching for something else. "It's so twisted." She landed on an episode of *Hannah Montana*.

The girls reluctantly agreed to watch this instead. Topaz and I made our way over them and cleared a spot for ourselves on the couch. We bummed some strips of Red Vines and watched with them, all of us laughing together at the cheesy jokes along with the comforting canned laughter. A light rush of contentment spread throughout my body.

TWELVE

A few nights later, your dad went rummaging through the bedroom closet, looking for something.

"What about something really simple," I was saying from bed. "Maybe rent out a Chinese restaurant, one of those red banquet rooms. In case it rains. We could hire a small band, maybe jazz or something."

"Since when do you like jazz?" he asked from the closet.

Though I still hadn't managed to say yes to his proposal, we'd begun playfully planning our wedding as though it were happening.

"I don't know. Isn't that what people have at weddings? Nothing too offensive. Oh, and about your grandmother's ring . . . where is it?" I asked, glancing at my bare finger. He'd offered it to me the night of our anniversary, but it had been slightly too big, and Shiro had promised to get it resized. "I just want to make sure you still have it. I haven't seen it since that night, have you?"

He emerged from the closet with a dusty old VCR machine. "Yeah, I have it," he said, but he was distracted, pulling a VHS tape off the bookshelf. "Want to watch with me?"

I thought maybe the tape was one of his early video projects. I got out of bed, made myself a cup of tea and sat on the couch while he fumbled behind the TV, hooking up the old machine.

It ended up being a PBS documentary from the 1980s about nisei—second-generation Japanese Americans—men, and their struggles with early heart disease. According to the show, nisei men suffered early heart attacks over two times more often than their Japanese counterparts. The show posited various theories about this discrepancy, one being that it might have something to do with the internment camps of WWII.

Your dad and his family had been surprised when his grandfather, whom everyone called Pops—a quiet, retired auto mechanic and die-hard baseball fan with an impish grin—had agreed to being interviewed for the documentary when his heart surgeon had suggested him. No one had ever heard him speak about Camp.

It was the same in your grandmother's family; for the most part, people never spoke about Camp, except in brief, obscure references, usually cheerfully. "Oh, it was a nice break!" they'd say. "Like year-round summer camp!" As a kid, I used to think my family had been allowed to attend some special, government-funded summer camp for free.

Dressed in a freshly pressed shirt, his hair combed to one side like a boy on school picture day, Pops sat erect in the large TV studio chair across from the more relaxed-looking interviewer, a white man with a fluffy head of gray hair, who looked to be in his late fifties or so—around Pops's age. Pops fiddled with his clip-on microphone, cleared his throat, looked at the interviewer and began.

"Yeah, so . . . when I was a kid, I had no idea where Japan was." He chuckled and stared into space, then pulled his shoulders back, looked back at the interviewer and continued. "In high school, FDR was my hero. Me and my friends drove Chevys, greased our hair, played baseball. Real all-American kids, you know? The Yankees were my team—still are. Even after the Dodgers moved out here, I stayed loyal. But anyway, after school, I worked on the farm with my parents. We had one of the most successful fruit farms in the Stockton area—apples, nuts, the sweetest strawberries you ever tasted." He took a handkerchief from his pocket and dabbed at his mouth, as if it watered at the memory.

"At the height of the season we hired up to fifty workers. Our farm was so productive, people wanted our secrets. Every so often, we'd get visitors from the bigger agricultural companies. Hakujin—white people. We always welcomed them." He spoke slowly, choosing his words carefully.

"Yeah, so, one time this hakujin guy came by. All dressed up in a nice suit, hat, everything. My parents invited him inside for lunch—sent him off with a big box full of berries. Before leaving, he poked around a while, asking questions about our farming techniques. My parents were trusting people, you know?" He leaned toward the interviewer. "*Naive* is more like it.

"But still, we knew they had their eyes on us. Oh, sure. Even before

Pearl Harbor, our phone line was tapped. FBI, you know? At first Mom thought Dad was paranoid, but no—he'd be on the phone to one of his friends, and he'd hear some guy's voice interrupt: *Speak English.*"

He pointed a solemn finger at the interviewer.

"You know those big corporate farms making so much money nowadays? There's no way they could be what they are today if they hadn't taken our farms yesterday. That's no coincidence, you know? Those big companies have a lot more weight with the government than you might think. Oh, sure, lobbying and all."

He seemed more comfortable now, leaning to one side, speaking less formally.

"Ever wonder why they split all the farmlands down the middle during evacuation?" he asked, drawing a vertical line in the air with a finger. "Intermixing farmers and city-folk like that? So we farmers wouldn't all get together and *organize*, that's why. You think it's a conspiracy theory?"

He paused for the interviewer's response. The interviewer dutifully shook his head.

"No way. They ain't no dummies!" Pops proclaimed. "They got what they wanted!" He laughed thickly, dabbed at his mouth with his handkerchief again, folded it neatly and rested it on his lap, returning to his slightly more formal tone.

"Yeah, so. In high school, my English teacher invited me to enter a patriotic youth poetry contest. My poem was called, 'Where Freedom Grows.' Nice title, eh? It won first place. I guess I was a pretty okay poet. The principal shook my hand.

"Then the war came. I received a letter from FDR—my *hero*—telling me I was an alien spy. An *alien*—" he stopped, widening his eyes. "I pictured a funny green frog-guy going around with dark glasses, hiding behind buildings with a laser-beam shooter or somethin', you know?" He dropped his head back and laughed again, then sat up and cleared his throat.

"Yeah, so. After the notice, we had to get rid of all our things. Destroy—burn, bury, whatever. Everything. Especially Japanese things. We had to; people were disappearing. Oh yeah, the FBI came into our house one night while we kids were sleeping. Ransacked the place. We didn't know what they were looking for. Someone disappeared at our temple. Everyone was paranoid—thought they might be next. Forget about freedom; people were *disappearing*."

He leaned forward and pointed at the interviewer again.

"Imagine men with guns barging into your house while your family's asleep. Then being sent off to prison, no trial or nothin'."

The interviewer crossed his legs and made a short, sympathetic sound.

"It affects you, you know? In ways you can't explain. They call us the model minority now, and sure, we're doing pretty good, I guess, but it still *affects* you, you know?"

"Well, sure," the interviewer hurried to agree, "an experience like that, especially when you're young, must have certain lasting effects."

Pops nodded, sat back, stared briefly into space, then continued.

"Yeah, so . . . in Camp, it was like living in a fishbowl." He motioned up to the corners of the interview room. "Eyes everywhere, always watching you from up on those guard towers, you know? No privacy. We had no idea how long we'd be there, what our fate would be. Some of the older generation went nuts. They couldn't handle it. Broke some of 'em—went *nuts*," he repeated, tapping his head.

He trailed off and shook his head sadly, seeming momentarily lost in a particularly haunting memory.

"Now, you and your family were interned in Rohwer, Arkansas, correct?" the interviewer asked. "The farthest relocation center from the West Coast?"

"Yeah, yeah, that's right," Pops answered, straightening his shoulders. "Arkansas—way out in the swampland. But not so long after we arrived, I received another *friendly* note, telling me I'd have the *opportunity* to fight for *my* country," he said, drenching his words with plenty of irony. "Go fight for my captors while my family's home in prison? For what crime? Looking like the enemy? Oh, sure, sure! No thanks—*no thanks!*"

He let out a harsh laugh and broke into a loud coughing fit. The interviewer pointed to a glass of water on a table. Pops took a sip and coughed a bit more.

"Anyway, I didn't go," he said, punching his chest. "Heck no. I was a 'No-No Boy.' You know us 'No-No Boys'?"

"Yes," the interviewer answered, sitting up, seeming happy to explain the term. "No-No Boys: you men were given a form to fill out, a loyalty questionnaire, asking if you'd be willing to fight for America and to un-conditionally swear your allegiance—"

"Yeah, yeah, right, right," Pops cut in, nodding and waving a hand impatiently. "So, anyway, they sent me off to Tule Lake," he said, point-ing to a wall of the room, as though Tule Lake were just on the other side. "High security, you know? My mom . . . she didn't take it so well."

He looked off into the distance, then dabbed at his eyes with his handkerchief.

"But you know, in the grand scheme of things," he concluded, looking back at the interviewer, returning his handkerchief to his pocket, "we can't complain. What we went through was nothing, compared to, say, what went on over there. Systematic genocide—the obliteration of a people on a mass scale. That's something I'll never comprehend. Or even right here, like what the Indians went through, or the blacks. In the face of some-thing like that, what we went through was nothing. I would perhaps call it, in the face of, say, the bombs—Little Boy and Fat Man; nice names, eh?—what we went through was more like a case of a single rape. Just one, single rape." He coughed once into his fist.

"Well now, I'd hardly say . . ." the interviewer started, pausing awk-wardly, but Pops cut in again.

"Still, you have to remember. That's critical for your sanity."

"Indeed. Now, you said your family lost its farm?"

"Yes, sir, that's right," Pops answered, nodding quickly. "After the war, my folks went back to Japan." He paused, as though searching for the right words, placing his fingertips together carefully. "They never returned home. Their hearts were broken. Navigational specificity became unclear," he said, pronouncing these last, perplexing words slowly.

The interviewer tilted his head as though waiting for an explanation, but none came.

When the show ended, Shiro let the picture run to static, resting his head back on the couch and looking up into the broken heating vent, which was temporarily quiet.

"Our whole clan had this big potluck dinner at my aunt's house when the show first aired," he reminisced. "We were all excited, piling big mounds of food on our plates, gathering around the TV—my dad set up the VCR so we'd be sure to get it on tape. We were sitting there, counting the minutes till it started, like, aw man, our family's gonna be famous!

"At first everyone's watching intently, bursting into cheers when Pops comes on. People slapping his back, laughing, saying, 'Hey there you are! Uh-oh, Eddy, man, you gotta lose some weight—lookin' a little chunky around the middle there!'

"After a while, though, people start getting distracted and bored, coming and going, helping themselves to more food, popping open beers and sodas and, you know, talking over the slower parts. But when Pops says that part about his parents going back to Japan—everyone just looks at each other, like, okay, *what the hell did he just say?* 'Cause, course, in reality, his parents never went back—being from Hiroshima, they couldn't, least not then. Then the bit about 'navigational specificity'?" He slapped his thigh, guffawing. "Aw, man, that was hilarious! Everyone thought he'd gone certifiably nuts! But he knew what he was talking about—in a poetic sort of way."

He paused, still staring up at the vent. I thought maybe he was dozing off, but then he continued.

"When the show's over, Pops just keeps sitting there, looking stunned, like he can't believe he's really just been on TV. Then someone flips the channel back to the football game and that was it—no one ever mentioned it again. In the next few years, he and his two brothers were all dead from early heart failure."

"Wow," I said, unsure what else to say. It had been the same in Mom's family, the men dying before their time. "Yeah, my mom's brother died in Camp."

"Oh yeah?" He sat up. "She had another brother?"

"Yeah. But he was just a baby." I was dimly surprised I'd never mentioned this to him before.

"How'd he die?"

"I don't know. It's kind of a mystery. No one ever talks about it. I guess babies just died more often back then."

The heater began to blow down on us.

"It's funny, sometimes I forget your mom was in Camp with Pops. In the very same block, no less. You're even closer to the whole thing than I am, but you never talk about it. Very *Japanese* of you," he teased, elbowing me lightly. "For someone so white."

"Ha ha." I elbowed him back. "It's such a shame about your family losing its farm."

"It wasn't lost, it was *stolen*," he corrected, irritation in his voice.

"I guess you could say so. Indirectly."

"Um, no, quite directly. Just like Pops said, those big agro giants wanted us Japanese farmers out of their way."

"Your Pops was so cute," I said, tracing a finger along his cheek, attempting to lighten the subject. "He looks so jolly, like a laughing Buddha. I wish I could've met him."

Our heads leaned into each other and I closed my eyes. An image came to me: an old, black-and-white photo I once saw at Shiro's parents'—your grandparents'—house, of a boy and a young man standing together in the middle of a large field, each holding a box overflowing with strawberries. They pose for the camera earnestly, but their eyes smile. The boy wears a Yankees baseball cap. A young woman in a light-colored dress stands over to the side, smiling coyly, a hand on her hip, the tip of her elbow cut from the photo. A wooden house with a large front porch stands in the background.

When I asked Shiro about it, he said it was taken at their old family farm in Stockton, before the war, and the man and woman were his great grandparents, and the boy was Pops. I'd been struck by the resemblance between Pops and your dad—same eyes, same chin; they were practically twins.

"So," Shiro said, sitting up, suddenly energized, his eyes bright in the near dark. "I'm gonna do it. Enough thinking; time for action."

"Huh? Do what?"

"Expose all the illegal shit at work. I've started a detailed log of all their crap."

"A *log?*"

"Yup—documenting everything: dates, times—"

"What exactly are you planning on doing with it?"

"Not sure yet," he said, leaning forward, running his hands through his hair. "Probably contact the ACLU first, to get their advice, get clear on my rights. Then I'll contact the press, publish stuff online. This whole scene's getting too much like what happened to us." He pointed at the TV which was now playing static. "Gotta do right by Pops. He dared to say no."

"To *us*? Shiro, that was years ago. It didn't happen to *us*." I placed my hand on his thigh and squeezed. "Come on," I said gently, "you're not serious, are you? This is the *US government* you're talking about. Taking them on like that would be foolish." I chuckled to show how preposterous such a notion was.

He frowned at me. "So, what, we just sit back and watch *this* happen over and over?" he asked, motioning to the TV again.

We watched the frantic gray dots on the screen, the heat from above making us groggy.

"I was alone with him the day he died," he eventually said, leaning into me, as though giving into the heat.

"Who?"

"Pops. I was staying at his place one week while my folks were out of town. One morning I walk into the kitchen and he's lying there on the floor. I can still see him lying on the green linoleum, his eyes wide open. Still has his Yankees cap on. I run over to him and ask if he's okay, but he doesn't say anything. He's just staring up at me, like he can't believe what's happening. I mean, yeah, he's shocked his heart's finally breaking and he's actually dying, but more than that, too . . . like he can't grasp something at an essential level. And like he's counting on me to help him understand."

I wiped a bead of sweat, or maybe it was a tear, from his cheek.

THIRTEEN

Shiro crawled around our attic on his next day off but couldn't figure out what was wrong with the heater.

"Come on down," I called up to the dark square in the ceiling of our bedroom closet. "You don't want to break anything more. I left another message for management. I'm sure they'll get back to us any day now."

"*Any day?* Meanwhile how long are we supposed to live in this *hellhole?*" he called from above. "You know, it smells really foul up here, like something died." I heard rustling and a couple of clunks. "You haven't been up here recently, have you?"

"Me? Of course not. Come on down," I urged again.

"I could have sworn I stacked your old childhood boxes over in the back corner there, but now one's right here, in the middle of the floor, with the lid off. It's like someone was up here looking for something. Maybe during the break-in."

"You probably just forgot where you put them. I really doubt whoever broke in would know about our attic space," I reasoned, chilled by the idea.

He started down the ladder. "Stranger things have happened," he said from behind his painter's mask—a precaution against mouse poop. He looked quite silly; I had to hide my smile.

"Did you even find any signs of mice up there?"

"Never hurts to be safe."

We decided to shut the vent until we could find a more permanent solution, so we shoved the couch aside and carried the ladder into the living room. But the vent was jammed in the open position. In trying to force it shut, Shiro cut his hand.

"Fuck!" he yelled, jumping down from the ladder as though he'd been bitten.

I ran to get some first aid supplies.

"Let's not get all worked up here. It's just a scratch," I reassured as I dabbed at the surprising amount of blood on his finger.

"It's not right," he declared, his voice muffled behind his mask. "Do you notice how sleepy we get in here at night while that thing's on? Something's not right in this apartment."

"Now, now, don't be so paranoid," I teased, applying some antiseptic cream and a Band-Aid to his wound. "Heat does that. Hey, I think it's safe to take your mask off now."

He slipped it off and wiped the sweat from his face. I went to the kitchen for a couple glasses of water and the box of aluminum foil.

"So, what, you think monsters are lurking up in our attic, breathing down noxious fumes on us?" I called. "Or wait, maybe someone from your work's camped out up there spying on us. Probably whoever broke into our apartment that day! Probably Chuck!" I said, laughing, returning to the living room with our waters.

"Very funny."

"Hey, Chuck?" I called sweetly up to the vent. "How's it going up there? Need anything? Some cereal?" I waved and curtsied. "Can you see me? Do I look like a terrorist from up there?" I twirled around and flashed my boobs at the ceiling.

"Okay, Jane, joke's over," Shiro snapped, sipping his water. "All I'm saying is, something's not right in here. Something's . . . fishy. And I'm gonna figure out what it is."

"And just how do you intend to do that?" I asked, kissing the red line on his cheek where the elastic of the mask had been.

He drank more of his water, ignoring my question.

"Look, I agree it's really annoying," I said, making my way up the ladder. "*I'm* the one going crazy, suffocating in here all day. I can hardly concentrate on my sewing anymore. But that doesn't mean there's some evil conspiracy."

I battled the hot wind, holding my breath as I attempted to seal the vent with foil. Twice the foil was blown off before I finally managed to tuck it securely around the metal slats.

"Genius, eh?" I asked, climbing down the ladder, proud of my fix.

"Hey, put that mask back on. You looked sexy. I've always wanted to do it with a surgeon."

He walked to the kitchen, examined his orchids, then grabbed the watering can, filled it, and stepped onto a chair to reach a high-hanging spider plant. I watched the muscles in his back relax as he gave the plant a slow twirl, picked off a few brown leaves and watered it, his movements graceful and assured. I loved watching him care for his plants; there was something at once invincible and delicate about him then. He stepped down from the chair and began watering the ones in the living room.

Sometimes he fantasized about having his own plot of land, where he could plant things into the ground, not just pots. It was a fantasy we shared: We'd move somewhere more affordable where he'd plant us a huge garden, which he'd tend to all day. From the plentiful harvest, I'd cook culinary masterpieces. You and your siblings would run around underfoot, eating berries by the handful, staining yourselves red as you played and fought and helped around the house and garden. We knew it was a whimsical, entirely old-fashioned fantasy but loved it just the same.

Growing up, the idea of motherhood had terrified me. Once I met Shiro, though, suddenly it seemed natural, and I actually found myself craving it.

I took the watering can from him and ran my fingers through his hair. He was so sweaty he looked like he'd just gone for a swim. He lifted up my blouse, his fingers still smelling of soil—then things got nice and steamy. We devoured each other right there on the living room floor, as though we hadn't tasted each other in months.

It *had* been a while since we'd had so much fun—since our anniversary, if I'm remembering correctly. Come to think of it, the morning of our anniversary, our lovemaking had been extra luscious, extra intense—divine, I remember thinking at the time, as though the cosmos had been smiling down on us.

That must have been the day we produced you!

I hope you don't mind my telling you all this. The last thing I want is to disgust or burden you. On the other hand, I don't want you suffering in ignorance. Believe me, I know how that can be. At least this way you can draw your own conclusions and, if it's possible where you are, make your own choices . . .

FOURTEEN

The girl wakes in her cot, covered in sweat, panting, as though she's been running. "Papa! Papa!" she's shouting.

A hand covers her mouth. "Shh!"

It's her brother, leaning over her. His lanky teenage body blends with the shadows of night. "You're dreaming again."

She pushes his hand away and sits up. The stench of horse manure mixed with the nearby outhouse makes it difficult to breathe.

"Where's Papa?" she asks, as she does every night.

"I've told you, Sumi, we don't know, okay? We don't know, we don't know, we don't know—all we know is there's been some mistake. He's done nothing wrong. So, we don't need to worry; he'll join us here eventually."

"What if he doesn't?" she whispers so softly she barely hears herself.

"Quiet!" he says, gruffly shoving her back down on her cot. "Don't say stupid things. Don't think such stupid things. Go back to sleep. Don't wake Mama. She needs her rest, for the baby."

His harsh voice reminds her of the guards' voices and their rifles. A few days ago, one of them barked at her when she took too long at the washbasin. Since then she's tried to avoid washing.

She and her brother look through the dark at their mother, curled on her side on her cot, facing away from them. She looks smaller than she should— like a large child. It's hard for the girl to believe a baby still grows inside her.

Before they came here, they heard stories of pregnant women being separated from their families, so her mother has been dressing in an oversized smock, bending forward when she walks, as though she has a slight disability, in order to trick the guards. Miraculously, none of them has noticed her state yet. She barely showed when they arrived here at the racetrack, so she managed to slip through the initial screening.

She has instructed the children, if asked, to say that she recently gave birth to a stillborn, to explain why her stomach appears large. Luckily, the girl and her siblings have not had to use this story yet, which the girl fears will not be believed and might be met with anger. She hopes the baby will come soon, so they can stop pretending—and so she can finally meet her new sibling. But she also fears what punishment may await them when it finally arrives.

Her brother returns to his own cot, lies down, and turns away from her. She can't sleep, all the strange night noises of the stadium forming a disturbing symphony.

She recalls passing this stadium once before, with her father. They had been in the car and she had asked him what it was, the building with the rounded, fortresslike walls. He had explained that it wasn't a place for children but had promised to bring her when she was older, to see a race. The place had possessed a romantic allure to her then, and she'd longed to see the fast, sleek animals inside.

Now we're the animals inside, *she thinks as she shifts in her cot,* but not fast or sleek—only small and scared. Me and the mice, *she adds, as one scurries past in the near darkness, stops, looks at her squarely, then, seeming relieved to see it's just her, begins sniffing around their things.*

She finds her toy boat in her tangled sheet and clutches it to her chest, singing softly to herself, a song her father used to play on his flute. Eventually her sister comes and sits beside her, placing a hand on her shoulder.

"Time to sleep now, Sumi-chan," her sister whispers warmly. Ever since they arrived here, she's been acting more like the mother than their actual mother, who's been quiet, often staring darkly into space. "Don't worry, Sumi-chan," she continues, "time to sleep. Papa's gonna be okay. Mama's gonna be okay. Baby's gonna be okay . . . everything's gonna be okay, I promise."

FIFTEEN

That Tuesday morning, I awoke to the most lovely sensation of your dad snuggling up to me from behind. His arms were wrapped around me and his skin felt soft, smooth, and warm on mine. His hands slid from my waist up to my cheeks. Eyes still closed, I savored this blissful, seductive feeling. The fingers remained there, resting lightly on my cheeks, for some time. But when I opened my eyes, I realized I must have been dreaming. Shiro had already left for work, and the hands had been much too small.

I jumped out of bed, showered, made myself a light breakfast, and set up my sewing station at the kitchen table. But I couldn't fully shake the sensation of those little hands. I also had the feeling, as I pinned the pattern to the fabric for a new dress, that whoever had broken into our apartment the other day was still there, and at that very moment watching me work. I became so preoccupied by this notion that I couldn't concentrate and kept accidentally jabbing my fingers with the pins.

Eventually, needing to get out of the apartment, leaving pins and half-cut fabric pieces splayed across the table, I grabbed a shopping bag and headed down the hill to the farmers market.

The sun was almost unbearable, but still I took my time wandering up and down the aisles, sampling this and that, surrounded by moms and kids, a few gray-haired retirees, and plenty of tattooed, pierced hipsters who, from the fact that they were out here in the middle of the week, were either mostly unemployed, like me, or techies working remotely—the type Shiro called "the new corporate drones disguised as rebels."

Ever since the accounting firm where I'd done administrative work after graduating college had downsized, I'd been looking for a job. Before he'd gotten his TSA job, your dad had worked at a small, family run garden-supply store, which he'd loved, but it went out of business when a

Home Depot opened across the street. While we were both unemployed, we spent many afternoons together, parked at café tables around town, nursing our drinks as slowly as possible while looking through job listings and preparing résumés, growing more despondent as the months progressed. We knew it wasn't just us—the entire country was still suffering after the 2008 collapse—but that didn't make the scarcity, and the rejections, feel any less demoralizing.

After Shiro had found work, I'd gotten more discouraged. I liked my part-time sewing job, but it didn't pay the bills, and I had no health benefits. My real dream was to become an architect. I've always wanted to build big things. But investing in graduate school now was impossible and, with the economy the way it was, maybe pointless.

Walking through the farmers market, beneath the clear blue sky, surrounded by all the freshly harvested, colorful produce and jars of homemade goodies, greeted by friendly smiles as the farmers offered samples of their goods, my body began to relax, and I started to feel invigorated, even hopeful for myself and the world.

Inspired by some small, shiny eggplants, I decided I'd try a Thai curry for dinner. I found some red and yellow peppers, some bright green chilies, and gathered bunches of basil, cilantro, and lime leaves, and finally a long, woodsy bundle of lemongrass, breathing in each fragrant herb before dropping it into my bag, my brain quickening with each scent.

As I was looking for a particular stand I'd passed with perfect-looking pears, my phone vibrated in my pocket.

It was a text from Topaz:

That's so horrible about your mom.

What do you mean?

Losing her home like that. Especially after all she's been through.

Huh?

You know, when she was a kid. Wasn't she
taken from her home as a child? Part of the
whole Japanese American Internment thing?

What does that have to
do with anything??

Sometimes Topaz jumped all over the place, expecting everyone to read her chaotic mind.

Losing her home. She's losing her
condo—it's foreclosing.

No, I don't think so.

Yes, it is. She just posted it on FB. You
really should get an account.

Too distracted to find the pears, I left the market, crossing the busy street under the freeway, texting Mom as I started back up the steep hill.

What's this about your
condo foreclosing?

Halfway up the hill I got a response:

Don't worry, sweetie, it's for the best.
Super busy now. Have fun!

I didn't know you were having
financial problems. Why didn't
you tell me?

Approaching our building, the sun still beating down, the strap of my bag cutting into my arm and my heart pounding, I paused to catch my breath and called her.

"Hi there, you've reached me!" her militantly cheerful outgoing message announced. "But please no voicemail messages here; text or Facebook communication is best—thanks!"

Upstairs I drank a glass of water, unloaded my groceries, stripped to my underwear and, not wanting to return to the bedroom or my sewing, lay on the couch and continued trying to reach Mom. We had recently bought an electric fan, which now stood in the corner, hopelessly stirring the hot air.

I thought about Shiro's recent suspicions that someone from his work, from the government, was rummaging through our apartment, searching through our personal items in hopes of finding evidence against him. How ludicrous.

And not just that—he'd also alluded to the idea that someone, perhaps the same ambiguous government-sanctioned villain, may have climbed up to our attic and tampered with our heating system to infect our air with some type of toxic gas! It would be funny, really, if it weren't so worrisome. In the past, even in the face of his political passions, he'd managed to think reasonably. Lately, it was as though he were looking at the world through a fun-house mirror.

On the other hand, these recent events *were* mysterious. How could one heating vent continue working when the unit was shut off? And why would someone break into our apartment while I was sleeping, searching for something without stealing anything? And build that tower?

It was true that Shiro had been subjected to more security checks than seemed reasonable recently. Maybe his work *did* have their eyes on him and, as far-fetched as it seemed, *would* go to outlandish lengths, like breaking into his home, to find something incriminating on him. Was I being naive to think otherwise?

Infected by the paranoid notion that the government might actually be watching our apartment, I covered my bare breasts and turned sideways to face the back of the couch.

The heater moaned on from above, and hot air blew down on me like an industrial hair dryer. The wad of foil I'd rigged to block the broken vent had fallen right off the next day. A new surge of sweat leaked from my pores.

My mind wandered back to the time your dad was considering taking his TSA job. He'd been adamantly against the idea at first, but his high school friend had gotten him the interview and, because jobs were so scarce and we'd both been unemployed for so long, I'd encouraged him, saying it would only be temporary. When Mom found out he was considering the job, she'd called several times with concerns, insisting it would be boring work and pointing out that the number of terrorists actually caught was statistically low compared to all the hassle—a surprisingly political comment coming from Mom, who considered herself apolitical.

"Plus, those *blue uniforms* are really hideous," she'd added. We all knew she had an aversion to uniformed government officials and would go to great lengths, no matter how ridiculous or morbid, to avoid them.

Once, not long after 9/11, Mom invited me on a trip to Hawaii with her second family. I was in my midtwenties and Chris was still a teenager.

As we all waited in the security line at the airport, I noticed Mom's hands were trembling. Just as it seemed we'd passed on through with everyone, a TSA worker approached us from behind and tapped Mom on the shoulder. She jumped and gasped, as though he'd held a gun to her head.

When the worker explained that she and her party would have to step aside for further screening, she began looking all around, as though considering her escape options.

"It'll be fine, Mom," Chris reassured her. "Don't worry, this is normal now."

"Yes, just relax, Sue," Jim, my stepfather, agreed. "We have nothing to hide."

"You know what, let's just get out of here," Mom muttered through clenched teeth, grabbing her single suitcase—she always traveled lightly—from the conveyor belt.

"Excuse me, ma'am," the young worker in the blue uniform started, following Mom as she quickly walked toward the nearest exit.

But Jim caught up to her and grabbed her shoulder.

"Don't be silly, Sue," he scolded, gently guiding her back. "You're just making this worse!" Laughing apologetically to the security worker who was now speaking into his walkie-talkie, he said, "Look, son, it's the *uniforms*. They make her uncomfortable. It has to do with her *past*," he said in a confiding tone, as though getting personal with the guy might help.

"It's just a random search, sir," the worker replied blankly.

We were escorted to a small room where different workers opened, unfolded, and refolded each of our personal items, their white-gloved fingers moving efficiently, like independent, trained creatures. As they worked, Mom stared down at her sandals, rubbing her upper arms, looking like a frightened child. I started spinning stories of how perhaps she wasn't the mom I'd always known; maybe she did in fact have something to hide, and we were about to spend our vacation at Guantanamo Bay instead of sunbathing on the beaches of Oahu.

But what, I wondered, was her crime?

I thought about calling Mom again now, as I lay with my face pressed into the back of the couch, the heat from the broken vent continuing to blow down on me, eroding the surface of my brain.

Sometime later I jolted upright, gasping for air. I stumbled to the kitchen to splash my face with water and only then realized what had shaken me from my dreams: that cat again. The shrieks sounded so close, were so shrill and persistent, it felt as though the small animal's teeth were gnawing at the surface of my skin, aiming for my bones.

Walking around the apartment, trying to ascertain where in the building the cries must be coming from, I realized, on listening closer, that the crier wasn't actually a cat, or any kind of animal; these were the cries of a human baby. A newborn, it seemed from the thin, desperate quality of the voice. Our next-door neighbor must recently have given birth.

In the bedroom, I saw that our drawers were pulled open and our bedding and clothes were strewn all over the floor. At the center of the bed stood a stack of random objects: some pillows, a couple of books, a jar of lotion. Like the tower before, it looked as though it had been built with a purpose in mind, like an object in some sort of primitive ritual.

I waited for that same sense of panic that I'd felt after the last break-in, but, for some reason, it didn't come.

I climbed onto the bed and studied the tower, then gently knocked it down. Then, slowly, I rebuilt it, just as it had been: the pillows, the books, the jar. Again I knocked it down; again I rebuilt it. I found myself stuck in this loop for some time, building, destroying, building, destroying, that newborn baby in the building continuing to cry out for help.

These actions, building and destroying, struck me as familiar, as though my body knew them well. I recalled playing around the house when I was a little kid, building similar structures from random household objects. We would work for hours, imagining we were building all sorts of large, monumental things, then insist that Mom and Dad tiptoe around them, leaving them untouched for days. Eventually, when the whim struck me, I'd take Dad's baseball bat, and go on a destructive rampage, knocking down all of the towers, laughing and shrieking with a wild, brutal glee.

SIXTEEN

Dad still lives in my childhood house in Albany, a small, mostly white, affluent town just north of Berkeley. It had been about two weeks since I'd learned of Mom's foreclosure when I went there for dinner. Dad greeted me with a lackluster smile, dressed in jeans, an untucked, pale-blue, button-down shirt, and slippers. I asked if he was well and he mumbled something about how, in the grand scheme of things, he supposed he was just fine.

He and his long-term girlfriend had split up the year before, and he'd been in a low-level funk ever since. But even so, this evening he looked a shade paler and more haggard than usual.

He'd cooked us a simple dinner of pasta and asparagus, and we ate on stools at the kitchen counter, along with glasses of an incongruously nice cabernet he'd brought out from his collection. At first our conversation revolved around Mom's foreclosure, Dad rolling his eyes at what he saw as her perpetual bad decision-making.

"We all knew buying that condo—as if just buying a *condo* weren't bad enough in the first place—but buying one at that time was absurd," he asserted, twirling his wine. "It was clearly the peak of the market; any fool could have seen that. But then again, I suppose it's par for the course with anything involving that character she chose to marry."

"Well, Dad, no one really knew we were in for such a crash. You can never know something like that."

"Nonsense. Any number of people could have told her, including myself, if she'd have asked. Well, I'm not bailing her out again. This time she'll have to face the consequences of her own poor judgment." He stuck out his chin defiantly.

"No one's asking you to bail her out. I'm sure she'll be okay, at least as far as the condo's concerned. So far she's managed to keep herself from homelessness."

"Which only encourages her reckless behavior," he said, pointing his wine at me.

"By the way, you haven't seen her lately, have you?"

"Just on Facebook."

"But not in person?"

"In person? No, why?"

"It's just, I can't get in touch with her. I mean, I've gotten some texts, but she's stopped our lunch dates and now she's not answering her phone. I'm getting worried. I'm thinking of writing her an old-fashioned letter, just to see if she receives it."

His laughter annoyed me as he finished his wine and, his laughter stopping abruptly, poured himself another half glass. "Ah, the days of letters," he said wistfully.

"You seem a bit down tonight, Dad . . . Anything wrong?"

"Oh, do I?" he asked, looking surprised. "Nothing to worry your pretty head about," he said, twirling his wine again, his Louisiana accent faintly slipping back. "Just somethin' that's bound to happen as one gets older, I guess—least to any half-cognizant, thinkin' individual." Dad had worked hard to lose his southern drawl when he moved out west, though every so often, especially when he was feeling uneasy, it would briefly sneak back. I liked the soft, wide-open sounds of the vowels and never understood why he'd spurned his old way of speaking.

"What's bound to happen?"

"Oh, nothin', nothing," he said, clearing his throat, returning to his somewhat stiff Northern California accent. "Just . . . reflections, I suppose. Basic philosophical questions one might not have taken the time to ask previously, when one was so busy." He set his wine glass down and looked at it. "Such as, for example, how useful one's life has been and such. Versus how hurtful, and so on and so forth." He stood and began clearing our dishes.

"What do you mean, 'hurtful?'"

"It's nothing, nothing. Just . . . well, when one spends so many years of one's life on a particular project . . . and that project comes so closely into one's focus that certain complexities and . . . larger ramifications, let's say, are overlooked," he stumbled on, rinsing a plate at the sink, "the gray area between pure research and certain other, more questionable applications that one had no intention of aiding . . . well, let's just say sometimes obsession with one's work, and a certain naive idealism—an almost religious faith in the purity of the field and such—can get the best of one." He glanced up at me as he placed the plate into the dishwasher, looking tired from his circuitous speech.

I was about to say something to comfort him, but he continued speaking as he filled the dishwasher with detergent.

"It's perfectly natural, of course, but it's been on my mind lately, is all. The other day at Monterey Market, for example. I found myself watching the young girl, probably in her late teens or early twenties, bagging my items—she was hapa, like you, I believe—and when she looked up to ask if I wanted my milk double-bagged, I heard myself apologizing to her."

He pressed the on button and the hum of the dishwasher filled the kitchen. We raised our voices to talk over it.

"Apologizing? For what?"

"Well that's just it. Nothing exactly—and everything. It's difficult to explain, the sense of responsibility one ends up feeling, deservedly so or not . . . She was a very nice girl, it seemed; she just smiled and said, 'It's okay, sir. No worries.'"

He looked at me, his eyes seeming extra blue. I felt he was hoping for some type of redemption, though for what I had no clue.

One of the sweetest people in the world, with his shy, stilted social demeanor, it was hard to believe that Dad had spent over thirty years as a nuclear physicist at one of the top nuclear programs in the world. He had never discussed the details of his work with me or Mom when I was growing up, and we never asked. It was as though the three of us had entered into a silent pact around the subject. Mom had admired that he was a successful scientist but had mixed feelings about the fact that he worked with nuclear energy, not to mention for the government.

"I'm just glad he doesn't have to wear a *uniform!*" she'd say with a shudder.

Sometimes I'd have the urge to ask him if he ever worked on any type of weapons, but then I wouldn't. Whether or not he has, I still don't know.

"Don't be silly, Dad," I reassured him now, grabbing an apple from his fruit bowl and wiping it on my blouse. "I'm sure you've only contributed to good in the world. Anyway, no need to dwell on the past; isn't that what you and Mom always taught me? Look toward the future?" I bit into the juicy fruit.

"Right," he said, chuckling at himself. "You are absolutely right, Jane."

He smiled at me gratefully, and at that moment I saw the young man I remembered from my childhood—I could see him coming home from work, tall and hurried, dressed in his dark-blue suit, his body brimming with energy, placing his briefcase by the door, picking me up and twirling me high in the air.

I had the impression that Dad was also seeing me as I was in the past: a scrawny, quiet girl with overgrown bangs.

"But enough about me, Jane," he said more brightly. "How are you these days?"

"Me? Oh, just fine. Just really tired, is all." I watched as he spread plastic wrap over the leftover asparagus. The feeling that we were back in the past was intensifying, and now I imagined Mom was there in the kitchen with us, dressed in the frilly, rose-print apron she always used to wear around the house. I imagined her taking the broom from the pantry and sweeping the floors, chatting nonchalantly about this and that.

"So," I said, trying to ignore my imaginings, "I've been meaning to ask Mom about this, but like I said, I just can't seem to find her. I was wondering, do you remember what she was like before she started up with her antidepressants?"

The Mom in my mind stopped her sweeping and placed a hand on her hip, waiting with tense amusement to see what Dad would say.

"Oh, gosh, dear, that was a long time ago . . . too long for this old fart to remember," he deflected, chuckling and placing the leftovers in the refrigerator.

"I mean, she must have been pretty stressed to need medication, especially back then, before it was so popular."

Dad shut the refrigerator door and the feeling of the past faded; Dad was old again, Mom was gone, and I was a grown woman in my midthirties.

"Well, dear," he said, still facing the refrigerator, "this is perhaps something you should discuss with your mother herself, don't you think?"

"But like I said, I can't find her. And it's not the kind of question I want to ask in a text. Anyway, you know she doesn't like talking about these kinds of things."

"No, she doesn't," he agreed.

He returned to the sink and washed the pots and pans in silence as I ate my apple. Eventually he cleared his throat and looked out the window above the sink, where the sun was setting, bathing his stooped profile in pink and gold hues.

"Well, Jane," he said, projecting his voice loudly over the dishwasher. I had the sense that he was about to relieve himself of something weighty he'd been carrying for a long time. "Your mother was perfectly normal, most of the time. But then there were other times . . . I think you know she inherited a rather heavy load. Her mother struggled with mental illness— or I should say chemical imbalance. I think you've heard about the baby?"

"Not much. But what little I heard sounded so sad." I placed the apple core on the counter.

"More than sad—a real tragedy. In retrospect, it's clear that Bachan needed professional help. Medical, science-based help."

"But didn't Bachan have reasons to be depressed? I mean, things in her life that were hard? Like leaving her homeland, Jichan being taken away, losing the hotel . . . not just chemical imbalance? Nothing you can inherit, right?"

"Well, sure, there's always play between the interior and exterior worlds, of course. One never knows for certain which holds more influence, ultimately. Humans are complex, convoluted organisms. But, from what your mother's told me, with Bachan it was more than a natural reaction to challenging circumstances, in terms of what happened to the baby . . ."

"How did it die, exactly?"

"Naming you after him never seemed like a good idea to me," he continued as though he hadn't heard my question, his voice now muffled and echoing as he leaned into the large pasta pot to scrub its bottom. "It seemed, well, morbid, to say the least. But your mother insisted. She claimed she had no choice. Some superstitious, ancestral belief. She insisted that naming the baby—you—after him would appease him somehow."

"*Him?*"

"The baby." He glanced nervously over his shoulder at me, then continued scrubbing the pot. "It's ridiculous, I know. But she was determined to stop her episodes. Paranoid, delusional episodes. As a child she used to believe she'd find him and the two would play together. Strange games, by a river. When they were interned in Arkansas, during the war. But then one day she couldn't find him anymore. She began sleepwalking—looking for him in her sleep. She'd have elaborate hallucinations, horrid stuff—great *monsters* with *horns* and *multiple eyes* or some such, if you can imagine," he said, shaking his head and laughing, as though embarrassed by Mom's childhood visions.

"Even as an adult, these episodes continued. She thought her brother's spirit was stuck in some sort of limbo-land—a kind of purgatory, I suppose—and was calling to her for help. She'd talk about a fire at her family's old hotel, after her father was taken by the FBI—something about the burning of an effigy and lost protection. A curse of some kind. She and her father had been close, according to Michi, so his disappearance affected her strongly. Of course, your mother never spoke about any of this, except during her episodes, when she was incoherent—I could never follow her logic, if you could call it that. It was difficult to live with, frankly." He shook his head, his back slumped over the sink.

"But Mom doesn't believe in spirits or superstitions or anything religious. She's always been against anything like that."

"Yes, well, that wasn't always the case."

"So, did it work?" I asked, the pit in my stomach pulsing disconcertingly. "Did naming me after the baby stop her episodes?"

"For a while, yes," he said, straightening his shoulders as he ran water over the pot. "But then they started up again. She'd hear him crying for her—around when you were in middle school, I believe. In the end, nothing worked but medication. Thank god for science, I tell you. Ironically, I think that's when she stopped needing me so much. Life's funny, isn't it?" He took some time to balance the pot atop the other dishes in the dish rack, then looked over his shoulder at me, smiling sadly.

"So, she took the medication to quiet the ghost?" My question surprised me.

"*Quiet the ghost?*" He let out an amused snort. "If you believe in that sort of superstitious nonsense. No, no, your mother came to terms with the fact that she inherited a chemical imbalance and treated it as such. Though nothing cured her restlessness . . ."

Mom naming me after her baby brother who died in Camp had always seemed like some sort of sick joke to me—a way to remember what no one wanted to remember.

When I was twelve, on one of our family visits to LA, late one night when everyone else was asleep, Aunt Michi paused our movie and walked in front of the TV.

"Don't tell your mom," she began quietly, glancing up at the dark staircase. "But I'm gonna tell you about your namesake."

"My *what*?"

I'd never heard the word before, and certainly no one had ever told me I was named after anyone.

She launched into her story right there, her short, stocky figure framed by the glow of the TV.

"It was after Pearl Harbor, maybe, I don't know, three, four weeks, when the FBI came to the hotel and took Papa—your Jichan. No one knew where or why or what. Our friends and neighbors said, well, maybe since he was such a good businessman in downtown LA, and such an active member at his temple—he used to carve these beautiful Buddhist statues—so maybe the authorities saw him as some sort of *threat* or something, they said.

"We kids and Mama, we just so happened to be out somewhere, I don't know, maybe school or an errand or something. But when we got home, he was gone. All his things were still there, just not him. They didn't take nothing else—they just came up to the top floor of the hotel, where we lived, and took him." She pointed up at the cracked plaster of her living room ceiling, as though we were in one of the lower floors of the old hotel.

She sat next to me on the couch and looked down at her fluffy pink slippers. I looked around her living room at the art deco–inspired curves of the ceiling corners. The home had been almost grand when she and her husband had purchased it in the early sixties, in a neighborhood locals once referred to as "the Black Beverly Hills." They'd saved for years for the down payment, no easy feat on my uncle's delivery man's salary and my aunt's wages as a nanny. The place still had an elegance to it, despite the wear and tear.

"Well, Mama was pregnant when they took him," she continued, "so now she had to run the hotel and care for us kids all by herself, no help. You're just a kid, Aki-chan, so you can't really understand, but that's a lot of work—running a hotel and restaurant and taking care of kids, plus being pregnant, with no help! Then, I don't know, maybe three or four months later, we got a notice saying we had to evacuate. Leave everything. I remember your uncle Tak reading that notice out loud ten, twenty times—none of us could understand it; it didn't make no sense. Leave everything in ten days. We still didn't know where Papa was. They put us over at Santa Anita racetrack." She pointed to her living room window. "We slept there while they built more permanent facilities—about six months. God, it stank!" she exclaimed, wrinkling her nose.

"Your uncle Tak, oh my god, he was so mad, and Mama, she got so quiet. We never saw her like that before. She wore this big, baggy dress, so the guards wouldn't notice she was pregnant. She thought if they found out, they might take her away. It scared us kids. Of course we all wanted Papa.

"Then one night right there in our stall, with the help of this nice neighbor woman from the next stall, she gave birth. He came during Obon. You know Obon?"

I shook my head.

"It's like . . ." She searched for the right words. "A celebration—each year. To visit with the dead. People light lanterns and dance with their ancestors. We kids used to have such fun at the old temple—we'd dance, eat shaved ice, play. I guess it seems fitting now that he was born during Obon, eh?"

I shrugged awkwardly.

"After he was born, Mama was scared the guards would take him away— like they did Papa. She'd hide him down in her dress whenever we left our stall. Poor little guy never saw the light of day. It didn't make no sense, and we tried explaining to her it would be different with a baby, but she wouldn't listen. She went kind of *crazy*," she said, tapping her head. "I don't think she ever even registered him for a birth certificate."

Our movie resumed loudly. She grabbed the remote and paused it again.

"When we got to Camp, she stopped eating, talking, everything . . .

I can still see her sitting there on her cot, just staring into space, not seeing nothing, no one. Oh, god, her arms were so *emaciated!* Just hanging there like noodles." She dangled her own arms at her sides to demonstrate.

"And poor Baby Aki, god, he was such a tiny, pathetic little thing— but oh man, could he *wail!* God, he had some *lungs!*" She let out a piercing laugh, a sharp mix of pain and pride.

"*Aki?*" I asked in disbelief. "I'm named after him?"

But she was too caught in her memory to hear me.

"I can still hear him crying, lying there next to her on that cot, just *screeching his tiny head off,* his mouth wide like this." She opened her mouth wide, like a baby bird. "But Mama's body wouldn't make no milk. He was so hungry, and mad, too—mad at being born into such a situation! Me and Tak, we were just teenagers, but of course we tried to help—we'd walk him up and down our barrack, try to sooth him. But there were times he had to be left alone with her . . ."

"Aki? Michi?" a voice called from the staircase. "You're still awake?"

Mom appeared in her white nightgown in the dim light of the living room, her hair disheveled. "What on earth are you two talking about this late?"

"Oh, nothing, nothing, Sue," Michi said forcefully, laughing, hurtling us back into the present. "Nothing at all, we're just finishing our movie—it's a stupid movie, anyway, real bad, real boring. Go back to bed, we'll be up soon."

Mom looked suspicious but obeyed Michi's instruction. "Okay," she said, heading back up the stairs, "just don't be much longer—it's so late."

"Whatever happened with Jichan?" I asked quietly, once Mom had returned upstairs.

"Oh, they finally sent Papa to join us, but we barely recognized him. He'd grown so thin. And quiet. They broke him in two: his Japanese side and his American side. They emptied him. We never knew how, what they did to him.

"He and Mama never talked about the baby. Papa never saw it, anyway. It's like he was erased. We stopped celebrating Obon—your mom doesn't even remember the old temple."

We then awkwardly finished our movie, but as we went upstairs to bed, she murmured softly from behind me: "But you know, Aki, babies died more often back then. It happened all the time. Mama wasn't thinking straight . . . you can't blame her . . . *infanticide is much too strong a word.*"

I remember gripping the staircase railing as she uttered those confusing words.

Suddenly I was slipping off of my stool, my hands clinging to the counter.

"Good heavens—are you all right?" Dad was asking, bending over me. His shirt was wet from the dishes and his cheeks were flushed; he looked as though he'd just been wrestling a large, slobbery animal.

"Fine, fine, just light-headed lately. Did you get new stools or something? These ones seem higher." I laughed, embarrassed.

"Same stools as always—you're sure you're not hurt? Can I get you some water? Coffee?" he asked, his softly wrinkled face concerned. "You've seemed tired all evening."

"I'm fine," I assured, waving him away, standing, settling back onto the stool. "I think the heat's been getting to me. I'll have some tea, thanks."

This was the second time I'd almost fainted recently. I made a note to visit a doctor if it continued.

"Well, Jane," Dad said tentatively, filling the kettle, looking out the window where the sun had now set. The sky was a tired purple, smudged with wild streaks of neon orange. "I suppose there *is* something I wanted to talk to you about."

"Oh?"

"Well, dear, it's just that," he began nervously, "apart from the bit of sewing you do for Jackie's shop, you've been unemployed for quite a while now. Over a year, in fact—"

"Yeah, have you noticed the whole country's in a recession? More like a *depression*, really. You can't just believe the numbers you hear on CNN."

"There's no reason to get defensive, dear, and yes, I read the newspaper. I'm well aware of our country's economic situation." He flicked on the kitchen lights, turning the sky to a black square. "I just want to make sure you're still motivated, is all. You never mention looking—"

"Well, lemme tell you, Dad, it's grim out there, real grim. Liberal Arts degrees are a dime a dozen around here. But I still check listings all the time, and I have a few decent leads," I exaggerated.

"That's good to hear." He went to the cabinet and pulled down a box of Trader Joe's cookies. "It's just, well, I promised I wouldn't say anything—please don't tell Jackie I did—but the other day I happened to run into her at the market, and she mentioned that you missed your last sewing deadline. She said she had to remind you—that you didn't even call to explain. She's just concerned, of course, wanting to make sure everything's okay."

I was taken aback by this; it took me a moment to realize that it was true.

"It wasn't exactly a *deadline*, per se . . . at least I hadn't thought of it that way. I guess I'd thought of it as more like a ballpark time frame," I stumbled. "But yeah, everything's fine. It's just been so hot, and our heater's broken. Can you believe it, in this heat wave? And, like I said, I've been so tired. So, it's been hard for me to concentrate."

Dad frowned.

"Oh, hey, and guess what: Shiro asked me to marry him!" I blurted, grabbing a cookie from his box.

I don't know why I hadn't told Dad about Shiro's proposal until then. I suppose I'd been waiting until I accepted it.

Dad's eyes widened; he leaned over and gave me a self-conscious hug. "Well, my goodness, how about that—well . . . *congratulations!*" He sat back at the counter beside me, hugging his cookie box. I couldn't tell from his body language if he was happy for me or not.

"He's a good man, that Shiro, a good man—good, strong morals. Of course, sometimes that's a blessing *and* a curse. But it's certainly a blessing when one meets the love of one's life, that being so rare these days. I'm assuming you said yes?"

"Not yet, but I will soon, definitely."

He raised an eyebrow. "You're not fully decided?"

"I am, I am—I just haven't said so yet."

He squinted suspiciously. "Does your mother know?"

"No, and please don't mention it. I'd like to tell her myself. That's partly why I want to find her, actually. I want to talk to her about a few things that've been happening lately."

"Now of course he'll have to keep that job of his he hates," he said, grabbing a cookie from the box. "One can't be overly idealistic when it comes to bread and butter, especially if one wants to be starting a family." He popped the cookie into his mouth.

"Well, we're not starting a *family*, exactly, at least, not yet, but I just hope he doesn't do anything foolish. He's thinking of blowing the whistle on his work for all their so-called transgressions. Racial profiling and things like that."

His eyes bulged and his mouth opened; I realized he was choking. I jumped up and whacked him on the back several times, until he burst into coughing. He gulped a glass of water.

"Blowing the whistle on *Homeland Security*?" he asked, still coughing, as he set his water down. "Surely Shiro's not that naive? Does he have any idea how aggressive this administration is on whistleblowers? When it comes to national security? One's career—one's *life*, really—can easily be ruined! Believe me, I've seen a thing or two in my day. Idealism is one thing, but stupidity's another!"

He coughed more, then shook his head and sighed loudly, as though he'd suspected something foolish like this from your dad all along.

"I know, I've tried telling him—"

"You're not pregnant, are you, dear?"

"No! Jeez, Dad!" I cried, rolling my eyes, feeling like a teenager. "Not everyone gets married 'cause they got knocked up, you know. Remember to chew, there."

His cheeks flushed.

Neither Mom or Dad had ever admitted that I was an accident, or at least a surprise, and that they'd gotten married when Mom was pregnant, but the timeline spoke for itself.

Dad handed me a cookie, but as I went to take a bite, that pit in my stomach felt bloated beyond what could still be called a pit. Now that I paid more attention, I realized it felt more like an absence than a presence—a steadily growing, amorphous outline of something missing at the center of my being. I placed a hand on my belly (on you, though of course I didn't yet know it) and set the cookie on the counter.

SEVENTEEN

A couple of afternoons later, Shiro showed me his newest video projects.

I was sitting beside him at the kitchen table, biting into a buttery slice of hamachi and sipping a cup of cold sake, wonderfully refreshing in the oven of our apartment. The meal was a special treat for us; I'd finally finished a dress, and Shiro had recently worked some extra shifts, so I'd splurged on some sashimi-grade fish and several of our favorite fixings.

There was a cozy feeling in the air as we played footsie under the table and he showed me various clips. I imagined myself walking down the red carpet alongside him at the Cannes Film Festival for his first big nomination, him in a tux and me in something slinky.

"Okay so this newest one's pretty rough," he said, wrapping an octopus tentacle into a bright green shiso leaf and dipping it in soy sauce and wasabi. "So, be kind—but I'm just curious to get your reactions."

"Me? I'm always kind," I teased.

He popped the wrap into his mouth, eyes widening and nostrils flaring as he chewed, shoveled some rice into his mouth with his chopsticks, and pressed play on his laptop. At first I thought he'd accidentally started that PBS special with Pops again, but when I turned to question him he held a finger to his lips.

It begins with a clip from the special—Pops straightening the clip-on microphone on his shirt, clearing his throat, saying, "Yeah, so . . . when I was a kid, I had no idea where Japan was . . ."

Then his voice becomes muffled and warped, his movements slow motion, as though he's fallen under water. This image slowly cross-fades with an image of a living room—our living room—in disarray, our things strewn all over. The room looks just as it had the day of the break-in.

I reached to pause the video, but he stopped me.

The camera pans down the hall and into our bedroom, where our clothes and other belongings are splayed everywhere as well, drawers open, the potted palm by our bed toppled onto its side, soil spilling onto the floor.

I realized my hands were trembling. I expected to see that tower there on the bed.

Had the break-in been a fake? Staged by Shiro? Was I about to see myself, reacting to the frightening mess?

By now Pops's voice has resumed: "Oh yeah, the FBI came into our house one night while we kids were sleeping. Ransacked the place. We didn't know what they were looking for."

The camera zooms out and we see the bed, to my relief, tower-free. We also see the back of someone standing in the room.

The figure, dressed in jeans and a hoodie, begins walking away from the camera, slowly, looking around, as though surveying the scene—it's unclear if this figure is the intruder, admiring his own work, or the victim of this crime, trying to understand what's happened. The figure turns to face the camera: it's Shiro.

I snapped the computer shut.

"Why'd you do that?" he asked.

"When did you do this?" I asked, suddenly light-headed.

"I guess . . . about a week ago? There's more—"

"So, what, you went through and destroyed our apartment? Just for fun? Is this some kind of weird, sick joke?"

"*Joke?* Um, it's *art.*"

I glanced all around the room, looking for what, I'm not sure.

"Sorry," he said, less defensively, "guess I should have realized seeing our apartment like that again would be upsetting for you."

"It's not upsetting," I lied, my hands still trembling. "I just don't get it. What's your point, exactly?"

He shook his head and held up his hands. "I mean, point? I . . . I can't say it has one definitive *point* . . . but after what happened here the other day, then hearing Pops on that old tape the other night . . . I'm just trying to make sense of things, is all. You know me, that's how I try and . . . put things together, I guess you could say," he said, pointing to his laptop. "But again, I'm really sorry, I didn't think it would trigger you—"

"It didn't trigger me," I insisted, standing. "I just need some fresh air."

I hurried down the hall and into the bedroom, pushed open the huge window and stepped onto the fire escape. Unlike the air in our apartment, outside was pleasantly crisp. The heat wave had finally passed. I took several deep breaths, feeling my body relax.

A few minutes later, Shiro joined me on the escape, spooning me. Our arms brushed against a branch of his lemon tree.

"You okay, babe?" he asked softly.

We stood like that a moment before I turned to face him; his innocent, concerned look melted me. This wasn't the first time he'd taken what I found to be unusual interest in random aspects of our life and incorporated them into his videos, I remembered. Maybe this one was no exception and bore no deeper, ominous meaning.

He took my hand, which had stopped trembling, and guided me down the escape stairs and into the garage. There was just space for four cars—we'd been lucky a spot had been available when we moved in—and no other cars were parked there now. I got a bit excited, thinking perhaps we might go for a drive, something we hadn't done in a while. Maybe I'd run back upstairs and grab us sweaters, and we could go back out to Tomales Bay, where we'd had our anniversary dinner, then return home by a different, safer route, I foolishly thought . . .

But a drive wasn't what he had in mind. Instead he disappeared behind his old Toyota that we called "Junior"—short for "Pops Junior," since Pops had left it to Shiro when he died—and emerged, holding a pair of antlers.

"Do you recognize them?" he asked, as though it were the most natural question.

"*Recognize* them?" I stammered, stunned. "What am I, some . . . some kind of *antler specialist*?"

He lifted them up into the amber, late afternoon light streaming into the garage, giving them an otherworldly glow. "Aren't they something? I've been meaning to show you."

Despite my urge to look away, I couldn't help but study them. Rough and dark at their base, like old growth tree bark, they grew lighter and smoother as they ascended, the tips bleached almost white and perfectly smooth, like bone. Then I realized of course that's what they were: bone. Except unlike bone's usual private nature, these were bold, public assertions of strength. The top of my head itched.

"When I drove back that day, they were still there. The body was gone. No trace, like I told you. But when I saw these things lying there in the morning sun—so goddamn majestic—I don't know why, but I had to take them. Sorry I didn't tell you sooner. Guess I just thought you'd think I was crazy."

"You've been hiding them here this whole time?"

"Not *hiding* exactly. They've just been right here in the corner, behind Junior. I guess you never looked."

"Shiro, this is really weird."

"Okay, so I'm weird, life's weird; that's been established," he snapped. "Can you think up another adjective? Look . . . you're right, I . . . I know it's weird. But I just keep seeing that deer lying there, its heart splayed there on the pavement, practically still throbbing."

"How could you tell which organ was which? It all looked like one huge, gross mess to me."

"Didn't you take an anatomy class at that fancy college of yours?"

"Nope. By the way, did you wash them?"

"*Wash them?*"

"Yeah, they might have all kinds of germs. You'd better wash them. Who knows where they've been! Use something strong, like bleach."

He shook his head dismissively and went back to admiring the antlers.

From their impressive size, the owner must have been a fully mature male. They struck me as still alive, as though they were somehow still pulling energy from their owner, wherever he was at that moment—perhaps sleeping under a tree in a dark wood, or grazing in a meadow. I had the impression that, if Shiro held them long enough, they would eventually graft themselves onto his hands and resume their growth.

"They just seem so rife with symbolism, don't they?" he asked, holding them over his head dramatically. "That broken deer, these fallen antlers—you know the deer's a common animal in mythology. Often appears as a messenger of gods. I just keep seeing that heart, and Pops lying there on that kitchen floor, staring up at me with the same exact look: helpless, shocked—like he was hoping I could help."

"Who, Pops? Or the deer? What are we talking about here?"

"Hart—H-A-R-T—that's an old word for a male deer. The heart of the hart." He placed the antlers back on the ground and began muttering in circular, cryptic riddles, the way he often did when he was working on one of his projects. "The heart of the hart. The broken heart. Hearts were broken."

His nonsensical poetic ramblings making me dizzy—still shocked by his disturbing video and now by these vestiges of some animal's life, which had been haunting enough that night, but which I had thought belonged to the past—I leaned into Junior to steady myself, feeling comfort in its solid, metal frame.

"So, Shiro . . . I've been thinking, about that night . . . maybe we're remembering it wrong. I mean, it was late, we were tired, it had been a long day. I mean, great, but really long."

"*Remembering* wrong?"

"Yeah. Memory's weird like that; you can't always trust it. Or maybe we were seeing things that weren't really there."

"What—like hallucinating?"

I shrugged. "Maybe."

"How do you explain these antlers then? They seem pretty real to me."

"The point is," I continued, still dizzy, leaning farther into the car, "sometimes things just *happen*, Shiro, without any real meaning. Some events are just random. Life's random bad luck. And looking back all the time, trying to connect all the dots is pointless. Memory can drive you crazy. I mean, I definitely understand the desire for everything to be connected, for everything to have happened for a reason, and it's hard to reconcile, the chaos of it all, but—"

"Okay, whatever, then," he snapped. "Guess it's all totally normal. Guess animals just naturally get disemboweled like that. And antlers just disappear, and then fall from the sky."

"What are you gonna do with these, anyway? Mount them on our wall? Above our bed?"

"They're not a trophy. More of an antitrophy, if anything. They might end up in a project."

"Hey, I know, maybe you can attach them to the front of the car. A warning to other deer? We can take them on our honeymoon!" I said, laughing, feeling not only dizzy but loopy.

"You know, Jane, you can be really sick—you seem so nice, but it's deceptive," he said, walking toward the garage door, his disgust surprising me.

"You don't have the corpse stashed away somewhere too, do you? In the attic, maybe? Hey, is that what's been giving off that rotting smell? Are you gonna perform an autopsy for your next video?" I laughed more, unable to control myself, practically falling into Junior, my voice sounding maniacal.

Just as his video had triggered me, my joking must have hit a nerve in him. He stomped out of the garage, leaving me alone with the disconcerting, deciduous things.

Over the next few days, as I went about my routine in the apartment, trying to get started on my next batch of dresses, all I could think about was that video of our ransacked apartment, and those antlers sitting, or more like growing, in the dark of our garage.

Was your dad losing it? I wondered. Here he was, hatching far-fetched conspiracies about the government, entertaining foolish notions about whistleblowing, making videos simulating our break-in, taking the day off work to gather random animal parts from road kill—could this be classified as worrisome, even clinical behavior? And if so, did he need professional help, and quick? Yet would he ever seek that help himself?

I knew he was skeptical of therapy, and that he'd never be open to something like psychiatric medication. He believed the overmedication of our country was a mass conspiracy to keep the people passive victims of the "new corporatocracy," as he put it. And yet, I'd heard of cases where just the smallest dosage of the right medicine could set things straight, correcting a faulty chemistry. Like Mom, for instance, who hated the idea of therapy and opted to take medication with the most minimum of visits to a psychiatrist.

On the other hand, in his defense, these antlers were stunning. They had a mysteriously strong gravitational pull to them. In fact, several times, in the middle of trying to modify a new dress pattern, I found myself overwhelmed by the urge to go down to the garage to look at them.

And men did seek their trophies. I remembered walking into an uncle's house during our family's only trip to Louisiana. His living room walls had been plastered with animal heads and antlers of all shapes and sizes. Mom and I had been repulsed, but Dad had quietly explained it to us as man's primal need to show his triumph over other males. I guess that was supposed to make it normal, but the mounted animal parts had still made us queasy.

But for Shiro, not exactly your typical guy-guy, an "antitrophy" from this incident was perhaps an understandable spin on the traditional need. Maybe it was even a healthy, positive way for him to make peace with that horrible night.

EIGHTEEN

After a few more weeks of not getting Mom on the phone and only receiving a few texts, I borrowed Dad's car and drove across the Richmond–San Rafael Bridge to Marin. It was a clear day, and the continuous blue of sky and water encompassing me as I drove across the bay filled me with hope.

First, I stopped by the country club where she "worked." I hadn't been out there in years—not since Mom and Jim had been members. After their divorce, when they split the income from the sale of their home and she bought her condo, the club had offered her a part-time job, greeting people at the front desk and generally keeping things in order, in exchange for a small salary and unlimited membership privileges. I thought the people at the club must have felt sorry for her and wanted to make sure she had a place to go every day. Mom was a natural cleaner—she hated clutter and would often toss things into the trash with relish, proclaiming: "You can't take it with you!"—and she loved the club's facilities, so the arrangement seemed to be working great.

"Really? You're *Mrs. Linden's* daughter?" the gal at the front desk asked when I explained who I was. "Funny, you look nothing like her!"

She looked to be in her late teens—or maybe everyone in their twenties was just starting to look like a teenager to me—dressed in a pink tank top and black spandex shorts, her near-white blond hair, dark roots showing through, pulled into a tight bun.

"Well, even so, I am," I said curtly. "Is she here?"

"No, not today. I haven't seen her in a month, at least. Things are a complete *mess* around here without her," she said, giving me a wink. I glanced around. The place seemed tidy enough. Then she said something really perplexing: "I guess she's just really busy with all her singing lessons."

"*Singing lessons?* No, I don't think so. My mother doesn't sing. I've never heard her sing. You must be thinking of someone else."

She tilted her head. "Don't you see her on Facebook or anything?"

"No."

She tilted her head more, as though asking why.

"I don't like spying on people, or being spied on." I wasn't sure why I was taking a slight pleasure in being rude to this perfectly nice-seeming gal.

She scrunched up her face and laughed a little. "*Spying?* Okay . . . well anyway, she's been preparing for some recital for a while now." She closed her eyes and held up a hand. "I just think it's *so* inspiring, all the different things she does at her age. You must be so proud of her."

Before I could get my bearings enough to ask if she could give me another example of one of these many "things" Mom did, a pair of older men dressed in pastel-colored polo shirts, holding tennis rackets, stopped by the desk and began flirting with the gal. She flirted back, playing with the straw in her purple Vitamin Water. I glanced at the door, beginning to doubt my impulse to come here.

"Oh, hey guys," she eventually said, remembering my presence. "Guess who this is—Mrs. Linden's daughter!"

They turned to me, raising their gray eyebrows, as though surprised to find me standing there.

"Oh, you mean *Sue?*" one of them asked. I nodded. "So, *Mysterious Sue* has a daughter? Well how about that—I always thought she was just a singular, free-floating spirit," he said, chuckling. "No strings attached."

"Nope. She's a mother, all right," I said. I wondered what about Mom had given him that idea.

"That's Sue for you, always keeping us guessing," the other man chimed in. Everyone laughed knowingly.

Annoyed, I turned to go. "Well, if you see her, please tell her I stopped by," I called over my shoulder.

"Of course—it was really great meeting you!" the gal called after me. As I was halfway out the door, she added, "Oh, hey, wait a sec, I actually have something for her."

I turned. She was looking for something under her desk, then held up a key.

"She left this here a while ago. She called the other day looking for it."

I took it. It felt heavy in my hand, like the metal of old cars. As I returned to Dad's car, I slipped it into my pocket.

I drove up the wide road a ways, then turned onto a narrower, quiet street and followed it up a hill covered in condos, ranging in muted tones from beige to pale greens, inducing a medicinal calm. As I drove, not passing a single pedestrian, growing confused by how identical each block looked to the next, wondering if I would actually find Mom at her condo, my mind wandered to a summer night from my childhood.

Mom was sitting at the foot of my bed, staring out my open window. She'd been commenting on the heat when she absentmindedly mentioned something about how unbearable the summer nights had been when she was a kid in Arkansas.

"Arkansas?" I asked. "Where's that? I thought you grew up in LA?"

She looked down at me, as though surprised by my presence.

"Oh . . . when I was a girl, for a short while, we lived out there. In the swampland. It was nice—so much nature all around. Like summer camp all the time!" She gave a short, shrill laugh, then resumed her stare out the window.

I had the sense that only her body was there in the room with me— that the rest of her was tromping through that far-off swamp. "At night . . . I'd lie awake in my cot, pressing my hands over my ears."

"Why?"

"The cicadas. They never stopped, like an angry chorus stuck on just two notes—it drove me crazy. Sometimes I couldn't stand it. I'd get out of bed and wander."

She looked down at me again. It seemed the part of her still in the far-off swamp was straining to see me, but the distance made it too difficult. I remember wanting to reach for her hand—even more, I longed for her to reach for mine.

But she just murmured, "Go to sleep, Aki," and wandered out of my room.

After meandering in circles, my determination to find Mom turning to anxiety, I finally found what I was pretty sure was Mom's building. I parked, climbed the stairs to her unit, rang the bell and, getting no response, knocked on the door and called her on the phone, only to hear her cheerful voicemail greeting. I climbed onto a planter box beneath the window and peeked inside.

Even then I wasn't 100 percent certain I had the right place, though it did look more or less how I remembered your grandmother's living room: spotless, with nondescript cream-colored walls and carpet, a sleek black-leather couch, and a round glass coffee table sporting a few magazines and a vase of what looked like fake tulips. It looked like one of those Ikea living room models; no sign of recent human life. It was impossible to tell whether anyone had stepped through the door an hour, a day, or a year ago.

I thought of the key the gal at the club had given me and tried it in the door. It didn't fit, but, my hand already on the doorknob, I turned it; the door swung open.

"Mom?" I called inside.

No one seemed to be home. Leaving the door half open, I kicked off my shoes and walked lightly across the soft, immaculate carpet to the small kitchen. No sign of life there either. Like the living room, it was spotless and there was no way to tell when it had last been used. I opened the refrigerator. There were very few items: a couple of Chinese-style take-out containers, a few condiment bottles, and a half-drunk bottle of wine. I opened the garbage can and peered in: nothing but an empty white bag.

Nervous to be invading her private space like this, and part of me still not entirely convinced this *was* Mom's place, I made my way into the bedroom. As expected, everything was tidy, the bed made, the light-colored drapes closed, allowing sunlight to filter through. The only disruption to the sparseness was, at the center of the bed, a brown suitcase.

I approached it slowly, calling out "Mom?" once more before opening it.

Its contents were also sparse: a cashmere sweater of hers I'd always admired, some makeup, a Polaroid snapshot of her and me from long ago, a Baby Ruth candy bar, and two floral-print silk scarves. I held one of the scarves up to my cheek, thinking of that black scarf she'd attempted to loop over my head at that warehouse the last time I saw her.

I ran my fingers over each item several times and along the satin lining of the suitcase, as though touching these shapes and textures might somehow impart information as to her whereabouts, and maybe more.

NINETEEN

The girl lies on her cot, playing with her toy boat, singing softly to herself. Her brother kicks the metal rail at the opposite end of their stall, a tinny, echoing sound she's grown accustomed to over the months.

A sudden grunt startles her; she stops singing and sits up. She tucks her boat under her pillow, which is just her rolled-up sweater, and stretches her damp, sore body.

Her mother is kneeling on the floor a few feet away, leaning against a bale of hay, breathing loudly. A young woman from the neighboring stall squats beside her mother, stroking her forehead, murmuring: "Good, good, that's it— breathe like that, breathe like that." Every so often her mother curls forward into a giant, gnarled fist.

The breathing grows louder and faster. Eventually the neighbor woman says, "Watch her," and rushes from the stall.

The girl's sister sits across from her, on her own cot. Together they watch their mother drop to her hands and knees, breathing through gritted teeth, every so often making frightening, muffled, barely human sounds. Her brother continues to kick the metal rail, his legs moving in and out of the single shaft of light sifting in through the stadium rafters.

Her sister mutters what they've all been thinking: "If only Papa were here."

Soon the neighbor woman returns with a middle-aged man, another internee, who tells them he's a doctor. He and the neighbor woman try to move the girl's mother to a cot, but she refuses, insisting on remaining there on all fours on the horse-stall floor. With the assistance of this stranger doctor and the neighbor woman, the girl's mother, biting on a balled-up scarf to suppress her screams, pushes her new baby into the world.

As the tiny, wet body slips into the neighbor woman's hands, there's a moment of quiet—then a thin, high-pitched whimper enters the air. The girl and her two siblings, now standing together stiffly, let out nervous giggles. Then everyone, except her mother, bursts into laughter. The stranger doctor pulls tools from a bag and cuts the umbilical cord.

Her mother lets out a short cry and collapses onto the floor.

The neighbor woman holds the baby up into the single shaft of light. "He's beautiful, ne?" she asks. A strikingly red streak of blood runs across its pale belly.

"Dame!" the girl's mother calls from the floor. No! The others look down at her, surprised. "No light!" she cries, followed by words in Japanese, most of which the girl doesn't understand.

The neighbor woman lowers the baby out of the light. Her mother relaxes.

A shadow passes over their stall; they hear the drumbeat of a guard's boots on the floorboards over their heads. They wait, frozen, until it fades. When only the other noises of night can be heard again—random creaking of wood, the shifting of neighbors in their stalls, a child calling for its mother from the other side of the stadium—the neighbor woman holds the baby up again, this time away from the light. In the dark of the stall, the small being seems to possess its own rosy glow.

"So much hair!" the neighbor woman exclaims softly. "And so lucky, to be born during Obon—your ancestors must be happy!"

The girl and her siblings exchange glances; they'd forgotten it was Obon.

Unsure how to react to this most unusual welcoming of their newest family member, the girl runs to her mother's side and crouches beside her. She pushes a few wet hairs from her moist face, straining to see her features in the dark.

"Mama? Do you want to hold him?"

But the eyes seem not to see her.

"Don't worry, she's just tired now," the neighbor woman explains. "Let's let her rest. She'll be fine tomorrow. It's hard work, pushing one of you into the world!" She and the stranger doctor share a knowing laugh.

The neighbor woman wraps the slick body tightly in a piece of fabric and offers him to the girl's sister, who cradles him and kisses his thick black hair. The baby lets out another small whimper. The girl's older brother approaches, peering into the bundle in her arms.

"Hey—he's looking at me!" he exclaims. "Hey there, buddy boy—it's your big brother here. Tak. Sorry you had to be born in this here dump, buddy, but don't worry, we'll getcha outta here in no time—just stick with us, okay?" He beams as the baby grips his finger. "Whoa there—you're a strong one! Man,

you're gonna be a pitcher, I bet, eh?" He laughs. The girl's sister laughs, too. "Or maybe a boxer? So, little fella, what'll we call you, eh? Johnny? Joey? Frankie?"

"Aki. Namae wa Aki desu." His name is Aki.

They turn to see the girl's mother pushing herself up to sitting, her arms shaking. The neighbor woman rushes to prop her against the wall.

For the first time, the girl's mother looks at the baby. A sparkle of something the girl hasn't seen since before Papa was taken returns to her mother's eyes: hope.

"Aki desu," she repeats, adding words the girl doesn't understand.

"She says Aki is the name Papa wanted him to have, if he was a boy," her sister translates.

Her sister hands the baby to her mother. The girl leans down and looks at the tiny, wrinkled, blood-stained face. She gasps; it's the most beautiful face she's ever seen. Her chest swells with a love so huge it hurts.

"Welcome to the world, Baby Aki!" she proclaims loudly.

"Shh!" her mother warns, squeezing the baby to her chest, her eyes flashing with fear. "They can hear us."

TWENTY

A few days later, I was sitting at the kitchen table, trying to get back to my sewing. The apartment was still a sauna. The fan helped somewhat, now that it was November and the air outside was cooler, but I had to keep it on the lowest speed now, so as not to upset the heap of fabric, patterns, and pins splayed across the table. I still had the disconcerting feeling that someone was watching me.

Eventually, unable to focus, I called my stepbrother. I'd been meaning to call him for several days but hadn't yet been able to muster up the nerve.

He answered immediately. "Yo, Chris here."

"Oh, Chris. Hi, it's Jane."

There was a pause. "*Jane?* No way. Wow. How many years has it been?"

"Hi."

I bit my lip, squelching the desire to hang up, and played with my scissors, cutting tiny bits of fabric. I'd chosen a light-weight cotton blend for this batch of dresses, and cutting into it was strangely enjoyable.

"So, Big Sis, how's it going over there in *Oaktown?*" he asked jovially, but I detected a darker note. I knew he'd always been confused by the distance I kept between us.

"Heh-heh," I heard myself chuckling awkwardly. He had a knack for making me feel uncomfortable in myself. "Just fine, thanks," I said, continuing to snip the fabric. "How are the kids?"

"Oh, we're all okay, but I mean, not the greatest honestly. Did Sue tell you we're moving?"

"Yeah, she did mention something about moving to Texas, so your company won't have to pay taxes?"

He let out a surprised laugh. "You're kidding, Sue actually *said* that? Well, that's Mom for you, right? Always dotting things with half truths."

I hated it when he referred to Mom as "Mom." His own mother was alive and, from what I knew, perfectly well, living in a luxurious senior community not far from him in San Jose.

"Half truths? Are you calling my mother a liar?" I challenged.

"Just joking, just joking, Big Sis, calm down there, calm down." He and Mom both liked telling me to calm down. I wasn't sure which of them had started this, but the other had soon followed. "But come on, you know how Sue is. Ever elusive—always covered in a convenient shroud of mystery, am I right?"

"What's that supposed to mean?"

I recalled the language the older men at the country club had used to describe Mom the other day: "free-floating," "mysterious," "always keeping us guessing." All this talk of Mom as some secretive, evasive woman bothered me, not to mention seeming a bit racist, coming from all these white men—the stereotype of the cunning, opaque, Oriental demon-lady—but also, and most annoyingly, it struck me as true. Mom *was* a mystery, not only to them, but to me, too. The fact that I was just as mystified as they were, or maybe more so, bothered me most of all.

In my irritation, I accidentally shredded what was to be the facing for my next dress. I'd been extra skimpy on my last purchase at the fabric store, so didn't have much to spare. Now I'd miss another deadline. I tossed my scissors onto the table and pushed the ruined fabric pieces onto the floor. Chris was explaining something about his move to Texas.

"They're really thrilled to have us out here—I mean, hello, we're bringing the twenty-first century with us! Oh, and believe me, we pay our fair share of *taxes*, all right," he added defensively.

I walked to the living room area. Out the window, San Francisco was picturesque across the bay, the Transamerica Pyramid pointing up at the sky from a layer of mist.

I pictured Chris, his limp, brown hair hanging almost to his shoulders, looking out from a window in one of the brightly colored walls of his tech company, the whole compound enclosed in a giant bubble, floating through the sky, like Glinda the Good Witch, landing lightly in a dry, flat landscape similar to Kansas, awaited by the promise of low home prices, and perhaps no taxes. The idea of him bringing the Silicon Valley out to

Texas with him seemed as surreal as bringing the Emerald City to Kansas.

"Well, I'm just calling because I'm looking for my mom," I replied, blinking a few times, snapping myself back to reality. I went to the kitchen to take a sip of my iced tea, but the ice had melted. "I can't seem to find her. She says she's been helping you with your move?"

"You can't *find* her?"

"Right. I can't find her. At least, not in the flesh."

"*In the flesh?*" He belly laughed. "Well, Big Sis, she just texted me a few minutes ago, and she's been checking in constantly on Facebook. I don't know if that's *in the flesh* or not, but it seems pretty accurate. It's a new feature—maybe you're not using it?"

"So, where did she last check in? I'm on a landline; my cell phone's not working today," I quickly lied, not wanting to explain to him that I wasn't on social media.

"Okeydokey, let's take a look-see here . . ." He paused, I suppose to check Mom's whereabouts on his phone. I sensed his relief at having a tangible way to solve this imaginary problem of mine. "Hmm, okay well it actually looks like she hasn't been checking in a lot recently, but she just posted something, and a few days ago she was at a Costco in Novato . . . and a Starbucks."

"I didn't know she was a Costco member. And I didn't know she liked Starbucks."

"Does anyone really *like* Starbucks? Isn't it just a place we go, 'cause it's there?" he jokingly philosophized. "No, but seriously, before that it looks like she was at a gas station in San Jose, right near our place."

"Did you see her then? The day she got gas near your place?"

"Did I see her the day she got gas?" he repeated. I couldn't tell if he wasn't hearing me due to a bad connection, or if my words were just alien to him. "No, like I said, I've been here in Texas this whole month, working my butt off night and day. Jen and the kids are still out there a few more weeks. We had our identity stolen, did Mom mention that? Major fucking pain in the ass. Don't recommend it. This whole month fucking sucks."

"Wait, so you haven't seen her since when, exactly?"

"Well, *Miss Nancy Drew*, I guess now that you mention it, I haven't actually *seen* her—*in the flesh*, as you say—for about a month or so, maybe more. But I'm about to buy her a ticket to Texas. She promised to be here when the kids arrive, to help us get settled. I certainly hope she's wearing her flesh suit when she arrives! JK."

"Well, I wouldn't count on her actually showing up, if I were you. Or staying too long when she finally does."

I immediately regretted my words. I pictured him thinking of how best to respond to my statement, embarrassingly full of childish, scarred resentment—something of course I hadn't intended. I sat back down at the table with my melted iced tea, kicking at the ruined fabric bits on the floor.

"Look, Jane," he said softly. "I know it was hard when she left you guys. And then moved in with us. I mean, I do, believe me, I do. Remember, my parents split up, too. It feels like you've been replaced. It feels like complete shit." His tone was frank and sincere. "And then even my dad and Sue broke up. So, it totally sucks, I know. But that was years ago. Time to move on, right? Anyway, she's in her *seventies*, for god's sake; people don't change in their friggin' seventies. Go easy on the lady. Mom's a little nutty, maybe even nuts, but we love her, right?"

I wondered how long he'd been waiting for the chance to give me these words of great wisdom—and how he managed to be insulting even to those he was trying to defend.

"Easy on her? I'm just trying to *find* her, Chris, that's all. I'm not being hard or easy or anything on her, really. I'm just trying to find her. Is that all right with you? That I find my mother?"

I twirled my glass, staring at the undrinkable light-brown water, realizing that this pause was going on for too long. I had the feeling that Chris was somehow watching me through the phone and that he was genuinely concerned for me.

"Big Sis, Sue's fine. Trust me. She's a big gal. I'll be seeing her here soon, I promise."

I made some excuse to get off the phone.

About an hour later, as I was folding laundry on the couch, that next-door baby started crying again. The pitiful, aggressive complaints sounded near enough to be coming from the bottom of my laundry basket. Though

I knew it was ridiculous, I emptied the clothes onto the couch to take a look, feeling idiotic as I traced the white plastic bottom with my fingers.

I wondered what sort of parents they were, ignoring their child like this. Or had the child been abandoned? Was there some type of abuse going on? Should I call the authorities? Most likely, though, the poor thing was just colicky, whatever that meant. And from what little I knew, there wasn't much one could do to silence a miserable infant.

Without a plan, despite my general aversion to confrontation, I opened our apartment door, stepped into the hall, and walked toward the door of our next-door neighbors' unit. Our paths rarely crossed, and I couldn't even remember what they looked like. But the cries—their grating tone and relentlessness—were genuinely starting to affect me. Surely something should be said to them? I decided to knock on their door, introduce myself, and politely request that something be done. But as I approached the nondescript brown door, a mirror image of our own, there was something that kept me from touching it. What would I say, exactly? "Excuse me, I'm your next-door neighbor, please tell your baby to be quiet"?

Also, the cries were quieter out here in the hall than inside our own apartment.

I found myself walking past the door to the end of the hall, and down the steps to the garage. I'd been fighting the urge to return there to look at those disturbing antlers ever since Shiro had revealed them to me. My footsteps echoed in the stark, mildew-smelling staircase as I descended, the cries now imperceptible, and when I pushed open the door, my breath left me, and my heart stopped: seated on top of Junior, the old Toyota, was a naked little boy with thick black hair and rosy cheeks. His dark, doe-like eyes looked directly into mine as he held the deer antlers, enormous compared to his small body, above his head. They looked both absurd and natural, as though he were some mythical, half-human, faun-like creature. The garage was dark except for the dim light coming in through the doorway I stood in, yet the little being on the car seemed to possess its own, almost blinding glow.

Then, before my eyes, the image vanished, and I was, of course, standing there in the doorway looking into a dark garage. I was unable to decipher a thing, as though the mirage I'd just witnessed, or imagined, had shrunk my pupils to tiny, ineffectual pinholes.

I shut the door, blinking and shaking my head as I hurried back upstairs, my mind racing to make sense of this odd, strikingly believable hallucination.

Inside our apartment, the next-door baby was still crying as loud as ever. I found some earplugs and returned to the laundry. As I was gathering up a new load, the earplugs not helping, I heard the click of something falling into the laundry basket: Mom's pill jar. It must have fallen from my jeans pocket. I didn't know why I'd taken it from her suitcase that day, except for plain, old-fashioned curiosity. I could only hope that she'd easily be able to get herself a fresh stock.

I had the urge to open the jar and take a few of the pills right then. Here I'd thought Shiro was going crazy, having irrational, paranoid fears about the government, making strange videos and collecting roadkill body parts, and now here *I* was, having hallucinations of naked young children in our garage! Were we both certifiably nuts? And these nonstop cries . . . I remembered what Dad had said about Mom taking medication in order to quiet her baby brother's ghost. It had helped, he'd claimed, though of course he didn't believe in ghosts. Who knew, maybe these pills would silence this next-door baby? And stop me from having any more disturbing hallucinations?

Before doing anything so rash as to take unprescribed medication— and just for the heck of it—I went to my laptop and did a product search for the curious name: Exilcon.

It turned out to be a new product, on the market for less than a year, aimed at helping people to manage anxiety, paranoia, and depression. The most I could find on the company's website, besides an array of hopeful promises, was a list of possible side effects, ranging, as with most drugs, from slight rashes to death.

I came across several articles about the recent skyrocketing of prescription drugs in America, then a site with glowing customer reviews:

"I was making long laundry lists of all the horrible things in the world, past and present, and how they were all connected to each other and to me," one user stated. "My friends and family were calling me paranoid. Now I can finally see things for what they are: random, unfortunate occurrences."

"I'm not quite as passionate as I used to be," one mother said, "but believe me, for myself and others, that's a good thing! In fact, my kids call them my 'Mommy vitamins'! If I'm grumpy, they ask, 'Mommy, did you take your Mommy vitamins today?' ☺ But I'm not emotionally dead, either—I've found a sweet balance, where I can actually enjoy my feelings instead of being overwhelmed by them."

"I used to dwell on the past all the time," someone else shared, "always thinking 'oh, what if I'd done this' and 'oh, what if I hadn't done that.' Exilcon has helped me to turn that around. Now my eyes are set on the future."

Some wrote poetically about their relief. "My life was an Escher painting, brilliantly surreal, but dark and dysfunctional. Now it's an impressionist landscape, with me the foreground and my troubles the puffy clouds in the background."

The more I read, the stranger the reviews became.

"A heavy headdress I never knew I was wearing has been lifted off."

"The demons are decapitated. The spirits are singing. The past is buried. The future is free!"

I must have fallen asleep, because the next thing I knew, hot air was blowing on me and I was lying tangled up on the couch, drenched in sweat, hearing my own name called out.

"Jane? *Jane?* Are you there?"

Wiping moisture from my mouth and cheeks, I saw the pill jar still in one hand, my phone clenched between my fingers in the other.

"*Mom?* Is that *you?*"

"Who else would it be, sweetie?" she answered calmly, as though nothing was out of the ordinary.

"I don't know, maybe your evil twin who's kidnapped you?" I sat up, pulling the earplugs from my ears and tossing them, along with the pill jar, into the laundry basket.

The next-door baby had quieted.

"Oh, sweetie, you're so funny. You sound strange."

"I was asleep. Must have dozed off while I was reading."

"But you called *me*."

"Did I?" I stood and stretched, my joints loose and achy.

"Oh jeez, you don't do things in your sleep now, do you? *Sleepwalk?*"

"What? No. It's just always so hot in here, it makes me drowsy. Our heater's broken."

"What about your imaginary friend? I hope he hasn't reappeared?"

"My *imaginary friend*? Of course not. God, Mom, I'm *thirty-four years old!*" I blurted.

My imaginary friend—that's who that little boy in the garage I'd just seen was! I hadn't thought of him in years, and in all my shock, I hadn't recognized him. The two of us had spent hours playing together, building things around the house, especially during the summer when Dad was at work and Mom was busy in the kitchen. I'd all but forgotten about him.

But why had Mom mentioned him now? Did she know I had just reimagined him—and if so, how? What on earth could explain this uncanny timing?

"Oh, good! I'm so glad to hear he's still gone," she said with relief. "So, is there something you wanted to tell me, sweetie? You keep calling but never leave messages. Very mysterious."

"*Me* mysterious? You've got to be kidding; I've been trying to track you down for weeks now. Months! And your voicemail greeting says not to leave messages."

"Oh, that's true. Sorry, it's just these days I really prefer text or Facebook communication." Your grandmother, who for the longest time had barely understood email, had recently become a die-hard social media fan. "I've just been so busy, you know? Helping Chris and the kids with their move to Texas, their identity theft, plus the club, and my singing lessons."

"I literally just talked to Chris, and he says he hasn't actually seen you in over a month. And I went by your club the other day, and the gal there said you haven't been in for—wait, so you're really taking *singing lessons?*" Was I still in a dream?

"Oh yeah, it's a real hoot! I sound like a dying cat, but at least I can try, right?"

"But that just seems so random; *singing?* You never sing."

"I'm not so old I can't try new things, am I? Anyway, I always sang when I was a little girl, until one day I just couldn't."

"Why not?"

"I have no idea, my voice just left—*poof*. Oh, and I might be going to China soon—wouldn't that be interesting?"

"*China?*"

"Yes. I met someone in a chat room. We've been messaging a lot—she works in a factory there."

"Someone in a *chat room?*"

I realized I had that same annoying habit as Chris: repeating what people said as though I hadn't heard them.

"Oh, she's really a fascinating gal. You should hear all that goes on in those factories over there!"

"But you met her in a *chat room*, Mom. Who knows if she's really who she says she is? She might actually be some, I don't know, some old lonely guy in Iowa, or some psychopath, or some bored little kid who knows where . . ."

"Well, Jane, what would be so horrible about that?"

"Mom, seriously, you have to be careful these days, meeting people online like that. Think of Chris's identity theft."

"I know, I know, but I just thought, hey, now that I don't have a mortgage, I might as well travel. See the world! And China's just so at the center of everything *future* these days, don't you think?"

"But where would you get the money? And I thought you hated international flights? All that security hassle?"

I walked over to the fan and turned it on the highest speed. My wet skin tingled in the sudden wind. Pattern and fabric pieces flew through the air, like scattering leaves.

"Sure, sure, but what am I gonna do, live my whole life in fear? At . . . certain point . . . move on . . . sorts of ways . . . out of places . . ."

"Wait, I can't hear you. So, when can I see you?" I asked, panicking that we might lose our connection. Who knew when I'd have another chance to speak with her again?

I rushed toward the back of the apartment, where reception tended to be stronger. "I'd like to see you soon."

"... your ... ever Skype?"

"No, I need to *see* you, Mom; your actual body," I insisted. "You *are* still inhabiting planet earth, yes?"

"You're so funny, Jane—it's not like it's been *that* long since we last saw each other."

Our connection seemed to have stabilized. I walked into the bedroom and peered out the fire escape window. Through the slats in the escape steps, I thought I saw the blur of someone running along the sidewalk. Could it be my imaginary friend again? I shut my eyes.

"So ... the other day, when I was looking for you at the club, that gal gave me a key for you. Then I went by your condo and your door was unlocked. And a suitcase was on your bed. Were you packing for somewhere? Texas? China? ... *Mom?*"

"Calm down, sweetie; I'm right here. Oh, the suitcase? I was just starting to pack, for when I have to leave."

I felt suddenly sheepish, picturing her returning to her condo and looking for her pill jar. I wondered if she knew I'd taken it.

"So, are you really losing your condo?"

"Don't worry about that. You really do worry too much, Jane. You always have. I was thinking of moving, anyway—maybe with Chris and them to Texas, or wherever they end up. You know, you can get a whole mansion and swimming pool out there for the price of a crappy one-bedroom in the Bay Area."

"But Texas gets so hot in the summer. You hate that, remember?"

"Welcome to the modern world, Jane. *Air-conditioning!*" she chirped.

I moved back to the bed and leaned against it.

"Well, I'm really glad to finally talk to you. I had a conversation with Dad the other day. He mentioned some things I'd never heard before that I wanted to ask you about. About your past."

"Oh?"

"He said you and Jichan used to be close. Before he was taken away. And that got me thinking ... that must have been really horrible for you, the government taking him away when you were just a little kid. So suddenly like that." The back of my throat began to tighten, but I forced myself to continue. "You never mentioned that to me. How come?" She didn't answer. "That must have been so scary for you. As such a little girl. Your dad disappearing. Mom? Can you hear me?"

There was such a long pause, I thought I'd lost her. But then she said, "I just don't understand why on earth Doug would be bringing all that up with you now. That man can be so strange. That all was so long ago, my goodness, I can't even remem—"

"He also mentioned something about a fire at the old hotel," I pursued, pacing the bedroom. I felt compelled to extract as many answers from her as I could, as swiftly and efficiently as possible, as though I were performing a surgical procedure. "And . . . lost protection . . . or a *curse* of some kind. What was he talking about?"

". . . just . . . illy . . . point . . . *that*?"

"He mentioned other stuff, too. About my namesake. Mom?"

She didn't answer. Unsure if she was still there, I continued flinging questions into the phone.

"How did the baby die, exactly? Do you know? Did you see anything?"

There was a clunk, followed by some crackling noises and what sounded like rushing water, as though she'd just tossed her phone into a river.

I stared at the phone, which now felt weightless. I felt weightless, too. I imagined myself as a small boat, floating out to sea.

A wave of nausea passed through me and I ran to the bathroom. I bent over the toilet to puke, but nothing came. Setting the phone down on the sink, I noticed the medicine cabinet door was open, its contents scattered all around. I closed the cabinet door and looked in the mirror. My eyes were red and puffy, as though I'd been crying—which of course wasn't true, unless I had cried in my sleep. And I rarely cry. Almost never. When I was little, if something bad happened, my imaginary friend would cry, not me.

Sunlight streamed in through the window behind my reflection, giving the diaphanous effect of running water. I turned; there, along the white bathtub floor, the little decorative stones we kept along the tub ledge had been arranged into several stacks, each about five or six stones high.

I climbed into the bathtub and knocked down the little towers with my bare feet. Spreading the smooth, cool stones along the tub floor with my toes, I was surprised by how satisfying this simple, destructive act was.

It occurred to me then what already may be quite obvious to you: it was *I* who had been building these towers. Just like the structures my imaginary friend and I used to build. And *I* who'd been tearing the apartment apart, searching for something. The intruder wasn't the government, kids looking for drugs, or anyone else; just me, sleepwalking.

But why was I building these towers again now? And what was I searching for?

I heard myself laughing aloud at these unnerving, confounding revelations and questions—a high-pitched, wicked cackle that frightened me.

TWENTY-ONE

The summer Bachan fell ill for the last time, when I was thirteen, your grandparents and I flew to Los Angeles and stayed with Aunt Michi and her family for a week. We all drove out to the nursing home every day, sometimes caravanning if there were too many of us. One morning everyone decided to take the day off, but for some reason I was still determined to go, even though it meant taking the bus—of course an unusual thing to do in LA. Your grandmother reluctantly agreed to accompany me.

The nursing home was far from Aunt Michi's house, at least by our Bay Area standards, and by bus it turned out to be a whole day's adventure. Mom and I sat side by side toward the front of the bus, passing through Hispanic, white, Korean, and black neighborhoods, and vast stretches of shabby shopping centers.

As the bus entered a trendy area in the heart of downtown, nowhere near the nursing home, Mom suddenly stood and pointed, her mouth open as though she'd momentarily lost language. I followed her finger across the street to a large, nondescript, beige box of a building wedged between a seafood restaurant and a Wells Fargo. The mammoth structure looked like an abandoned warehouse, seeming out of place in its drabness, and it was unclear from its facade what the business was.

"See that big building there?" Mom asked as the bus drove past. "That's the hotel. It's gotten so run-down."

The corner was already shrinking behind us. I stood as well, straining to see.

"You mean your family's old hotel? You're sure that was it?"

"Yes." I doubted Mom had been by the location in decades; I was surprised that she could be so certain about it.

"Seems like a super nice area," I observed. "Too bad you guys lost it."

"I wonder if that old bathtub still exists," she mumbled. "Those things must be indestructible."

"What's that?"

I waited for an answer, but she seemed transfixed, looking out the back of the bus. We stayed standing for some time, hanging on to the overhead handles, surfing potholes, both of us continuing to gaze out the back windows, even as we passed through new neighborhoods, as though we were leaving behind mental breadcrumbs.

The hotel had been bought in my uncle Tak's name, since aliens couldn't technically own property—apparently Bachan had been a shrewd businesswoman before the war and had known how to get around certain bureaucratic red tape. For a while it was a thriving establishment with over fifty rooms, housing many permanent tenants and a popular restaurant on the ground floor, where Jichan cooked—according to Aunt Michi, his specialty was seafood. But then he was taken away and they were sent to Camp, so Bachan had been forced to sell it for next to nothing.

The bus let us off several blocks—or whatever you call those vast stretches of concrete in LA—from the nursing home, so by the time we arrived we were sweaty and hungry. The place was a typical LA design: a one-story, white stucco structure with a Spanish tile roof, and a few palm trees and cacti with garish pink flowers decorating the grounds. The nurse, who knew us by now, ushered us through the depressing halls.

Bachan looked frail but cheerful enough in her bed, propped up with a few extra pillows so she could eat her lunch. Her hair, which had always been jet black, swept up into a Japanese-style bun, had finally retired and was now cropped short, sitting on her head like a white string mop, making her look a bit like a Muppet.

When we walked in she seemed not to recognize us, as usual, and I had the urge to do an about-face and leave. On our recent visits, Aunt Michi had done most of the talking. Mom had never learned much Japanese as a kid, since by the time she'd been born, speaking it had been dangerous.

Bachan smiled now as she might at any nice strangers and motioned us to chairs. We stumbled over a few pleasantries, Mom doing her best to chat about the weather, before we fell into an uncomfortable pause.

Eventually, Bachan squinted at Mom. "Sumiko-chan."

"Yes—of course it's me, Mama," Mom said, laughing, looking relieved. "Michi couldn't come today, so it's just us. This is Jane here—little
Akiko-chan. Remember Baby Akiko? Look how big she is now! She's the
one who insisted on coming today."

Bachan studied me suspiciously. "Aki?"

"You saw her yesterday, Mama, don't you remember?" Mom said, suddenly irritated.

"I go by Jane now," I added.

"Papa coming?" she asked, looking from me to Mom. "Papa coming
home?"

"*No*, Mama, Papa's been dead for ages," Mom told her bluntly.

Bachan pursed her lips and nodded. "Dead, dead," she said knowingly.

Then her eyes lit up and she leaned toward me. "Cigarettes?" she
asked. I let out a nervous laugh.

"Goodness, Mama, *cigarettes*? No!" Mom exclaimed.

This was new. Bachan must have known Aunt Michi would never
have tolerated such a request.

"Hai, hai. *Cigarettes*!" Bachan insisted impatiently.

"No, Mama—bad for your *health*!" Mom scolded. "Since when do
you *smoke*, Mama? *Bad for health*," she repeated loudly.

Bachan leaned back into her pillows and waved a purple, veiny hand
at us as she looked down at her fish sticks and canned peaches. Tears
formed in her eyes. I wasn't sure if they were tears of sadness, or if her eyes
were just watery.

Then she looked up again. "Candy?" she asked.

Mom always kept a couple of Baby Ruth bars in her purse. It was a
habit she'd started long ago, when Aunt Michi had gone to work in a Baby
Ruth factory in Chicago, right after the war. Bachan flashed us a decayed
grin as we presented her one. She ate slowly.

"Oishi," she whispered, eyes closed.

Perhaps high on sugar, Bachan changed, sitting up and speaking to us in
rapid Japanese. We listened, smiling and nodding politely though, as usual,
we understood little to none of what she was saying. At one point Mom

turned to me and said she was pretty sure she was telling us stories from her childhood in Japan. Finally Bachan leaned back and closed her eyes.

"All gone now," she concluded. "All gone."

Mom and I looked at each other, wondering if this was our cue to leave, but as we stood, Bachan's eyes popped open.

"You married?" she asked Mom.

"Married? Oh, god, Mama, I've been married forever now! You know my husband, Doug. You were there at our wedding, Mama. *Doug.* He was just here visiting yesterday. Jeez, Mama, you're so *senile!*"

It wasn't just her senility that kept Bachan from remembering your grandpa; she'd never liked him and had never bothered learning his name.

Bachan took a hanky from a frayed silk pouch she wore around her neck and spit into it.

"He hit you?" she asked Mom.

"Oh, Mama, are you really gonna start up with *that* again?" Mom asked, rolling her eyes. "Listen to me once and for all: Doug is the nicest guy you could ever want to meet. *Nice guy.* A little boring sometimes, maybe," she joked, winking at me, "but no one can say he's not nice. *I* have to kill the bugs—he can't even smash a *flea!*" she said, laughing loudly.

But Bachan looked skeptical. "Dad hit you?" she asked me, making punching gestures at the air.

"No, never," I assured, laughing with Mom. "Dad's a good guy, Bachan, just like Mom says. Not violent at all; harmless, never hurts anyone—"

"Yes *violent!*" she insisted, cutting me off. "Make *bombs,*" she said, frowning, pointing a finger at me. "*Nuclear bombs!*"

Mom and I gasped.

"Oh, god, no!" Mom cried. "Is *that* what you think, Mama? Why you've always hated Doug? No, no, there's all kinds of uses for nuclear power these days. Jane's dad does research. *Research,* Mama. Not bombs! For energy. *Energy.* Very peaceful. He works for the government, yes—but *no violence.* You know, *energy?* Doug's not the enemy; he's the good guy. *Good guy,* Mama."

"Nuclear *no* peaceful. *No good. Demon work!*"

She began to cough, a horrible, deep-throated hack. She pulled out her hanky again and held it to her mouth until she finished. After stuffing her hanky back into her pouch, she glared at Mom. "*Why you marry oni?*" she asked.

"Oh jeez," Mom muttered, pacing the room. "So, if Doug's an oni, what does that make my Jane here then, *half demon?*" she asked, gesturing at me in frustration.

I let out an awkward laugh, tucking my hands into my pockets.

"Anyway, isn't it better to marry an oni than someone helpless, Mama? Yes, Doug's hakujin, and he works for the government—he's a powerful guy, Mama. Isn't that *good*? We're safer, this way—we have someone on the other side looking out for us now. At least he doesn't have to wear a uniform!"

Bachan frowned and turned to me. "You sleepwalk?"

"Sleepwalk?" I asked, confused by this non sequitur.

"No, Mama, Jane doesn't *sleepwalk*," Mom snapped, sighing loudly. "That was me—*me*, Mama, Sumi. Okay, that's it, we're leaving."

She made the cuckoo sign for my benefit, then walked to Bachan's side and placed a hand on her arm. "Don't worry, Mama, everything's okay now. Are they giving you your medicine?" she asked less angrily. "I'll make sure, okay? We have a long trip back to Michi's now—the buses here are awful. We'll see you tomorrow with everyone else."

I followed Mom out the door, but as we were halfway down the hall, we heard Bachan's voice. "*Aki*," she was calling. "*Aki . . . Aki . . .*"

"Let's get out of here," Mom urged, grabbing my arm. "She's totally crazy."

I wanted to leave with Mom but found myself turning around. I pulled my arm free, walked back down the hall and pushed open the door. Bachan was standing in the middle of the room, arms hanging at her sides, her lunch spilled onto the floor.

"Aki?" she asked, looking at me hopefully.

"Uh-oh, you'd better get back in bed, Bachan."

I rushed to pick up her food, but she grabbed my shoulders. I was surprised by her strength, her bony fingers pressing into my flesh.

"*Aki?*" she repeated, anxiously searching my face.

She was so close, I could smell the Baby Ruth on her breath. I was frightened but also felt an unfamiliar pang of joy, perhaps because she seemed to be truly seeing me for the first time.

"Yes? What is it?" I asked.

She continued searching me, then, seeming disappointed not to find what she was looking for, released me.

Her eyes darkened. "Baby die. He die. You know baby?"

I shook my head.

"Neighbor's baby. You know next-door neighbor woman? She had baby." She pointed at her neighbor's hospital bed, which was empty. She spoke a few sentences in Japanese, then, seeming aware of my confusion, changed back to English. "Sad, sad neighbor woman. Her baby always, always crying. So *loud*. So *hungry*, ne? Never stop. *Never stop!*" She looked at me with desperation. I was nervous she might fall over, she seemed so distraught.

"Careful, there, Bachan," I said, touching her elbow to steady her.

"Then he die."

She leaned into my hand, a tear forming in her eye.

"Oh, god, Mama!" Mom exclaimed, surprising us. She entered the room, rushed between us, grabbed Bachan's shoulders and roughly steered her back to the bed.

"It wasn't the *neighbor's* baby, Mama! Don't you know that? And he didn't *just die*; babies don't just *randomly die*! My god, Mama, don't you realize you're talking about *yourself!*" she nearly shouted, her cheeks, already pink with rouge, flushing.

Bachan looked suddenly smaller as she allowed Mom to guide her back into bed and under the sheet. I'd never seen Mom so shaken up before; her temples twitched and her hands trembled as she pulled the sheet up over Bachan's body and tucked it in firmly on all sides.

"Jeez, Mama, you spilled your lunch. Now I'll have to see about getting another one! No more getting out of bed, okay? Do they need to tie you in here? Don't worry, everything will be fine. We'll see you tomorrow, okay?" she called over her shoulder, pushing me out the door.

We saw Bachan just once more, the next day, with Aunt Michi and the rest of the family, before we flew back to Oakland. About a month later, she died.

TWENTY-TWO

That weekend, I decided to prepare a feast. Every so often I'd do that—spend the day shopping and cooking, for no special occasion, especially if I was feeling aimless. Cooking has always helped me to feel more solid about the world and my place in it.

I took the bus downtown to A-1 Fish Market, where I took my time perusing the selection, finally splurging on some plump scallops and two bright-eyed red snappers. On the way home I stopped by the farmers market for some fresh herbs and veggies. I returned to the apartment, energized, my arms brimming with produce, and spent all afternoon cooking an Indian meal, one of Shiro's and my favorite cuisines.

Heating the ghee, which is so pure it never burns, throwing in the cumin seeds, cloves, and cardamom pods, watching them darken and expand like fists releasing, breathing in their essences, I felt myself relax. Everything felt perfectly whole—even the next-door neighbor woman's baby was quiet.

When Shiro got home that night, our apartment steaming with spices, he announced he could smell the meal from the street, gave me a hungry kiss, showered, threw on a cotton yukata robe I'd made him, and settled at the table to read the newspaper while I finished cooking.

I liked that he still subscribed to an actual news*paper*; there was something wonderfully old-fashioned about him reading the paper while I cooked. To some it might have seemed outdated—the man reading about the world, the woman preparing the meal—but the fact was, I loved cooking, and he loved the news. I enjoyed being independently embroiled in our own passions, while being just across the kitchen from one another. Except for it being the middle of the night, and us being Asian, I felt like we were characters from some old sitcom, like *The Dick Van Dyke Show*; I could almost hear the comforting laughter from the studio audience.

When dinner was ready, he set the table, switched off the lights, and lit a few candles, which I thought uncharacteristically romantic of him. It was perfect, because I was planning on giving him an answer to his proposal that night.

As I carried a plate of steaming chapatis to the table, I noticed he was leaning over his orchids at the kitchen window.

"What's up?" I asked.

"Oh, nothing. It's just, see that bird out there? On the plum-tree branch?"

"It's so dark out there, how can you see anything?" I went to the window and strained to see the bird he was referring to: just an average-looking robin sitting on a branch under a streetlight. "So?"

"It just seems oddly still, don't you think? I've been noticing it sitting there for a while now. Like it's watching me. And it's pretty late for a robin to be out."

We both stared at it a while. It didn't move.

"Maybe it's asleep," I suggested.

"Nah. Birds sleep with their eyes closed. In their nests, right?"

"How can you see its eyes? And do they even have eyelids?"

"Don't some have multiple pairs?"

"I have no idea. Google it."

"Never mind," he said, closing the curtains. "Let's eat!"

With the broken heater blazing away, it felt like we were dining in the tropics. We partook in all the dishes, which I must say turned out extra tasty, and chatted cheerfully about this and that, slipping from one subject to another easily, in a way we hadn't for some time.

"Amazing. Fucking. Meal," he said after polishing off his second helping. "Genius."

With the romantic lighting and mood, now seemed like the perfect chance for me to bring up his proposal.

"Yeah, so I was reading an interesting article," he said as I was opening my mouth to speak, "about these drones they're making to look just like birds and bugs—surveillance bots. Have you heard of them?"

"Huh?" I asked, flustered at the distraction.

"Surveillance bots. Military's working on 'em—that's how all these things start, like the internet. Some air force dudes. Totally fucked up. Insect and bird *spies*, can you believe?"

"Wait," I said, placing my fork down, looking at the kitchen window. "Did you think that was a *fake* bird out our window just now? *Spying* on us? Sent by your work, no doubt? Chuck's avatar?" I laughed but was also genuinely concerned about his growing level of paranoia.

"Ha-ha, hilarious. That's not why I'm mentioning this, no," he said, wiping the juices from his plate with a chapati, "I just thought you might be interested. Biomimetics—mimicking nature. They study animals in their natural habitats, then mimic their behavior in computer technology. They've been studying dozens of species of birds using these high-speed cameras. Apparently normal drones are clumsy landers, but birds . . ."

He stuffed the bite of chapati in his mouth and used a hand to demonstrate a bird's graceful swooping, perching motion, the sleeve of his robe swaying gently beneath.

"So now these new bird-drones can land lightly and precisely, even waddle around, if necessary," he added, scuttling his hand from side to side on the table, "so they can go indoors for optimal spying. And get this—they can *recharge* themselves from the sun, so they can keep spying forever. Creepy, eh?"

"That's pretty weird," I admitted, pouring myself another glass of cheap white wine. "Want some?" I asked.

"No thanks, I'm good with beer."

"So, what do people use these for? These little spying creatures?"

"Who knows, really? That's just the thing. We *don't* know."

"Well, I guess it's good to be ahead of the game with all that," I reasoned, sipping my wine. "It's not like they're gonna be used on civilians or anything."

"Oh, no, surely not," he mocked. "Only on card-carrying terrorists."

He leaned toward me and I recognized a lecture coming on. I sat back in my seat and drank more wine, my desire to bring up our engagement dampening.

"But that's the most obvious, extreme version of all the crazy surveillance that goes on. Most of it's way more subtle. See, here's the thing: tech isn't just fun, like they want us to think. It's not just some neutral science project. It's how they watch us, track us, sort us." He held up a fresh chapati and ripped it in two. "They divide us into two groups: consumers and criminals. Poor folks, they squeeze all the consumer out of them, then, when they can't pay their debt, off to the criminal side they go." He tossed half of the chapati onto his plate. "Once your file's in the criminal database? You're screwed; it follows you around forever.

"As for us, the so-called middle class?" he said, holding up the remaining piece of chapati and inspecting it. "They watch our every move, track our tastes to feed us what we want, to keep us consuming, so we're living paycheck to paycheck, never able to build assets, stuff you can *hold, touch*. Any attempt at building something solid keeps getting knocked down again." He dropped that piece onto his plate as well. "But people don't see the scam—how they have nothing real to hold on to. Why?" He paused for dramatic effect. "*Fake freedom*."

"Okay . . . so what's that?" I reluctantly encouraged him.

"The freedom to *consume*." He took a sip of beer. "Ever heard of Edward Bernays?" I shook my head. "Freud's American nephew. I might do my next film on him—the guy's at the center of modern American culture. He masterminded that ad campaign in the 1920s calling cigarettes 'torches of freedom' to get women hooked on nicotine. Brilliant, evil guy. He linked *buying* to this popular new concept of his uncle's: the *self*." His eyes were all lit up and he shifted back and forth in his seat, so excited he could barely sit still.

"Suddenly ad companies are pitching the idea of shopping as freedom—as *self-expression*! We don't need just *one* house for the extended family anymore, hell no, we each must have our *own*! Each our *own car*! Our *own everything*—to *express ourselves*! *To liberate ourselves*!"

"So, like the *I* in iPhones and iPads, that's part of all this, right?" I asked, getting a bit excited about these ideas as well. There was no denying, he had some interesting points. "Identifying with our products?"

"Exactly! Steve Jobs was the king—Bernays incarnate! We keep throwing our money at these tech companies, surrendering ourselves to them in digital format, reducing ourselves to binary—nothing to touch, nothing to *hold in your hands*."

He ran a finger back and forth through a candle flame. "I just want to feel more connected to things at their *source*, you know? Even if it's less convenient. Not always have everything displaced. We're so separated from the basic elements of things nowadays . . ." He looked at the piece of chapati on his plate, studying it as though it were a sacred object. "You made these chapatis by hand, right?"

I nodded.

"See? That's what I love about you!" he cried, beaming proudly at me. "You make fucking *chapatis by hand*! Who does that these days? You may not realize it, Jane, but in your own quiet way you're a fierce, righteous warrior." He winked and held up the piece; it was in the shape of a half-moon.

"Oh, great. You see my cooking as some kind of war?" I challenged, though honestly, his hyperbolic admiration of my cooking—even seeing me as some kind of fierce cooking warrior, as over-the-top and ridiculous as that sounded—*did* actually turn me on a bit.

"Not just that—you're not on Facebook or anything, right? You're one of the only people I know who isn't part of all that virtual crap." He gave me a knowing look. "You and me, we have *history* that keeps us real."

"*History?* I hate history," I blurted childishly, not sure where my intense opposition was coming from. "I just don't want to bother with all that stuff."

He narrowed his eyes and pointed up at the corners of the room.

"If we could just see them in their uniforms up there on their watchtowers, looking down at us, hear the click of their rifles, smell their sweat—we might rebel. But no. We don't see them, 'cause . . ." He leaned closer and lowered his voice. "They've moved into our *heads*. And we love it. That's what gets me most—the enthusiasm. We all rush like fucking lemmings to trade any trace of real freedom for a one-way ticket to Cyber Limbo-land."

"*Cyber Limbo-land?*" I asked, sipping my wine, resigned to getting pleasantly tipsy and bringing up our engagement another time.

He nodded.

"And who's 'they'? *Big Brother?*" I let out a shrill little laugh.

"Basically—the government, corporations, working together. Mussolini would've loved it." He stared at the candles on the table. "Course, for this whole *self* thing to work, we have to have an *other* . . ."

The flames wavered in a slight breeze coming in through the living room windows, casting shadows across his face.

"That's where the racial profiling at my work comes in—what better *other* than folks who look different, have a different religion? The more scared of *them* we are, the more quickly we'll trade in *real* liberties for *fake* ones. Oldest trick in the book. Keep one half imprisoned, the other half scared . . . We let these demons run rampant, spy on us, sell our data to who-knows who for whatever evil purpose, destroy the planet, whatever the hell they want, so long as they keep the *other* away and we can keep buying our *liberation* . . ."

He looked up at me, his eyes wide with alarm.

"Do you know how easy it would be for this to go way wrong? We're a greased machine beyond Orwell's wildest dreams, but we don't worry, 'cause, I dunno, I guess 'cause Obama's such a nice guy. But all it would take is the wrong guys getting their hands on the wheel—"

"Hey now," I chirped, standing, hearing Mom's voice. "Calm down there, you. To hear you talk, the whole world's coming to a cataclysmic end tomorrow!"

I laughed again as I walked to the sink to get myself a glass of ice water.

"Isn't this all a bit conspiracy-theorist? You're not planning on blowing anything up in protest, are you?" I joked, though honestly, I was growing uncomfortable with his mounting agitation at the world and worried about what lengths he might go to in order to find justice.

"Hello, I'm a peace-loving dude—don't you know that by now?"

He blew me a kiss. I blew him one back.

"So, what's this whole evil plot then?" I asked, sitting back at the table with my ice water. "It's all about money in the end, right?"

"Yeah, sure—but more than that, too." He looked back at the candles, his jaw tense. Shadows danced across his cheeks. I remember feeling afraid of him for the first time. "Going back to Freud . . . he said we all have this animal side. This dark, bestial hunger that knows only to keep feeding."

"Then what *is* real freedom? I mean, okay, it's not buying, or the internet, but does it actually exist?"

He took a sip of his beer and thought a moment. "I'd say it's a direction, not a destination. And awareness. We have to open our eyes. Wake up. Can't battle demons we can't see."

"I think freedom's an illusion. It's all fake."

He looked surprised by my cynicism. He shrugged. "Maybe so."

It's funny, I always fancied myself as the optimist between the two of us. But looking back now, I see how wrong I had it: *I* was the pessimist, not your dad.

"So, you know my latest post, the one about Obama's continuation of extraordinary rendition and torture? It's getting lots of attention—just hit a hundred thousand views. It may cost me my job and possibly much more."

"Then why not take it offline," I cut in, "if you're so sure it's a problem?"

"And let them win? No way. I'm telling you, I'm almost ready to blow the whistle." He finished off his beer and set the empty bottle on the table. "I know we need the money, and I'm gonna start looking for something else. But until then, I'm collecting documentation. Now, I know you're not gonna like this, but . . . I've been sneaking some video footage at work—just to add to my documentation. To build my case."

"*Sneaking* video?" I asked, my whole body tensing. "At your *work*? You're kidding, right? Shiro, that sounds totally illegal."

"Wanna know what's totally illegal?" he shot back almost angrily. "You should see what goes on in that IO Room. Some of the guys literally have their buddies out on the floor make hot women go through the scanners again, so they can watch their naked bodies! They can jerk off, do whatever the hell they want back there—no security cameras, for public privacy, so they say. Everyone knows this shit goes on, but no one'll *say* it."

"Okay, it's horrible, but Shiro—"

"That's not all—you should *see* some of the footage I have, Jane. Oh, man, the other day I got one of Chuck actually explicitly explaining *how to racially profile*. It was classic—he's like, 'Yeah, so, anyone wearing a turban,'" he said in his exaggeratedly nasal, dorky Chuck voice, "'or, you know, Middle Eastern–looking, you gotta check 'em. It's not race, it's just statistics, ya know? And Mexicans—pull aside the Mexicans.' When I asked, 'Oh, is this official policy? Some immigration quota?' he got all squirmy and was like, 'Look, man, we're here to protect Americans—you got a problem with that?' I'm telling you, I can't wait to watch them try and defend—"

"You're telling me you have personal cameras hidden around the *airport*? Including places you're *forbidden to have cameras*?"

My stomach contracted and I was suddenly nauseous.

"Nah, I'm not that dumb. I bought a tiny camera I secure on myself."

"Get rid of it. Erase it. Now."

I stood—I thought I might have to run to the bathroom to puke.

"Hang on—okay, okay, you're right, I should probably be more careful." He reached out a hand to me. "I won't erase the footage I have, but I'll take more steps to make sure no one finds out. Sorry, I should have told you earlier. But you have to admit, the shit they're getting away with—"

I stepped away from the table. "Shiro, this isn't some thriller you're starring in; this is real life. This is the *United States government*. You could go to prison for this. *I* could, too, as your accomplice. Have you even thought of that?"

"I said I'll be more careful," he mumbled, looking away.

A few silent, tense moments passed as he pushed the remaining bits of his food around on his plate with his chapati. I took a deep breath. The wave of nausea was passing, but the wine and heat were making me drowsy. I sat back down.

"Why do we always have to talk about such big, serious things all the time?" I asked quietly. "Why can't we just talk about something light-hearted for a change?"

"Fine. Bring something up yourself," he challenged. "Anything. I'd love it."

I opened my mouth to rise to his challenge, but no sound came. My cheeks flushed with anger at both him and myself.

"Maybe something you read, or heard in a conversation, or show—just *something*," he pressed. "An interesting idea you came across. You have plenty of free time for new experiences these days, don't you? I'd love to see you acting more, not just *re*acting.

"Like my proposal to you," he said, looking me directly in the eyes. "You can't even bring that up to give me an answer. I mean, I assume your answer's yes, and it seems like now we're making wedding plans, but I just have to *assume* so, from context clues. It's like we're gonna end up married by *default*. You can't even say 'yes' about what I'm hoping is one of the most important things in your life. That's worrisome, don't you think?"

Of course, he was right; it was obvious I had some disability in this area. Some block to taking life by the reins and galloping joyously forward. It's a block I've always had, but for some reason it had come to an excruciating head since the night of our anniversary.

Why couldn't I say yes to marrying him? I could hear the words in my mind: "Yes, yes, yes! Oh-my-fucking-god, yes! I've never been more certain about anything in my life!" But when I went to form them in my mouth, that nagging sense of absence at my center bubbled and swelled, as though it were intent on expanding until it inhabited all of me.

The last thing I wanted was to fall into the bogus stereotype of the passive, voiceless Asian American woman. And yet sometimes that's exactly how I felt.

On the other hand, who said being quiet was really such a terrible thing? All the loud men? Maybe being quiet in general wasn't the problem, per se. But not being able to say yes to what I wanted most in life—that *was* a problem, I had to admit.

"Well, ironically . . . I *was* actually planning on bringing that up tonight," I began, chugging down my water. "But then you started in with your whole mansplaining thing and . . . the moment didn't seem right anymore. But you have a good point, I *do* need to work on that. I agree. Bringing stuff up, taking more initiative. *Act*ing more than *re*acting. Definitely. I'll work on it, I promise."

He looked surprised and pleased.

"Cool. Sorry about the mansplaining." He grinned sheepishly.

"So," I said, setting down my water. "Speaking of taking initiative, the other day I borrowed Dad's car and drove out to Marin, to try and find

Mom. I decided I needed to get to the bottom of this. She's been missing for quite a while now—over a month."

"Oh? A whole month?"

"But it was weird—her condo was almost empty. It barely seemed like anyone was living there. I called her hair salon; they said she hasn't been in since that day I saw her at that warehouse. And I even talked to Chris. He says they communicate all the time, and he's planning on buying her a ticket to Texas, but he hasn't actually *seen* her. I mean, she still posts on Facebook, and even 'checks in' according to everyone, and I get her texts and emails, and I even finally talked to her the other day. So, she still exists, obviously."

"But where? Place matters."

"I don't know . . . it's like she's vanished . . . Jeez, Shiro, do you think she's okay?"

I hadn't realized just how worried I'd become about Mom's disappearance until then.

"Maybe she's finally managed to escape," he offered—I couldn't tell if he was being sarcastic.

"*Escape?* Escape *what?*"

"Or at least she *thinks* she's escaped. But really she's being held prisoner again."

"Prisoner? Where?"

"Cyber Limbo-land."

That was it—all at once I burst at the seams and out came peals of wild, hysterical laughter. I fell off of my chair, rolled on the floor away from the table, arched back, doubled over. I was sure my entire meal would come projecting out of me. I don't know when I'd last been so consumed by any emotion, let alone such full-on, unabashed hysterics like this. The outburst lasted for some time, despite my efforts to squelch it. Finally, completely drained, sides aching, I collapsed on the floor, moaning lightly. It was a wonderful release, honestly.

"Um, you okay there?" Shiro asked.

"Sorry . . . I have no idea where that came from . . . What were we talking about?" I took several deep breaths and managed to prop myself on my knees, resting my head on my chair.

"Something hilarious, apparently—your mom's disappearance."

"Right." I climbed back into my chair and gulped down the rest of my ice water. "You were speaking metaphorically, I hope? About Cyber Limbo-land?"

He raised his eyebrows.

I tried to laugh again but couldn't. The absence at my center seemed to have expanded during my fit of laughter and was now winding up toward my chest.

"No, but seriously, I guess she's just really into her new online life and her singing lessons, or whatever . . . and I'm sure being at her condo is too depressing now that she's losing it . . ."

"Don't say 'losing'—say stolen. By our predatory banking system."

"Yeah, whatever. I guess our schedules must just really be incompatible."

"Neither of you *has* a schedule."

"Well," I stammered, placing my cool glass on my cheek, a pool of sweat collecting at the small of my back, "I admit, I *am* getting really worried. She used to sleepwalk when she was young . . . I hope she's not doing that again and didn't wander off somewhere? Do you think I should call the police?"

He shrugged. "I mean . . . you say you just talked to her?"

"Yeah, a few days ago."

"And she's been checking in on Facebook? What evidence do you have that she's actually missing?"

"Well . . . I don't know about *evidence*, really. It's just, I haven't actually seen her since that day at the warehouse. And I just have this funny feeling. Kind of like the day I came home from school and she was gone."

"I mean, as far as the police are concerned, she's probably not missing. A funny feeling won't get you far with them. But that doesn't mean she's okay."

"I'm gonna mail her a letter," I announced, suddenly hopeful. "An old-fashioned letter, through the postal service. As a test, I'll ask her to write back by hand, since I know her handwriting. And I'll include questions only she could answer. If I don't hear back, I guess I'll just have to call the police . . . or hire a private investigator."

"A letter—yeah, good idea." A bead of sweat dripped off his eyebrow, aggravating him. "Jesus, this heat's too fucking much."

He jumped up from his chair and crossed the kitchen to turn the fan onto the highest speed. The candles blew out, and in the darkness, the rectangles of streetlight from the living room windows became more prominent, like eyes opening. The sleeves of his robe fluttered in the artificial breeze.

"Have you called the building manager recently?" he asked. "We ought to report this damn broken heater to the rent board. Our gas bill must be outrageous."

Everything we'd done to rig the vent shut—tin foil, cardboard, duct tape—had blown right off again, as though the heat had a will of its own.

"Actually, it's really weird, but our bill's been normal. But yeah, I've left tons of messages, and I'll keep trying. Oh, and Shiro . . ."

I poured myself more wine.

"About . . . about your sneaking those videos at your work. You'll stop that, right? I mean, it's just too risky. And you'll delete whatever files you've already taken, right? Please?"

He walked to the sink, turned on the faucet, and stuck his head beneath.

"Fine, at least no new footage for now," he relented from under the faucet, water soaking his hair and the top of his robe. "But I swear, I *am* gonna expose those fucks one of these days."

TWENTY-THREE

The girl stands in the doorway, watching her sister walk the baby up and down the floor of their new home: a cramped room in a newly assembled, army-style barrack, which they are told will soon be divided into two, to share with another family.

They arrived just a few days ago, so everything is still strange. Even the air is different here—heavier, thicker. The hotel was just a short distance from the beach; no matter how warm it got, the air always carried a hint of the sea's spaciousness. Here, the air smells of moss and trees, and she can almost taste the mud from the swamp that people say runs along the back border of the facility, though she hasn't yet seen it herself.

She had never ridden on a train before coming here, and it could have been fun, except for the tension that gripped the shoulders and jaws of the adults, and the soldiers with rifles patrolling the aisles, their darting eyes always watching, their laughter amongst one another ringing out menacingly.

Her baby brother's cries pierce her ears now. She looks at her mother, sitting upright and rigid at the center of her cot, staring straight ahead. She resembles a skeleton the girl once saw hanging in a museum on a school field trip. She can't remember when she last saw her mother eat—at the racetrack she often skipped meals, and now she refuses to walk to the mess hall with the family, for fear that someone will take the baby.

"He's hungry, Mama," her sister pleads, bouncing the baby, naked except for a makeshift cloth diaper. She repeats herself in Japanese, leaning down and offering the baby, but her mother just continues staring straight ahead, as though she can't see or hear.

Her sister speaks more loudly and quickly, still in Japanese, so the girl only catches short phrases. Something about needing to take the baby to the mess hall for some rice porridge, and Tak waiting for them.

The girl and her sister are slipping into their zori sandals by the door when her mother's eyes widen into focus. Suddenly she stands and grabs the baby from her sister.

For a moment his cries stop. The girl and her sister sigh with relief.

Her mother sits back on her cot, her frail arms arranging the baby on her lap, and unbuttons the top of her dress, revealing a small lump with a dark swollen circle at its center. She presses it into the baby's mouth, and for a moment he attempts to feed. But soon he becomes frustrated and begins to cry again, louder and more angrily than before.

"Shh!" her mother hisses. "Shizukani! Kikoeru!" Be quiet! They can hear!

She shifts him on her lap and presses her other nipple into his mouth, but again he protests. She keeps trying, shifting him back and forth, shoving her dry nipples into the baby's shrieking mouth, continuing to cry desperately for him to quiet.

The girl wonders if she's actually trying to feed him, or just silence him.

Her big brother appears. He's so tall his hair grazes the barrack doorframe. Hands on his hips, he shakes his head with disgust at the scene before him.

"This is pathetic," he mutters. He only speaks English now.

He marches to her mother. "Cover yourself," he instructs. "We're taking him to the mess hall. You're being paranoid, Mama. No one's gonna take him! What would they want with a baby?"

"Tak's right," Michi adds in English—she only speaks English in front of Tak now; ever since the racetrack, he gets angry when she speaks Japanese. "And what would Papa think, both of you starving to death while he's gone? You can't make no milk if you don't eat!"

But her mother turns away from them, clutching the baby protectively, scurries to a corner of the room, crouches down and places him in a wicker laundry basket, draping him with a pale-blue blanket. She looks up at the girl's sister with the eyes of a frightened mother animal and mumbles something in Japanese.

"Neighbor woman?" her sister asks. "What do you mean the neighbor woman can help? What neighbor woman?"

"Our neighbor at the racetrack," the girl explains from where she stands by the door. Her mother has asked for her before—the nice woman who helped with the birth—even though she was transferred from the racetrack long before them. "She's confused. She thinks she's still here."

Her sister walks to the laundry basket and lowers the blanket from the baby's face. "That woman's not our neighbor no more, remember Mama? We're all the way in Arkansas now. She was sent somewhere else—we don't know where."

Her mother seems saddened by this news and walks limply back to her cot, the baby continuing to cry from the laundry basket, his tiny fingers poking up at empty space.

"Don't worry, Mama, even if they hear him, they won't take him," her sister insists, scooping the baby into her arms again. "Like Tak says, what would they want with a baby?"

Her mother sits and resumes her stare into space.

Her sister sighs, frustrated. "Just go on without us again, Tak. I'll stay. Bring Sumi. Say your mother's still sick. Bring us home two plates. And be sure to bring something for Aki—a cup of milk or rice porridge."

The girl squeezes her toy boat in her dress pocket as she walks down the barrack steps into the evening. It would be a relief to leave the cries if it weren't for the cicadas. Every evening at sunset, the baby's voice and the cicadas become one, screaming in wild unison.

The world outside is just as humid as their room, but at least the sky is enormous—a radiant swirl of pink and orange.

Her brother strides past her, swatting away mosquitoes, his long legs carrying him quickly along the dirt path between the barracks. He turns a corner. Except for a guard standing on the nearest watchtower, his rifle resting against his thigh, no one is in sight. Many of the barracks are still empty, though more families arrive each day.

The guard, as though hearing something, turns in her direction. The wooden structure he stands on seems to become his body; she imagines him as an impossibly tall, angular beast, its long shadow slicing the ground in front of her. His eyes land on her. She feels them burning into her skin and soul.

"Tak! Wait for me!" she wants to shout, but her mouth is frozen. Her body feels as though it belongs to someone else. Her feet feel tethered to the ground.

Finally, the guard glances away, releasing her from this spell. She pries her sandals from the dirt path and runs after her brother.

TWENTY-FOUR

The next morning, I woke to the same sensation as that other morning: soft, tiny hands resting on my cheeks. The feeling was so sweet, so blissful, so seductive, I found myself lingering there in my half-sleep state, afraid the feeling would pass, until my stomach turned and I nearly puked. I sat up and pulled myself out of bed.

It occurred to me that I hadn't had my period in over a month. But I'd never been regular in that department, so I wasn't too concerned. In fact, my period had always been so light and irregular, I'd always wondered if I might be infertile.

Seems funny to confess this to you, of all people.

The next-door baby was sobbing, and Shiro was howling some hard rock song at the top of his lungs in the shower, the two voices harmonizing dissonantly.

I considered giving the wall above my dresser a good bang, as a warning to whoever was on the other side that this was getting to be too much—that no one should be expected to put up with such nonstop racket—but ended up only placing my hand there. The wall was warm. The cries seemed to seep through the porous material of the wall into my palm. I could almost feel the small, determined creature on the other side attempting to crawl inside of me. I imagined reaching through to the other side, pushing the small being back to wherever it had come from—

"*Aki!*" a voice called.

The cries stopped; the baby must have fallen asleep.

"Huh?"

"Aki—if we ever have a baby, let's name it *Aki!*" Shiro was shouting down the hall from the shower. "You know, after you," he called over the water. "Since you don't use the name, it's kind of like, wasted. And it's such a cool name."

"What on earth made you think of that right now?" I yelled back down the hall. "And no way; naming our baby after myself would be the last thing in the world I'd ever want!"

"Fine," he called back and went back to howling his song.

Shaken up by his disturbing inspiration, and by my equally disturbing experience at the wall, I busied myself with searching my dresser drawer for a decent pair of undies. Noticing they were all stained and ratty, I thought maybe I should spice things up a bit and buy something new, maybe red and lacy—our sex life wasn't anywhere near what it used to be. As I rummaged around, my fingers felt something cool: Mom's pill jar. I'd hidden it there the day I'd discovered it in the laundry basket.

I lifted it, unscrewed the cap, and shook several capsules into my hand. They were almost weightless, and quite cute, half pale blue and half yellow, split neatly down the center, like miniature Easter eggs. I poured all but two capsules back into the jar.

I went to the kitchen and took your dad's Cap'n Crunch from the cabinet, the loony sea captain on the box offering up an explosive, sparkly spoonful of the golden squares, along with an ecstatic, military salute. I shook a heap of the squares, smaller and less gold than they were on the box, into a bowl, poured in the milk, opened the blue-and-yellow capsules and sprinkled the white powder on top. I added two teaspoons of sugar, the way I knew he liked it, gave the concoction a stir and placed the bowl on the table next to his newspaper.

I didn't even think much about it, to be honest; it just seemed like the right and natural thing to do at the time. And, after all, Shiro himself had requested that I *act* more, not just *react*.

It was getting close to unbearable, his ranting about all the horrible things in the world and how they were all connected and, worse, how they were all connected to *us*. Not to mention the serious risks he seemed willing to take to personally put a stop to them, like sneaking video footage at work, which could be a felony. From my research, albeit limited, this miraculous new substance seemed like it might be just the thing to help contain his paranoia, maybe even turn it around.

I would have confronted him with the idea directly, which of course would have been the more noble thing to do, but I knew it would be a lost cause.

Putzing around the kitchen, waiting for him to emerge, I thought about how difficult it was to determine whether to approach a problem from within one's own mind or "out there" in the actual world. It was certainly easier to address problems from within one's mind, at least in the short term—way less messy than attempting to locate their external sources, which had so many moving parts and could be so dangerous. Especially if those parts lay within the government.

Still, trust me, it's not as though I was proud of my actions. I certainly regret them now. If I'd acted differently, it's possible I wouldn't be here at this old strawberry farm now, talking to you.

Just then, he appeared, keys and bike pump in hand, backpack slung over his shoulder, hair uncombed.

"Hey there, foxy mama," he greeted me.

"Are you *biking* to work?" I asked.

In an effort to rely less on fossil fuel, your dad had recently taken to biking more and driving less.

"No way, just to BART. But I should—need to start getting in shape. With the male genes in my family, I'm gonna be lucky to make it past sixty—all that heart stuff. You're having *cereal*?"

"No, I made it for you."

"Really? Sweet—you never do that."

I shrugged. "Just felt like it this morning. What, can't I make my favorite fiancé his favorite breakfast?" I said in a sultry voice, puckering my lips and placing a hand on my cocked hip.

He laughed. I walked to him and combed his hair with my fingers.

"I love you," he mouthed.

"I love you, too," I mouthed back.

This was a joke of ours: neither of our families ever said the phrase out loud, so we always just mouthed it to each other. We didn't need to say it; we knew it was true.

"Well, it shouldn't take you long to inhale a bowl of cereal, the way you do," I teased. "I doctored it up the way you like."

"Nah, gotta jam. You have it." I wrinkled my nose. We both knew I never ate Cap'n Crunch. "I'll grab something at the airport. FYI, next time don't doctor it for me; gets all mushy."

We kissed and he walked to the door.

"Oh, meant to tell you," he said, slipping into his shoes, "some folks are going for drinks after work today—thought I might join. Want to meet up with us? Might be good for you to get out of this oven now and then."

"I thought you hated everyone over there?"

"Nah, some of the lowly workers like me are decent enough."

"You're not gonna tell them about your secret spying, are you?"

"Course not. So, you'll join us?"

I shrugged. It was true, I needed to get out of the apartment more, but hanging out with his coworkers, none of whom I knew, didn't sound like much fun.

"Maybe, but I might want to stay in and get some sewing done. I've been falling behind again. By the way, have you been hearing that baby crying?"

He looked at me funny. "Baby?"

"Yeah, the one in the apartment next door. I've been hearing it all the time. It's been driving me bonkers, actually."

He stood still a moment, listening. "You hear it now?"

I listened, too. "I guess not now, no. It must be asleep. But I'm surprised you haven't been hearing it. It was practically singing a duet with you this morning when you were screaming in the shower."

"Ha—well, maybe its voice is in some register only you can hear," he joked. "Alrighty then—off to fuck with Chuck!" He pushed a gust of air from his bike pump toward me as he strode out the door.

I walked to the table and looked down at the wilting bowl of cereal. I almost dumped it, but instead took a seat at the table and lifted the news-paper, which was open to an article your dad must have been reading earlier. I didn't know the last time I'd actually sat down and read an article in a physical newspaper.

Until recently, the region of Fukushima was relatively unknown outside of Japan, though locally it was famous for its rolling green hills, natural hot springs, and summer peaches . . .

I scanned down the page:

Recent data revealed that the concentration of radioactive cesium on children's shoelaces was astronomically high. When the children tie their shoes, their hands become contaminated, and when they eat . . .

Only more bad news, of course. This is why I never read the newspaper, I remembered—it was too depressing, and I always felt so helpless.

Why can't they ever say anything positive? Mom's voice sounded in my head, the question she always asked whenever anyone expressed interest in current events.

I heard a small whimper; the next-door baby must have woken.

I folded the paper, picked up the spoon, dug it into the cereal, scooped up a dripping mound, and placed it into my mouth. I suppose I was simply curious what so many Americans were finding so appealing. I'd thought I might detect a bitter taste, but, despite the mushy texture, the medicated cereal was actually quite delicious. I scooped a second, third, and fourth bite into my mouth, quickly, each bite more fulfilling than the last. That amorphous absence within me seemed to stir and stretch itself up toward my throat, opening its wide, hungry mouth, as though this was exactly what it had been craving all along.

TWENTY-FIVE

About a week later, Shiro was on his computer at the kitchen table. I came up from behind and saw an image of our living room on his screen.

"What's this?" I asked.

"Oh, nothing. Just working on something."

I didn't think much of it, assuming it was just an odd photo or another of his video projects, but after a few minutes he let out a sigh. "Come," he said. "I have something to confess."

I sat beside him and he scooted the computer so we both could see.

"I've set up a camera in here."

"A what?"

"A camera."

"A *camera*?"

"Yeah."

"Where?"

"In here."

"In *here*?"

"Yeah. A mini surveillance camera."

"A *surveillance camera*?"

"Could you stop with the parrot thing?"

I looked all around the room, suddenly light-headed.

"But I asked you not to. Is this for one of your projects?"

"No, at least, not directly. Sorry, I should have mentioned it. But I didn't want to freak you out. After what happened that day, with someone breaking in and all, I figured it wouldn't hurt to be safe."

"*Safe?* To *spy* on me?" I couldn't believe it. He'd never so directly betrayed my trust like this. "Just like you're spying on your work?"

"I'm not spying on *you*, silly—this *is* me spying on my work. Or whoever the assholes were who broke into our house and went through all our stuff—and could've attacked you! Anyway, *they're* the ones spying on *us* . . . maybe. Who knows what really happened? That's the whole point here—"

"So, since when? Yesterday?"

He thought. "I guess it was last Tuesday I got it up and running. Yeah."

"*Last Tuesday?* But you installed it when?"

"Probably a couple days before. Why do you care so much?"

"Why do I care when you started *videotaping* my living space?" I stood and began pacing the kitchen floor. "Gee, let's see, maybe because I don't like being spied on in my own home? After all you go on about hating your job and technology and our fishbowl, Big Brother society? Talk about *hypocrisy*!"

He was intently studying the screen, not seeming too concerned with my feelings.

"Are you really gonna sit here and watch this? Our apartment, just sitting there?"

The image went blurry. He was fast-forwarding. A figure passed across the screen; he paused: it was me—no big surprise there.

"Yup. There I am. Wow, what do you know? You caught me. Shocking exposé."

But he was too engrossed to pay me much attention. He rewound and played the same footage again. Sure enough, I walked past the camera, from the living room toward the hall, holding a cup of tea. The time stamp read 2:45 p.m.

"This is great. Are we gonna watch me making lunch now? Can we watch me sleep? Do you have cameras in every room?"

"No, just one, so far—just captures the living room and part of the kitchen." He was fast-forwarding again. "I'm determined to catch those motherfuckers."

I felt more light-headed. "Where is it?" I asked, looking all around, trying to guess where the camera would need to be to get the angle we were seeing, suddenly nervous it had caught me emptying those medicine capsules into his cereal the week before.

"Up there," he said, pointing to a hanging plant up in the corner by the doorway to the hall. "Same kind we use at work, but smaller. I bought it about month ago—you know, to sneak footage at work. I was wearing it on me, but then the other day it occurred to me I should be using it here at home, too. So, I mounted it up there."

I squinted up at the spider plant; he'd hidden it well.

"Surveillance *plants*? Wow, really? Like those surveillance bots you say you hate? And I had to catch you in the act?"

He looked down. At least now he looked slightly ashamed.

"You're right, I should have told you. Like I said, I'm sorry. I just wanted to try it out for a while—I was afraid you'd veto it."

"So, is it recording us right now?"

"Nah, I only turn it on during the day."

"Because you don't want to keep an eye on yourself, just me."

"Jane, the break-in happened midday, when you were home *alone*. This is for your own safety, babe—"

"Okay, so if you insist on this, show me how to turn it on and off myself."

He was staring at the screen again, as though it were the most riveting thing he'd seen. "Yeah, okay. I'll teach you how to work it. But just don't forget, especially if you take a nap. I want to track this for a while. Something's wrong here."

I sat back down next to him—he must have fast-forwarded, because the time stamp now read 3:20 p.m. There it was again: our living room. Here I came again, passing from the hall into the living room. But this time I was pitched forward a little, arms dangling at my sides.

I reached to fast-forward it, but he stopped me.

"Wait." He pressed the back arrow, and we watched the me-on-the-screen run jerkily backward.

"I thought we weren't spying on me?"

I wanted to shut the computer, but on the other hand, I was also curious.

"Yeah, I know, but I just want to see something. You're walking kind of funny there, aren't you?"

We watched my entrance again. My walk was definitely off from my normal one. My steps were clunkier and I was leaning forward, looking down at the floor.

"See?" He rewound and played it again. "You're leaning forward. And kind of . . . lumbering. Look."

"Yeah, I do look a little funny," I admitted. "Like I'm looking for something. I must have been looking for something."

"Maybe you really had to pee," he suggested. "People walk funny when they have to pee."

"Yeah, probably." I noted the time stamp again. "This footage is from when?"

"Yesterday." The me-on-the-screen passed out of view. He fast-forwarded again, hoping to find something a bit juicier, I suppose. "What did you do yesterday? Did you go out at all?"

I thought a moment. "No, I don't think so, not yesterday."

When I reappeared on the screen, I slid the computer in front of me, rewound, then hit play. Again, I was walking in that strange way, this time from the living room to the hall, bent forward, my arms hanging in front of me, apelike. The time stamp read just a few minutes later: 3:28 p.m.

"Yeah, I probably just really had to pee," I said.

He reached across me and continued fast-forwarding. When I appeared again, I brushed his hand aside and pressed play. The me-on-the-screen was now stooping down in front of our bookshelf, sitting cross-legged on the floor, and quickly, one by one, removing books from the shelf and tossing them aside. I was almost out of the camera's view, so it was difficult to make out details, but I seemed to be running my hands all around the edges of each book, and behind on the shelf, as though searching for something. My back was curved forward and seemed to be slightly shaking.

"What were you doing there?" he asked.

"I have no idea. Let's stop this."

I reached to shut the computer, but he swiveled it back toward him and leaned in closer.

"Were you *dusting* or something? And maybe listening to some show? You seem like you're shaking, like you're laughing—or crying?"

"No. I mean, I don't think so. I don't think I was, but I guess I just forgot."

He eyed me sideways. "You *forgot*? You don't think you were asleep, do you? Like sleepwalking?"

"I don't think so, no."

"You said your mom used to—something like that couldn't be hereditary, could it?"

"I have no idea."

I thought of myself ransacking our apartment and building those strange towers in my sleep. Part of me wanted to tell him the truth, or at least, my suspicion of the truth, but I was still too confused, and terrified of what that actual truth might be.

"But I'm sure we'd have noticed if I was doing that. Sleepwalking, I mean."

He turned up the volume on his computer.

"Listen," he said, "you can even hear your voice a little. The camera was too far to catch much, but it sounds like you're saying something."

I slammed the computer shut. "All that talk of pee, now I have to go," I announced, standing.

As I headed to the bathroom I imitated the forward-pitched walk I'd seen myself do on the tape; it felt only slightly familiar.

Sitting on the cold toilet, gripping the edges of the seat with clenched fingers, I wondered why I was so afraid to admit to Shiro that yes, I'd probably been sleepwalking—maybe even sleep-crying. And that it seemed, during these episodes, that I searched for something and built those strange structures. If I *had* admitted this all, the two of us could have taken on the problem together, as a team.

I suppose I was too afraid of what else I might see myself doing on that screen to admit any of this. And of him thinking I was insane—and of the fact that I might actually *be* insane, and following in Bachan's footsteps.

"Don't watch anymore, okay?" I shouted from the toilet. "It creeps me out, your watching me like this. It's invasive. You make such a big deal about tech and privacy."

"I know, I know," he called back. "But don't you want to know what's been going on in here?"

"You say you hate spying on people at work, that it's below your dignity, and now you're doing it in your own home. Who's the bad guy here?" I continued shouting from the toilet.

"Sorry. Point taken."

"Get rid of that video, okay? I don't want random footage of me lying around. Destroy it right now, okay?"

"Can we finish this talk later? I can barely hear you."

"*Erase it!*" I yelled angrily, my belly cramping.

"Okay, fine—I'll delete it right now if it makes you happy. But you have to promise to turn it on when you leave. And nap. We're gonna get to the bottom of this, okay?"

"Yeah, okay. So, no more secret spying on your fiancée, right?"

"My *fiancée?*"

"Well . . . girlfriend, I guess."

"Right. No more secret spying."

"Promise?"

"Promise."

TWENTY-SIX

The next day I mailed a letter to your grandmother. I'd included a few questions I was sure only she could answer, ending with: "If you're unable to see me in person, for whatever reason, I ask that you please send me a handwritten response, answering all my questions, within the next two weeks. Say by December 15th. This will help me know that you're okay, so I won't have to involve the police or any private investigators. I know you post on social media, and we sometimes speak on the phone, but I want actual proof that you still exist in the physical world. Also, I have some things I've been meaning to ask you. Some things that might help me understand what's been happening around here. Oh, and guess what, Shiro and I are getting married. I was going to tell you in person, but it seems that's not happening. And isn't it your birthday soon? Also, I think I might be pregnant. So, please get in touch."

I figured that last part would catch her attention. Since my period hadn't come for longer than usual, I'd finally made a trip to the drugstore and had the test waiting at home. Though Shiro and I often fantasized about having kids together, I hadn't yet been able to summon the courage to pee on the silly stick.

As I left our apartment to walk to the mailbox, I nearly bumped into a woman in the hall. It must have been our neighbor with the baby. I had never seen her before and almost stopped to introduce myself, but she seemed preoccupied, barely noticing me as she struggled with her bags and keys at her apartment door. Her long black hair obscured her face, and I noticed her arms looked quite thin. I thought of congratulating her on the recent birth of her baby and also of asking if the baby was okay, if its constant cries were anything serious. I wondered where it was. Had she left it inside the apartment with a sitter or its other parent? But before I could decide whether or not to speak, she'd already disappeared inside her apartment.

I walked down the steep hill to the mailbox. As I dropped the letter inside, a gust of wind whipped at my back, and I turned to see a large, empty cardboard box blowing down the center of the street like an unmanned chariot, its open sides flapping around wildly. At the end of the block it stopped, shifting in the breeze, looking confused as to what to do next. I had the urge to run to it, crawl inside and mail myself to Mom. Imagine her surprise, opening the box and seeing her own daughter pop out!

As I made my way back up the hill, panting, recoiling at the thought of going back inside the stuffy apartment and facing all the sewing I'd fallen so behind on, I decided to go for a little outing. I knew Shiro had taken BART to work that day, so, carefully—praying not to see my old imaginary friend—I went into the garage and, avoiding looking to see if those antlers were still lurking in the shadows, quickly got into Junior and started up the motor. Luckily, I saw no antlers and no naked child.

I thought of Pops, and how much he'd loved this old Toyota. Shiro once told me how Pops had fawned over his cars as though they were living beings. Apparently he'd spent many of his last days cleaning and maintaining this one. Shiro had joked that the old guy's spirit probably still hung out inside the car, and that's why it was still in such unusually good shape.

Imagining Pops himself sitting next to me in the passenger seat, chuckling in the voice I'd heard on that old PBS special, I drove around town aimlessly, then decided to go by my favorite bookshop near the Berkeley campus, figuring I'd browse and get a cup of tea. But when I drove by looking for parking, I saw that the bookshop was gone. For a moment I thought I'd come to the wrong place, as I often do. College students streamed by the boarded-up doors as though nothing of note had ever been there, even though the place had been a landmark on Telegraph Avenue as far back as I could remember.

"Nope, it's gone all right," I heard Pops's voice say.

I drove the streets some more, heading vaguely back in the direction of the apartment. The feeling that Pops was sitting beside me was becoming stronger.

"Akiko-chan. It's a nice name. Aki. Named after your uncle, right?" he asked.

"I go by Jane now," I corrected.

"Yeah, yeah—but Aki's your *real* name," he insisted. "That's the real you."

"Real's relative," I murmured.

"Maybe so. But still, you have to remember."

"Best to look to the future," I heard myself blurt.

I realized now that I had passed our neighborhood and was driving down Broadway toward downtown Oakland. I was not far from that warehouse with the roving clothes store—the last place I'd seen Mom. Knowing it was a foolish idea, that there was no logic or sense in going back there, I nevertheless felt compelled to return to the site. I had the ridiculous feeling that I might find some type of clue there, the way retracing your steps when you've lost something can sometimes help you find it, or at least bring you closer to the point at which it was lost.

I thought of that black scarf Mom had been holding up to herself in the mirror that day, the one she'd tried to tie onto me. When she'd crumpled it and tossed it onto that accessories table as we left, I'd glanced back to see it unfurling, covering everything in its midst like a dark, viscous liquid.

I wondered what she'd meant on the phone that morning when she'd said: "No one can afford to live *here* anymore." Was it really just the San Francisco Bay area she'd been referring to? Or something more than that?

I continued down Broadway and turned onto the small side street, which was just as deserted and depressing as the last time I'd been there. I parked Junior next to the drab, beige, run-down warehouse. It was even taller than I'd remembered, looming high into the sky.

I got out of the car and approached the barbed wire fence. The air was chilly, and I wished I'd brought a sweater. I saw no trace of the hole I'd wriggled through that day. Instead, the gate was ajar. Looking around for potential muggers or stray dogs, I slipped through and, feeling dwarfed by the towering, industrial wall, walked around the corner, where I expected to find that old claw-foot bathtub. But it was gone, too. I tried the doorknob on the green metal door, but this time it was locked. The roaming, chic boutique must have found a new home.

I looked up at the white security camera mounted above the door. At its base, a small red light was blinking. Gazing up at the lens, I had the impression, as random and ludicrous as it was, that whoever was watching me through this camera was also watching Mom at this same moment, wherever she was.

"Mom?" I said softly.

I recalled a day in high school—a day I hadn't thought of in any detail in some time. I was playing volleyball in the school gymnasium my freshman year, the first game of the season, and I'd invited Mom, who was a stay-at-home mom at the time. I kept peeking at the gymnasium door, wondering if she'd make it. Toward the middle of the game, she appeared in the doorway wearing dark sunglasses, her long black hair swept up into a mini beehive. She was dressed in her typical, overly fashionable way—who wears high heels, a fitted black dress, and a fake fur cloak to their kid's school volleyball game? She waved at me and, instead of removing her sunglasses and heading for the bleachers with all the other parents, leaned against the wall right there by the door, arms folded impatiently across her chest, watching the rest of the game from there, slipping out again as soon as it was over.

After the game, I decided to cut my afternoon classes—I don't remember why now; maybe I'd gotten a minor injury. I arrived home a good two hours early. Using my key, I opened the door and, before calling out, saw something puzzling: on the stairs, Mom's black dress lay immodestly, looking more like a hovering, dress-shaped hole than an item of human clothing. It was then that a weightless, clammy feeling spread throughout my body. I walked from room to room, calling for her, at first quickly, then slowly, looking around at all our household things as though I were a fish in a tank gazing out at the dry world. When Dad came home from work that evening, he took one look at my face and knew she was gone.

She didn't go far. Except for a few mysterious absences now and then lasting only a few months or so, she was always more or less around, living here and there in different apartments, never more than a few hours away, working various odd jobs and dating several different men until she remarried. We always kept in touch, though there were a few key occasions—a birthday here, a Christmas Day there—when she couldn't be reached.

I slipped back out through the gate, hurried to the car, and drove back toward the apartment in silence. I thought my impression of Pops sitting beside me had fully faded. But as I approached our hill, he cleared his throat.

"Yeah, I spent many an afternoon sitting at the edge of that river," he said, fiddling with something on the dashboard.

"Oh yeah?" I asked, not sure which river he was referring to.

"Yup. It was the only place I could think straight. I used to fish there, until they sent me away." He was silent a moment. "Used to make my own fishing poles. Sat there for hours. You wouldn't believe some of the things I pulled out of there."

As I was turning into our driveway, he coughed once into his fist.

"Lately I've been fishing again. Just recently, in fact, I pulled something up. Yeah, it was all twisted and bent out of shape. Practically unrecognizable. What was I gonna do?" he asked, turning to face me. "Let it stay stuck down there for all eternity? Fighting those demons all alone?"

"That was nice of you," was all I could think of to say.

"Course, I can't take him where he needs to go. The fella needs help I can't give."

I turned off the car motor and sat for a few moments in the dark of the garage.

Back in the apartment, after scrubbing the floors, cleaning the stove, paying bills, even fixing a zipper on a dress I'd botched earlier—basically every task I could find to divert myself, all the while cursing the neighbor's screeching baby—I finally peed on the pregnancy-test stick. Waiting for the lines to form, I plucked my eyebrows, my hand unsteady. Leaning on the bathroom sink, I took a deep breath and held the stick up to the light.

Two blue lines had formed into a cross, proclaiming: yes, I was pregnant.

I tossed the stick into the garbage and took another test, the result the same.

I carried my computer to the bed. First I did a search for "pregnancy tests false positive." When nothing promising appeared, plagued by the feeling that someone was watching me from over my shoulder, I did a search for "morning after pill." Though even as I typed, I realized, due to my stupidity and denial, I was much too far along for any such thing.

I found myself excited, giddy, even thrilled, at the prospect of motherhood—and a deeper, life-long bond with Shiro—yet also, I must admit, alarmed, terrified, and horrified, even. I felt myself split in two, the part of myself that instantly loved and utterly wanted you more than anything disconnecting from the part of me frightened beyond logic.

Looking down at my hands, I watched—as though over my own shoulder—my fingers move across the keyboard, typing the words "abortion options."

TWENTY-SEVEN

I suppose I should back up and explain the night of our anniversary.

I've avoided it until now because the details have a way of eluding me. The more they elude me, the more they haunt me—this is a perfect example of one of those random memories that, because we don't fully comprehend it, festers and grows unmanageable, taking up much more space in the mind than it warrants.

Or maybe it's the opposite; maybe the reason it haunts me is that its significance is larger than I'll ever comprehend.

I'm hoping that today, my mind being clearer as I speak to you, I can finally get the details straight and extract them from my consciousness.

The day started out nicely enough. We had a wonderful, carefree afternoon at the beach—picnic, sandcastles, cuddling, gazing out at the Pacific.

Afterward, we drove to a restaurant near Tomales Bay, where we got a great table overlooking the water and ordered grilled oysters, garlic fries, and champagne. We were both giddy, from the champagne and the fact that we'd made it as a couple exactly five years that evening.

At one point your dad leaned in close to me, almost knocking over the ketchup. I closed my eyes and he planted kisses on my lids, sealing them like old-fashioned wax stamps.

When I opened them, he was holding a small box out to me. I lifted the lid to find a gold band lying on light-green tissue paper.

"Well?" he asked.

I wanted to speak, but no sound came; my heart had sprung to my throat.

"What's wrong—cat got yer tongue?"

I laughed, my cheeks flushing. "It's . . . it's lovely," I stuttered, suddenly shy, reaching for the edge of the box.

He lifted the band and held it out to me. "It was my grandmother's. Want to try it on?"

"What for?" I wanted him to come directly out with his question.

"Well . . . we've been together for five years . . ." Now his cheeks flushed.

The waitress approached, but he waved her away.

"Cat got *yer* tongue?" I asked. We laughed; he never suffered from speechlessness.

He cleared his throat and looked down a moment. When he looked up, his dark eyes stared right into mine. He pushed our water glasses aside and took my hands.

"We have our differences—we see the world through different eyes. But that keeps things real. More exciting. We teach each other. I love how you obsess about finding the perfect produce." His face broke into his dimply grin. "I love your amazing cooking. The fact that you fucking *sew your own clothes* . . . What I'm trying to say is, the first time I saw you, I thought we should be together. It felt just like that, like fate. And you know me, I'm not a mystical, fate kinda guy. But we're meant to be together, simple as that. So—what do you say? Will you marry me?"

I opened my mouth to speak, but, again, no sound came.

"I love you," I mouthed instead.

"No rush," he quickly assured me. "I didn't even expect an answer tonight. Think about it, of course. I want you to be sure."

"Can I try it on?"

I stretched my hand toward him. He slipped the ring on easily—too easily.

"Who'd you get this sized for?" I teased.

We laughed, easing the tension of the moment. My throat relaxed.

"It was my grandmother's," he repeated.

"It's so lovely, just a bit too—"

"I can get it adjusted, no problem. Any jeweler can fix it, easy."

I admired it on my finger: an elegant, simple band.

As I went to hand it back to him, I accidentally knocked over his water. We laughed as he dabbed at the spill with his napkin. He took the ring and went to put it back in the box, but it had gotten wet. So, instead, he dropped the ring into his shirt pocket. I thought to ask if he was sure it would be okay, just loose in his pocket like that, but didn't.

I planned on giving him my answer later that evening, in the comfort of our home.

When we left the restaurant, it was chilly. We clutched each other as we rushed into Junior. He started up the engine and we shivered as it coughed a few times and steadied to a promising purr.

We sped along Sir Francis Drake Boulevard, blasting a new band your dad had recently discovered, the fall sky growing dark. I could smell the apples we'd bought from a farmer's stand earlier that day from the back seat. I rested my head on the window and placed a hand on Shiro's thigh, allowing my focus to soften as we came to the stretch of road I've always loved—a winding corridor of towering old redwoods alongside a creek, everything a dark, fertile green, like the entrance to some enchanted kingdom. The plaintive vocals and pounding bass of the music seemed to usher us through the trees—I remember feeling each tree was a sentinel marking the passing of something significant, guiding us from country to city, day to night, then to now . . .

Then the deer was standing before us, sideways, a big buck with great antlers, growing bigger by the millisecond, its head turned to face us, round eyes wide.

We hit it with a loud thud.

Next thing I recall, our car was on the side of the road and Shiro was frantically asking if I was okay. Then he was jumping out of the car. I quickly followed and caught up with him as he crouched over the deer. In the red glow of our taillights, the animal was looking up at us with the same shocked expression as when we'd sped toward it moments before.

"Let's go," I heard myself mutter.

Your dad ran back to the car and returned with a flashlight.

"Where are the antlers?" he was asking, shining the light on the dead body.

The chestnut fur on the deer's head was smooth, with no sign of any rupture, the long, sleek neck sloping up to wide, powerful shoulders.

In contrast to the pristine upper body, the lower half was splayed open, tangled innards spilling out onto the pavement, one side dotted by a light-pink, scummy foam. Steam rose from the grotesque mess and bones jutted from the corpse at odd angles, one sticking straight up toward the sky. My mouth tasted metallic, like fresh blood.

"Fuck!" Shiro yelled.

I ran to a nearby footbridge and puked. I could hear the rushing of the creek below.

"Let's go," I called, heading back to the car.

When I'd cleaned myself as best I could, I looked back to Shiro and couldn't believe my eyes—he had grabbed the deer's hooves and was laboriously dragging the fragmented body to the side of the road, the orange glow of his flashlight bobbing in his shirt pocket.

"Shiro, what the hell are you doing?" I shouted. "Stop! Don't touch it!"

But he continued dragging it across the road. When I joined him he was squatting next to the deer's face, as though listening. The deer's mouth was open, as though trying to speak.

"Shiro, come on. Who knows what germs that thing's carrying? It's freezing and I'm sick! Let's go home and get you cleaned up." I turned my back, covering my nose, afraid I might puke again.

"I don't get it . . . I don't get it," he murmured. "What the hell happened?"

"We hit a deer," I said through my hands. "You were great; you kept us safe. You didn't swerve . . . That could've been way worse." As I spoke, several cars whizzed by, their headlights appearing and disappearing into the night.

"But I hit the brakes. And this couldn't be the deer we hit. It has no antlers."

"Come on, let's—"

"No. No. No," he kept saying.

"No what?"

"Something's not right here."

"What do you mean?"

"Take a look!" he shouted. "Do you really think our car could do all *this*?"

I wanted to run back to the car, to speed all the way back to our apartment, to never think about this incident again, but something told me he wouldn't let it rest until I took in the details of the scene more fully. I turned around and peered down.

Indeed, it was an unusual sight for a road kill, to put it mildly. It looked as though some barbaric medical procedure had been attempted and failed, the belly cut down the middle, its contents—bluish-purple wormlike colonies and several dark, gelatinous blobs—extracted.

I had the sense that this deer wasn't just a deer, but something much bigger and all-encompassing, its frighteningly strong gravitational pull affecting both of us at our core.

"It does look like . . . something else happened," I managed to whisper.

This seemed to satisfy him somewhat.

He stood, I thought to go back to the car, but instead he went out to the middle of the road, shining his flashlight up and down. "Hello?" he called into the darkness. Another couple cars zoomed by—he jumped out of the way then ran back again.

Feeling like Scully from *The X-Files*, I decided to take command of the situation—clearly he wasn't thinking straight.

"Okay, Shiro, we're leaving now," I announced, running to him, ushering him out of the road, pressing him toward the car. "I'm so sorry this happened, tonight of all nights . . . It's horrible. So unfair. I feel so bad for that deer. But let's just go home and continue our night, okay?"

As we approached the car, we noticed something lying in the dirt, about knee-high—in the dark it could have been a small bush. Shiro lit the form with his flashlight to reveal a set of antlers. They looked like an enormous pair of claws pointing skyward, their shadows jerking in the trees beyond. We must have missed them before in the chaos.

Shiro moved his light back and forth between the antlers and the carcass, making me more queasy. The antlers, like the deer's head, were free of blood or any sign of impact. They lay there undisturbed, seeming carefully placed, somehow, as though whoever had left them might be planning on returning for them soon.

"They must have fallen off when we hit it," I said.

"No. There's no way we could've knocked them off so cleanly. These must be from a different deer. And that's not the deer we hit. But there must be some connection . . ."

"Maybe the deer we hit got away. Maybe this deer was hit before we even came along, who knows? And who knows when or how these antlers got here?"

I peeled the flashlight from his cold, rigid fingers, pushed him into the car, closed his door and took my place behind the wheel, my hands shaking.

"Cars can do crazy things," I said, more to myself than to him, starting the motor. "Think of all that momentum."

We drove the rest of the way home in silence, speeding through the night as though it were chasing us.

TWENTY-EIGHT

The morning after I discovered I was pregnant, Shiro and I sat across from one another at the kitchen table, sharing a package of mochi, while I filled out some unemployment paperwork and he worked on his computer on one of his projects.

"How's your job search going?" he asked.

It was a subject he rarely asked about. He was probably more concerned than usual, since earlier that morning, Jackie had called, wondering if I wanted to take a break from sewing for the shop. "Your dresses are really lovely," she'd tactfully said, "but, well, you've been missing several deadlines, Jane. And the last thing this arrangement was meant to do was stress you out."

I'd been mortified and, of course, angry at myself for being unable to hold even so casual a job, and had mumbled a stupid apology. Too tongue-tied to negotiate a better arrangement, I'd agreed to the break.

"Oh, you know, still grim," I answered, making a few more marks on my paperwork. "Thanks, by the way. For supporting us. I mean, I've been making a tiny bit, with my sewing, but . . . mostly it's been all you."

"Your rich dad's helping."

"He's not rich, really. But I'd really be up shit creek without you. So, thanks."

"We're a team, right?"

"Right." I felt my cheeks flush. The whole financial arrangement felt extremely awkward. "Sorry it's been so hard for me to concentrate in here lately . . ."

"Hey, it's not you—anyone'd go stir crazy, cooped up inside this oven all the time. We just need to get you out of this place more. We should sue our landlord about this fucking heater."

"Yeah, probably. Oh, and Shiro . . ." I swallowed hard, pushing my paperwork aside. "Guess what?"

I stood up and took a step away from the table, feeling silly and exposed. "I'm . . . I'm pregnant."

He looked as though he hadn't heard me.

"Yeah. I just found out. Yesterday. It's been a while, I think. Because, you know, my period hardly ever comes, I didn't even think my body could—"

"Wait—you're . . . *pregnant?*"

I nodded.

"We're . . . *pregnant?*"

He jumped to his feet, stared at me, then burst out laughing. We kissed, twirled together in a big circle, then he pressed his cheek against mine and we slow danced around the room in silence.

"Shiro . . ." I eventually whispered into his ear. I opened my mouth and, this time, my voice came. "Yes."

We stopped our dance.

"*Yes,*" I repeated, a little louder. It felt so satisfying to finally say that word. "I want to marry you. I want it so much." My body softened, and I let out a giddy laugh. Maybe it was you, Little One, who gave me the courage to finally give him my answer.

Emboldened, I continued. "And not just because of the baby. But because . . . I love you."

He pulled back to look at me.

"I—I—I love *you!*" he pronounced back loudly.

We broke into drunken laughter. Though we'd never for a moment doubted our love for each other, there was something wonderfully freeing about this first spoken proclamation. We danced around the room again, this time quickly, then stopped to grasp each other all over, kissing hungrily. Our cheeks were wet with his tears. This is perhaps the most blissful moment I can remember the three of us sharing.

But as we resumed our slow dance around the living room, I began to feel as though I were hovering above us, just under the ceiling, marveling down at us and the moment itself. And the more I marveled at the moment, of course the more distant I felt from it. I imagined myself floating through the roof of our apartment, a pale balloon disappearing into the sky.

"Let's keep it quiet for now though, okay?" I murmured. "About the baby. It's gotta still be my first trimester. I still have to see a doctor." I let go of his hands and stepped back. "I mean, from what I hear, the double lines on the tests don't lie, but still, I want to be sure. It explains a lot; I've been so tired and a bit nauseous. And kind of . . . claustrophobic."

"Aw, come on, let's tell the whole world!" he yelled, spinning around and throwing his hands up in the air. Then, noticing my worried expression, added, "That is, once we really know for sure, of course. Let's get you to a doctor. Like tomorrow. Can I come?" He dropped to his knees, lifted my blouse, and kissed my belly. I laughed.

"You have to work. Don't worry, I'll look into it."

"Don't put it off, okay?" he asked, kissing me more. "Hey, in there," he said. "How ya doin' in there, Little One?"

Little One—that's when we started calling you that.

"But . . . Shiro," I said, pulling him back to his feet. "I'm happy. But . . . I'm also scared. I mean, I have no idea how to be a mother. Absolutely none." My throat tightened. "I barely even know myself, really. I mean, look at my family . . . What if I inherited some horrible mothering gene or something? I just don't know about this."

"But . . ." He looked confused. "Isn't this what we've always fantasized about?"

"Fantasies are one thing; reality's another. Of course, I love the idea, but like I said, Shiro, I really don't know. What if I'm a horrible, *horrible mother*?" I almost shouted.

He looked scared.

"We didn't plan this." I said more calmly, letting out a nervous laugh. "I don't know, maybe we should just . . ."

He shook his head. "Just *what*?"

"I mean . . . maybe we should at least explore our—"

Then he stepped into me, pulled me back into his arms, and squeezed.

"Hey, listen, there," he whispered into my ear. "Shh . . . you're gonna be awesome. Completely. Fucking. Awesome. *We're* gonna be awesome—the three of us. Can you believe it? The *three of us*?" He lifted my chin and looked into my eyes. "Three for *now* . . . eventually four, five, six, seven . . ." he joked.

I couldn't help but smile. "I don't know . . . I guess . . ."

"Don't worry, fears are totally natural," he soothed, his breath warm on my cheek. "Come on, everyone's terrified of parenthood. You think I'm not fucking terrified? But just wait . . . remember that kick-ass garden we're gonna have?" he continued, guiding me back into a slow dance. "That big porch you're gonna walk down each morning, your hair hanging all over your shoulders, all sexy, a big basket in your arms, like a goddess—like Inari, the harvest goddess . . . you'll harvest whatever strikes your fancy for your big ole hungry family. Especially *daddy-bear*," he growled.

"Hey, you know," he said, stepping back, suddenly inspired. He turned to look out the window, placing his hands on his hips. The sky out the window was a perfect, swimming pool blue. "I'm gonna quit my stupid job. If we're getting married, starting a family—that's just bad mojo, that place. We don't want that." He turned back to me, his eyes all lit up. "Not for Little One—right, little guy?" he asked my belly.

"Hey now, it might be a girl."

"Of course. I mean *guy* in the nongender way. But nah, it's a boy . . . I just have a feeling."

We laughed again.

"But about my job—no way. Let's start afresh. We want to be proud of our family, right? For Little One."

He got down on his knees again and placed the side of his face on my belly.

"The other day I was in the IO Room, watching this family go through the scanners, listening to the guys jeering, making twisted, lewd jokes, and this girl, probably just eight or nine years old, her naked body there on the screen for us all to see, just stands there once the scan's done. Her mom tries to call her off, but it's like she's frozen; she just keeps standing there. One of the guys says something nasty about grabbing her—you know. The other guys laugh. I thought I'd puke. It was just a moment or two until she joined her family again, but I swear, in those moments, I had the feeling she was looking back at us, through the camera. Her big, wide eyes just staring at us, unblinking—but not just back at us, *into* us. Like she was seeing us for who we were—and judging us. Ashamed for us. Deeply ashamed. I can't explain it, Jane . . ." He stood to face me.

"Come on, I'm sure she wasn't judging *you*—"

"No really, I gotta get out of there. For my sanity. It's killing me. I'll quit, report the bastards, get a job we can both be proud of. Even in this economy, I've gotta find something—then eventually you can go back to school. Get your degree in architecture. We'll have that house, that garden . . . the little ones . . ." He smiled, melting me. "Whaddya say?"

"Well, of course, I like all these ideas," I said, running my fingers through his hair, loving him, even his stalwart idealism, insanely. "I understand your concerns, but, Shiro, *reporting* them? Right now, of all times? That's just not safe."

"It's true, Obama loves throwing whistleblowers in jail, but—"

"Idealism's one thing, but stupidity's another."

"Look, sometimes you have to make sacrifices for the greater good. By the way, I called the ACLU the other day, just to get some advice about how to proceed with my story—"

"Your story? What *story*?"

"You know, all the illegal shit I've been—"

"You didn't give them any of our personal information, did you?"

"Um, no, I don't think so. But don't worry, they're the good guys—"

"Do you *hear* yourself, Shiro? You think the government broke into our apartment. If that's true, who knows what else they'd do? We have to think of all *three* of us now—"

"Shhh," he said, touching a finger to my lips.

A shadow crouched over his brow, then flew away.

"Sorry, sorry, I shouldn't be bringing all this up now. There's time enough to discuss all this. The important thing—the goddamned important thing is: *we're getting married!*" he hollered at the top of his lungs. "*And having a fucking baby!*"

He burst into some freaky hybrid between break dancing and Irish clogging, then we laughed, hugged, and he led us in a clumsy, swing-type dance throughout the living room, though this time our dancing felt strained.

TWENTY-NINE

Today is hot again, like the first week they came here. The girl tells her teacher—a friendly hakujin woman who arrived only last week—that she isn't feeling well. She finds her sister in the other classroom and tells her she wants to return to their barrack; she has a bad feeling. Her sister agrees to accompany her.

As they approach their block, the noon sun hot on their heads and shoulders, they hear a baby's cries. But as they get closer, the cries stop. They find their barrack empty. Their big brother is working his shift at the mess hall, but their mother and baby brother should be here. Her sister says they should return to the school, but the girl refuses, insisting on looking for them. Impatient, her sister returns, leaving the girl to wander alone through their block until, at last, in the narrow alley behind their barrack, she discovers her mother. She knows her mother sometimes comes here, as it's one of the only outdoor places in the residential blocks out of view from the watchtowers.

She's struck by the silence of the alley.

"Mama?" she calls.

Her mother is crouched over something, involved in some laborious task, and seems not to hear her. Back stiff, shoulders braced, she seems to be struggling.

"Where's Aki?" the girl asks, walking closer. "Who has Aki?"

Suddenly her mother appears to relax. Her shoulders fall.

She stands and staggers backward, then sits on the ground, her back to the outside wall of their barrack, gaunt face tilting up to the sun, eyes closed. Her long black hair cascades down her back, emaciated arms splayed at her sides. It's unclear if she's awake or asleep; she wears a look of pure, blissful relief.

The girl feels herself tumbling into the silence of the alley.

She looks to where her mother had been busy. There on the ground lies their laundry basket. Within it, something is sealed under a pale-blue blanket. She can barely see the contours of the small body: gentle slopes of a nose, knees, toes. Just one hand pokes free, the tiny fingers reaching for the toy boat balanced at the edge of the basket.

The girl bends down and shakes her mother's shoulders.

"Mama! Wake up, Mama! Wake up!"

She continues to shake her and shout. Finally, getting no response, she throws her head back and wails: "PAAAAPAAAAAA!"

Her voice reaches for the sky, reverberating off the barrack walls, lingering in the hot air of the alley a few moments before fading.

Her mother's eyes pop open.

These are someone else's eyes, *the girl thinks.* Ever since we've come here, these eyes have belonged to someone else. Not my mother's. A stranger's. No, an animal's. Not human. Wild. Possessed.

The girl steps back and points to the basket. The possessed eyes shift to the sealed bundle. They remain there; the girl wonders what, if anything, they see.

The eyes widen, as though suddenly comprehending.

Her mother jumps to her feet, lunges at the basket, and pulls back the blanket. The toy boat tumbles to the ground. Apart from being a funny shade of purple, her brother looks peacefully asleep.

Muttering Japanese words the girl doesn't understand, her mother scoops the baby into her arms. She holds him close, whispers into his ear, strokes his thick black hair, sings him the beginning of a lullaby, squeezes him, shakes him—lightly at first, then so vigorously the girl fears something will break.

"Mama, stop!" the girl cries.

Her mother stops. The girl, her mother, the baby—and all the world— hang suspended.

Finally, her mother's head drops back and she lets out a short, horrible sound the girl has never heard before.

She drops the baby back into the basket as though it's now contaminated.

She puts a hand over her mouth, stumbles back into the barrack wall, and vomits through her fingers. The girl watches steam rise from the clumpy mess on the dirt ground.

The eyes shift to her. The two share a look of horror.

What has she done?

Now her mother is stooping down, again scooping up the baby, rewrapping it in the pale-blue blanket, tucking the bundle beneath the fabric of her own dress, disappearing around the corner of the alley. The girl stands a moment, startled, before chasing after her.

Toward the end of their block, her mother collides with a teenage boy— another internee, wearing a Yankees baseball cap and holding a handmade fishing pole.

"Whoa there, you okay, ma'am?" the boy asks as her mother pushes him aside and continues on, pitched forward crookedly, clutching the bulge beneath her dress.

"You okay there, kid?" the boy asks as the girl follows. "Need some help?"

But she keeps running after her mother, past the mess hall, through the residential blocks beyond the makeshift hospital, through the woodsy swampland at the back border of the camp, slipping and sliding on the muddy ground in her sandals as she struggles to keep up.

At the river's edge, her mother pulls the bundle from her dress, bends down among a cluster of tangled vines, and again involves herself in some complicated task the girl can't understand.

When she rises, the girl sees what she was doing: tying the bundle to a rock with a vine.

Her mother lifts the heavy package, presses it into her thin body, and carries it into the river, navigating her way through the brown, mossy water up to her knees, fallen leaves and branches slowly drifting by. The girl thinks how her mother looks like one of the swamp trees from behind, growing straight out of the water—long, rigid, lonely.

Without warning, her mother gives another horrible, barely human cry and heaves the package into the river, disturbing the water with a great splash, expanding circles marking the vanishing spot, reaching toward the girl on the shore.

Her mother's body begins to shake. First her arms, then her shoulders, then all of her. She bends forward, her face dipping into the water. Then suddenly she gasps, throws her head back and loud, wailing sobs echo throughout the river. The trees, water, air, sky—and all living creatures here in the swamp— seem to sob along with her mother.

The girl backs away, disappearing into the woods.

THIRTY

Later that week, we had Topaz and a new guy she was dating over for dinner. I spent the day cooking, trying as best I could to ignore the next-door baby's cries. I looked forward to when everyone arrived, as they always quieted when others were around.

Topaz was decked out in a black, silky pantsuit and high heels, her blond hair ironed straight, her makeup giving her a veneered sheen. Roger, her date, was short with a slight build. His head and face were shaved clean except for a precisely shaped, meticulously maintained orange goatee—a funny mismatch of tough and dainty.

"How's work?" I asked Topaz as she kicked off her heels and twirled an ankle.

"Oh, great," she answered. "I'm literally running from showing to showing—most of them short sales. It's a shame, all these nice folks losing their homes, but what can you do? Speaking of foreclosures, how's your mom? I see her on Facebook—seems like she's doing great, considering."

"I guess so. I wouldn't really know."

She raised her eyebrows disapprovingly. "I know social media sucks, Akiko, but you really should give in and get an account already." She had taken to calling me by my old name for some reason, and it was deeply annoying.

Shiro arrived after them, coming straight from work. He rushed in, gave Topaz a hug, shook Roger's hand, ran to the bedroom to change his clothes, and returned to the kitchen to offer everyone drinks. Topaz wanted wine, but Roger declined beer, wine, soda, even water.

"You know," he explained, standing in the middle of the kitchen, his hands dangling at his sides, "it turns out drinking during meals actually hinders digestion. If we chew enough, our saliva breaks down our food much more efficiently."

"Man, sounds like a lot of work," Shiro said, opening himself a beer.

Dinner conversation went well enough at first. We didn't tell them about the pregnancy, but Topaz proposed a toast to our engagement, and we brainstormed possible wedding scenarios: a potluck picnic, a Zen center ceremony, a mountaintop gathering that no one except our most rugged guests could attend.

"Isn't it great, not having any religion or anything you have to follow?" Topaz asked dreamily. "I mean, what freedom—you just get to choose what feels right in the moment."

"On the other hand, a little more structure might be nice," I suggested. "A little guidance or . . . a belief system or something."

She nodded half-heartedly.

The conversation moved to Roger's job at Pixar and the impressive facilities there, including a soccer field, swimming pool, movie theater, even cereal bar—it sounded like a forbidden city within the city of Emeryville, where one could happily live out one's life.

"Sounds like a frat house for royalty," Shiro commented, chugging his beer. "What's it like now that Disney owns you guys?"

"*Shh,*" Roger said, smiling at Topaz. "We don't talk about that."

"Ah—don't ask don't tell?" Shiro asked.

"You know, you two a have a lot in common," Topaz told Roger, giving him a quick peck on his goatee. "Shiro's a filmmaker, too. He makes these way-cool short videos—very edgy and political. He's modest, but he has a huge following. I'll show you sometime."

"Awesome. Where do you have them produced?" Roger asked as he patiently chewed a piece of broccoli.

Shiro shrugged. "Nowhere, really—just YouTube and stuff."

I wondered if he was jealous of Roger's job at a big film studio.

"It's warm in here," Topaz remarked, slipping out of her blazer and draping it over the back of her chair, revealing bare shoulders and a fitted pink blouse.

"Sorry, we should have warned you," Shiro said. "Our heater's broken and the building manager's MIA. Feel free to get naked."

Topaz giggled. "So, what's your next project about, Shiro?"

"The evils of technology and how we're all enslaved by Big Brother," I answered for him with a little laugh of my own, hoping to keep things on the light side and move on.

"*Corporate* technology," Shiro corrected. "Technology funded by neo-liberal capitalism."

"Fascinating. Tell us about it," Roger said, leaning forward. "What do you find wrong with *corporate* technology?"

I pictured him, dressed in the same black turtleneck he was wearing that night, sitting at a conference table at one of his artistic brainstorming sessions at Pixar.

"Well, let's see . . . what's wrong with a tiny sliver of the population designing tech to make as much money as possible for themselves, while the rest of us are at their mercy, hoping they'll design tech that benefits us rather than enslaving us? Hmm, can't see any potential problem there."

Roger smiled, as though amused by Shiro's hyperbole. "Sure, sure. But can't you also say tech can be part of the solu—"

"I mean, what's tech actually gotten us in the past, say, hundred years that's really so great?" Shiro asked, cutting him off. "The destruction way outweighs the benefit. Anyone who thinks otherwise at this point is an idiot."

Roger let out a startled laugh. "Well, I don't know about *y'all*," he said, "but I'm sure enjoying your electric fan here—wonderful invention of the twentieth century, I'd say."

Topaz and I laughed, nodding in agreement.

"The reason we need the fan is 'cause the fucking heater's broken," Shiro pointed out grumpily.

"Well, I see Shiro's point," Topaz offered diplomatically. "Tech *does* suck. I mean, look what just happened in Fukushima. Nuclear power's a nightmare."

"True. I won't argue with anyone about nuclear power," Roger agreed. "We're all aligned on *that*."

"Now, now, not all nuclear power's bad," I chimed in, waving a finger at everyone. "It's an easy target, but we're gonna be grateful for it someday when we run out of gas."

There was an awkward pause as everyone looked unsure what to say.

This was a loaded subject for me and Shiro, what with Dad's lifelong work at the lab, and Shiro's family coming from Hiroshima.

"Anyone want any more of anything?" I asked, standing. "I got the veggies from the farmers market today. I'm loving the kabocha: Japanese pumpkin. I'd never used it for this recipe, but I think it works okay in place of the pork?" I'd gotten creative since Topaz had told me Roger was off animal products.

"Delicious," they all sang in unison.

"Akiko's a phenomenal cook," Topaz told Roger. I sat back down, irritated at hearing my old name.

"But come on," Roger continued to Shiro, holding his hands out in a good sportsmanly gesture, "can't tech be part of the solution? Doesn't it have to be?"

"Sounds great, but it's a slippery slope," Shiro answered. "Remember, no matter how fun computers are for us average joes, they were started for the military. Take drone warfare; how many kids have to die before we see that our favorite pastime goes hand and hand with murder?"

"Wait—isn't that a Bob Dylan song?" Roger joked. Topaz laughed nervously.

"Oh, that's a great one! Did you just think of that now?" Shiro shot back. I wondered if he was drunk. Roger and Topaz looked momentarily stunned.

"But even physical warfare's gonna be obsolete soon," he went on. "We all clamor to put our lives online, not realizing how simple it'll be to have them erased. Nuclear power's bad, sure, but Silicon Valley is just as destructive, and more insidious . . ." He was now lifting bits of tempeh high over his plate with his chopsticks and watching them plop down again like little bombs, an act that struck me as incredibly rude.

"So, whose laptop's that?" Roger asked, motioning to the silver machine sitting open on the coffee table. The glowing apple with its missing bite looked ominously biblical.

"Mine," Shiro said. "Hey, man, I'm just as addicted as the next user; never said otherwise."

"Ah, I see." I could almost hear the trace of a bell in the air—from his satisfied grin, Roger seemed to think he'd scored a point.

"Hell, where I work, we use technology to spy on people daily," Shiro added. "See their naked bodies, pull aside anyone who looks like the enemy—we love turbans, man, those Sikhs are a great target, even though they had nothing to do with 9/11."

Roger raised his eyebrows. "You're not one of those 9/11 *conspiracy theorists*, are you?"

"Um, it's not really a conspiracy theory that Sikhs weren't involved with 9/11," Shiro said in a mock whisper, then went back to rudely playing with his food, a bead of sweat trickling down his cheek.

I could see from the twitching of his jaw that your dad was getting really pissed. Compared to Roger, Shiro looked dangerously macho that evening. It was clear that between the two, Shiro would easily win in a fistfight. But Roger's smugness came from the fact that he knew he would never *be* in a fistfight. He was digital, I decided; your dad was analog.

"Huh. No—you know, this is actually interesting," Roger said, adjusting himself in his seat and crisscrossing his chopsticks on his plate, something my aunt Michi would have said was bad luck. I admired how quickly he recovered from each of Shiro's little attacks, as though he found a healthy intellectual spar energizing. "I took a class on postmodern philosophy in college about this stuff . . . There was this one philosopher who talked about how the invention of any technology is also the invention of that technology going wrong. The invention of the train is the invention of the train *wreck*."

"Paul Virilio," Shiro said, surprising us all.

"Oh, you've heard of him?" Roger asked. He seemed unsure if he was being mocked.

"He looks at the violence of modern-day speed, and of representing ourselves in miniature, digital form. Turns out some of us noncollege folks actually read these esoteric books just for fun—strange, huh?"

Your dad prided himself on his working-class background, even though he'd taken a few community college classes out in Modesto and was better read than most people I knew.

"Good for you, man, good for you," Roger said with a condescending chuckle. "But in the end, it seems to me, like with any tool, it's *how* we use it."

I found myself praying Shiro could be magnanimous and relent to a compromise. But he stared straight ahead as though at a dark road.

"When you're driving really fast . . ." he said in a patronizing tone, "there's no margin for error. Even the littlest slip, the most imperceptible bump in the road, can have exponential impact."

I stood and began clearing the table. "So, how many teas? Coffees?"

"Coffee—thanks, Akiko," Roger said.

"Call me Jane," I corrected stiffly. "I go by Jane."

Just then the heater began to blow down on us more forcefully.

"Aw, really?" Topaz pouted. "But Akiko's so purty—I never got why you didn't like it."

"This fucking heater's driving me nuts," Shiro said, peeling off his T-shirt and tossing it across the room. "Like I said, feel free to get naked."

Rogers eyes widened. "It *is* quite warm in here," he said, tugging at the neck of his sweater. His smooth scalp glistened with sweat.

"Shiro, you're right; the modern world totally sucks," Topaz said, clearly admiring his muscular torso. "I can't even listen to the news anymore—way too depressing. I wish more people had your idealism. And passion. We should probably all stop driving, using computers, everything, like on *Little House on the Prairie*—that would be so nice. But even back in Laura Ingalls's day they were killing Indians, so someone's always killing someone, right?

"Maybe what we need is a more . . . *spiritual* approach," she suggested to us all in a serene tone. "I mean, maybe it's not about right and wrong, good and bad—it's all about the *middle path*. If we dwell on the dark side, we get sucked into it. We need the dark, the light, the yin, the yang—"

"Was that the Buddha or Yoda?" Shiro asked in a deadpan.

"Hardy-har," she retorted, seeming only slightly offended. "Well, I for one recommend drugs to deal with the modern world. My new medication's a miracle!" She gave a nutty guffaw, an exaggerated happy face and the thumbs-up sign.

I thought of Mom's new medication and wondered if she was taking the same one.

Then she touched her finger to the air as though opening a new app. "Oh, hey, I almost forgot, we brought ice cream!"

"I thought you were vegan?" Shiro asked Roger.

"Not when it comes to desserts. I guess this is where my murderous streak comes in," he joked.

"How deviant," Shiro muttered. I could tell he was fuming; he despised tempeh.

Instead of having ice cream, Shiro prepared himself an enormous bowl of his cereal and ate it standing, leaning over the kitchen counter. Every now and then Roger glanced over at him, no doubt fascinated by the beastly way he shoveled down his food with hardly any sign of chewing.

"Yo, dude, you should come work at Pixar," he called to him at one point. "You'd love the cereal bar. I can keep an ear out for openings for security guards."

"Wow, man, thanks," Shiro answered, grinning, his mouth leaking milk. "I'm not really technically a security guard—but gee, thanks for looking out for us blue-collar-types, bro."

"Oh, I forgot—you're an *artist*," Roger fired back. His patience with Shiro's hostility had ended.

We finished out the evening awkwardly but thankfully uneventfully.

As he got into bed later that night, Shiro let out a big groan. "Man, that little Pixar dude was a piece of work! Talk about the definition of a douchebag."

"Well, we can't all be Mr. Self-Taught Working-Class Guy like you," I snapped, flipping through a sewing magazine.

"Oh, come on, you have to admit he was annoying. I'm getting tired of white people. The only way to open their minds is to crawl in and stretch them from the inside—and that's the last place I want to be."

"Wow, how racist," I said lightly. "Are you sure you're not jealous of the fact that he gets paid to do his art?"

He sat up—this clearly hit a sore spot.

"His *art*? What kind of art can possibly escape from that Disney factory alive?"

"Top's been through a lot lately, the least we can do is be welcoming to her new guy."

"So, what, I should never state my true beliefs?" he asked. "Just make nicey-nice all the time, so no one gets offended?"

"There are times and places for everything."

"Not for you, Jane. It's always the same time and place for you. And that's called Repressed City."

A tense moment later, he peered over my magazine with a sheepish smirk. "How'd you get so freakin' *Japanese* anyway? You're the diluted one, after all. You should act more white."

Your dad took pride in being more Japanese than me and took any chance he could to rib me about my whiteness.

"You know," he continued, "people in Japan aren't as repressed as us Japanese Americans, from what I hear. Our Japanese mannerisms are way old-fashioned, from the early 1900s, when our families moved here. Plus there was Camp—mass cultural oppression."

"Well, from what *I* hear there's still plenty of repression in Japan. Anyway, I'm more white than Japanese."

"How's that? You're fifty-fifty last I checked." He peeked down at my crotch. "Wait, which half is which?"

I hit him on the head with my magazine. He laughed.

"Yeah, but I just *feel* more white," I said, to rankle him.

He whacked me back with his pillow and leaned into me, shoulder to shoulder. We pushed against each other like a pair of lame Sumo wrestlers, until finally I let him fall on top of me.

"Is this okay for Little One?" he asked.

"Of course. It's probably still no bigger than a flea."

He tried lifting up my tank top.

"Hey, can I ask you something?" I asked, stopping his hand.

"Huh?" He looked at the clock. "You know I have to be at work in just a few hours?"

"So, what, you have time for sex but not talk?"

"Basically." But then he could see I was serious and sat up to face me. "What's up?"

"Well . . . do you believe in ghosts?" I heard myself asking.

"*Ghosts?* Why?"

"Just answer the question."

"Nah—at least not in the normal way people think of them."

"What do you mean?"

He looked around our bedroom. "I mean . . . the past is always with us, affecting us in all sorts of ways . . . but ghosts—nah, that's just a cop-out."

"But don't you think there might be something more than we can see with our eyes? People all over the world believe in spirits . . . what if our apartment's haunted? Maybe that's why our heater's broken?"

"Wow, quite the active imagination there! And you make fun of *my* conspiracy theories? Nah, I don't buy it. Our problems are right here and now, in the real world. The *real world, baby,*" he teased, placing my hand on his hard-on.

I pulled my hand away. "I just wish sometimes we could relax more . . . worry less. Do fun stuff. Like we used to. Cuddle on the couch. Go to the movies. Even dumb ones. You've seemed so stressed about everything lately."

"Sounds good. Let's go to the movies." He kissed my neck.

"I just feel weird lately. Like there's this hole in me that keeps growing."

I longed to explain to him about the sad neighbor woman and her baby, about my sleepwalking—my searching and the towers. Any number of words flew around at the back of my throat, but I kept swallowing them.

"You pick a movie and we'll go," he was saying, reaching under my tank top and squeezing my breasts, which had been growing fuller. "We can invite Topaz and Roger and I'll be nice, I promise . . ."

"Sometimes I just feel . . . cursed or something. I can't explain it, but it's like I'm always looking for something. To protect us. And I'm looking for it everywhere, but I can't ever find it. Maybe a higher power, or—"

"Yeah, well, religion's a hoax. But there's plenty of good out there—folks sticking out their necks to make the world a better place for the rest of us, to protect us. Civil liberties groups and all. We can feel good knowing that. I know *I* feel good knowing that . . ."

He turned off my bedside lamp and gave me a tender kiss. I kissed him back, pulled my tank top over my head, pushed him down, and crawled on top of him.

"Top was right about one thing," he whispered as he slipped inside me, "you should go by Akiko. *Akiko . . . Aki . . .*"

My given name had always turned him on, and, funnily enough, during sex was the only time I didn't mind hearing it.

I hope you don't mind hearing this, Little One?

That night, though, I was distracted, and as things progressed, my mind began to wander . . .

I wondered why it had been so important to me, in middle school, to erase my old identity and take on a new one. Mom had been so upset when I did—was it really, as Dad had recently said, related to the spirit of her baby brother? Naming me after him to sooth his outrage at his miserable fate?

Despite my anxious musings, pangs of pleasure pulsed from my center throughout my body as Shiro rolled me onto my back and began nibbling his way from my throat downward. But my mind wandered again, this time, of all places, to an anecdote Aunt Michi had once shared with me.

Apparently when Mom announced to her family that she was leaving Los Angeles to move up north to the Bay Area in the late 1960s, Bachan had been horrified. Your grandparents had met a few months before, at a self-realization workshop at the Esalen Institute, an early New Age retreat center on the rocky cliffs of the Pacific.

"LA's just too Hollywood for me, Mama—too shallow. I need to find myself," Mom had proclaimed.

"Find yourself?" Bachan had asked, wrinkling her nose. "You're right here!"

"My new self, Mama—my *real self*," Mom had explained impatiently.

Bachan had looked to Aunt Michi for help.

"You have to understand," Aunt Michi had attempted, "Sumi-chan's from the new generation, Mama. They have all kinds of new ideas about things. You know, civil rights, identity, stuff like that." She elaborated in Japanese, ending with: "*finding themselves*, ne? Everything's changing, especially up in San Francisco."

"No *self*," Bachan had asserted. "No such thing. Just self*ish*. So American. Lonely-desu. People here so lonely, ne? In Japan, we just have family. Think what's best for *family*."

"But look at you, Mama. You came all the way here—you left your family behind in Japan," Mom had pointed out. "Changed your whole identity, like a butterfly!"

"I came here *for* family, *for family*!" Bachan had responded indignantly. "Family send me here, and I go! No complain, I just go! I help family, send money back to family!" Then she'd turned to Aunt Michi and unleashed an angry tirade in Japanese.

"Was that okay?" Shiro whispered, panting, kissing my forehead, and rolling off of me.

"Yeah, amazing," I said, staring into the dark of our room.

THIRTY-ONE

The next day, I found myself more exhausted than usual. I couldn't focus on anything. After forcing myself to eat a few bites of breakfast, I wandered the apartment aimlessly, eventually ending up in our bedroom, where I noticed a large, unusual insect traveling across the ceiling.

Metallic, dark bluish green, with long antennae, it looked like a cross between a beetle and a grasshopper, about one and a half inches long. It moved slowly, stopping every few inches at regular intervals. I stood there studying it, hoping it had no wings, or that it wouldn't suddenly plop down onto me. As silly as this sounds, I had the impression that it was also watching me—maybe assessing my physical abilities in order to calculate any sudden movements I might make. I thought about getting some tissue and smashing it, but kept hearing the crunching sound its shell would make.

I opened the fire escape window, hoping it would leave on its own, and went to take a shower. When I returned to the bedroom, it was no longer on the ceiling. Maybe it had found its way out the window. Momentarily relieved, I lay on the bed, my damp, naked body wrapped in a towel. I was drifting toward sleep when I heard the vent in the living room start up. I'd tried tracking its on and off patterns over the past months to see if there was any schedule to its madness but hadn't been able to pinpoint one.

Caught in this limbo-land between waking and sleeping, my mind flitted here and there, eventually finding its way back to that insect. Suppose it hadn't gone out the window? Chances were that it was still somewhere in the room, maybe even close to me now—maybe it had dropped right onto the bed.

Where had it come from? It was unlike any bug I had seen before. I thought of Shiro and his bird from the other day. Had he really suspected his work was spying on him, using drones designed to look and act just like birds? How hilarious! If only it weren't so disturbing. And hypocriti-cal—with his very own surveillance plant in our apartment!

I kicked myself for not putting an end to the stupid insect while I'd had the chance. If I didn't want to smash it, why hadn't I just captured it in a jar?

Perhaps our apartment *was* being surveilled by the government. Just because I was the one who'd been ransacking our place in my sleep didn't mean some other entity wasn't present. Was I naive to be so dismissive of Shiro's suspicions? I *had* been feeling watched each day. Maybe I'd just been sensing Shiro's camera. But my feeling had begun before he'd set it up—at least, I thought so. Or maybe he had successfully planted the seeds of paranoia within me and now they were taking root.

I gazed up at the tall palm growing by our bed. The leaves were wilted and brown at the edges; one looked about to fall right onto my head. This struck me as odd. Shiro always took such good care of our plants. I thought of his words from the other day: "Something's not right in this apartment."

The baby in the apartment next door was fussing, as usual. But on lis-tening more closely, I noticed the cries sounded a bit different now—older and more indignant, more like a toddler having a temper tantrum about something specific, not just a newborn protesting life in general.

It was then that I decided to try something new. I peeled myself from the bed, cleared my throat, took a big breath, and let out a loud squeal right back at the wall.

Sure enough, the cries stopped.

I imagined the little fellow was startled and was listening for what I might to do next. I admit I was startled myself. In fact, what most sur-prised me was how much my own voice and the baby's sounded alike.

In a more natural tone, I asked what was so upsetting.

The silence continued. But I could have sworn the little being on the other side was thinking about my question.

"What's the matter?" I asked again through the wall, soothingly, plac-ing a hand on my own belly. "You can tell me, little one. I'm listening . . ."

After a minute, I heard it cooing back, like it was actually comforted. I had the impression no one had ever spoken to it like this before. I smiled to myself, proud to have made a difference.

I thought of my childhood imaginary friend, the little boy with thick black hair I'd seen in the garage recently, and of how he used to follow me around the house and help me build things, seeming content to be in my presence.

"That's it," I continued, my confidence growing. After all, now that I was going to be a mother, I needed to cultivate my empathic, nurturing side. "I know you must be feeling so scared and lonely—and abandoned. Has your family abandoned you? But don't worry, they'll be back soon. You're okay now . . . everything will be fine . . . Shh . . . you're not alone. I know how lonely and hopeless it can seem, but don't worry, things will be fine, I promise . . ."

I climbed onto my dresser and pressed my ear right up to the wall to see if I'd receive an answer.

"Ma," it seemed to be saying. "Ma. *Ma?*" Taken aback, I froze.

"*Maaa!*" it began shrieking, seeming angered by my silence. Soon it was back to wailing again, more harshly and desperately than ever.

"*Shut the goddamned hell up!*" I shouted, my voice cracking, slamming my hand against the wall.

But the cries kept coming.

Stunned, I scrambled down from the dresser and, overcome by a sudden, frightening rage, the likes of which I'd never felt before, I climbed back into bed and pulled the covers over my head, stifling the urge to hurl something through the wall and break the bones of whoever was shrieking on the other side.

When my eyes next opened, it was pitch black and a sulfuric stench filled the air.

I felt upside down and inside out, my head where my feet should be, elbows pushing out my ears, knees caught up in my ribs, hair and skin inverted, my middle a floating abyss. There was a humming sound, as though a storm were brewing nearby.

It seemed I'd fallen into some wet, prehistoric hole near the center of the earth.

Struggling to orient myself, wiggling what seemed to be my fingers and toes, opening and closing what I was pretty sure were my eyes, wiping sweat collected at what felt like my hips, I eventually emerged from this amoeba-like state, beginning to sense which way was up and down, what was me and not me.

The ground felt warm and soft beneath my skin, like moss.

Gradually taking in the scant light, I could vaguely make out long, blue shadows moving along a horizon. The shadows became more distinct as I watched—for how long, I have no idea—until I perceived several humanoid figures, looming and strangely misshapen, wielding some sort of long, rounded objects. A white, lacy mist curled up around their gnarled knees and ankles.

They seemed to be working together intently, pounding at the ground repeatedly. Each time they bent with a sharp, violent blow, I felt a shooting pain deep within, as though these monstrous beings were hammering away at something inside me. Honestly, I had the sense that they were set on destroying you.

I also sensed, as they consumed themselves with their task, that they were acutely aware of my eyes on them, and were effortlessly, and scornfully, watching me back, through the dark and mist.

Opening and closing my eyes, telling myself that this vision was a ridiculous fantasy, nothing more than my active imagination, along the same lines as the recent vision of my childhood imaginary friend, these entities eventually faded. In their place, I began to discern the outline of my own naked body—arms, elbows, breasts, knees, curiously emanating subtle hues of blue. One arm was suspended above my head; slowly I lowered it to see that my hand was clenched into a fist.

I tried standing but banged my head and fell back down again. I heard a faint chuckle. Someone *was* watching me, it seemed, taking a wicked pleasure in my misery. The chuckle came again, louder, then a third time. That's when I realized, to my horror, that the person laughing was me.

I gasped, covering my mouth with my hand.

Just then something brushed against my ankle. In the dim light I saw several cardboard boxes, their lids removed, newspaper wrapping scattered about on the floor. I was in our attic. It seemed that, in my sleep, I had set up the ladder and climbed up here, once again looking for something.

The sound of wind was the broken heating unit, howling away just a few feet from me.

My eyes straining, I saw my own handwriting on the nearest box: *Jane*. Beside this, another name had been crossed out. I remembered doing that when I changed my name in middle school, taking a sharpie and crossing out my old name on a few boxes Aunt Michi had given to me, replacing it with my brand-new one.

Blood singing in my ears, I noticed something standing a few inches to the left of the box. At first I thought it was a small person, and I feared it was my imaginary friend. But on looking closer, I saw it was inanimate: a tower, made up of about five or six objects stacked one atop the other. The structure seemed to grow smaller and larger, closer and farther as I blinked sweat from my eyes; this foul place seemed to be the source of all illusion.

Finally, steadying my hand, which was still faintly glowing blue, I reached for the topmost object. Cool and light, rounded, smooth as skin. I looked closer: it was a wooden carving in the shape of a boat.

The little boat seemed to vibrate with a certain vitality as it perkily balanced in the palm of my hand—as though it were happy to see me, trying to convey something about all the waters it had known.

A warm hand touched my shoulder.

My eyes closed and my body softened. I tried not to move or breathe, for fear the hand might just as quickly disappear.

I knew the hand belonged to your grandmother.

How did I know, you might ask? It's a good question, and I know you may think I'm crazy, and I can barely believe it myself, but trust me, at the time it was clear: Mom was squatting on the floor there in the attic beside me, also looking at that toy boat in my hand. I could feel her breath, smell her skin, even hear her voice softly humming a childish tune.

I held still, cherishing this peculiar intimacy. Ironically, this was the closest I had ever felt to her.

The girl runs through the morning mist, singing a song she recently learned at school, her sandals click-clacking in the mud as she slips in and out of shade and sunlight.

I kept my eyes closed. I felt certain I wasn't in the attic anymore.

The smells from the mess hall have faded, and now smells of the woods—moss, earth, rotting leaves—fill her nostrils. She's almost to the river. The last time she saw him, he was there on the misty shore waiting for her. If she hurries, they can play with their boat before she has to be back for breakfast, before anyone's noticed she was gone.

The hand released my shoulder and I felt something brush past me—I reached out and grabbed a hand. It was small, warm, and moist.

She turned to face me: a young girl of about six years old in a tattered dress, bangs cut bluntly across her forehead.

"Is he here?" she asked, breathless. "Have you seen him?"

"Who?" I could barely whisper.

Her dark, shiny eyes flashed with impatience. "Baby Aki, of course. Come on! He's waiting at the river!"

I heard things rustling; a bird cawed from above.

She turned and tried tugging me with her, the spongy ground shifting beneath my feet.

I tugged back, thinking of those monstrous blue shadows I'd just seen on the horizon. I wanted to warn her, "No, don't go there—I don't know what they are, but they're awful!" but only a small squeak escaped my lips.

She looked at the boat in my hand, eyeing it suspiciously.

"Where'd you get that?" she asked.

Not waiting for my answer, she grabbed it and ran away, her small body bound with conviction as she headed through the woods for her river.

I lunged after her, tumbling into darkness.

"*Mom!*" I shouted, opening my eyes.

But I was alone in the dark of the attic again. She was gone.

Had I been dreaming? Hallucinating? Both?

The boat I'd been holding and the other objects from the tower had toppled to the floor.

Just then I heard a loud bang. I froze, listening. There were shuffling noises. Footsteps. Someone or something was moving around in our apartment below.

PART TWO:

THE RIVERBED

THIRTY-TWO

Two white butterflies flit past my face. A mosquito hovers above my left arm. I try to swat it but miss. The sun is crawling higher and my shadow on the road is shrinking.

The day Shiro brought me here to this orchard, almost six years ago—just a few weeks after we met—we got out of the car and he immediately started down the ravine.

"Come on, let's cross over," he said, turning to offer his hand.

"Won't the people who live here get mad at us for trespassing?"

When he pointed out that there were no cars in sight, so it was a safe bet that no one was home, I made up some other excuse.

"Anyway, why don't you just use the bridge?" I asked, pointing to a footbridge leading from the road to the house.

"More fun this way. My pops and his brothers used to play down here by the creek when they were kids. Let's check it out—don't worry, we'll cross together!"

The truth was, I had desperately wanted to take his hand—I remember feeling swollen with the desire to the point that my body ached. But at the same time, I felt stuck, just like I do today, as though my feet were tethered to the road.

He pressed a bit more, then shrugged and bounded down the ravine, leaping across the water on rocks, climbing up the other side and into the orchard. I watched as he walked among the walnut trees, disappearing and reappearing, thinking how naturally he blended in with them.

When he returned, he offered me a handful of soil, holding it up for me to smell.

"Mm—can't ya just taste the yummy garden this land could grow?" he asked.

I think that was the moment I fell in love with him.

We held hands and walked along the road, delighting in the fresh air. I remember him bragging that, unlike most Japanese farmers who'd leased or sharecropped their farms before the war, his family had actually owned this land, purchasing it in the children's names, the way Bachan and Jichan had with the hotel. Though the mood was light, I could sense the regret in his voice as he looked out at the land that might have been his.

I light another cigarette now—I've never burned through so many cigarettes before, or so many memories. Sweat trickling down the back of my neck, still leaning against Dad's car, I think again of my first memory. I have to admit, over the years it's taken on a certain sinister quality.

The details just don't add up. In my version of the story, Mom is most definitely alone outside the car—not surrounded by the concerned strangers of her version.

Not that I mean to suspect her of anything. But on the other hand, why would she have taken the time to smoke a cigarette while I could have been suffocating in the hot car?

Of course, her fear of uniforms kept her from acting as any rational mother would have. But if she'd been concerned for my safety, wouldn't she at least have been looking back, making funny faces to reassure me that everything was all right? And just to make sure I was still breathing? In such heat, a small body is vulnerable.

Or had motherhood been too much for her? Had she, overwhelmed by the weight of another helpless human being's soul, momentarily considered the unthinkable?

Aunt Michi's horrible words echo in my mind: "Mama wasn't thinking straight. Infanticide is much too strong a word . . ."

Future! that bird chirps again from somewhere in the orchard.

Looking across the ravine at the old strawberry field, I feel a certain tug—a nudging back and discarding of the superficial layers of things, and an insistent beckoning to what lies beneath. I manage to overcome the stuck feeling enough to pull the heels of my pumps free from the dirt road and step toward the creek. I peer down: it's dry.

I take a few steps down the steep slope. My ankles wobble. I kick off my pumps, toss them up to the road, gather up the ends of my skirt, and make my way farther down toward the creek bed, enjoying the soft, clumpy ground beneath my bare feet.

About halfway down, holding onto a large, twisted root for balance, I hear a loud bang and look up. The front door of the old house, which is just barely in view from my vantage point, has swung shut and a little blond boy appears on the porch, followed by a large man in overalls, maybe his father. The two descend onto the orchard, one after the other—the little boy and the fat man—their steps bearing a strangely ominous weight. They seem to be moving in slow motion, as though time has come under some spell.

I watch them walk across the footbridge, climb into a raised, metallic-blue pickup truck, and slam the doors. The engine roars on and the truck drives down the dirt road, a massive dust cloud billowing up in the air behind them.

Just then a bird swoops into view and alights on a branch of the nearest tree in the orchard. It's the only bird in sight—unusual looking, brown with orange markings on its head and chest. I've never seen one quite like it. Is it the one that's been singing that hopeful song?

It looks around jerkily a few times—mechanically, even—then looks down into the ravine and seems to spot me. Is this a real bird? Or one of those drones Shiro used to worry about? Perhaps a high-tech security service to guard the orchard? I know it's a foolish thought, but I still find myself panicking.

"Come on down here; it'll do you good," a kind, soft voice calls to me from below.

At first I think it's Pops, but no. The voice is similar, yet different.

Obeying, I slip and slide my way down the rest of the ravine, the new outfit I bought for the interview—I haven't been sewing these days—getting all smudged with dirt. The ravine is deeper than it had appeared from above. I crane my neck to see that bird in the orchard, but it's now out of view.

Still, I have the sense I'm not alone down here.

The creek isn't completely dry after all. A single ribbon of water meanders between the rocks, as though determined to mark its path.

Suddenly claustrophobic, I hurry across the rocks and begin to climb up the other side of the ravine.

But after only a few steps, I slip. I try again, this time finding a good foothold. How hard can this be? Shiro had made it seem so effortless that day. Just as I think I'm making headway, I grab a rock jutting from the dirt wall, but it comes free in my hand, and once again I slide backward. My arms, feet, blouse, and skirt now covered in dirt, I make a few more attempts, each more sloppy than the last.

Maybe it's better to return to the road, after all. Why bother climbing up to the old farm?

Why did I come here today?

And why am I talking to you?

Either you already know everything I'm saying, or you don't, in which case perhaps knowing all this only burdens you, makes your journey to wherever you're going more difficult, or even halts it altogether? Perhaps sometimes ignorance is better. Is this little confession of mine just an excuse, my selfish way of relieving myself of guilt, and of keeping you here with me?

If so, I'm sorry—I'm so, so sorry!

I should say a final goodbye, let you, and myself, move on.

Fly away, fly away, fly away!

This insistent thought beats through my head as I try climbing back up to Dad's car and the road, but again, I keep slipping backward. I grab a root and attempt to hoist myself up, but no luck. I try again, and again. My muscles are limp, my heart pounds wildly. I try to call out for help, but my voice just emerges as a pathetic "eh!" I tumble backward, my body slamming painfully into the rocky ground.

Is this it? Am I stuck here forever? Am I such a failure, having fucked up my life so thoroughly in every possible way, having lost everything of significance—including you—that it's hopeless for me to break free from the repressed, lonely cycle of my life?

I close my eyes against the noon sun and rest my cheek on the creek bed, resigning myself to an eternal sleep in the underworld.

THIRTY-THREE

"Jane?" a voice was calling.

The shuffling below continued.

"Jane—are you there?"

"*Dad?*"

"Where are you?"

"Up here."

"Up where?"

"In the attic."

"The *attic*? What on earth are you doing up there, dear?"

"I guess I was looking for something. What are you doing here?"

"Oh, well . . . sorry to pop by like this, but I got a very concerned text from your mother—she suggested I come check on you. You once gave me a key for emergencies, if you remember, so I hope you don't mind I used it to let myself in. I called and rang the doorbell a few times, but no one answered."

"Hold on . . . can you wait in the living room?" I made my way on all fours toward the patch of light on the floor.

"Of course, but first let me hold the ladder stable for you."

"No thanks, I'll be fine."

"But it looks like it's about to fall, the way it's set here. You didn't set this up very well, dear. I'm surprised you made it up at all." The top of the ladder shifted around as he adjusted it from below. "Okay, you can come on down now."

"Please, I'd really rather if you waited in the living room. I'm naked."

"*Naked?* My goodness, Jane, what are you doing up there naked?" I didn't answer. "Well, come on down. I'll just hold the ladder for you. I'll close my eyes."

"Please, Dad?"

"I'm holding this steady for you, Jane," he insisted sternly. "Come down."

I resigned myself to the humiliation and fumbled my way down. When I reached the floor he hurried out of the room, calling, "I'll just be out here, then."

I grabbed my towel from the floor and wrapped myself in it. My breathing beginning to stabilize, I threw on some clothes and ran a brush through my damp hair.

A few minutes later I came out to the kitchen, where Dad was sitting at the table, tapping a nervous foot. "Everything okay, dear? What were you doing up there?"

"Like I said, I was looking for something. Can I get you anything?" I asked, opening the fridge door. "Tea? Sandwich?"

"No, no thanks, I've had my lunch. I didn't realize this place had an attic. Do you and Shiro keep much up there?"

"Not much, just some old boxes. Well, I'm starving," I said, grabbing a loaf of bread and tossing together an avocado sandwich.

"Why is it so hot in here?" he asked, seeming irritated. "And it smells sour—have you taken the garbage out recently?"

"It's our heater, making things go bad so fast. It's broken, remember, I told you? And . . . actually . . . it was strange up there . . . I think there must be something dead and rotting." I cut a wedge of lemon, dropped it into a glass of water and chugged down half the glass.

"*Dead?* Must be a rodent. Call your landlord right away. Or maybe Shiro can look into it when he gets home. But that doesn't explain why you were up there in the first place." He was studying me now. "Are you sure you're okay, Jane? Goodness, have you been *crying?*"

"No, I don't think so." I fished the lemon from my water, shoved it into my mouth, and flashed him a yellow monkey grin.

"I don't think I've ever seen you cry, certainly not since you were a little girl."

He folded his hands on the table and straightened his spine.

"Well, Jane, as I said, your mother texted me today saying she was concerned. She said you sent her a strange text message earlier."

"Text? I never sent Mom texts today."

He took out his phone from his back pocket and set it on the table. "Yes, you did. It made her very concerned."

"So, now *she's* concerned about *me*? I seem to remember *my* being concerned about *her* the other day, and you thinking nothing of it," I said, taking a seat beside him at the table, sucking on my wedge of lemon. "Not enough for you to go snooping around her house."

"Concerned—you mean about her foreclosure?"

"Not just that; the fact that she's nowhere. That she's evaporated off the face of the earth. Did she mention anything about that?"

"Don't be silly, Jane. She's in Texas, helping Chris and his family with their move, I believe, or en route. Anyway, I'd hardly say I've been snooping. As I said, I called but—"

"Well, I didn't text Mom today. She must be confused."

"No, she's not," he assured, finding something on his phone and handing it to me.

> Hi, I got this funny msg from Jane
> today. Maybe you should go check it
> out. I would if I were in town. I have a
> very bad feeling about this. Please go
> check on her immediately.

Then below, a message forwarded from me:

> I can't find it. Where is it?
> Where is it? Where the hell is it
> wherethehellwhereeeeeererrrrissss-
> sithavetofindithavetofindithavetostopit-
> stopitstopppppppppppppptwdn12iu3RYg

I handed the phone back to him, drinking more of my water as I tried to decide how I should explain things to him—since I was still so confused myself.

"Remember how Mom used to sleepwalk?" I asked.

He looked surprised. "Yes?"

"Well, I think I must have done that. Sleep-texted. And sleepwalked. Up to the attic. Maybe it's hereditary."

"You sleepwalked *up a ladder*?"

"Apparently."

He looked at a loss for words. "Does Shiro know about this?"

"Shiro? No. It's only happened a few times that I know of, and I don't want to worry him. That's the last thing we need. He's already so paranoid about his work and how the whole world's coming to an end—"

"He's not still planning on making trouble there, is he? You know this administration is notorious for how it treats whistleblowers. They've excavated an arcane law from 1917, the Espionage Act, in order to put the fear of god into anyone thinking of challenging them. Just the other day a man was charged for—"

"Also," I cut in, unable to focus on his words, "I know this sounds crazy, but I think there might be some . . . ghost or something up there. And some type of . . . supernatural beings. Monsters or something." I laughed nervously, placing my glass on the counter, my hand shaking slightly. "Maybe I should talk to Mom about it. Maybe it's related to all her childhood visions. I know this sounds totally crazy, but I'm telling you, I felt something . . . weird. And, I know this sounds crazy, too, but I felt Mom was . . . up there in the attic with me. I can't explain it. But I felt her with me. I saw her."

I wanted to say more but suddenly realized how absurd I must sound.

Dad stared at me, speechless, confirming my fear.

"Jane," he finally said, pulling his shoulders back and sticking out his chin, his tone firm, "I want you to know that I've set up an appointment for you."

"An *appointment*? What kind?"

"A doctor's appointment. Just a regular doctor's appointment. A family health practitioner. My own doctor referred her to me, in fact. He says she's really wonderful. You don't have insurance, do you?"

I shook my head. My medical insurance had gone away with my employment.

"That's what I thought," he said, looking hopeful. "So, you're probably overdue for a routine physical, right?"

I nodded. "Yeah. Yeah, a doctor's appointment would be good. I've been meaning to." I placed a hand on my belly—on you.

"Wonderful. It's my treat. And then, well, if there's anything that needs more looking into, like this sleepwalking issue or anything else, psychological or physical, you can discuss it with a professional. She can make referrals. If not, fine. Your mother found great relief when she finally took her mental health seriously."

"So, now because I mentioned ghosts, I'm crazy?" I asked, shocked and hurt at his insinuation.

"Goodness, Jane, the only one who keeps mentioning the word *crazy* is yourself. It's just, well, if you're experiencing fears—and even visions— with no connection to reality . . . it's just that some of these things *are* hereditary, is all, dear. And you seem to be having a difficult time getting things done, isn't that right?"

I nodded.

"And from what you've been saying about Shiro—his paranoia and all his rash ideas about his work and so on—perhaps he should be seeking some professional help as well. My point is simply this: one mustn't be irresponsible when it comes to one's health. Science can be our friend. At any rate, I'll email you the appointment information."

I looked at the bright purple, pink, and white orchids your dad kept by the kitchen window, which seemed to be smiling encouragingly in the sunlight coming in through the half-open curtains.

THIRTY-FOUR

Dr. Sharma is a South Asian woman, probably in her midthirties—petite, with prominent eyebrows, glittery eyes, and abundant black hair swept back into a large hair clip. When she entered the room, dressed in a white lab coat and green skirt, I was struck by how pretty she was. She shook my hand firmly, then closed the door and leaned back against it, arms folded across her chest, looking for a moment like a teenager.

"How can I help you?" she asked with a slight British accent.

The general nature of the question threw me. I found myself flipping through all the settings it could apply to—a hair salon, a café, a tech-support phone call—until I rested on the right one.

"Well . . . I'm here for a routine physical. Plus, I'm pregnant."

"Yes, I see from your chart. Congratulations!" she said, smiling abruptly. "We'll make sure to schedule you with an OB-GYN. Other than that—any questions? Concerns?"

"Not really, no."

"Really? Nothing at all?" She looked at me patiently as she continued leaning against the door.

"Well . . . I have been feeling a little tired lately."

"Ah—I noticed that on your questionnaire," she said, walking to her computer and calling up something on her screen. "You checked the box for 'abnormally fatigued.' But you know this is quite normal for pregnancy."

I nodded.

"But I see you've also checked the boxes for 'anxiety' and 'depression.'"

I nodded again.

"So, you've been feeling anxious and depressed? Both?"

There was something about her no-nonsense manner that I appreciated. I could feel myself relaxing in her presence.

"I guess so. Maybe. I'm not sure I really know the difference."

"Well, anxious, we'd say, is being more or less extremely stressed—like perhaps you have too many things on your plate that are making you very overwhelmed and worried, or perhaps you find yourself worrying over apparently nothing. Depression is more like if you are feeling very down, maybe sad, hopeless. Perhaps finding it difficult to get out of bed in the morning and go about the normal day-to-day routine. Beyond just plain fatigue—you know? But of course they can be interrelated. One often goes with the other."

"Yeah, I guess I'd say a little of both, maybe? But I don't have too many things on my plate. I'm unemployed at the moment, so . . ."

"I see," she said, typing something on her computer. "And you are very anxious about not having employment?"

"Well, yes, especially now that I'm pregnant. I don't have any medical insurance. I received unemployment checks for a while, but that ran out. I'd been doing a bit of sewing, for this family friend's boutique, but that ended. Obviously I need to find a real job, eventually. For now my dad and boyfriend—I mean, fiancé—are helping out."

"Your *fiancé*? Congratulations," she said, smiling again, typing more, I guessed onto my chart. "You say 'eventually.' But you've been actively looking?"

"Not as actively as some would like," I said, laughing. She raised an eyebrow. "But that's part of my anxiety. It's been difficult for me to actually *do* things. That's why I lost the sewing job; I couldn't concentrate. And now that I'm pregnant, it'll probably be even harder to find a job, and to keep one."

"And how are you feeling about your pregnancy, Miss Thompson?"

"Oh, happy, of course. Thrilled. Very thrilled. But, I mean, to be honest, it was a surprise. A big surprise. And of course, like anyone, I'm nervous. I've been worried about what kind of mother I might be. I know it sounds silly, but my worst fear in the world is that I've inherited some type of . . . disorder or something."

She frowned. "Disorder?"

"You know, some type of horrible mothering gene or something. Being a horrible mother." I laughed again, too loudly. "I know it's irrational. And normal, right? I mean, having fears about parenthood."

"Of course," she said, smiling, making another note on my chart.

"It's not just the pregnancy," I continued. "Everything has felt off over the past few months, like my life needs one big chiropractic adjustment. I've been really tired, as I mentioned, and feeling . . . it's hard to describe, but this sense of . . . absence, I guess I'd call it. Almost like instead of a baby growing inside of me, I have some slow-growing hole. I'm worried it will keep growing until . . . until nothing's left."

She studied me a moment. "A hole. Interesting. Can you give me an example of something you've felt was *off*, as you put it? Something concrete, perhaps?"

I sat up straight on the exam table and tried my best to explain all the things—from the mundane to the significant—that had been feeling off, ever since the night of our anniversary, leaving out only my disturbing visions. She nodded as I spoke, every so often entering something on my chart. When I mentioned the broken heating vent, she looked at me, interested.

"A dysfunctional heating vent?"

"Yes."

"And is this vent real or metaphorical?"

I looked into her dark, glittery eyes. "Sorry?"

"The *vent*. Is it real or metaphorical?" she repeated, as if this were the most normal question in the world.

"Oh, no. No metaphors, here; everything I'm talking about is real. Real as this room we're in right here. We're talking actual, physical matter." I patted the paper on the exam table, which made a louder crinkling sound than I expected.

She glanced around the room, as though confirming its contents were indeed real.

"My fiancé and I have *both* been very disturbed by it," I continued, assuring her that the broken vent wasn't just in my mind. "He's actually the one most worked up over it. At one point he thought the government was camped up in our attic to spy on us and infect us with toxic fumes!" I said, choking on a sudden burst of laughter. She handed me a tissue. "I mean, he's a great guy, don't get me wrong. Just a little paranoid sometimes."

She made another note on my chart.

"You're not writing that part down, are you? I mean, about him thinking those things about the government. I wouldn't want that on his—or my—record, or anything. I mean, I wouldn't want anyone to see that who could twist it around or—"

"Don't worry, Miss Thompson, I didn't mark anything down about that. After all, this visit is about *you*, isn't it?" I nodded. She squinted at her screen. "And you two are happy? You and your fiancé?" she asked.

"Yeah, for the most part. I've just been so tired," I said, playing with my tissue. "I mean *really* tired. His work schedule's always changing and we eat at the strangest hours, so my sleep's all out of whack. And I think I've been sleepwalking."

"Sleepwalking? When did this start?"

"I'm not sure, exactly. Recently, I think. Like the last few months. My mom used to, as well. I've even daydreamed, or hallucinated, I guess—but that's probably much too strong a word. Just very vivid dreams, probably, while half asleep. Only once or twice."

She typed something on my chart and looked at me. "This is definitely something you'll want to discuss with one of our mental health specialists. Any other sources of anxiety or depression you'd like to discuss with me today, Miss Thompson?"

"Well . . . another thing is—speaking of my mom—she, my mom, that is, has been . . . missing, I guess you could say."

"*Missing?*"

"Not exactly missing. It's not like I've called the police or filed a missing person report yet. That would be the last thing she'd want. And I mean, my friends see her on Facebook, and she texts and calls every so often. But I can't seem to find her. At least not here, in the physical world." I patted the paper on the exam table again.

"And you normally see your mother often? In the *physical world*?" she added with a slight smile.

"Well, not so often, really, but around once a month. She did mention she'd be going away for a while, but still . . ." I felt my cheeks flushing, realizing that my worries might seem more extreme than necessary.

"So, she told you she'd be traveling, yet you still imagine she's *missing*?" She was studying me suspiciously now.

"When you put it like that, I guess my concern does sound a little . . . paranoid. I guess my fiancé's not the only one." I laughed again. "Also, our next-door neighbor has this baby that cries incessantly. It's the most annoying thing in the world. Really, it never shuts up."

Now she laughed. "Miss Thompson, I'm afraid you'll have to get used to that—babies cry. That's what they're programmed to do best. It's for their survival!"

She quickly entered something more on my chart and scrolled back to the top. I figured she was wrapping up this portion of the visit. I hesitated a moment before mentioning what had been on my mind all along—after all, she was a medical doctor and didn't have all day. But on the other hand, the subject had been nagging me almost constantly over these past months and seemed somehow pivotal to where I was now, here in the exam room, with you inside me. Nothing had been quite the same since. And she had acted interested in everything else, including the broken vent. So I went ahead and risked sounding insane.

As I began speaking, she scrolled back down to where she'd been in my chart and resumed her note taking. Throughout my story—including the splayed, grotesquely disemboweled corpse; the alarmed, pleading eye; the steaming entrails sliding along the road in the flashing headlights; the mysterious antlers—she kept nodding, every so often saying, "Mm, yes," as though everything I was saying made perfect sense and was helping to clarify my situation.

"It was like the deer was more than just a deer," I told her. "It felt . . . like its body was sent there just for us, somehow—or *was* us. Or even bigger than that. I can't explain."

When I got to the part about the antlers in the garage, she left her computer and moved to the swiveling chair across from me, leaned back into the blue canvas, crossed her slender legs, and adjusted the hem of her skirt.

"Yes," she said, cutting me off midsentence, "it's wise of you to consider, when so much in your environment is off-kilter, that the problem might be stemming from *yourself.*"

"Well, I wasn't implying that so much; more like vice versa."

"Chicken or egg." She pulsed her thick eyebrows suggestively.

"I don't understand—"

"All I'm saying is, I'm glad you came today, Miss Thompson," she said, reminding me of some sinister character from an Agatha Christie detective novel. "It's good to get the help we need. Especially when children are involved."

"Yes, for sure," I rushed to agree, though I still wasn't sure what she was implying.

I guessed we'd move to the part of the visit where she'd examine me, order lab tests and write any necessary referrals, then send me on my way. But instead she settled farther into her seat.

"I'm going to tell you a story," she said, smoothing her skirt over her lap.

"When I was first married, and my husband and I had just moved to London from our home in Delhi—many years ago now—we lived in a small but nice penthouse apartment. Lots of windows, lovely morning light; it faced east, you know? But across the street, there was a construction site, and night and day, people were working. It was so loud, dusty, and generally obtrusive, it was impossible for one to have any peace of mind.

"From the beginning, my husband kept asking when they would be finished, but it went on for years—three, to be exact—with no end in sight. We couldn't even tell what it was exactly that they were building, and they were unable or unwilling to tell us. Sometimes it seemed a certain section that was nearing completion would actually be taken down and started all over again, as if someone at the management level couldn't make up his mind. We were used to projects getting stalled by various bureaucratic glitches back home, but this was beyond anything like that—and somehow we had thought that in London, things might be more functional in this regard . . ."

She gazed at the exam-room wall, as though she was picturing her old London apartment and the noisy, dusty site out her eastern-facing windows. I glanced at the clock—it seemed time for her to be seeing her next patient, yet she showed no sign of even starting my physical examination. She seemed indifferent to the passing of time.

"It was really awful. I mean—maddening. The construction invaded every possible space within me: physical, mental, spiritual. In fact,

I became obsessed with watching them work and would spend hours, sometime days, glued to my window. I became almost suicidal, I confess. Then, when the self-destructive urges passed, I found myself filling with violent urges toward my husband, and, of course, the workers themselves. At first I was afraid of these urges, and would attempt to talk myself out of or around them. I'd say things like, 'Well, just because one has such violent thoughts doesn't mean one will act on them. On the contrary, isn't it healthy to allow oneself to feel one's rage—and even to think the occasional dark, taboo thought, rather than repressing it?'"

I wanted to stop her somehow, without appearing rude. What was the point of this long, disturbing tale? This was what your grandpa's doctor had considered "really wonderful?"

"I'm telling you, Miss Thompson," she continued, "these urges in me became so forceful, once I was seriously tempted to offer the workers a tray of fruit juice laced with poison at their lunch break. Of course, I had access to any number of drugs, because of my medical internship at the time. But in the end, I knew that would be futile—naturally the workers would quickly be replaced. How many murders would I have to commit before I could have any peace of mind?" Her eyes shifted from the wall to me, waiting for an answer.

"Not sure," I answered weakly.

"There *is* no answer to that question, Miss Thompson," she said, seeming smug that I'd failed her test. "Attempting to solve something from our basest instincts only leads us to infinite destruction. Don't you agree?"

I nodded.

I had no idea what her point was, but, in spite of myself, I found myself asking, "So . . . how did it end? Did they ever finish the construction? Or did you just move?"

She smiled, standing and again smoothing the wrinkles from her skirt.

"It ended as all things do—in its own peculiar way. But let's just say that I had to take matters into my own hands. I could no longer be a victim of outer circumstances beyond my control. In darkness, one must create one's own light. I had to look *within*. I wouldn't be here today if it weren't for what happened over there, now would I?"

"You didn't kill the poor workers, did you?" I asked, laughing nervously.

Her eyebrows lifted impressively high and she let out a huge laugh. She seemed to think this was the funniest thing she'd ever heard. "Of course not!" she managed, leaning against the wall, wiping away a few tears, looking like a teenager again.

Once she'd recovered from her outburst, she inhaled and exhaled deeply, then straightened her posture and looked back at me with her pretty eyes.

"Come, let's take a look," she said.

The rest of the visit was more or less routine. She resumed her semiprofessional manner and examined me, ordered some blood tests, scheduled a visit with an OB-GYN, then wrote a referral for mental health counseling.

"Just remember this, Miss Thompson," she said as she handed me the pink slip of paper, "these unseen things have a way of persisting, even thriving—until they are satisfied. But we *can* perhaps manage them, at least for the time being."

All I could do was nod dumbly.

Halfway out the door, she called, "Happy Holidays!" and let the door slam shut behind her.

I thought I might report her; her behavior was way off—not only very creepy, but maybe even illegal. In the end, though, I handled it in the way I usually do: I made some lame excuses to myself and forgot about it.

The other appointments were more normal, thankfully. After a short interview with the mental health specialist, which included considerations about the risks of medicating while pregnant versus not medicating under my circumstances, I left with a small square of paper that I handed to the pharmacist on my way out.

THIRTY-FIVE

The girl kicks off her sandals and stands barefoot among the roots and vines growing from the mud. Mosquitoes, butterflies, and dragonflies flit about as she reaches for a large stick poking out from the river. A thin, white, lacy mist covers the water like a loosely knit baby's blanket.

It's early morning—she slipped out while everyone was lining up for bathing—and the insects and birds are already singing loudly. She sings along with them, enjoying the way her voice bounces off the canopy of trees and the water. She pulls the stick and drags it along the shore, carving a slow line in the mud, the air humid, sweat trickling down her brow.

Something shifts; she stops and listens. She spots ripples in a patch of bright-green algae beneath the mist and jabs her stick in. A bullfrog jumps into the air and reenters the water with a light splash. She resumes her walking and dragging, every so often stopping again to jab her stick between the reeds into the water.

She notices a stillness in the air and stops. All the life of the swamp seems to have paused in anticipation.

She turns and sees him squatting there at the other end of the shore, his naked body partially submerged.

He seems unaware of her as he plays, gathering clumps of leaves and mud and forming them into little balls, stacking them one on top of the other. At one point he slips and falls backward into the water, his tiny toes pointing up toward the low-hanging vine drooping from a branch above. She tosses her stick aside and makes her way to him.

By the time she reaches him, he's back on his feet, unfazed by his fall, his little body moving swiftly, his full head of black hair stark against pale, smooth skin.

She pulls the toy boat from her dress pocket and holds it out to him. He glances up, his eyes meeting hers briefly, but continues his game. Normally they play with the boat together, in the puddles between fallen branches, imagining they're out at sea.

Without speaking—they never speak—she sets the boat down and joins his game. The two play side by side like this for some time, gathering mud clumps and stacking them along the shore. The sounds of the river are still suspended; only her own voice rings above the silence as she continues to sing her song.

Out of the corner of her eye she sees shadows dart past. She looks up to find that her playmate is gone. Only the boat and mud clumps are left; the warm brown water laps lazily at them and her toes.

She senses motion beyond a patch of cattails. She stands and wades into the river up to her thighs, the bottom of her dress now wet and heavy. Moving carefully, so as not to disturb anything living in the water, she peers through the stalks and stiffens.

Several looming figures, taller than humans but shorter than trees—their posture crooked and twisted like the cypress knees growing from the river, their rough, warty skin a deep, ocean blue—stand together in the low mist. Each creature has two white horns and several large, bloodshot eyes that seem to burn holes into the air as they glare out in all directions. They carry black clubs, raising them high over their heads and plunging them down into the mud, ruthlessly, repeatedly.

She takes a step forward, bending a cattail out of her way, and takes a closer look. There are more than she first thought—she can't tell how many, as they're spread along the misty shore far into the distance.

One of the nearest creatures, its club lifted to the sky, turns its horrible, blistered face toward her, as though hearing something. She hears it too: her own voice. It's only then that she realizes she's still singing.

She claps a hand over her mouth.

The ground shifts beneath her and she slips, making a large splash.

Struggling to regain her footing on the riverbed, grabbing onto cattails and a floating, mossy branch to steady herself, she looks back at the creatures. They're still intent on their rhythmic, destructive task, except the one, who has now spotted her.

Its red-and-white marbled eyes, bulging from their swollen sockets, fix on her as she huddles between the cattails—she stares back helplessly, feeling a burning deep within.

The gnarled figure lowers its club and straightens its back, revealing itself to be much taller than she had first thought, its stunningly blue form blocking her view of the darkening sky, its horns brushing against the leaves of the nearest tree.

Slowly it approaches, moving easily through the water, towering above the cattails and floating debris, emerging on the shore where she and her playmate were just moments ago.

The fierce eyes still glare at her, and everything else, all at once.

Opening its black mouth, thunderous laughter tearing through the suspended air, the creature lifts its club and, with one crashing blow, destroys her and her playmate's work—the little stacked mud clumps disappear into the water.

The toy boat, dwarfed by the creature's thick ankles and feet beside it on the shore, looks as though it's trying, with all its might, to sail away.

The girl wants to scream, but she opens her mouth and her voice is gone.

Trapped thigh-deep in the decaying river, under the spell of these searing eyes, she realizes, deep in her bones, that this creature has taken her for its own.

THIRTY-SIX

Your dad's new bedtime ritual was to shave, brush his teeth, strip to his underwear, do a series of jumping jacks, push-ups, sit-ups, then some stretches. It seemed he was getting his body into perfect shape to greet his new life of fatherhood. That Sunday as he was finishing up his routine, I sat in bed, knitting a pair of yellow baby booties for you.

I'd never really learned how to knit but had spent the past few days watching how-to videos on YouTube. I had expected the skill to come easily, as I'm generally quite good with my hands, but for some reason the task of knitting these booties was proving difficult. I kept making them in odd, inhuman shapes, and having to unravel them and start all over again.

Shiro's shadow moved up and down on the bedroom wall as he did his sit-ups. Though he was only a few feet away on the carpet below, the distance between us felt much greater. My left hand, abandoning its task of knitting, walked along the mattress toward him. I imagined my fingers as tiny people traveling across a desert while the edge of the bed was the edge of the earth. Shiro was an alien in some other galaxy below, doing alien exercises. I listened to the steady rhythm of his exhales mixed with the hum of the broken heater down the hall, as well as the faint, muffled whimpers from the apartment next door, cars off in the distance, the more-felt-than-heard drone of electromagnetic frequencies traveling through the air, the city and beyond, communicating with each other in a language all their own . . .

I wondered if I should tell him about my new mental health program. I knew it would bother him. Especially since you were coming along for the ride with me. In the past he'd talked about how wary he was of so many people placing something as critical as their brain under the management of pharmaceutical companies. I thought back to an ad campaign when I was in college where all BART stations—even the floors and ceilings—had been plastered with images of gigantic purple pills looking like grape candy, along with the words: "Don't be alone. Just ask your doctor." They'd looked quite tempting.

Over the past week, I'd begun noticing the product's soothing effects. It so happened that I'd been prescribed the same new drug that I'd swiped—and yes, sporadically sampled—from Mom: Exilcon. Just as the online reviews had promised, the effects were subtle but profound. It wasn't as though that sense of absence was gone; it was still there, just instead of being nebulous and free to travel throughout me as it wanted, it had shrunk to a more manageable shape and size, like a shirt that could be neatly folded and placed inside of a drawer. My exhaustion and uneasiness had been replaced by a general, gentle buzz of well-being. Shiro's paranoia about his work and those surveillance creatures were no longer bothering me.

Best of all, I could barely hear that next-door baby crying anymore. Only the faintest, muffled whimpers if I really listened carefully. Maybe the cries had quieted, or maybe the pills were just helping to block them out. Or were they softer now because they had always only been in my mind? Would this drug eventually erase them entirely?

Whatever the case, at last I was able to be more productive during the day, looking through job listings with more enthusiasm, planning the wedding . . . I was even considering going back to my part-time sewing job.

But tonight was different. I was finding it difficult to focus and kept looking up from my knitting.

The absence seemed to be leaking out of its tidy, assigned storage space, seeping into the complicated, mysterious landscape of the rest of me. I felt like a freshly bleached sheet onto which a drop of blue ink had spilled, and now the ink was spreading, starting at my center, trickling down into my hip creases, down my legs to my ankles and toes, and upward as well, traveling along my rib cage to my chest and throat, pouring down over my shoulders, collecting in little gooey pools at my armpits, sliding in rivulets down to my wrists and fingertips . . .

I wanted to describe this sensation to Shiro but felt so saturated by this strange, blue liquid absence that there was nothing left in me to form the words.

THIRTY-SEVEN

A couple weeks after my appointment with Dr. Sharma, just after Christmas, the building manager finally stopped by. Phil, a tall, skinny white guy in maybe his forties with reddish skin and greasy, florescent blond hair, showed up hours late in shorts and a wrinkled Hawaiian shirt, looking as though he'd just spent the past months, or perhaps years, sleeping on the beach.

As if to spite me, the heating vent behaved itself throughout his visit. Phil sighed impatiently as I explained the problem. After finding nothing apparently wrong with the heater, he said all he could do was to replace the vent cover so at least it could close properly.

"It'll basically be a metal Band-Aid to shut out the heat. You'll still hear the muffled screeching you're describing, but at least it won't get as hot. Will that satisfy you?" Despite his laid-back, beach-bum appearance, he had a gruff, impatient manner.

"I guess a new vent cover will work, if that's all you can do. Band-Aids are better than nothing, right?"

While he was up in the attic, he found some mouse droppings, so before leaving he reluctantly made a run to the hardware store and set some traps. I figured I wouldn't mention this part to Shiro, since it would only encourage his paranoia.

"I'd clean up that attic, if I were you," he remarked as he descended the ladder. "Stinks to high hell . . . smells toxic."

As he was leaving, I asked him about our next-door neighbors—if he knew if they had recently had a baby. I was back to thinking it must have been an actual baby crying on the other side of the wall and not just some figment of my imagination.

"Next-door neighbors? This is a corner apartment and that one unit next door's been vacant five, six months, at least. There's still some things need fixing before we can rent it—but I'll get it done soon," he said defensively.

"You mean no one's been living there?" Obviously this couldn't have been true.

"Not a soul—unless someone's been squatting in there illegally. Have you really been hearing noises from there? Do you want to call the cops?"

"Oh, no, there's no need for that. I just could have sworn I heard a family living there."

He raised his eyebrows, lifted his toolbox, and rushed out the door, as though he had several more appointments to catch up on after his long hiatus.

The next day, Shiro danced around the apartment, whistling as he watered his plants. He had just finished repotting one out on the fire escape and had soil all over himself—his hands, forearms, even his hair and cheeks—he looked freshly harvested.

"Thank god that fucking vent is closed!" he cried, trailing little clumps of dirt down the hall as he danced his way to the kitchen. "That was *insane*! I can't believe we let it go on so long. Of course, now it's already winter."

"You know what the manager said that was so weird, though?"

"What's that?"

"He said the apartment next door's been vacant these past months. But that's impossible; that baby was crying all the time."

"Baby?" he asked, watering a perky, wide-leafed plant on the bookshelf. "Whoa, slow down, lady—Little One's not even out yet; don't tell me he's already whining," he teased.

"No, silly. You know, the baby next door."

He headed back to the bedroom. I followed him. He handed me the watering can and climbed back out onto the fire escape.

"Hey, speaking of babies," he said through the window, "we'd better start thinking about reorganizing things around here. I mean, where's Little One gonna sleep, anyway?" He peeked into the bedroom. "Maybe I'll build him a nice sturdy bed—or a crib. Do babies still sleep in cribs these days?"

"But it was so loud," I pursued. "That next-door baby. Or maybe I was just imagining it," I quickly added.

"Maybe it was across the street, or in another unit, with some killer lungs." He picked up a plant, rotating it as though trying to find its most attractive angle, sunlight falling on the leaves and his shoulders.

"You know," he said, carrying the plant in through the window, "I almost got used to this place being a sauna. I was having to give these guys so much water, it was crazy. That's why that fern died." He pointed to an empty spot on his dresser.

"Oh, was there a fern there?"

"You're funny," he said, carefully setting the new plant in the empty place. "You never notice our plants."

"Hey now, that's not entirely true; I notice you caring for them."

"It's okay, it's okay," he said, giving me a hearty kiss on the neck, smudging me with soil. "I plant things and get them growing, you harvest and cook them. We're a perfect team, like that. That's why we need each other, right?"

"So, you give life, I take it?"

"Hey, creation and destruction—the cycle of life."

He was right. I've never been good at growing things.

THIRTY-EIGHT

When I was a freshman in high school, a few weeks before your grandmother left, she and I flew to LA and visited her brother in the hospital after one of his last heart surgeries. An old army buddy of his also happened to be visiting that day. Unlike Pops, who had been a "No-No Boy," Uncle Tak and his friend had answered yes to all the questions on their loyalty questionnaires during the war and had been "allowed" to fight in Europe.

Since Uncle Tak was still groggy with medication, Mom and his old army buddy did all the chatting. It turned out the guy's family and ours had been at the same Camp—of all places, in Rohwer, Arkansas, a tiny town along the woodsy swamps of the Mississippi River. I'd never heard Mom talk so much about Camp; normally she did her best to avoid the subject altogether. Maybe she liked the fact that this man had been there, too, yet was a relative stranger.

"What block were you guys again?" the old guy had asked Mom.

"Oh, I don't remember. That was so long ago. Wait now—seventeen. That's right, Block Seventeen. Jeez, I can't believe I still remember."

"Seventeen, seventeen . . . okay." I could see the old guy walking through the map of Camp in his mind. "So, you knew the Saitos?"

"The Saitos—oh, Johnny Saito?"

"No, Herb and Mary. Wait now—I think maybe Herb did have a little brother named Johnny . . ."

They reminisced like this a while, the old guy recounting a few mundane anecdotes, before he brought up something I'd never heard before.

"Hey—so, you must be the one that got shot?"

Mom's eyes widened. "Shot? Oh, no. Wait—*shot?* Goodness, where did you hear *that?*"

"Your brother here told me—always said his little sister was that famous escape artist. Wasn't that you?"

Mom glanced around the room, as though trying to find something. "Jeez, I haven't thought about that in ages. But I guess it *did* happen, now that you mention it. Funny how some memories just kind of go away—I haven't thought about that in *ages*," she repeated, tucking a loose strand of hair behind her ear.

"So, that was you, eh? Trying to escape!" He let out an admiring chuckle.

"Oh, well, jeez, that was so long ago, I can barely remember—what was I, just six years old? But, oh, no, no, no, you heard it all wrong. *Escape?* How could a little girl ever hope to escape a place like that? No, no, I was just sleepwalking, after curfew, I think it was, and a guard shot in my direction, from up on his tower."

"Thought it must be you . . . knew it wasn't Michi." The old guy looked impressed as he took off his baseball cap and rubbed the few gray hairs he had left. "Yeah, you know, I was off in combat with your *lazy brother here*," he said wryly, "but we all heard about it. So, this is your famous *escape artist*, eh, Tak?" he said loudly by Uncle Tak's ear. "The sister who eventually escaped up to San Francisco?" he joked.

Uncle Tak's eyes crinkled, his thin arms at his sides.

Mom laughed and blushed, waving a hand. "*Escape artist?* No, no, please!" she cried, seeming a bit enticed by the idea she was so vehemently protesting. "My goodness, I was just *six years old*—like I said, I was sleepwalking. How could I *escape?*" She paused a moment, then pointed at the hospital wall. "Do you remember the river?" she asked. I had the feeling that, suddenly, the river was just beyond the wall.

"Oh, sure," the guy said, looking at the wall as well. "All those cypress trees growing out of the water. Cypress *knees*, we called 'em, cause they looked just like an old man's knees. We used to fish back there, before I got sent off to Italy with Tak here."

There was a moment of silence as the two stared at, or through, the wall.

"So, the guard shot from up there on his watchtower, eh?" the guy finally asked, placing his cap back on his head. "He didn't hit you?"

"Oh, no, no—he was practically just a kid himself, just doing his job. I'm sure it was only a warning shot."

"Just happened once?"

"Oh, yes. The shooting, that is." She glanced at me, clutching her upper arms. "But that's enough about all that. My Jane here doesn't need to hear about all this *past stuff*—jeez, young people don't need that! No one does, right? My motto is: *Look to the future!*" She laughed uncomfortably. "Anyway, Camp was mostly fun, don't you think? For us kids, I mean. We didn't know any better—for all we knew we were on a long vacation, right? Like summer camp!"

"Oh, yeah, sure, for the little kids," the guy rushed to agree.

There was another pause.

"But aw, man, sleepwalking in that fishbowl," the guy pressed, not picking up on Mom's cue to change the subject. "Lucky you didn't get yourself *killed* or get your family sent off to Tule Lake, you know? Must've scared the hell out of your folks!"

"Well, Papa wasn't there yet." She glanced at me again. I grabbed a magazine and pretended to read it. "But yes, Mama was afraid I'd keep wandering." She lowered her voice and took a step toward the old guy. "She started this thing where . . . at bedtime, she'd push a table in front of the door and tie me to my cot with her scarves." She rubbed her upper arms, as though still feeling the restraints. "Still, sometimes I'd manage to break free. I guess *that's* why they called me the escape artist . . . I'd get stuck between worlds, I guess you could say. Between waking and sleeping, I mean. I'd go to the river." She walked to the window, where a few white-haired patients sat on a patio, eyes closed, resting in the sun. "We used to play together there. Strange games. Mama didn't like it."

"Who, you and Michi?" the old guy asked.

"No, a boy. From another family, I guess. Isn't that funny, I can't remember? Isn't it so random, what we remember and what we don't?"

The old guy looked confused but nodded anyway.

On our flight home, I asked Mom to elaborate on these sleepwalking episodes, but she laughed, put on her sunglasses, pulled a Baby Ruth from her purse, ripped off the wrapping, and shoved half of it into her mouth.

"Oh, how on earth could I tell you about that, Jane?" she asked, chewing. "The whole point is, I was asleep! I honestly have no idea what really happened!"

That was our last trip down to LA together. After that, she always came up with some excuse whenever I suggested we visit her family. As a result, I haven't seen any of our LA relatives in years. It's almost as though we don't have a family anymore.

THIRTY-NINE

Dressed in her nightgown, the girl walks down the barrack steps and into the night. Traces of incense from the Obon festivities linger in the air, but the music and dancing have stopped, and the other internees are asleep. A few unlit lanterns still hang from strings between the barracks. The full moon looks like an enormous lantern.

The girl has only the vaguest memory of the Obon celebrations at their old temple, before the war—bright colors and laughter and people moving in a circle.

She had wanted to partake in the festivities this evening, or at least to watch, but her mother didn't allow it, insisting she and her sister stay in their barrack.

Now she walks—more like floats, like the visiting spirits—through the blocks of barracks, past the school and hospital, toward the back edge of Camp, where she hopes he is waiting, the ground getting cooler, spongier beneath her bare feet, the closer she gets to the river.

Before she enters the woods, a second moon swoops down, painting a white track in the dirt, revealing night creatures flying or scurrying or slithering out of view. But the girl keeps walking, unaware, even as the bright light lands on her shoulder, sweeps across her feet, casts her long shadow before her.

The guard shouts from his watchtower.

"Hey, you! You—stop, ya hear?"

Getting no response, he shouts again, and again.

"I'll shoot, I swear, I'll shoot!"

He fixes his rifle near the small figure and hesitates.

"I said, I'll shoot!" He pulls the trigger.

The first shot snaps the night in two; the second slams it back together again.

The girl drops, her open eyes shrinking into focus. Dizzy, nearly blinded by the searchlight, she can barely make out her own hands, nightgown, the flying insects, the dirt ground.

She hears footsteps—a woman is running toward her, still dressed in her summer kimono from the festival.

"Stop, she's just a child!" the woman is shouting up toward the light.

The woman leans over the girl, touches her cheek, asks if she's hurt. Tiny drops of moisture twirl in the glaring light between the girl and the woman's face, like snow. The woman smells of incense.

More footsteps—the guard is running toward them.

"Step away now!" he barks. "Stand back!"

The woman obeys.

The guard squats down into the white circle of light, grabs the girl's wrist roughly, asks if she can hear him. When she blinks, he sighs, his body softening.

"All right, ma'am, show's over," he tells the woman. "Nobody's hurt here."

He scoops the girl up into his arms and stands, stepping out of the light. He's taller than she had first thought, and more muscular. From his voice, it's clear he's quite young, probably not much older than her own brother.

"Nobody's hurt," he repeats to the woman. "They were just warnin' shots, is all. She shouldn'ta been out this late—what are you doin' out past curfew?"

The woman bows, stepping backward. "I was finishing cleaning up. From the festival."

"Well, lucky for you, I'm gonna let it go this time. I knew it was a bad idea, lettin' y'all do that strange spirit festival a yours—figured it'd get everyone all riled up, and now look. A little girl was almost killed. Get goin' back to your barrack—now!"

She doesn't move, but instead eyes the guard suspiciously as he holds the limp, nightgown-clad girl in his arms.

"I said get goin'!" he shouts, his voice cracking.

The woman scurries off into the darkness, like one of the night creatures.

The girl, now alone in the arms of the tall, angry man, shuts her eyes, her body rigid. When he whispers in her ear, asking for her block number, she can barely manage to mumble it.

As he carries her for what feels like much too long through the vast night, she imagines herself in the arms of the blue demon, the large hands like claws clutching her flesh too tightly, the hot, sour breath burning her face, the rough cloth of his uniform like the creature's warty skin rubbing abrasively against hers, his rifle like the creature's club pressing rhythmically and painfully into her ribs.

She wonders if they'll ever arrive at her barrack—is he deliberately torturing her, walking circles through the night around her block, delighting in her anguish?

Eventually they arrive. He climbs the steps, pounds on the door, and waits, like a deliveryman bearing a medium-sized package.

Her mother opens the door. The guard places the girl onto her legs. His hands squeeze her ribs once more as she wobbles a moment before gaining her balance.

"Evenin', ma'am," he says, now sounding like a gentleman. "You'd better keep better track of this here daughter a yours—she almost got herself killed tonight."

Her mother grabs the girl's wrist and pulls her inside the small room, stepping between her and the guard.

"Now I just fired warnin' shots, mind you," he assures. "I couldn't see so good, from up on that tower, in the dark and all—couldn't see she was just a kid. Still, she can't be wanderin' off like that after curfew. Seems like she was headin' out for the woods. Good thing I got to her; who knows what all's lurkin' back there by the river this time of night? Ain't nowhere for a child." He eyes her mother up and down, running his tongue over his teeth with a disturbing sneer.

The girl senses he's waiting for some type of reward for his good deed.

Her mother bows, holding the door open, not speaking.

"What's happening?" the girl's sister asks from her cot.

"Shizukani," her mother mutters over her shoulder. Quiet.

"Now, I'm gonna have to make a note of this, you understand," the guard says, his voice deeper. "If I ever catch her—or any of y'all—out after curfew again, y'all'll be sent off to one of those maximum-security places. Not so fun as here—no singin' and dancin', I can guarantee you that. You'd better keep this one tied up in here or somethin'." He points to the girl. "Lucky nothin' worse happened to her out there tonight, wanderin' around like that in that little nightie a hers."

Her mother stays bowed in the doorway as the guard lifts his rifle, rests it on his shoulder, pauses a moment, then returns down the steps, his feet landing heavily. He spits onto the dirt path before making his way back into the night.

Her mother shuts the door, turns, and slaps the girl's face.

"Crazy!" she cries softly. "You get us killed!"

The girl only now finds herself fully awake.

"What's happening?" the girl's sister repeats from her cot, sitting up.

"Nenasai, Michi!" her mother instructs. Go back to sleep!

Her sister lies back down.

Her mother yanks the girl into a corner of the dark room.

"Why you keep going back there?" she demands. "What you looking for?"

The girl recalls something she hasn't thought of in over a year: the wooden statue that used to stand at the family altar. The little smiling god in the bright red bib. Its pained grimace as it had vanished in the fire.

"Are you looking for Papa, Sumi-chan?" her mother asks, more gently now, kneeling, taking her hands, looking into her eyes with sympathy.

She begins speaking in Japanese, her words flowing freely, expressively. The girl allows her mother's mother tongue to wash over her, warm tones of love, sadness, fear; for a moment she feels deeply bonded to her mother.

But then, realizing she's not understanding most of the words, the girl stiffens. She hopelessly chases each word in her head.

Her mother stops speaking. They look at each other helplessly.

"Papa's not here," her mother states stiffly in English, releasing the girl's hands. "We don't know where he is. We don't know—"

"Aki," the girl interrupts. "I was looking for Baby Aki."

Her mother stands.

"It's his birthday, remember? Obon?"

Her mother makes a vague gesture with her head.

"He needs me," the girl continues with more confidence. She pauses, listening. As usual, she hears the faint, high-pitched cries in the distance. "Can't you hear him? He's calling for us—he's by the river, with them—he's in danger, Mama! We have to find him! We have to—"

Her mother slaps her again, and again. "Wake up!" she commands, grabbing the girl's shoulders, shaking her. "You're sleeping. Wake up, wake up, wake up!"

"Mama, stop!" her sister cries from her cot. "She's still a kid, Mama, let her be!"

Her mother releases the girl's shoulders, stumbling backward into the barrack wall, covering her face with her hands, as though fearful of what she might do next.

"It's okay, Sumi-chan," her sister says, hurrying to the girl, taking her hand, guiding her back to her cot, where her toy boat waits for her. "Go back to sleep now, okay?"

"Yes, go to sleep," her mother repeats, releasing her face, her hands trembling. "Everyone, go back to sleep."

The girl is confused. Does her mother want her to wake up or go to sleep?

Her sister returns to her own cot. The girl lies down, curls onto her side facing the barrack wall, hugging her boat, pressing her eyes shut.

Her mother paces the floor until she's sure her daughters have fallen back to sleep. Then, quietly, she pushes their small table in front of the door, takes two silk scarves from her suitcase, rolls the girl onto her back, takes the toy boat from her clenched fingers and, despite her own trembling hands, ties the small arms, as gently but tightly as she can, to the frame of the cot.

FORTY

That weekend we celebrated the New Year with Shiro's family out in Modesto. Shiro had been taking BART to work, so Junior hadn't been driven in some time, and when we went to start the motor, the battery was dead. When the AAA guy lifted the hood, he was amazed to find the original battery.

"Whoa, no way," he exclaimed. "The battery from *1984*? These guys don't usually last but forty, fifty thousand miles tops," he said, holding the thing up for us to admire, as though it were an impressive, dismembered organ.

"Way to go, Pops," Shiro said proudly, patting the side of the car.

I was relieved the guy didn't notice the antlers lurking in the corner.

When we arrived, his dad met us in the driveway and immediately took my hand.

"No ring?" he asked, looking to Shiro.

Shiro looked flustered. "Oh, the ring—yeah, I thought I told you, Gram's ring was too big. I still have to get it resized, just haven't gotten around to it yet."

His dad frowned disapprovingly. We hadn't told them about the pregnancy yet, at my insistence.

As always, his mom served all the traditional foods for the holiday, plus a few extra goodies to celebrate our engagement: crab, sushi, egg custard, lotus root with shitake mushrooms, ozoni soup, and, my favorite, fresh mochi his dad and a few guys from their bingo club had pounded themselves.

Since they owned a small grocery store and could never get away, we rarely saw them, but whenever we did, we all got along nicely. His mom was small, hardworking, always smiling, and spent most of her spare time in her large garden. His dad was wiry and energetic, spending what few hours he wasn't at the store tinkering around in his garage, fixing and inventing things. He liked joking with me about what an understanding girlfriend I was, putting up with his quirky, headstrong son.

"He's always hatching some *eccentric, artistic ideas*, right?" he'd ask me. "Always so passionate about *this and that*!" We'd laugh together.

That evening, our bellies stuffed, Shiro and I wandered through his mom's garden. We admired her persimmon trees, the expansive branches bare, having just borne a plentiful harvest. As we sat together on an old, rusty glider beneath one of the trees, I noticed something near the tree trunk, almost camouflaged in the dim evening light: on a wide, flat rock stood a stone statue, about ten inches tall. It wore a serene smile, eyes closed, and a monk's robe, its hands pressed together in prayer. A bright-red baby's bib was tied snugly around its neck, the bloodred color, even in the faint light, a shocking contrast to the pale stone. Near the statue's bare feet stood a stack of small stones, reaching near to the statue's elbow.

"What's that?" I asked.

"What's what?"

"That," I said, stopping the glider. "That funny looking little guy there with the red bib."

"You don't know Jizo?"

I shook my head, feeling light-headed.

"That there's Jizo. Jizo-san, meet Jane. Jane, meet Jizo-san."

"Jizo?"

"A god—a bodhisattva. The protector of babies and children. I'm surprised you've never heard of him."

"You know my mom, she's not into that stuff. The more American the better."

"Right. Well, he protects all people, really, but his specialty's the weak and vulnerable. And travelers—folks crossing from one place to another. A cousin of mine gave birth to a stillborn a while back, so my mom set him out. He's supposed to make sure the spirits of folks who die before their time don't get stuck in limbo-land."

"Limbo-land? Kind of like Cyber Limbo-land?"

"Yup—maybe they're more or less the same," he joked. "The

netherworld between this one and the next. A kind of living hell. In the old myth, it's this riverbed where all those nasty oni live. What's it called again . . ." He snapped his fingers and hummed the notes of a haunting tune. "It's on the tip of my tongue—my grandma used to sing a song about it. Saino-something. Saino . . . Saino . . . *Sainokawara.* The riverbed where little spirits are doomed to spend all of eternity."

"Wow, sounds dramatic."

"Oh, hell yes—these myths are pure drama. The little spirits' cries are supposed to be unlike anything on earth, so pitiful they pierce through *flesh and bone*!"

We both laughed a little and sat a moment looking at the small statue.

"And the stone tower? What's that?" I asked, feeling more light-headed.

He started up the squeaky glider again.

"They're like penance, from what I remember. And redemption. The babies stack them along the misty shores of Sainokawara for good karma. To ensure their parents' safe passage to the next world. Plus to help themselves out of the river. People in this world are supposed to stack them to help the poor little guys. Sometimes people make other offerings too, like baby clothes—handmade bibs or hats or other baby things." He adjusted himself on the glider and lowered his voice.

"It's a good story . . . the not-fully-formed, abandoned little spirits spend their days sobbing, looking for Jizo, building stone towers on the misty banks . . . but every evening at sunset," he continued, his voice growing more dramatic, "the nasty *oni* come—big ole blue, hideous beasts with horns and tons of bulging, bloodshot eyes, always watching," he bellowed, really getting into it, bugging out his eyes, lifting and crashing his arms with gnarled fists, "and topple down the towers with their ginormous iron clubs!"

He made explosion sounds, stopped the glider and waited for silence.

"Then they laugh as the little guys have to start building all over again—*Myahaha!* The cycle's endless." He smiled, raising his eyebrows. "Good story, eh?"

"You sure know a lot about this."

"Yeah, well you know me, I like to read."

He started up the glider again.

"So, how does he protect the little stuck spirits?" I asked, my eyes fixed on the little statue in the bloodred bib.

"Well, *if* your family's paid him their respects, O Great Jizo here comes along and hides the little fellas in the sleeves of his robe and guides them safely across the riverbed. Kind of a reverse midwife. But without Jizo? Aw man, shit outta luck. Poor fellas are screwed—doomed to suffer on the shores forever. They just build those towers all day, then watch those nasty oni knock 'em down again. Sucks, eh? Eternity's a long time. That's why religion's ultimately a crock of shit."

I stopped the glider. "I think I've seen them."

He eyed me sideways. "Huh?"

I recalled those strange, blue, shadowy entities up in the attic— whether they had been in my dreams, real, or somewhere in between, it didn't matter; I could still see them moving, bending forward repeatedly, intent on some destructive task, still smell the sulfuric air, feel the moist ground beneath me, sense Mom squatting beside me, looking at that boat, grabbing it, running away.

"I mean, yeah, I think so," I stammered, closing my eyes. "The demons. I think Mom and I have seen them."

"How so? You mean in pictures?"

"Shiro . . ." I took a deep breath, opened my eyes, and cleared my throat. "I've been . . . meaning to mention. I was up in our attic and I found those old boxes Aunt Michi gave me when I was a kid. I came across this little toy boat. And I could have sworn . . . this is gonna sound crazy . . . but I swear Mom was there with me. But not *Mom*, Mom; Mom as a little girl. And she was looking for someone. The baby."

"The baby?"

"I'm pretty sure she was looking for her little brother, you know, who died mysteriously in Camp. Baby Aki."

"*Aki?*"

I nodded, feeling myself start to tremble.

"You're *named* after him?" He looked confused. "Why didn't you ever tell me?"

"I don't know. I guess it didn't seem important. Mom never mentioned any of it to me. I'd never have known anything if it weren't for Aunt Michi and Dad. And I don't know the details, but apparently Bachan went crazy in Camp and—" I couldn't speak anymore, I was shaking so violently— this was as close to crying as I'd come in ages.

"Whoa, whoa, slow down," he said, rubbing my back. "So, Camp drove your Bachan crazy?"

"Well, chicken or egg. She probably already had some kind of mental illness or chemical imbalance."

"Um, Camp happened—that was traumatic. Lots of people suffered mental breakdowns."

"Mom says it was like year-round summer camp, at least for the kids."

He kept rubbing my back gently. "No offense, babe, but look at your mom. It's called denial. Mega hardcore *denial*."

"There's something else," I continued. "I've been sleepwalking. I'm the one who ransacked our apartment that day. There was no robber, no TSA, no government. Just me. I've been . . . building towers, like this one here." I pointed at the tower as best I could despite my shaking. "And looking for something. But I don't know what. I haven't figured out that part yet." I looked at the stone statue. Despite its closed eyes, I could feel it looking back at me.

Shiro shook his head. "Wait—let me get this straight. You're saying that was *you*? *You* who went through all our things that day?"

I nodded.

He shook his head more, then stood, walked to the trunk of the per-simmon tree, and turned to face me. "When did you figure this out?"

"It's been slowly occurring to me . . . I just feel so strange all the time. Kind of . . . not fully *here*. It's hard to explain. Remember that feeling I mentioned of that hole growing in me? That's why . . . Shiro, the other day at the doctor's, when I went in to check on Little One, I started taking some medication. Just to manage that feeling. And the sleepwalking. And to quiet the baby I've been hearing. Or . . . the ghost of the baby . . ."

"*Ghost?*" He looked at me as though I were a stranger.

"Apparently Mom used to see her brother's ghost—or thought she did. She took medication to stop the hallucinations."

"Wow—shit. That's intense." He came back to the glider and sat next to me.

From his reaction to this news—concerned and surprised, yes, but not amazed—I could tell he was viewing it from a purely psychological standpoint; his disbelief in ghosts was complete . . . which was actually a relief. I leaned into his certainty, as though leaning into the wall of reality.

"Jane," he said, kissing my head, enveloping me in the cool sleeves of his jacket, "I'm so sorry you've been dealing with all this alone. You must have been so stressed—why didn't you tell me?"

My shaking had reduced from large, irregular jerks to tiny, hummingbird tremors.

"But ghosts—I mean, even if I believed in them—would that really work? Medicating a ghost?"

"Not the ghost—me. I'm the one who hears it. And now I hear it less, so it seems to be working."

I started up the glider, the high-pitched, squeaky sound scraping at the night.

"What about Little One?" he asked, placing a hand on my belly—on you.

"Oh, they said it was perfectly safe," I rushed to explain. "That's the very first thing I asked, of course. Little One's safety comes first. They said it was much better to be a capable, happy mother than a dysfunctional stress-case, when, you know, changing diapers and all." I forced a laugh. "And the sleepwalking seems to have stopped now, so that's good. And like I said, I'm not hearing the cries anymore. Or hardly at all."

He was nodding slowly, in rhythm with the glider, as though he were running on maximum comprehension capacity and was determined to stay calm and supportive, and in sync with reality, in the face of all this wacky news.

"Okay. Well . . . sometimes I guess people do need this . . . a little help. And if you're sure you do . . . well then, I trust you," he pronounced firmly, taking my hands in his. "I trust you, Jane. We're in this together. For the long haul. I don't want you to be so stressed."

"Thanks," I said, squeezing his warm hands, my body softening. "I was so scared to tell you."

It was such an enormous relief to finally confide in him. I felt closer to him than I had in months—perhaps ever. We slid back and forth on the glider, which now sounded less abrasive, soothing even.

"So, what's on the other side?" I eventually asked through chattering teeth. The garden suddenly felt cold. "What's across that mythical river?"

"Beats me. New life, next world—or enlightenment or some shit."

"So, you don't believe in any of this?"

He thought a moment.

"I mean, as metaphors, these myths are great. But all those realms are right here." He planted the heel of his shoe into the ground for emphasis, stopping the glider. "Here on earth. It's up to *us* to save ourselves, not some *god*," he said scornfully. "That's just a cop-out. Let's spare Little One all the religious mindfuck crap, okay?"

"But how do you explain that crying?" I asked, sitting up. "And my building those towers? And the monsters I saw in the attic? And Mom's—"

"Shh," he said, turning me away from him, massaging my shoulders. "I don't know. You must have heard the legend at some point in your childhood and just forgotten—and now you're dreaming about it. The mind is wild, illogical terrain. And the baby—just because it wasn't right next door doesn't mean it wasn't somewhere in the building. Someone probably *does* have a baby. You're home all day; it makes sense you'd be the one to hear it. And you've been stressed about motherhood, so of course the cries would grate at you, especially since they were so constant and annoying. Maybe it's gotten older now and a bit quieter, is all."

"Yeah." I closed my eyes, his words relaxing me, even as all my thoughts hurtled around us like objects in a hurricane. "Yeah, you're probably right."

That night we slept at his parents' place. I hope you don't mind my mentioning this, but we had the best sex we'd had in ages, tightly cramped together in Shiro's childhood bed. My mind was at last able to relax and let go. The branch of a tree scraped up against the window in the wind, as if cheering us on; a slight smell of mildew and sweet, wet earth permeated the air and everything else—the mattress, the sheets, even our skin.

In the driveway the next morning, his mom called for us to wait as she rushed back in the house and returned, smiling as always, with a boxful of her homemade jams for us to take home. His dad asked how Junior was holding up and Shiro shared the story of the miraculous, long-lived car battery.

"No way. That old thing was still ticking, eh?" His dad walked around to the front of the car, folded his arms and studied the body intently. We'd mentioned our anniversary night and the deer—which, surprisingly, had left no marks—and I thought his dad must be checking for traces.

As we got into Junior, his dad tapped the hood, signaling for us to wait, ran off, and returned with his garden hose. He proceeded to give the body a good wash, circling the car two or three times, every so often dropping the hose to use his own spit, lovingly, as though he were performing some type of cleansing ritual. After the wash, he lifted the hood and fiddled around under there a while, murmuring to himself, before closing it and giving it a final pat.

There was a sense of peace in the car as we drove home that morning. Your dad and I hardly spoke as we took in the spacious sky and stark tones of winter rushing by. Eventually we came to the windmills. Standing in long, single rows along the brown rolling hills, they looked like a welcoming committee of tall, white aliens, just landed.

FORTY-ONE

Over the next few weeks, life became much more pleasant. My paranoia about Mom being abducted by some intangible, evil force had diminished. I was finally settling into the twenty-first century, I suppose, feeling more comfortable communicating with her virtually.

My anxieties about motherhood had also eased up, and I was starting to feel positive, even excited about the prospect of being your mother. I could feel a genuine connection between myself and your little body growing inside me. I'd daydream about which of my features you'd inherit and which of Shiro's: would you get his super dimply smile? My eyes? His honey-colored skin or thick black hair?

At times I'd find myself speaking to you.

"Hello there, Little One. I'm so excited to meet you! I can't wait to see your beautiful face, to kiss your tiny fingers and toes . . . to look into each other's eyes. It's growing clearer to me each day that you're the most important thing in my world."

Shiro would speak to you, too. He'd rest his head near my belly at night and tell you long, rambling, nonsensical, hilarious stories he'd make up. All three of us would shake with laughter.

Needless to say, we were already in love with you.

My sleeping patterns had grown more regular, partly due to the fact that the apartment had quieted. I only heard the neighbor's baby's muffled cries if I really strained myself—and even then only for a few minutes, usually at sundown and in the early morning hours.

It made no sense what the building manager had said; clearly a woman and her baby had been occupying the apartment next door. I had even seen the mother that one day. Maybe they *had* been squatting illegally, as he had suggested—or maybe they lived elsewhere, or in another unit in the building, even, but the mother, knowing this next-door unit was vacant, had made use of it when the baby was particularly upset. Maybe she had a spouse who worked from home and needed quiet during the day. That would explain why Shiro couldn't recall hearing it; he was usually at work during the day, and he slept like a log at night.

As far as the idea of the cries coming from a ghost, which I'm sure you must be wondering about, I had crossed that off my list of possibilities. First, I agreed with Shiro that ghosts were most likely just cop-outs—a result of people not wanting to face their own current problems, projecting them onto some convenient past. Second, hearing the blood-curdling, angry cries of an actual ghost was not something I, or I would imagine most people, wanted to believe in. That would open up all kinds of cans of supernatural worms that I had no desire to deal with, not to mention I would be labeled as insane.

Shiro was doing better, too. The edges of his outrage at all the injustices of the world had softened. For instance, the other day we'd gone bowling with Topaz and Roger and had enjoyed pleasant, polite conversation with no stressful political rants. Afterward, Topaz texted me that we both seemed much happier.

We still hadn't told anyone about the pregnancy. I suppose some part of me was still holding on to the dim hope of telling Mom in person before she heard it on social media.

And maybe there was some small part of me that already sensed the future . . .

Thankfully, Shiro and I had come to the agreement that, what with you on the way, now wasn't the right time for him to cause a ruckus at his work and wind up unemployed or in prison. He still intended to blow the whistle on them at some point and had saved all his evidence—which I wasn't at all happy about—but meanwhile jobs were scarce, and we agreed there wasn't much we could do for the time being, other than simply to be grateful for what we had, and to adjust to the way things were. What a relief it was to finally relax.

The medication was working in just the way I had hoped. I know what you're thinking: medicating someone without his consent? But really, I was only giving him a very small amount—just half of what I had been prescribed. Yet it seemed to be working wonderfully. I knew he would actually thank me, were he less reactive and paranoid about Big Pharma and the world in general being out to oppress that very paranoia. And believe me, I was planning on telling him eventually.

His headaches were the only side effect I'd noticed. They made concentrating nearly impossible, so he hadn't been able to work on his videos.

One afternoon he was sitting at the kitchen table, holding his head in his hands, when I entered wearing the wedding dress I'd been working on. It was a simple, cream-colored satin minidress.

"So . . . what do you think?" I asked.

He peaked up through his hands. "Cool." Then he sat up, frowning. "They're a little . . . I don't know, crooked, aren't they? I mean, one's a lot longer than the other. Maybe you should stick to sewing." He smiled slightly. "No, but good work. I'm sure the more you practice, the better you'll get."

That's when I realized I was holding up those awful baby booties I'd recently knitted for you.

"Oh, these. I forgot I was holding them. I know, they're horrific. But at least they're kinda cute in a weird, deformed way, don't ya think?"

One was long and curved, the other short and bent at much too sharp an angle. The only thing they had in common was the yellow yarn, loosely and poorly knit. I'm afraid it looked as though I was preparing to clothe some sort of misshapen, monster baby!

As ashamed as I was of them, I was also proud of overcoming my fears about motherhood enough to make them for you.

"Well how 'bout the dress—you like?" I asked, blushing. I tossed the booties onto the counter and spun around, the satin heels I'd bought to go with the dress making me clumsy. "You can't see Little One yet, can you?" I asked, turning sideways, sucking in my stomach. "Pretty soon I won't have a waistline. Maybe never again, if we're gonna keep making babies."

He smiled again, but I could tell he was distracted from the pain. "Wow. Nice work," he said. "You look great."

"I was thinking a simple bouquet. Yellow roses, maybe, or something really unpretentious, like daisies. Or maybe those are so unpretentious, they're pretentious? What do you think?"

"Sure," he said, pushing aside his half-eaten bowl of cereal, placing his head back in his hands. "Looks great—you look great."

"You sure you don't want to finish that?" I asked. "You haven't eaten all day. Another headache?"

"Yeah—must be those scanners at work," he said. "Or who knows, maybe they're just random."

"Sorry. Want a massage?"

"It's like a bunch of birds have landed on the power lines of my brain," he said, tilting his head and shaking it.

"What kind of birds?"

He looked up at me, surprised. "What kind of birds?"

"Yeah, like, are they, I don't know, baby finches, with ruby-red chests? Or peaceful white doves?" I sounded perkier, more cheerful than I'd intended.

"Would that make any difference?" He pressed his fingertips around his scalp, as though feeling for the exact contours of the creatures—their heads, beaks, wings, talons. "Maybe something like blue jays. Definitely predators. Not friendly."

I walked up behind him and began massaging his scalp.

"Hey, when are you gonna get your grandma's ring resized?" I asked. "I haven't seen it since our anniversary. I'd better start wearing it while we're still engaged, ya know?" I kissed his hair. "It isn't lost, is it? Should we search the house for it?"

"No, I just keep meaning to, but then I keep forgetting." He nudged my hands away. "Thanks, but that's actually making my headache worse." He turned to face me. "You've been taking your supplements for Little One, right? Folic acid and all that stuff?"

I was taken aback, the question seemed so out of the blue. I was suddenly terrified that he might suspect me of medicating him.

"Of course. Why do you ask?"

He nodded and placed his head back in his hands. "Nothing—just wanted to make sure."

I breathed a sigh of relief.

I admit, as hard as it was to watch him suffer his headaches, I was thankful for the break from his art-making. In the past, whenever he was in the middle of one of his projects, he'd get so obsessed that it was all he could talk about, the only lens through which he could view the world. Suddenly everything became an accumulation of evidence proving the narrow truth of his project. It was claustrophobic.

I was enjoying spending more carefree, relaxed time with him, cuddling on the couch in the evenings, watching our funny shows, flipping through baby-name books, and planning the wedding.

I felt a little guilty, of course. But believe me when I say that I sincerely thought things were better for us now—for all three of us. It's not healthy to raise a child in an environment of constant stress and paranoia. Any sane person will agree with that, right?

Again, I understand one might wonder about the ethics of medicating someone without his or her consent, and under most circumstances, I'd also be skeptical, but, as I've said, I knew bringing it up with Shiro directly would be a lost cause. It would anger him, even, and trigger his anxieties about someone being out to get him.

The thing was, it was a double-edged sword. Your dad was less obsessed with all the negative and unjust aspects of life, but I noticed he was less excitable in both directions. He was less passionate about the world and everything in it, including me, and even you. He still loved us, of course, but his love had a more muted quality. That was something I hadn't counted on.

FORTY-TWO

A few days later, Shiro stood over me, shaking me awake. I sat up on the couch, wiped drool from my cheek, and looked around the living room. Like months before, our place had been ransacked.

"Jane? You okay?" he was asking, searching my body.

This was the first evidence of my sleepwalking since I'd started my medication. I looked around at our things strewn everywhere and was filled with a sense of dread. A tower of books stood on the floor beside me—without thinking, before he seemed to notice, I toppled it down with my foot.

"Have you been sleepwalking again?" he asked.

"I guess so."

He looked at the kitchen table, where his laptop sat open. "What were you doing with my computer?" he asked, going to the table. "It was in the bedroom, shut down."

"Was it? What time is it? I thought you were coming home late tonight?"

"I got off early." He sat at the table. "I was called into the office. I thought you were gonna run the camera when you took naps? But I'm not seeing any footage from today—not any for weeks." His computer was wirelessly connected to the security camera he'd mounted to the spider plant.

"Oh, I haven't been doing that anymore. Now that we knew there was no actual break-in, that it was just me that time, I figured there was no need."

He motioned to the mess in the apartment. "But there *is* a need. Aren't you curious what exactly you do in here?"

"Why were you called into the office?" I asked, standing, approaching him at the table.

He opened his mouth as if to tell me, then paused. "Nothing. Nothing big."

The muscles in his face twitched as he glared at the screen. The light glowed blue in his eyes—I had the sense that he was battling to see clearly through the haze of one of his headaches.

"What is it, Shiro? You're scaring me."

He jumped up, went to the bookshelf, and began looking for something.

"What are you looking for?"

"My flash drive—have you seen it?"

"What flash drive?"

"The one I always keep here. It's gone."

"I don't think so, no."

He ran to the bedroom; I followed. The bedroom had also been torn apart. He was in the closet, mumbling curses, setting up the ladder with a great clunk, climbing up into the attic.

"What on earth are you doing?" I called up into the darkness.

"My video footage of work—and all my files logging everything. Gone—it's all gone. Someone fucking deleted or stole it—or both. *Fucking shit!*" he shouted.

"*Gone?*"

"Yup. Gone. Man, it's a mess up here—and still stinks like hell." I heard him rummaging around, throwing things. Then a loud snap.

"Shit!" he exclaimed. "*What the hell are rattraps doing up here?*"

"Oh, oops, I forgot to tell you. They're mousetraps, not rattraps. Sorry, the manager set them when he was here. Are you okay?"

"Luckily, yes—but I could've lost a fucking toe with this thing! Jesus! How many of these things are up here?"

"I have no idea." I heard more rummaging. "You're sure you're okay?"

"*Yes!*" he exclaimed a minute later.

He climbed down the ladder as I held it steady. He was beaming, holding up a white envelope, waving it over his head victoriously.

"My backup drive—I hid it up there, just in case!" He jumped down from the last rung of the ladder and did a celebratory spin. "Good thing!"

Then suddenly he grew serious. He walked to our bedroom window and gazed out at the fire escape.

"They have it now. All my evidence against the whole fucked-up place, my footage from the IO Room, the racist profiling speech, everything—someone has it. They have it now," he repeated softly, as if to himself. "This is really happening. I'll lose my job. Probably a lot worse. Maybe they'll just threaten and fire me . . ."

He turned to me with alarm. "You were right, Jane. I'm sorry—like you said, I should have been more careful. I shouldn't have been so cavalier, leaving the files on my computer. When we discovered the break-in was just you, not my work, I stopped being so diligent. The last time I was looking over the files, doing some editing, I just kept everything right there . . ." He stood there limply, looking woozy, as though he might faint.

Then his eyes lit up. "Unless . . ."

"Unless what?"

He ran back to the kitchen; I followed. He was ripping open the envelope, pulling out the backup drive, spinning his laptop to face him—I hadn't seen him so excited in some time.

"Unless I post this right now! For the whole world to see!"

But before he could plug the drive into his computer, I caught his arm. He looked up at me.

"Are you kidding, Shiro? You're really crazy enough to do something like this?"

"Well, what else do you want me to do at this point?" he asked, looking at me desperately. "Just sit here and wait for them to come after me? And silence me?"

"Okay, let's just calm down here a second," I chirped, guiding him to the couch by the elbow. "Let's just think straight a minute before jumping to all these rash conclusions. Want something to eat? Some soup? Cereal?" I perched on the arm of the couch, hugging my knees to my chest. "Maybe your work didn't steal the files, or even delete them. There's lots of other possible explanations here, right?"

He squinted at me suspiciously. "Like what?"

I'd been trying to forget the day, last week, when he'd been at work and I'd opened his computer, just curious to see what footage he had stored there, waiting to be revealed to the world one day. Things were going so well between us, and with you growing inside me . . . I hated thinking anything could ruin that.

"I—I don't know."

I looked around at our disheveled living room.

"I mean, this mess was obviously me. I must have sleepwalked again. I haven't for at least a month or so, but . . . I was feeling a bit like my old self today. Really tired. And that next-door baby was crying again, just a little. Or maybe I was just imagining it. But either way, I was feeling like my old self. Maybe I need to up the dosage of my medication."

He frowned, tilting his head in confusion. "What are you saying?"

"I don't know, really. I mean, I don't think I would have done anything with all your files. I wouldn't do that. Unless I did it in my sleep. But I just really don't remember. I'm sorry, if I did. I thought my sleepwalking was over. Maybe I need to up the dosage of my medication," I repeated lamely.

"Delete my files in your *sleep?*" he asked, incredulous.

"Yeah, no, I probably wouldn't have done that. I don't see how I could have. I think in my sleep I just look for something . . . and build those towers."

He took a deep breath and shook his head. "No. Look, my work probably just hacked the files remotely. It could have been any time during the past couple weeks—I haven't been checking. And my flash drive—I must have just misplaced that. I'll find it. It's probably just a coincidence we're discovering all this now. You probably just sleepwalked and randomly carried my computer out here. And turned it on."

He eyed the backup drive in his hand and started back toward his computer.

"Maybe I *did* do it," I whispered.

I had been horrified that day, seeing all the videos on his computer, full of incriminating evidence against his manager and coworkers, and potentially the government itself. I still wasn't sure if it was my disgust at the content itself, or my fear of Shiro endangering our family, that most filled me with the desire to destroy the files.

"Did you delete the files, or didn't you, Jane?"

He took a step toward me, frightening me.

"Shiro, I don't know. I really don't. Maybe," I stammered, getting down from the couch, standing across from him. He glared at me.

"Maybe it's been weighing on me. All your talk of whistleblowing. I know you've agreed not to do anything for now, but like you said yourself, it's just not safe. It scares me."

I placed my hands on my belly and began pacing the living room.

"It's dangerous, Shiro. *Dangerous*. We need to think of all three of us now. We're not just single, freewheeling, twentysomething slackers who can do whatever the hell we want anymore . . ." My fingernails dug into my belly. "I'd love to stand up for all these great ideals, of course I would, but now's no time for some heroic revolution!" I shouted.

I stopped my pacing and looked at him. "Do you really want armed men in uniforms barging into our house, maybe in the middle of the night, while we're all sleeping?" My throat tightened and my voice became a strained whisper. "A night raid? Who knows what they might do to us during a *night raid*? They could do anything . . . then throw us all in prison and who knows what else? Take our baby? *Make us all disappear?*" I was shocked by my own words.

He looked shocked, too. We stood in silence.

"What then?" he asked finally. "Just let them win? The daily invasion of people's privacy, their civil liberties—people being harassed because they happen to look like the enemy, because they're women, brown, wearing a turban—you're fine with all that?" he challenged. "People hauled off to fill some racist immigration quota? Sure, standing up is scary, but—"

"Please, Shiro?" I let out a funny little laugh. "I'd love to stand for all these ideals, I really, really would, but . . . the world's a messed-up place . . . this is one of the *good* places. You're just one person. We can't all save the world . . ." Clichés seemed to be spontaneously leaping from my mouth. "Can't we just try and stay out of trouble? Live a normal, happy life?"

He turned sideways, his jaw clenched.

"Look," I said, suddenly bursting into loud, high-pitched laughter. "I really don't know what happened, anyway. I'm just guessing. We're getting all worked up here, maybe for nothing! I don't even know for sure I did any of this. That's the whole point here: I was *asleep!*" I was laughing so hard I could barely control myself.

"That's no normal sleepwalking," he snapped, suddenly grabbing my shoulders, halting my laughter. "Did you delete the goddamned files or not?"

"Ouch. Let go of me, Shiro."

"*Did you or not?*" he demanded, squeezing harder, his fingers pressing into my flesh.

"You're hurting me. I don't know. I was *asleep!*"

"Good thing I still have this," he said, releasing me, holding up the backup drive.

I tried laughing more, but only a hoarse breath emerged.

Then I was grabbing the stupid metal thing from his hand and hurling it across the room. It crashed against the wall with a satisfying smack, landing on the floor with a quiet thud.

We looked at each other, stunned.

"You're right, you'd better up your meds, because these are *not* working," he barked, then grabbed his skull in his hands. "Jesus, my fucking head. This is getting to be too much. I'm gonna have a fucking heart attack here."

FORTY-THREE

About two weeks later, I was sitting at the table, enjoying a snack of salami rolled around cream cheese and chocolate chips. Don't ask me why.

It was the beginning of February, and the branches on the plum tree outside our kitchen window were still naked.

Shiro hadn't been home in a few days. He'd called after work to say an emergency had come up at his parents' store and he needed to stay with them to help out. I'd thought it a bit odd, since he'd never stayed away last-minute like that, but I didn't think too much of it. Things had been strained between us ever since our fight, and I thought some time apart would do us both good.

Suddenly the door burst open and he entered, still wearing his blue work uniform, carrying his laptop, his hair disheveled. He zoomed past me to the hall, then a moment later was standing in the kitchen doorway, dark circles under his eyes, his cheeks a funny shade of purple.

"Hi there," I said, my mouth full of chocolate and cream cheese. "Everything okay?"

"How could you?" he asked.

"I know, it's a weird snack, but I was just in the mood—"

"*How could you?*" he repeated.

"What are we talking about here?"

That's when he marched toward me and began shouting full force, as though something had exploded in his brain.

"*What the fuck were you thinking? How could you possibly do that!*"

I stared up at him, nearly gagging on the cream cheese in my throat.

He knocked over a chair. "*Well?*"

"Do what? What are you—"

"Are you really gonna sit there and pretend you don't know? I thought I knew you! I trusted you!"

"Shiro, calm down," I said, barely managing to swallow. "I really have no idea what you're talking—"

"*Medicating* me?" Tears welled in his eyes and rushed down his cheeks. "What the hell were you thinking?"

He threw his laptop onto the table with a bang.

"I have a confession," he said, looking down guiltily, wiping away tears. "I placed more cameras. Ones that you weren't controlling—all over the apartment. I had a drug test at work and the results came back positive for a substance I hadn't listed. I told them it must be a false positive, so they agreed to do it again—results still aren't back yet. But I got suspicious after our fight the other day. I needed to figure out what the hell was going on in here. *Good thing I did!*" he yelled, his voice cracking.

The walls of the kitchen looked more prominent, as though they were falling in on me.

"I thought drug tests were only for illegal substances. Not prescription medications?"

He closed his eyes and pinched the bridge of his nose, as though only now believing what he had suspected.

"Okay, wait. Let me get this straight," I said, slowly standing, feeling that perhaps my only option at this point was to remain as righteous as possible. "You're mad at me about something you saw me do while you were secretly *spying on me*? Why didn't you just come out and ask?"

He stared at me as though I were some hideous monster.

"What the fuck? Would you have told me? *You* want to talk about *trust*? And who the hell cares how I found out—why the fuck are you slipping me pills in my cereal?" he yelled, his eyes wild.

"Look . . . okay. Yes, I've been sharing my medication with you. Don't worry, you've just been getting a half dose. But think about it, Shiro, hasn't it helped? Hasn't the past month been nice?"

He gaped at me, speechless.

"Come on," I continued softly. "Sometimes we just need a little help. From the *inside*. And you said yourself you wanted me to *act* more, not just *re*act. Remember?" I asked, reaching for his hand, but he jerked it away. "You've seemed so much more relaxed. Happier. We've both been happier. You've stopped being obsessed with all the horrible things in the world and hell-bent on your whistleblowing. It's been better for Little One. Don't you see? You were getting so paranoid, all that constant talk of—"

"It's not okay to mess with someone else's brain!" he shouted, backing away from me. "What the hell kind of pills have you been feeding me, exactly? For a fucking *month*?"

"I can show you the jar. It's a really great new product. It's been getting really popular. Mom takes it, too, actually. It helps manage anxiety and paranoia, it doesn't change you into someone else. You become more *yourself*, in fact, just a more peaceful version—"

"Stop with the fucking advertisement!"

He kept backing away until he stumbled into the counter, looking genuinely afraid of what physical harm I might cause him. In that moment, I felt maybe he was right; maybe I *was* a horrible, multiheaded monster.

"I won't do it again," I whispered. "I promise. I'm sorry. I would have told you eventually."

"Honestly, I'm surprised you're not using your sleepwalking excuse again, or sleep*searching* or sleep*erasing* or whatever the hell it is you do in here! What about my files? Did you delete them or not?"

"I think so, yeah," I said quietly.

The weight of this admission released from me, I plopped down in my chair. "Sorry. I should have told you, but I knew you'd be so angry. Again, Shiro, for your own good, our family's good—"

"And were you awake for that, too? Or asleep?"

I nodded, then shook my head. "Maybe half of each?"

"Jesus fucking Christ, Jane. Are you ever fully awake?"

"I'm not quite sure."

He opened and closed his eyes several times, shaking his head, as though not believing what he was seeing or hearing.

"It's like you have some psychotic need to erase everything."

"The footage was illegal, Shiro. And dangerous. It was endangering us."

"You know, speaking of illegal—I could probably have you arrested," he asserted, hands on his hips. "I could call the cops right now if I wanted.

This is probably some kind of felony, medicating someone without their consent. Course, you could just plead insanity."

"And I could have *you* arrested for spying on me and your work!" I announced, standing, mirroring him with hands on my hips, suddenly energized by a new surge of righteousness. "And for all your anti-American videos!" I added triumphantly.

"*Anti*-American?" He turned a shade paler. I could see his rage turning to bafflement. "I'm—I'm the one who believes in the goddamned constitution, remember?"

We stood staring at one another like two aliens from separate planets.

My righteousness quickly depleted, I sat back down at the table. The left and right sides of my body felt unrelated and my head felt drained of blood. I watched him through my hair, which had fallen from its ponytail. He was grabbing a paper towel, wiping the tears and snot streaming down his face.

"I can't believe you thought this was a happy month for us," he was saying, "while I've been suffering these fucking headaches!"

"Look . . . maybe you're right," I whispered.

He looked up at me.

"Maybe I shouldn't have done all this. I was just so scared. And so confused. It's been too much. The pregnancy. That next-door baby crying. My sleepwalking. Mom's disappearance. Your worries about your work. I—I needed some help. I thought we both did. I've felt stuck, these past months. Even longer. Like some curse is hanging over me . . . I can't explain . . . I want to move forward, Shiro, I really do, more than anything, but I just don't know how."

I wanted to say more, or at least to feel more—to cry, laugh, scream, collapse—but I just sat there. He turned away and held up a hand.

"Stop," he said. "Just stop."

I watched his back rise and fall as he leaned into the counter.

"It's so ironic, Jane. You try to suppress all negativity. But in the end, you just create it. You do need help. Serious help."

He turned to me and gave a strange cross between a grimace and a smile.

"Before? I was so here with you to get that help. All of me was here with you. All of me. But this is too much. You've crossed a line."

"Maybe I *am* crazy."

"Ya think?" he snapped.

He took several deep breaths, as though summoning the strength to continue, then straightened his shoulders and looked at me with a mix of love, hate, and mostly pity.

"You know it's over between us, right?"

"Shiro, please—"

"No." He held up a hand again. "It's over. But listen." He took a step toward me, his tone softer, almost loving. "No matter what, I promise you, here and now, to be a good dad to our Little One. Okay? Just promise me this: you'll take good care of him, or her, too. Okay? Can I trust you with that?" He took a step closer. "Being a good mother to our kid? Can I?" he implored, his eyes bright with tears.

"Of course," I whispered. "Of course you can."

He pointed to his laptop. "Watch, if you want. But I know that's not your MO. God forbid we have any self-awareness around here."

With that, he marched to the bedroom.

I looked at the dark screen and waited a few moments before touching the track pad. The screen lit up with an image of our kitchen. At first I thought the image was paused, and I was about to close the computer, but then someone walked on-screen. It took me a second to recognize myself.

My hair pulled into a sloppy ponytail, I open the cupboard, bring down Shiro's cereal box, a bowl, and a glass. The camera seems set on the wall beneath the cupboard, so it captures me up close. My face blank, my movements swift and methodical, I shake a large mound of cereal into the bowl, open the refrigerator, grab the milk, let the door swing shut, fill the glass with milk, and set it on the counter beside the bowl.

"Shiro?" I call, glancing away from the camera.

Hearing my own voice startled me. It felt as if the real me was trapped in the kitchen on the screen, and I—the me here on the outside—was an impostor.

The me-on-screen turns back to the counter, facing me-the-impostor, and begins to fiddle with something small in my hands.

I reached for the computer, found the file location, closed the file, opened the finder, found the filename, selected it and other files with similar names, dragged them all to the trash, emptied the trash, and slammed the machine shut.

FORTY-FOUR

The next few weeks are still a blur. I couldn't stand being in the apartment anymore, surrounded by the empty spaces where all of Shiro's things had been—especially the circles of dirt marking the spots where his plants had once lived. It turns out, when taken altogether, I *did* notice them. I missed them greatly.

So, most nights I stayed at your grandpa's place, on an air mattress on the floor of my childhood bedroom, now his cluttered office.

At first I couldn't get in touch with your dad at all. He wasn't answering my calls or texts. I desperately wanted to talk to him, to work things out, to try and understand what had gone so wrong. I swung back and forth between being furious and devastated that he wouldn't talk to me.

One afternoon, after almost three weeks of not hearing a word from him, having just found a new place to sublet, I returned to the apartment to collect the rest of my things. Most of the furniture, except the bed and my dresser, had belonged to Shiro, so the place felt hollow and barren. Thankfully, it was silent.

I've always been a minimalist in terms of stuff, so it didn't take long to pack. When I'd finished, I remembered my old childhood boxes up in the attic. I hadn't been up there since the day I sleepwalked and saw—or thought I saw—those monsters. And Mom.

Quite nervously, I set up the ladder in the bedroom closet and climbed up. I spotted them in the dark right away.

Several objects were still strewn across the floor where I'd left them amidst their newspaper wrapping that day. Holding my breath against the sulfuric stench, moving as quickly as possible while avoiding mouse-traps, willing myself not to have any encounters with supernatural visions, I thrust everything back into its box and carried the boxes, one at a time, down the ladder and into the living room.

Three boxes contained items from my own past that at one time had meant something to me. I shoved these aside.

The remaining two had been given to me by Aunt Michi when I was about ten, during one of her rare visits to our house in Albany. She'd given them to me discreetly, telling me to be careful with them, and not to show them to Mom, who hated things from the past and might destroy them. But I'd never taken the time to look inside—at least not when I was awake. There was always a certain ominousness about them. I felt the same way now.

Shiro was right, I did deny and suppress everything negative, or at all threatening to me. If there was any hope of changing that, and of saving our relationship, I needed to start turning that around. I forced myself to look inside the nearest box.

I found what appeared to be some of Mom's old things, including school yearbooks, photo albums, some loose photos, letters, a pair of silk scarves, and that little boat. It was lighter than I remembered, probably made from driftwood.

I lifted a photo and studied it: faded, frayed at the edges, a young girl with bangs stands in front of a tall building, holding a suitcase with both hands, looking straight at me with startled eyes.

I sat on the floor, picked up my phone and called Mom.

When, as expected, it went straight to voicemail, I hung up and found myself calling Aunt Michi. Though I hadn't spoken with her in nearly a decade, her contact information was in my phone. As the phone rang, I wondered nervously if she would even remember me.

"Hello?" A voice similar to Mom's, but older, softer, answered.

"Oh, Aunt Michi. Hi there. It's me, Jane . . . you know, your niece; Sumi's daughter—"

"Yeah, yeah, hi, Aki. Everything okay up there?" she asked naturally, as though we spoke regularly. She was the only one, aside from Bachan, who'd never called me by my new name.

"Yeah, everything's fine. I'm just calling to say hi . . ." My cheeks flushed. I suddenly felt ridiculous to be calling her so out of the blue like this. "Long time no talk."

"It's good to hear your voice, Aki."

"Good to hear yours, too. Jane. I go by Jane now."

"Oh, right, sorry. *Jane.*" It sounded funny on her voice. "Everything okay up there?"

"Oh, yeah, everything's fine," I repeated, trying to make my voice cheerful. It seemed we might go on with this circular conversation forever.

"How's Sumi doing?"

"Mom? Oh, she's okay, I think."

"Are you coming down for a visit?"

"A visit? Oh, no, no. That is, that would really be nice, but . . . actually, the reason I'm calling, Aunt Michi is . . . remember those boxes you gave me?"

"Boxes?"

"You know, those old boxes. Of Mom's old things—"

"Oh, sure, the boxes. The ones I gave you. Sure, I remember. What about them?"

"Well, I'm just looking at them now. For the first time."

"Oh, really? You never looked in them before?"

"No, not exactly," I stammered. "I was always . . . for some reason I was always a little scared to." I laughed. "But I thought maybe you could explain some of the things I'm seeing. For instance, there's a photo of a little girl, I'm guessing it's Mom? Standing in front of a tall building—"

"Oh, yeah, that was the old hotel. I took it with Papa's camera the morning we left for the assembly center. There was a fire in our bathroom that morning, but luckily no one was hurt."

"A fire? Huh. Interesting. And there's a little toy boat here." I returned the photo to the box and lifted the boat, running my finger along its smooth, honey-gold grain.

"Oh yeah, yeah, the boat. Your mom's favorite toy—she carried it everywhere. Papa carved it for her before Camp, but she snuck it with us—good thing she did, 'cause it ended up being his last carving. When the baby came, she shared it with him—your namesake. That's why I thought it was fitting you should have it."

"Now . . . how did he die, exactly? The baby?"

There was a pause.

"I thought I told you that story already?"

"I don't think you ever finished it. I mean, you don't have to tell me now if you don't want—"

"No, no, now's okay."

There was another pause. I pictured her walking to a chair in her kitchen and settling herself into it, or maybe to the stove where she was stirring one of her jams.

"Well, it's a sad story, Aki. You sure you want to hear it?"

"Jane," I corrected, clutching the boat to my chest. "And yes, I think I should."

"Right, right, *Jane, Jane,*" she strained, as though the name were difficult for her to pronounce. "Yeah, well, so, it happened not long after we arrived at Camp, I don't know, maybe a month or so. It was during the middle of the day, when me and your mom were at the new school they'd just built for us. Everything was built so fast, just quick, temporary structures. I remember it was hot that day. Tak was working his shift at the mess hall—this was before he went off to fight in Europe . . ."

I was surprised by how easily she slipped into telling this story, which made me think it must never be too far from her mind.

"Your mom—she was just five or six years old—she insisted on leaving school early. She'd get these feelings sometimes, I don't know, like premonitions or something. So, I said, okay fine, I'll go back with you. I can still remember that sun shining down on us, burning my skin.

"But when we got there, our barrack was empty. So, I said we should go back to school, not get ourselves in trouble. But your mom, she was so stubborn. So, I said, okay fine, I'll go back alone, you can keep looking for Mama and Aki if you want. I still don't know what she saw when she found them. But she was never the same after that."

"Wow . . . so she was the one who found him?" I asked.

"Yeah, your mom did, yeah."

"No wonder she's so . . . I mean, that's horrible."

"Yeah, me and Tak, we told our neighbors on our block the baby died in its sleep. Of course babies died more often back then, so no questions were asked. And, I mean, you should have seen him, such a tiny, malnourished thing—so no one was too surprised. We said we had our own little private ceremony by the river—said we cremated the body. But really, there was no ceremony, no nothing. We stopped celebrating Obon. It's like he was erased."

"So . . . what do you think Mom saw that day, Aunt Michi? When she found them?"

My phone began to vibrate. Shiro was finally returning my calls. My heart leaped to my throat.

"Oh, you know what, Aunt Michi, I'm getting an important call. I want to hear more, but I'll call you back in a few minutes—"

"Oh, okay. You're sure you're okay up there, Aki?"

"Yes, I'm fine. It's just, I was going through those boxes and . . . sorry to rush off like this—"

"'Cause you know, I keep calling Sumi, and she never returns my—"

"Yeah, Mom's terrible at keeping in touch," I hurried, standing, panicking that I might miss Shiro and not be able to reach him again. "Are you on Facebook? That's the best way to communicate with her these days."

"Oh, well, okay, talk to you soon—"

"Yes, thanks, goodbye!"

I hung up before I could hear her response, switching over to Shiro.

"Shiro, thank god."

"Hi, Jane."

"How are you?"

"I'm just fine, thanks. You?" His tone was crisp and formal.

"I've really been needing to talk to you . . ." My heart was pumping full force in my throat. I looked at the little toy boat in my hand, so perky and hopeful.

"Sorry. I just needed some space. I hope you can understand."

"Of course. Maybe it's good, because . . ." I began pacing the echoing floors of the empty apartment, clutching the boat to my chest. "Shiro, I've been doing a lot of soul-searching since you left. I know it sounds like just a coincidence, or like some lame excuse, but . . . I actually just got off the phone with my aunt Michi now, and . . . it's hard to explain over the phone, but I think I'm finally starting to understand some things about my family, and myself, that I could never really figure out before. I mean, not that I have everything figured out yet, of course not, but I think I'm finally ready to . . . look at a few things I was too scared to look at before. More closely. Get my head out of the sand and really face some of the things I've been hiding from."

"That's really great, Jane. I'm happy for you."

I'm not sure what I expected, but my heart sank at his coldness.

"Yeah, well, what I'm saying is . . . and why it relates to *us* is . . . I want to work things out. Together. Shiro . . . I think I'm finally ready to."

He didn't say anything.

"Maybe it's not too late for us. We could go to a couple's therapist together—"

"No, Jane," he said firmly. "It is too late. There's absolutely no way. You broke my trust. I'm sorry, but I'm already moving on." I could hear the definitiveness in his voice.

"Are you a hundred percent sure about this?" I asked anyway, my heart breaking.

"Yes. I'm sure. One hundred percent."

I'm not sure how the conversation ended.

When we hung up, I saw Aunt Michi was calling me back. But I had no more desire to talk to her, no desire to hear her voice ever again, no desire to hear another word of that haunting story. All my fears about motherhood came flooding back. I dropped the boat. As if in response, the absence at my center jumped out of its container and began to swell, larger than ever.

FORTY-FIVE

Your dad and I first met at a party. For some reason I was attracted to his intense, brooding expression as I watched him talking with someone across the room. A few minutes later, he walked right up to me and introduced himself.

I should explain. When your dad smiles, his face transforms to this celebratory network of dimples, like a ridiculously happy old man or baby, or one of those wrinkle-faced shar-pei dogs. He performed this trick for me and that was it—I was hooked.

"*Jane*," he repeated with a note of condescension. "Funny, you don't look like a *Jane*."

"Actually, my real name is Akiko."

I'd shocked myself; normally I never told people my Japanese name—in fact I had an aversion to speaking it.

"Ah, I *thought* you were Japanese." Now he surprised me; no one ever thinks I look Japanese, especially not Japanese people. In fact, people often look me over skeptically if I reveal my background.

"Akiko," he repeated a couple times. Something in me had stirred, hearing the name on his voice. "I like it," he announced. "It suits you. Aki. You should go by that."

I laughed, blushing. "Yeah, well, maybe I will one day . . . but I'm pretty used to Jane by now. Oh well."

We chatted on a bit more about nothing much, then the wave of the party pulled us away from each other, but before he left he asked for my number and called the next day. We met at a café and had one of those conversations where everything sparks with synchronicity. He touched the back of my hand as we said goodbye and I remember feeling as though he had planted a seed there that would keep growing forever. When we had sex the first several times, it felt as though two lost halves of some cosmic force had at last found each other—I know that sounds silly, but it's true.

When, a few weeks later, we realized our families had both been interned at the same relocation center during the war, Shiro said, "See? That clinches it. It's fate. And I'm not a fate kinda guy." He said it half-jokingly, but I think he meant it.

Still later, we realized the coincidence was even more uncanny: our families had not only been interned at the same Camp—the farthest from the west coast—but Pops and Mom had been housed in the same block. Block Seventeen. I'd had no idea about the layout of Camp until then, but apparently the living quarters had been organized into clusters, like little neighborhoods.

Even to me, there did seem to be some special significance about this unlikely connection. Maybe even—though this is probably just hindsight speaking, or the effect of being here at this old farm—a feeling that our happiness together in the present might, in some way, help to restore something lost in the past.

How ironic: Camp, the root of both our paranoia—and his obsession with injustice and my obsessive denial of it—first bonded, then broke us.

In any case, within a couple of months we were looking for an apartment together, already hatching fantasies, picturing our house, our garden, our kids.

Shiro had dated mostly Asian girls before me, from what I could tell from his sparse remarks on the subject. I was his first hapa girlfriend.

Mom had been surprised when I'd told her his name.

"Shiro?" she'd asked. "That sounds Japanese."

"It is."

"Really? You're dating a Japanese?" It sounded like she was referring to a species, like a cat or a unicorn.

"I guess you could say so."

"Both his parents are Japanese?"

"Yup. One hundred percent pure-blooded."

"Wow—your first Asian guy, huh?" She herself had dated only white guys—at least after high school, as far as I knew.

I hadn't been sure if she'd meant the first Asian guy I'd dated, kissed, or slept with, but decided to keep it simple. "Yup."

"Are his parents American?"

"I think so. I mean, yeah. Oh, his family was at the same Camp as you, actually. Funny coincidence, eh?"

"Really? *Rohwer?*" she'd asked in disbelief.

"That's what he said, yeah. I wonder if you might have known them? Yamamoto's the name."

"Oh, god, I'm sure no—there were tons of people there, and anyway, I don't have any memories from then."

"None? You used to have a few."

"Yes, well, not anymore. You're sure his family was at *Rohwer?*"

"That's what he said."

"Huh. So, is he sansei or yonsei?"

"I don't know. That wasn't something he just so happened to mention over burritos."

"Probably yonsei—most people your age are yonsei. So, what's he like? Is he cute?" She'd sounded mystified.

"Very. But don't get too excited; we only just started seeing each other. You might never meet him."

"Okay, okay—well this'll be interesting. It's just such a weird coincidence."

FORTY-SIX

The day after the procedure, I left Shiro a voicemail, saying I needed to talk to him in person, immediately. He returned my call and said he'd meet me in the garage of the apartment.

"Look, Jane, I don't want you to think I'll only remember the bad," he said when we met in the late afternoon shadows of the garage. His tone was softer than it had been on the phone, more like his regular self. "There's been plenty of good. Some amazing good."

"Our intense chemistry."

"Yeah, that was pretty amazing, all right." He flashed me the ghost of his killer grin. "For a while."

"And we do have things in common. We're like two parts of a whole, in some ways."

"Yeah, but we're opposite, too. It would never have worked for too long."

I swallowed this painful jab, nodding slightly to feign agreement.

"So, how's work going?"

"I've given my notice."

"Oh. Good for you. Hey, Shiro. I'm sorry about my sleepwalking. And all the trouble I caused . . ."

There was an awkward pause, both of us kicking at the ground.

"Yeah, well . . . I'm sorry for my parts, too. I guess we're all sleepwalking in one way or another, aren't we?" he finally said with a defeated sort of chuckle.

"I guess it's goodbye to all those plans, then," I said.

"Yeah. The house. The garden."

"The kids."

"Well—" He half smiled, then looked confused by what must have been my disturbing expression.

"Not anymore."

"Not anymore?" He tilted his head.

That's when I told him about the procedure. I'd gotten it the day before. Since I was in my second trimester, they'd had to do it surgically. I'd wanted general anesthesia so I wouldn't have to endure the event consciously, but they'd only given me local. They apologized for this afterward, because there were some minor complications, and it took longer than expected. They never told me exactly what was happening, and I was so light-headed it was difficult to focus on their words, but I do remember numb, disembodied sensations, and at one point the doctor saying something like, "persistent tissue . . . unusually tenacious . . ."

Even with these complications, the procedure took less than an hour and they sent me on my way shortly afterward.

"Oh, and Shiro . . . you were right. I thought you'd want to know . . . it was a boy. He was a boy."

We stood there not speaking for some time.

"It was a routine procedure. People do it all the time," I eventually said, I suppose attempting to lift our spirits. "It was a little later than normal, but not much. It was relatively painless. At least you can publish your exposé about your work now," I plowed on with militant cheerfulness. "You can be that hero you always wanted to be. But . . . still be careful, okay? I don't want you to end up in prison or anything." I let out a quick chuckle.

He looked at me with amazement, wiping away tears.

"Wow, Jane. You erase *everything*, don't you? Every. Fucking. Thing."

He turned and walked to a corner of the garage. At first it seemed he was planning on exiting through some secret door hidden in the dark. But then he emerged back into the light, holding up that pair of antlers—I hadn't realized they were still there—one in each hand. Carving their way skyward in a majestic, gravity-defying stunt, they reminded me of inverted plant roots. He carried them around Junior, holding them high, as though planting them into his head, looking like a mythical, wild prince. He opened the trunk, lay them carefully inside, slammed it shut, got into the car, and drove away.

"Shiro!" I called out from the dark as he disappeared into the sun.

FORTY-SEVEN

I returned upstairs to the apartment. I hadn't been back since the procedure.

The heat was hissing away from behind its metal Band-Aid in the ceiling and the next-door baby was shrieking its head off again, its cries louder, more violent than ever, so high-pitched and piercing I felt them cutting into my bones.

Had my medication stopped working? Had the procedure awoken something?

After hardly hearing the cries for months, having settled into the comforting belief that they now belonged to the past, they filled me with unbearable demoralization and dread.

Who the hell's baby was this?

Was it you, Little One?

Were you refusing to leave this world without a fight? If so, I admire your tenacity!

Was it the ghost of my baby uncle? Was he angry not only about his own fate, but now about what I'd done to you?

Was it *myself*?

Fists clenched, body shaking, I resolved to stop the cries forever.

I still don't know exactly what possessed me to do what I did next.

The boxes and the driftwood boat were still on the floor, at the center of the living room, where I'd left them the day I talked to Aunt Michi. I hurriedly carried them into the bathroom, Mom's voice darting around in my head like a frantic, caged bird: *Future! Future!*

Setting the boat on the floor beside me, I tossed everything else into the bathtub. As I went through these motions, I felt as though I wasn't alone, but that someone else, or perhaps multiple entities, were now joining me in this ritual. And not just multiple entities, but multiple moments, as though Time had tucked itself under my skin and was now careening forward at reckless speed, with no care for objects in our wake or other random effects, propelled by some violent wind from the past. There was a sense of freedom in this crowded, hurdling-forward sensation. As I tossed things into the tub I—or should I say we?—could practically feel the wind on my cheeks.

Folded neatly at the bottom of the last box was a kimono. Resisting the urge to throw it immediately into the tub, I lifted it, allowing the fabric to fall to the floor. Its hand-stitches were perfect, obviously made by skilled, loving hands; its bright, lush colors—forest green, lilac purple, cherry blossom pink—looked only slightly faded from what must have been their original shades. I breathed in its musty, vaguely sandalwood smell before tossing it onto the heap.

Finally, I lifted the toy boat.

The girl crouches behind a large cypress tree growing from the mud, clutching her boat to her chest. She knows the blue demon wants it; this is the last piece of her it hasn't yet managed to steal.

I placed it at the top of the pile. It looked small yet proud, balanced at the peak of the heap, as if crying, "Look, Mommy, no hands!"

She fears that without this boat, there will be no hope of finding her brother, or her father, or perhaps even herself, ever again

The crowded, flying-forward feeling intensifying, I ripped up the empty cardboard boxes, tucked the pieces amidst the objects in the pile, crumpled the newspaper wrappings, scattered them about the tub, ran to the kitchen, grabbed a lighter, returned to the bathroom, and lit the fire.

How long has she been hiding here with it? Hours? Days? Decades? She can't say. All she knows is that her fingers ache from grasping it for so long

At first it kept fizzling out, little puffs of smoke rising lazily to the ceiling. I had to light the cardboard several times, in several places, blowing on the flames and finally vigorously fanning them with a magazine, to get them going.

She peeks from behind the tree to see the blue figure moving toward her through the cattails, its impossibly long, crooked shadow slicing the lacy mist

The kimono was first to take, the bright colors fast fading to brown, black, disintegrating to ash. The letters, yearbooks, photo albums, and scarves quickly followed, crumpling, crackling, blackening. Flames danced around the tub, staining the sides like fresh bruises.

glaring eyes burning holes through the tree trunk

Only Jichan's carving resisted. The flames lapped harmlessly, almost playfully, at the boat's smooth, rounded surface. I admired its unlikely strength.

warming the boat in her hands

But soon, as the laws of nature would have it, smoke curled from underneath, like ocean waves, and the wood gave way.

She smells smoke

I imagined the boat was on its last voyage.

The boat ignites, flames bursting through her fingers

As the boat disappeared, I closed my eyes, relieved.

She begins to sob—but along with her pain and sadness is also relief . . .

Just then a painful cramp jolted me at my center. I stumbled away from the tub and felt something cool trickling down my leg. I looked down to see several drops of blood blossoming on the bathroom floor.

The smoke alarm sounded. Gagging on the smoke, clutching my center, I staggered down the hall and into the bedroom. Waving my arms around in vain, coughing, I climbed up onto the dresser and, my arms shaking so much I could barely do it, disabled the alarm. Then I scrambled back down, thrust open the large window, and crawled out onto the fire escape.

Clutching the iron railing, head pitched toward the sidewalk, a gaping, scraping-against-stone emptiness where you once lived in me, I tried not asking myself the question:

What have I done?

Please try to understand, Little One: how could I have gone through with it—with you—things being the way they were?

I was far too confused, too distraught, to be a good mother, or anything at all close.

Imagine me, a single mom, especially then, with no job, my sleepwalking still unresolved, and still being haunted by that baby . . . and Mom's disappearance . . . and always having to interact with Shiro while he'd moved on, with who knew who else, always reminding me of all my mistakes and what could have been . . . not to mention his paranoia and relentless anger at the world—even though we'd broken up, this stress would surely have followed us both around . . .

Would I have been able to love you properly?

The worst part of all this, looking back now, is that my most paranoid fear was true: I really *did* inherit some horrible mothering gene.

How do we walk right into the very traps we try so hard to avoid? Is life just cruel, taking some sick pleasure in watching us live out our worst nightmares?

The cramps and shaking and coughing began to subside as I sat on the cold metal of the escape, though my breathing was still strained and my chest burned. The crowded, hurdling-forward feeling was gone—instead, I felt utterly alone and still. A lone speck floating in stagnant space.

I had the sickening thought that perhaps I had made an enormous, irreversible mistake—that my fate, and yours too, had been sealed not only by the procedure, but now, more cosmically, and perhaps eternally, by this fire.

I stayed out there on the escape for quite some time, watching the sky grow dark, my chest and pelvis dully aching, terrified of going back inside the apartment.

My only consolation was that when at last I crawled back in through the window—and I can't express the degree of relief I felt at this—it was blissfully silent.

A pure, thorough silence.

I collapsed onto the bed and slept for more than twelve hours, as though I'd climbed inside the silence and into some ancient, subterranean slumber chamber.

When I finally woke, sunlight from the open window warming my face, I looked over at the dresser. And guess what I saw, crumpled into a little ball, looking like a cheerful clutch of baby chicks in the morning light? That monstrous pair of yellow booties I knit for you. The ones I could never get right. They seemed to be laughing at me as they lay there in the sunlight, amused by my failure—like a gift sent from some demon to taunt me.

FORTY-EIGHT

About a month later, your grandmother and I had lunch over Skype. I was doing a bit better by then, having fully recovered from the procedure, and was settling into my new sublet.

It was nice to finally see and talk to her in real time. Her hair was styled the way she'd worn it years ago, in a short pageboy cut, bangs cut in a high fringe across her forehead, making her look even more youthful than when I'd last seen her. The few wrinkles I remembered her having were invisible, at least on my screen; her antiaging products seemed not only to be slowing her aging process, but reversing it—unless she was using some filter on her computer camera to airbrush herself. She wore a dark blouse and matching scarf tied around her throat.

She was eating from a large bowl of noodles and seemed to be in some type of enclosed food court or mall. A steady flow of people streamed by behind her head, and I could hear muffled background noises. But it was difficult to ascertain much about the specifics of the place.

First she chatted nonchalantly about this and that—Texas, Chris and his kids, an upcoming trip to China. Things I already knew from her recent posts. At one point I interrupted to ask if she had ever received my letter, the one I'd mailed through the postal system. She said she hadn't, that she handled all her business online nowadays and never bothered sifting through the piles of paper junk. Any time she made excuses about her lack of presence in the physical world, I found myself nodding quickly, feeling we were both uncomfortable with the truth, whatever that was, and eager to take part in the deception.

"Why, was it something important, sweetie?"

"No, nothing really. Anyway, it doesn't matter now," I reassured.

I longed to tell her about you—how I'd fantasized about her meeting you, holding you, walking together with you along a beach or in a park—and about the procedure. But I pictured my words floating from my lips to the computer, popping lightly against the screen. Even if they did reach her, wherever she was, I felt certain she wouldn't have really understood them. And what would have been the point of burdening her with such depressing news now?

"Oh, excuse me a sec, I have to take this," she said, turning sideways and touching her ear, though I didn't detect any Bluetooth.

I was sitting at the kitchen table in my new sublet, having an uninspired tuna fish sandwich. I nibbled at it as she spoke in soft tones to someone else.

"Sorry, where were we?" she eventually asked, turning back to face me.

"Who was that?"

"Oh, no one important," she said, taking a hearty forkful of noodles. The bowl looked to be bottomless. The more she ate, the more seemed to appear. My mouth watered.

"Those noodles look great. But why are you eating them with a fork? I've always seen you eat noodles with chopsticks."

"Oh, I know, but they only have forks here."

"Are you at a restaurant?"

"I just love this place—you'll have to try it sometime!"

Just then her face blinked on and off the screen and her voice stuttered. Then she was frozen, her lips pursed around a noodle, eyes half closed. Geometric patches of light and shadow divided her face and neck, making her look like a cubist painting. I minimized her image and futzed with my internet connection, closing obnoxious pop-up ads offering me dating services, vacation deals, kitchen appliances, and other random things.

Then she was back.

"Oh, good—so where were we?" she asked again, shoveling another forkful of noodles into her mouth.

"I don't remember. What about your condo? Any news on the foreclosure?"

"Oh, god, believe me, I'm glad to lose it. I don't want to be tied down anywhere anymore. I'm through with all that. Now I can literally go wherever I want!" she chirped, dabbing at her lips with a napkin. "I'm *free*!"

She paused, her eyes flitting about. "So, you know, Jane . . ." She poked her fork into her noodles. "I'm not sure how to say this, but . . . I guess it's best to be honest, right? After all, you're my daughter." She laughed, embarrassed.

"Of course I want you to be honest with me, Mom. Always."

"Well, it's about your breakup with Shiro—I know that must have been so disappointing for you. At first I really thought you and he were made for each other—you just seemed perfect, like a match made by, I don't know, heaven or something. But then . . . he had that other side, too—that darkness." Her eyes narrowed. "That intensity, you know? Way too dark. All that negativity." She shuddered. "And paranoia. No," she said, shaking her head, "that's impossible to live with. Trust me.

"And I don't mean to be *racist* or anything," she continued in a loud whisper, "but men of color can be like that: so angry all the time. *Resentful*, you know? Even Asian guys, in their own way—usually they never talk about it, but sometimes they can't stop. It can be maddening—*relentless*." She shuddered again. "Like Shiro—he'd just get into that political rant, you know? That nonstop litany of complaints, this and that, broken promises, stolen land, forgotten lives, da-da-da—I mean, at a certain point you just have to move on, you know?"

"Look at me!" She straightened her spine proudly. "You don't see me dwelling on the past, do you?"

I opened my mouth to speak, but she went on.

"Plus, you know, Japanese American men specifically, they have so many heart problems. Just look at Papa, Tak, Uncle Billy, that lady's husband, what were their names again . . . anyway, my point is, they all die so young. It's so sad. I don't know what it is, exactly . . ."

"So, what, only date privileged white guys?" I asked in disbelief. "Is that what you're saying? Less *stressful*? How racist!"

"Oh, really, Jane," she scolded, rolling her eyes and clicking her tongue at me. "I didn't say that. You've always had a knack for making things sound so much worse than they are. Anyway, all I'm saying is, your dad and I are both relieved about Shiro. As much as we thought he was a sweetheart—I mean, the man loved you from here to the moon—we really think this is best for you. You'll be happier, you'll see."

"Right. I think so, too—"

"Just think how Bachan and Jichan must have felt when they left Japan . . ." She took another bite of her noodles. I waited as she chewed thoughtfully.

"I mean," she continued, swallowing, "each of them alone on a big boat, just teenagers, leaving their families and homeland and everything they knew, sailing across the Pacific Ocean, sacrificing their pasts for a brighter future . . ." She looked up as she spoke, as though looking at a screen featuring a romantic film about the hardships and triumphs of immigrants. "They must surely have thought their lives were over." She looked back at me, her eyes widening at the optimistic ending of the film. "And they were—their old lives, that is. But they kept their eyes on the future, no matter what. Only the future! They had us kids, started a business, da-da-da, I had you—the rest is history!"

She smiled with satisfaction, as though wrapping something up in bright-red cellophane.

"Right," I said.

"All I'm saying is, there's still plenty of history ahead." She raised up a forkful of noodles as though proposing a toast. "Forget the past, Jane. Really, just say goodbye and don't look back—everything's changing so quickly, anyway; we're practically a new species. *A brand-new species!*" She looked delighted at the prospect.

"Definitely." I looked down at the two remaining pieces of ice melting at the bottom of my glass.

"Remember Shiro's strange, silly videos?" she asked. "Is he still making those, do you think?"

The last video of your dad's I'd seen was melodramatic and nonsensical, like all of his art. But it had also been oddly moving. I'd found it on YouTube late one night, not long after he left.

It opens on a highway out in nature, apparently shot from inside a car, redwood trees whizzing past—I soon recognized it to be Sir Francis Drake Boulevard—then cuts to a pan from a clear blue sky to the tops of the giant trees, sunlight filtering through the branches in long rays, leaves gently wavering, to the dirt shoulder of a road, to a pair of fallen antlers. They seemed smaller, more lackluster than I remembered, lying there just the way they had been that night, only now in daylight, dwarfed by the gigantic redwoods.

The camera closes in on them as flies swirl around, every so often landing on one. We hear the sounds of nature: birds cawing, leaves rustling, the babble of a creek. Every now and then a car zooms by. A barely audible electronic beat begins, accompanied by the sparse, wandering notes of an electric guitar. From off-screen we hear a man's voice, at first too low to be understood, then we make out his words: "Hearts were broken. Hearts were broken." This phrase repeats as the camera moves closer in on the antlers, until we see their wood-like grain. The voice sounds like Pops from that old PBS special, but it's slightly distorted, so I can't tell if it's his or Shiro's.

Superimposed over the antlers comes the image of a man—Shiro—standing on the road, facing profile to the camera. He's dressed simply, in a white T-shirt and jeans. He stands there for some time, the electronic beat and guitar building. Then he begins, almost imperceptibly at first, to bend forward, his head bowing, shoulders slumping, spine curling, hips flexing—it looks like he might be falling asleep or crying or simply deflating—until he's bent in two. He continues to descend, eventually crumpling to his hands and knees, now looking like a man praying, or searching for something. He keeps falling until finally his body is prone, now looking like a dead, empty man. This image fades and we're left with just the antlers and the road.

"Navigational specificity became unclear," the voice says.

The camera zooms in so close on the antlers that they disappear and a dreamlike, psychedelic explosion fills the screen, then a blinding flash of white, fast fading to burnt sepia tones, saturated reds and golds, perhaps an enhanced sunset on the horizon, melting to brown, black, degenerating to static.

Today I remember these details clearly, but that day, my memory of the video was hazy. I paused, straining to recall even one or two images from it, or at least what I had found moving.

"Jane?" Mom was leaning into the camera, waving something—maybe her napkin. "Jane, are you still there? Something wrong?"

"Oh, yes. No. It's just . . . I've been really worried about you, is all."

"Worried? About *me*? What on earth for?"

I suddenly felt like a small child.

She leaned closer into the camera, making her nose look huge. "My goodness, Jane, are you okay? You look like you're shaking."

I put my sandwich down. "I guess I am, a little."

"Jeez, you've gotten so thin. Look at your arms—you're emaciated! Oh, god, I'm the world's worst mother, aren't I?" she asked softly.

"No, no, Mom, it's okay—"

She sat back in her chair and looked down, clutching her upper arms. For a moment I thought she had frozen again. But then she looked up.

"I always knew it," she said so softly I could barely hear her. "That's why I never wanted kids. You know you were an accident, right?"

She paused, and I thought she might change the subject, but then she gave a short gasp and continued.

"Oh, not to say I didn't want you—not at all, Aki. Meeting you was the happiest moment of my life. You were my everything . . . my heart's delight . . . I never . . . things are just so complicated . . ."

She turned away from the camera. "Chris is lucky I'm just his step-mom. But you—"

"I'm actually doing really well now, Mom," I rushed to assure her, attempting to rescue us both from this painful, horribly awkward moment. "I've made some new friends recently. You know I'm on Facebook and stuff now. Don't worry, I'm actually doing really well!"

But she didn't respond. She just sat there, profile to the camera.

Then suddenly the image of her and her noodles at the food court disappeared.

She now appeared, from what I could tell, to be in a dark, cramped space. Her face was turned toward me and glowed a faint blue. It seemed perhaps her computer was her only light source. This lighting was dimmer yet harsher, far less flattering, and I could see crinkly lines around her forehead, eyes, and mouth; she looked much older than she had a few seconds ago, and extremely tired. Her head and shoulders were scrunched forward, as though the ceiling and walls of the space were pressing in on her. Her mouth was open, but no sound came. I thought this might be a still image, but then she blinked and, a moment later, I noticed a tear rolling down her cheek.

Seeing her in this cramped, boxlike space, I immediately thought of the storage closet at the back of my high school gymnasium, where sometimes I was assigned to put away balls. One day my freshman year, after the first volleyball game of the season, I accidentally locked myself in there, the heavy metal door slamming shut behind me. I'd panicked and shouted frantically, banging on the door, nearly hyperventilating, until finally someone heard me. It had been the most terrifying hour of my life. Unless you count my very first memory. Ever since then, I've had a fear of industrial storage spaces.

That's funny, now I remember—that was that same day Mom came to watch my game, sporting her sunglasses, inappropriate black dress, and fake fur cloak, slipping out as silently as she'd come. That's why I returned home early that day to find her gone; I'd been so shaken from being locked up in that stifling storage space.

Just as quickly as it came, the view of Mom in that dim, cramped space vanished. She swiped a finger across her cheek, perhaps to wipe her tear, and all at once her earlier environment returned: table, noodles, people walking behind her in a steady, casual flow, muffled background noises—she was sitting at the table, cheerful and youthful again.

"Where are you?" I asked.

Such a simple question—I wonder why I'd never thought to ask her this before?

She answered me as she pulled a compact from her purse and began powdering her cheeks—something or other about Texas and being on her way to China, maybe. But I found myself unable to hear her words. As her lips moved, I was struck by the stark realization that Shiro had been right; she had finally managed to escape. She had transformed herself into a weightless, digitized version of her old self, and now seemed to be operating from this new, convenient, ever-elusive, ever-adaptable, postphysical state, untethered to any earthly, physical burdens.

But what holding cell was her actual body in?

And who held the key?

And what, or who, ultimately controlled her new operating system?

Had she purposefully shown me that dim, cramped space, as some sort of cryptic cry for help? Or had that been an accidental glitch in her otherwise perfect, airbrushed facade?

Or had I just imagined it?

I took a deep breath, resigning myself to the fact that I'd probably never know the answers to these questions.

As though hearing my thoughts, she paused her speaking and powdering. "Oh, don't worry so much, Jane—you really worry way too much! It reminds me of when you were a girl, how you'd always bring up your first memory. Remember that? It was such a random, morbid memory to obsess about, being locked inside a car. And to this day I'm not even sure it ever *happened.* I couldn't understand why you'd bring it up all the time . . .

"But no, really, I'm so much happier now, Jane—more than ever before, I can't tell you. It's like . . . like . . . someone's finally scooped me up off the bottom of a river and cleared away all the gunk and slime from my skin and lungs and, I don't know, all the little dead fish from my ears!"

I pictured her as that little girl I'd seen in the attic that day, her black hair bouncing on her shoulders as she'd grabbed that toy boat from me and hurried toward a river.

"What about your singing lessons? I never see you posting about those anymore."

"Actually," she said, smiling sheepishly. "I *can* send you a song—if you like."

"Yes, but can't you just sing it now?"

"Here? In front of all these people?"

She shoved her compact back into her purse and quickly typed on her keyboard. "Go ahead, check your inbox. It's a bit embarrassing, so I'm turning my camera off. I don't want to see your reaction when you hear it."

Her face disappeared on my screen as I found the file and opened it.

A lovely, lilting voice emerged from my speaker. I closed my eyes and quickly became lost in its swooping highs and lows, its graceful soaring. Now and then it hung suspended on a single note with such a gently pleading, heart-wrenching trill, I could feel my own chest tremble. I felt I was experiencing both the song and flight of some brightly colored, as-of-yet undiscovered species of bird as it playfully discovered its own talents.

Could this voice really belong to Mom?

It sounded unlike any famous singer I knew of, and I *did* recognize certain aspects of Mom's speaking voice. But I'd never heard her sing before. Perhaps she had digitally manipulated her voice with some type of application. But such technical ingenuity wasn't something I'd expect from her.

The song was "Waltz across Texas," the country classic Dad used to sing around the house when I was a kid. On Sundays, he'd bring out his old albums and fill the house with the yearning, twanging voices of Ernest Tubb, Hank Williams, and Jimmie Rodgers, and he and I would sing along with them, always a tad out of rhythm and off-key. Mom had hated this music and would often abruptly leave to run errands. I was surprised, not only that she was singing so beautifully now, but that she had taken one of Dad's old songs and made it something transcendent, and all her own.

When the last notes had faded, I opened my eyes. She was back on my screen.

"Not bad, eh? I can finally sing again!" She looked so genuinely happy I thought she might cry.

"Wow, Mom. That was beautiful."

We looked at each other for a nervous moment.

"Well, sweetie, I should really run," she said, touching the dark scarf at her throat, the passersby behind her continuing their steady flow. "I'm so glad you're finally online. And I like this, having our lunch dates again, I really do—things feel good again, don't they? Normal, right?"

She bunched her napkin into a ball, dropped it into her bowl of noodles, blew me a kiss, lifted her small white purse from the table, and tucked it under her arm, preparing for her departure.

FORTY-NINE

Maybe as a form of rebellion against my old life with your dad, whenever I'm not ramping up efforts on my job search, I've been immersing myself in social media, rediscovering and catching up with old acquaintances, making new friends, and generally making up for lost time. I hardly remember why I was ever so resistant to joining the whole world blossoming online—it's felt liberating!

Actually, I've started seeing someone, if you can call it that. He's just moved down to the Bay Area from Portland. It's nothing at all serious yet, and so far we've only been on a couple of actual, in-person dates, but we've been messaging and chatting a lot. He seems like a fun, easygoing type of guy, from what I can tell: thirty-seven, nice build, brown hair, computer programmer, into sports. White.

He's not an obsessive newshound, like your dad was. His Twitter posts are all politically benign—in fact I don't believe we've once talked about politics. The subject just hasn't come up. We like most of the same shows, even ones dating back to when we were kids and before. Just the other day we had a blast quizzing each other on plots from *The Brady Bunch* and *The Twilight Zone*. It's a funny phenomenon, being nostalgic with someone about a past we never actually shared.

Simply put, I'm enjoying life more, allowing myself to be entertained and distracted without guilt that I'm burying my head in the sand. I don't know the last time I read a full newspaper article. It's a relief, not being around someone always updating me about how horrible everything is, with so much skepticism about our government and the world—about "the system" being out to get us, rigged by some vague Big Brother.

Yes, life has certainly been more pleasant without your dad.

Now that I'm on Facebook, I can easily keep up with Mom, and though I still haven't seen her in person—times I've physically gone to a place where she's recently "checked-in," I've missed her—this goal is less relevant to me. I've accepted that our relationship has evolved to a new, more fluid realm.

That reminds me, just the other day I was walking downtown, along Broadway, not far from that warehouse where I last saw her, and I actually saw that old claw-foot bathtub. Of course I can't be certain it was the same one, but it was just too much of a coincidence, being so close to where I'd first seen it. It was now featured in the window display of a trendy new shop of some kind—it was unclear what they sold, exactly. A clothesline hung rustically above the tub, displaying vintage aprons. I went into the shop and stood by the window, tempted to step up into the display area and touch the cool porcelain, maybe even climb inside. But that would have come across as eccentric, or worse, to the shopkeeper and other shoppers—and anyway, what would have been the point?

I'm living in a cute, studio-apartment sublet, not too far from our old place, on the same side of the lake. It gets lovely morning light. When I first walked in, I thought of Dr. Sharma and what she'd loved about her old place in London. I've been there several months now. The only problem is, lately I can't cook or sleep well there. Maybe because I know it's just temporary. And because I find myself feeling as though I'm being watched—as though your dad's tiny cameras are still hidden about. When I last tried to prepare myself dinner there, I ended up burning everything. And it's just not as practical to cook for one.

So I've been living like a transient these days as I continue to look for work, without any real place to call home, living off of frozen food and takeout, alternating between staying at the sublet, Dad's place, Topaz's couch, and, occasionally, Airbnb. There's something nice about this, actually—not being pinned down to any one physical location.

And just my bad luck: my new next-door neighbors are, yet again, another woman and her baby. Just when I thought I'd finally rid myself of the others. I was sitting on the couch one day at around sunset, folding laundry, when I first heard the faint cries. Another newborn, it seems from the thin, shrill sound of its voice, still just barely arrived into this world.

But I find myself dreading the day it grows louder. I may have to up the dosage of my medication yet again. No wonder this product has been getting so popular—it really has worked wonders for me. According to the company's website, so many people are finding it helpful for managing stress in today's challenging world. And it's a relief that the old social stigmas about taking such products barely exist anymore.

Sometimes, though, I do wonder if this peace I've been feeling has much depth to it. Is it simply a chemical Band-Aid? If my surface were probed, what would be awaiting me?

No matter how shallow, though, I find this functional, pleasant peace much preferable to any alternative. I never want to see those shadowy demons again.

The product's one shortcoming is that it doesn't help the absence.

At first I thought it did; the amorphous, hole-like feeling would shrink down to a manageable size that could be easily contained. But it's been slipping out of its box again, and once it's free it expands, as unattended negative space will. I have the sense that it won't be happy until it's taken up all of me, becoming an impressively convincing hologram of myself. I often have the sense lately, while laughing or otherwise enjoying a perfectly pleasant moment, that I'm sitting across the room from myself, or even further, observing my own actions.

The absence is affecting my memory, as well. With the exception of today, many past events, even ones I used to hold dear to my heart, seem fainter.

This detachment has a seductive, addictive quality. To live free from the past or the body.

But as I lie here in this creek bed, one hand on my ribs, the other capping the cool tip of a stone, my eyes closed against the sun, I worry I may be starting to disappear.

FIFTY

The girl is standing in line at the mess hall when he appears. A hush falls over the people near her. An older woman gasps and others whisper as they move aside to create a path from her to him across the large, echo chamber of a room.

She knows it's him. He's been permitted to write them letters over the past few months, which she and her siblings crowded around, reading hungrily over each other's shoulders. The letters never said much, just sparse details about the weather, the terrible food, and his cellmates. In his last one, he said he would be joining them within weeks.

But now that he's finally standing here, just feet away from her in the mess hall, she hesitates. Is this really her papa?

Someone nudges her forward; she walks slowly toward him.

He's not wearing his hat. This is the first detail that tells her something is not right. He always wore his hat, set back on his forehead, his thick, wavy hair poking out from beneath. Now, hatless, he looks foreign to her. Smaller. His hair has grown thinner and has a gray streak. The bones in his face are too prominent, and there are dark caves beneath his eyes and cheekbones. His hands hang at his sides, as though disconnected from the rest of him.

When she reaches him, she looks up at his face, searching for the papa she knows—the laughing twinkle in his eyes.

But empty eyes stare back at her.

She's waited for this day for so long, dreamt about it countless nights, wished on stars, grown accustomed to the burning fear in her belly that it would never come—but now that it's here, she feels betrayed. She wants to strike his face, yell out in anger, run from the mess hall, throw things against the walls, perhaps ignite the life back into his eyes in this violent way.

But instead she forces a smile.

"Papa," she says.

"Hello, Sumi-chan. You've grown, haven't you?" His voice is hoarse. His tired face manages a smile.

She pulls the boat from her dress pocket and holds it out to him. She wants to tell him how she's kept this with her since the day he was taken. She wants to explain everything that's happened to them while he's been away—everything she and the boat have seen.

But her father looks down at the carving as though he doesn't recognize it.

Over the next few days, she and her siblings mostly stay away from him, afraid of what they'll find if they get too close. But when she has the chance, she continues to search his eyes.

On the fifth day of his return, it occurs to her: her papa is gone.

More than when he was taken from the hotel, more than when they moved to the racetrack without him, more than when they took the train across the country to this place without him, more than when his letters appeared in the mail room. His body has been delivered back to her, all in one piece, as she had hoped and prayed for, but her papa no longer lives there.

What have they done with him? *she wonders.*

Where is he now?

FIFTY-ONE

About a month ago—the week of my due date for you, oddly enough—I had just finished a job interview and was walking along College Avenue in Berkeley, amidst gaggles of upscale locals and college students, and guess who I saw having lunch at a sidewalk café?

He wasn't alone. Sitting across from him at a table for two was a petite redheaded woman, about my and Shiro's age or maybe a little younger. Her hair was styled in a self-conscious, 1970s, Mary Tyler Moore sort of way, sprouting out the top of her head and swooshing down on either side, lifting up at the ends. She wore a thick, sunflower-yellow headband and matching minidress. The whole get-up was very anime, somewhere between adorable, spooky, and comical.

Shiro looked mostly like his old self, dressed in a T-shirt and shorts, though his hair was longer than his work had allowed him to wear it. Their styles looked incongruous together, like one of those early trick-photography photos of two different fruits miraculously under one skin—a half strawberry–half kiwi under a banana peel.

There was no visible communication between them, and for a moment I thought they were strangers who'd randomly been seated together. But then your dad must have mumbled something, because, without looking up, she handed him the salt. Then he slid something—his pickles, maybe, which I know he hates—onto her plate. She picked one up and ate it. They had the air of an old married couple.

But how could anything like that be remotely possible?

I did the math—we'd broken up at the beginning of February. It was only mid-June. If anything, I'd have expected them to be at the giddy height of their honeymoon. Or maybe they were just friends? I strained to see if there was anything on her ring finger, but of course I was too far away.

Realizing I'd been staring for too long, I thought about crossing the street and saying hi. Maybe meeting the new person in his life would be just what I needed to help me move on. After all, we were all mature thirtysomethings, weren't we? Look at Topaz and Frank. Just last month they had shown up to the same party with their own dates. It had been awkward for a moment, but then the evening had progressed with an air of sophistication, and we'd all been proud of ourselves.

But as I stepped down from the curb, I noticed something about her I hadn't caught from farther back: she was Asian. Her elaborate red hairdo had made me think otherwise, but now I saw she was probably Japanese, or maybe Korean. I'm not sure what it was about her, but she looked to be actually from Asia—maybe it was something about the way she was sitting, or eating, or her meticulous, Tokyo-inspired fashion that made her seem to me distinctly not American.

Unsure why this revelation threw me so strongly, I dislodged my foot from the curb, spun around, and, nearly running into a parking meter, speed-walked in the direction I'd been heading—or maybe the other direction, I have no idea. The world was suddenly a convoluted maze. Passing the restaurants and shops, I told myself it was best this way. Why bug them? It would only be an unpleasant trip backward. And the important thing for all of us now was to focus on moving forward.

Future! Future!

New species, new species!

I made my way back to my sublet and promptly threw up.

FIFTY-TWO

Today's date is July 12, 2012. Not so very special a date, but when I jotted it down at the top of my notes during my job interview this morning, it stuck out to me; I realized it was exactly ten months since my and your dad's last anniversary—or two months from when we would have had our sixth.

I borrowed your grandpa's car for the interview, and afterward, found myself wanting to take advantage of the wheels. I've been feeling restless lately, and the idea of a spontaneous road trip appealed to me. I was out near Tracy and my first instinct was to drive west, maybe across the bay and up to Mount Tam or Point Reyes.

Then my mind went to Sir Francis Drake Boulevard. I hadn't thought about that night in some time.

I wasn't sure why I had the urge to return there now, except maybe for some type of symmetry, what with Shiro having returned there once. Also, I had the nagging thought that something was lost out in the chilly dark that night, and that, without realizing it, I'd been looking for it ever since. For some reason today seemed like the day I might find it.

Perhaps his grandmother's ring. I'd never seen it again after that night. He'd dropped it into his shirt pocket so casually after his proposal to me at the restaurant, and what with all the chaos, it could easily have dropped out as he'd stooped over that deer. Maybe he'd taken the next day off work to return there in order to look for it, and he'd felt too bad about not finding it to tell me. Maybe he'd taken its disappearance as some kind of bad omen—an omen that had snowballed into grandiose paranoia about everything—and its reappearance would set everything straight.

Weren't we, after all, fated to be together? And wasn't this fate stronger than any of the stupid miscommunications and deceptions that had happened this last year? Maybe even strong enough to win us one more chance at meeting you?

I'd return to the site, find the ring, bring it to my sublet, and write him a handwritten letter—he'd surely get a good kick out of that.

"Hey there, hope all's well," I'd write. "I know this is so weird, but guess what I found the other day when I just so happened to be out in Marin? It was right there in the dirt—right where it must have fallen that night!"

But as I drove onto the freeway, I laughed at myself. How could I hope to find something so small almost a year later? I probably wouldn't even be able to find the right spot; it had been too dark for me to notice any landmarks. There had been trees, a creek, and a road—but there are so many trees and creeks and roads.

So I thought of all the other places I could go. I had a credit card, a car with AC and a GPS, and no obligations in the foreseeable future, other than eventually bringing Dad's car back, and he had another, so it's not as though I'd be leaving him stranded. I could float off in pretty much any direction and not have to consult anyone, not be missed by anyone—what a wonderfully freeing thought!

I entertained the idea of heading east; within a couple days I could be in Texas. Maybe I'd have more luck finding Mom out there. Then maybe, just for the hell of it, while I was already out that way, I could go a little farther east and stop by Dad's hometown in Louisiana. I still had a few cousins out there—it might be fun, popping in and saying hi, just to see if they still remembered me.

In fact, if I'd made it that far, I might as well keep going until I reached Arkansas—how interesting that would be, to wander anonymously in that tiny town where Mom had spent a few years of her girlhood. With all its woods, rivers, and swamps, it sounded like it must be a beautiful place.

Realizing how unrealistic a three-day drive was, I thought maybe I'd just head down Highway Five—I could visit Mom's family down in LA. Maybe Aunt Michi could help me to make more sense of things. She had such a clear memory for details. And I'd been meaning to pay her a visit for years now.

Suddenly gripped by this idea, I picked up my phone, turned it on speaker and balanced it on the steering wheel. It only rang a couple times before her voicemail picked up.

"Please leave a message," a digital voice instructed.

"Oh . . . hi, Aunt Michi. It's Jane here." I stammered. "Sorry I never called you back that day, I just . . . well, just calling to say hi again, and I was just wondering . . . well, just give me a call back when you get the chance. Okay, I hope all's well with you and everyone, thanks." I hung up, flustered.

I continued down the freeway, looking out at the dry rolling hills, so many shades of brown. Why was I being so morbidly nostalgic today, craving to visit all these old, irrelevant places, when there were endless new places I could go? I resolved to go somewhere entirely new.

Just as I was about to pull up Google Maps on my phone and get wildly adventurous, I saw a sign for, of all places, Stockton.

Ten miles, it read.

It occurred to me how close I was to your dad's old family farm.

Maybe it was the unexpectedness of this, and the absolute about-face on my own resolution of less than a minute ago, that enticed me. Impulsively, I veered across three lanes, people honking at me, to take the turnoff.

Passing the downtown district, I took an exit I half recognized and drove along the frontage road, then turned onto one of the thoroughfares, surprising myself at how easily I seemed to be finding the way. I kept on for a few miles, the countryside getting greener as I passed small vineyards, gardens, and small to midsize orchards. Just when I thought I might be lost, I found myself crossing over a small bridge, turning down a dirt road, and pulling over onto the shoulder alongside a ravine and, beyond, an orchard.

I felt a rush of excitement as I recognized the old, run-down house with the large porch and green door.

As I stepped out of the car, the heels of my pumps sinking into the dirt road, crisp, sweet-smelling air entered my lungs. A little blond boy was playing on the porch. He paused his game and eyed me suspiciously. I waved to him and smiled. He didn't smile back but seemed assured enough that I was no psycho killer to resume his game.

My phone vibrated—a message from Dad, wondering how the

interview had gone. I glanced at a recent post from Mom—apparently she still wasn't in Texas, but was hovering somewhere ambiguously between here and there. Typical.

I was struck by the sudden urge for a cigarette. That's when I remembered having bought a pack the week Shiro left, when I'd been desperate for some extra relief. I'd only smoked a few, then had forgotten about them.

As I rummaged through my purse looking for the pack, my fingers wrapped around something soft stuffed at the bottom of my purse. It felt like a tiny, frightened animal. I pulled up a tangled wad of yellow yarn—that horrible pair of booties I made for you. Shuddering, planning on throwing them away as soon as I could, I shoved them into my skirt pocket and grabbed the cigarettes and matches.

***

Actually, you've caught up with me.

Or maybe I should say I've caught up with myself. I'm not sure how long I've been stuck down here at the bottom of this ravine, lying on my back, talking to you.

"Looks like you might need a hand there, Aki?" a voice asks—the same one that beckoned me down here a few hours earlier.

I open my eyes, push myself to sitting, then to standing, a bit dizzy, blinking as my eyes adjust to the sunlight. Wondering exactly how long I've been down here, I stretch, my lower back aching where a rock was digging into me. I walk up the creek a ways, kicking around a medium-sized stone, appreciating the silence filtering through the gentle, rustling sounds of nature.

Just as I'm about to make another climbing attempt back up to the road, I bend down and pick up the stone I'm kicking. Its smooth, round form and modest weight settle in my hand.

I place it on top of another, larger stone nearby. Sun beating down on my head and shoulders, my body sticky with sweat, even as the creek bed cools my bare feet, I contemplate these two stones stacked together.

I lift another, smaller stone and place it on top of these two. I do this several more times, stacking stone upon stone, until I've created a tower six stones tall. It stands there at what now looks like the center of the creek bed with a certain dignity.

I recall the legend your dad told me last New Year, when we sat together on that rusty glider in his parents' garden, about that funny-looking statue in the bright-red bib. The god that protects the vulnerable.

I build another stone tower, a bit farther up the creek. Then another, and another.

As I work, I'm possessed by an unfamiliar clarity of purpose. I hear myself breathing. My skin tingles and my chest begins to ache. My throat yawns wide open, as though waking from a long, deep sleep, and I have the sensation of a tiny hand reaching down my throat, into my chest cavity and deeper, into the darkest, most remote region of me, and placing something solid there.

I hear my voice, first soft, then loud, wailing out in all directions, reverberating off the rocks and ravine walls, reaching for the sky. I must be laughing wildly. But now I taste salt and realize tears are streaming down my cheeks—I'm sobbing, like never before.

I continue to stack stones, my chest aching and throbbing, my face a mess of tears, snot, and dirt.

It occurs to me that I've actually gone through these same motions—sobbing and stacking—many times before, but always just in my sleep.

At last, placing a final stone, wiping my face with my blouse, I take a few steps back and regard this collection of towers. The short, bulbous structures seem imbued with their own life force and appear to be looking back at me. I have the sense that we've all come together here for a spontaneous family reunion.

The creek seems louder, as though its weak current has strengthened.

I reach into my skirt pocket and pull out the yellow booties. Feeling their extreme lightness in the palm of my hand, I smooth them out as best I can and set them on the creek floor at the foot of the nearest tower. They look like two opposite ideas lying together: one long, curved, and pointy; the other short, wide, and crooked. For the first time, I'm not ashamed of these ugly failures.

Then it hits me, with the weight of a thousand stones, whose booties these are—and whose towers.

First and foremost, I've made them for you, Little One.

But I've also made them for someone else—someone whose presence I've felt, on and off, without always knowing it, in various forms and degrees, throughout my life.

Scenes from my life flash before me, only instead of memories, the images are fresh revelations, their colors vivid, edges crisp—textures, sounds, and smells coming back to me with distinct clarity, each scene making a bit more sense than it ever has before.

Maybe it's been my baby uncle's elusive, rejected, persistent presence that's always kept me from fully sinking into the heart of absence.

Hello, Uncle Aki.

These offerings are for you, too.

Why have I been so afraid of you?

I hated being named after you—but of course, you already know this. Hated, reviled, despised! I knew that when Mom looked at me, she often only saw the awful shadow of you. I tried running from you, and for a while I thought it had worked—but you wouldn't let me alone, would you? Will you? You keep following me around, relentless—is this stubbornness a family trait? Or just the universal stubbornness of all those we abandon?

I'm so sorry for what happened to you.

I'm sorry we forgot you.

I'm sorry I forgot you.

I place my forehead on the rocks and feel their coolness seep into my skin. My eyes closed, I see that god in the bright-red bib.

Hello?

I'm sorry, I don't remember your name . . .

But if you're watching me now, if you can hear me, I ask you: please help Little One across the river. Please, oh, please, help my and Shiro's Little One to cross the riverbed of Limbo-land and to arrive safely on the other side.

Please keep him from becoming an abandoned, hopeless spirit!

And please help my uncle Aki. He's been waiting for so long.

And maybe Mom, in her own way, is also stuck here in the riverbed. Please help Mom to cross over to the other side.

And please help me, too.

I stay this way for some time, my head pressed against the cool ground. I have no idea how long; time has become meaningless.

Finally, I stand up. I feel at once heavy and light, weighted in a refreshing sort of way. I take one more look at the yellow booties and stone towers, then turn to face the orchard side of the ravine.

With a determined shout and a running start, grabbing onto roots and rocks, grunting, moving quickly so as not to lose momentum, I ascend the dirt wall. As I climb I have the uncanny sensation that a pair of hands is beneath me, pushing me upward.

Soon I'm up top on the soft, wet ground of the orchard, heaving great sighs of relief. I'm covered in dirt, as though I've just been harvested. I picture your dad standing a few yards away, also covered in dirt, waiting for me, smiling, arms outstretched.

The old house looks larger and even more run-down up close than it did from the road, the once-white paint peeling, the porch steps collapsing in places, the green door cracked. Still, there's an inviting, humble hospitality and an admirable tenacity about the structure. I have the urge to walk up the porch steps and go inside.

I realize now that all the times Shiro and I had imagined our future together—the house, the garden, the kids—we'd both been picturing this place. Really, our fantasy wasn't so much a fantasy, but a sort of reverse déjà vu: a specter of a future that wasn't to be.

Well, Little One that wasn't to be, I guess it's time for us to say goodbye.

Goodbye.

I love you!

That same bird I saw earlier, or one just like it, is perched on a branch of the closest walnut tree. Again it tilts its head to look at me. But now that I'm so close, I see it's not as strange-looking or robotic as I'd first thought; thankfully, it seems to be just a normal, old-fashioned sparrow. A few others like it suddenly swoop down from nowhere to join it—the clutch of them flutter here and there among the branches, chatting playfully, cheerful flashes of orange and brown flitting through shimmering green.

Then, as if collectively hearing some distant call they have no choice but to answer, they pause briefly and fly away.

My focus shifts across the ravine to the road, where Dad's car is waiting.

I see Mom standing there now, leaning against the back-seat window. She's as she was in my first memory—a woman in her forties, dressed in a short, 1960s-style lime-green dress, smoking a cigarette. Except instead of watching her from inside the hot, suffocating car, I stand here in the shade of this tree as she tilts her head back, gazing up at the smoke rising into the empty blue space above her. This time, I have a clear view of her face; her brow is furrowed and her mouth stretches open, the smoke from her lips like a twirling, translucent voice.

Rather than the police coming and rescuing me from the car and everyone clapping, the way her version of the story ended, she takes her time to finish her cigarette, then drops it and stamps it out with the toe of her black high heel. She glances up toward me and the ravine. Seeming intrigued, she takes a few steps in my direction, peering briefly down toward the creek, then looks back to where I'm standing. I see now that she isn't the still-youthful, round-faced woman from my memory; she has aged, naturally.

I'm about to wave and call to her: "Mom! Yes, it's me. Come! Cross over, it's safe here—it's beautiful! *Come!*"

But she shields her eyes with a hand, as though the sun is too bright for her here on this side, and turns away. Clutching her small white purse in one hand, the other hand dangling at her side, she walks down the dirt road. Her walk is neither brisk nor slow, not that of a young or old person, just steady, intent on its far-off destination.

I imagine the ending credits of a film scrolling across the screen, the femme fatale having finally carried out her plan. I watch her fade into the distance, until she's no more than a green speck on the road—then she's gone.

Once we were running along a beach together, holding hands. I must have been five or six years old. I looked up at her—she was so beautiful and carefree, running beside me, her long black hair flying all around her laughing face—and I remember feeling complete, utter happiness.

I turn back to the orchard and wander among the trees. The bright green leaves burst out in all directions, trembling slightly, reminding me of constant flux—even as I'm overwhelmed by excruciating pangs of anger, grief, and regret.

When my legs are tired, I make my way back to the house, cross the footbridge, collect my shoes by the side of the road, and return to Dad's car. Limp, smeared with dirt, I take a seat behind the wheel and start up the motor. My phone is vibrating in my purse. I dig it out and see that it's Aunt Michi. It looks like she's called several times.

"Hello?" I answer, somehow surprised that she would have gotten my message from earlier and be calling me back.

"Hi, Akiko—you called?"

"Oh yeah, hi, Aunt Michi. I just wanted to . . ."

"Everything okay?"

"Oh yeah, everything's fine, fine. How are you?"

"Oh, I'm fine. How's Sumi?"

"I . . . I don't know. I don't see her anymore."

There's a pause.

"You're sure you're okay, Aki?"

"Oh yeah, I'm fine. I just wanted to say sorry for not calling you back."

"That's okay. Are you coming for a visit?"

"A visit? Well . . . that's funny, Aunt Michi—that's funny you should mention that again. Because that's actually why I called earlier. What . . . what are you up to today?"

"*Today?*" I can see her wrinkled face scrunching.

"Never mind, I know it's way last minute, and I haven't been down there in ages. I bet you're busy. I just have Dad's car and happen to have the week off work," I fib, flustered, "and randomly thought maybe I'd drive down, but never—"

"Sure," she interrupts. "Sure, come on down, Aki. I don't got no plans. Come on down today—it's actually good timing, 'cause my bingo game got canceled because of the Obon festival tonight. They're using the room at the senior center for the dancing. You can stay in Angie's room. It's all set up." Angie is her daughter, my cousin, who now has her own family.

"Today is *Obon?*"

"Yeah, yeah—you know Obon?"

"Yes. You told me about it a long time ago."

"Oh, right, well anyway, don't worry, it's perfect timing. Come on down today, Akiko-chan."

"Really? Are you sure? But I know it's so last minute—"

"How many years has it been now? Way too long. Come. We can catch up."

"Well . . . that's funny you say that—because that's what I'm wanting. Aunt Michi, I . . . you know those boxes I was asking you about the other day?"

"Oh yeah, the old boxes. What about them?"

"Well . . . Aunt Michi . . . I'm not sure how to say this but . . . they're gone. The kimono, the photos, everything. I destroyed them. Even that toy boat."

There's another pause.

"Why'd you do that?"

"I'm . . . I'm not really sure. I felt I had to. But now I wish I hadn't. It was a big mistake. I'm so sorry—"

"It's okay, Aki. Don't worry. Those are just things. Just things, ne? You just come home, okay? Just come home."

I nod, tasting salt.

"You there, Aki? Aki? I mean *Jane*. Sorry, I can never—"

"Actually . . ." I turn off the car motor. A few leaves float past the windshield as my throat yawns open. "Actually, keep calling me Aki. Jane doesn't suit me anymore. It never really did, now that I think of it. I'll be going by Akiko now—again."

"Oh, okay."

"You know, Aunt Michi, maybe I will come down for a visit. It's actually been kind of rough over here lately. I guess I'm not really fine after all. I guess you could say I've hit rock bottom, actually. Things have never been worse. My life's a horrible, shitty mess." I can barely talk over my tears. "I've—I've lost everything of importance. Everything."

"Oh, Aki. I'm so sorry."

"Our baby."

She pauses. "What baby?"

"Mine and Shiro's. It was never born. But it's gone."

"Oh, Aki."

She waits as I choke on my tears and catch my breath.

"You still there, Aki?" she eventually asks.

"Yes. Yes, I'm here."

"What about you and Shiro—are you two okay?"

"No." That's all I can manage to say.

There's another pause.

"You know, Aki," she says, as though she just thought of something. "You should really come on down here today. You can stay with me. As long as you want. Like I said, Angie's room is all ready."

"It's not too much trouble?"

"Are you kidding? It's no trouble at all. We're all waiting for you."

We finish the conversation, saying goodbye for now.

I turn off the phone, toss it onto the passenger seat, and sit here behind the wheel, wiping my face with my hands and blouse. I start up the motor again, roll the windows down, and take one last look at this old farm.

Would I do certain things differently if I had the chance to do them over again? Most definitely. But perhaps that's a pointless question.

Was it pointless looking back today? No. It was necessary. How else would I have crossed over to the other side?

As your dad would say, we must face our past, our demons.

I make a slow, wide U-turn on the dusty dirt road.

***

Singing at the top of my lungs along with the radio, my hair whipping at my face in the wind, I drive down Highway Five toward Aunt Michi's house. I should be there by sundown.

But look at me—here I am still talking to you, even after saying goodbye.

Maybe, then, goodbye forever isn't the answer?

Shall we make a plan to talk every so often? How about once a year, around this time, you can come visit me from wherever you are. We can spend a little time together, catching up about anything important. Then you can return to whatever journey you're on, and I'll move forward with my life here. What do you think?

I actually feel ready to move forward with my life—it's a wonderfully unfamiliar feeling.

So, my Little One, goodbye for now.

And goodbye for now to you, too, Uncle Aki.

Until we meet again: safe journey to us all!

ACKNOWLEDGMENTS

Before undertaking this project, I never fully grasped what a truly collaborative process writing a novel is. I am awed by the kindness and generosity of all those who contributed to the manifestation of this one.

First and foremost, thank you to my parents, who have loved and supported me at every step of the way. Thank you to my mom for sharing her life experiences with me and for giving priceless feedback and spiritual support throughout this process. To my dad for being a solid rock of intellectual rigor and unconditional acceptance, and for patiently line editing several early stages of the manuscript.

Thank you to my aunts Reiko Sheppard and Fumiko Ito for always believing in me, and for cheerfully stopping whatever they were in the middle of to answer calls from me asking for their advice or recollections. To my mother-in-law, Ramona Rath, for her passion for books and constant giving. To Lily Storm and Claire Bove for reading the manuscript multiple times, offering clarity and wisdom, and encouraging me not to be afraid to say "too much." To Michelle Kellman, Eric Kupers, John Jacobsen, Nadia Oka, Debby Kajiyama, Jeff Sheppard, Dawn Holtan, and David Ryther for giving important feedback. To Michael Palmer, the Suczek-Kuos, Ondine Young, Chingchi Yu, Heather Lukens, Roxanne Bellotti, Sierra Filucci, Leigh Eisenman, Mito Kodera, Sheena Koyama, and others I am no doubt forgetting, for supporting me in various crucial ways throughout the process.

To my dream-come-true agent, Aimee Ashcraft, for her tireless positivity, professionalism, and expert midwifery, assisting me with loving hands creatively, editorially, and practically to realize this story and to bring it into the world. To Vikki Warner, my acquiring editor; Ember Hood, my copy editor; and all the other wonderful people at Blackstone Publishing—Jeffrey Yamaguchi, Lauren Maturo, Mandy Earles,

Greg Boguslawski, Kathryn G. English, Josie Woodbridge, and everyone else—for believing in and working on this project with such integrity and dedication. To Michael Signorelli for his sharp, thoughtful editing.

To my daughters, Mariko and Kaela, for bringing me so much joy and always inspiring me.

Finally, thank you to my husband, Brian, for being at the center of this story alongside me from its inception—for countless insights and contributions, endless love and support, and all the late-night, revelatory brainstorming sessions. This novel would not exist without him.

This story, while inspired by my family's experiences during the Japanese American internment, is a work of fiction, born from my own personal experiences and imaginings, and is not meant to represent the actual lives of others.